Praise for
Beauty and the Bounty Hunter

"Austin's finely drawn characters and riveting tension will knock you out of your boots! Her books are like the smoothest whiskey—they go down easy but pack a punch. Everyone is sure to fall in love with the fiery Cat and the wily Alexi."

> —Sabrina Jeffries, *New York Times* bestselling
> author of *'Twas the Night After Christmas*

"Riveting, poignant, and unforgettable, *Beauty and the Bounty Hunter* by Lori Austin is a page-turner that reminded me why I love Westerns. I adored the unique characters and the depth of their story lines. Lori Austin is a brilliant and talented storyteller who doesn't disappoint."

> —Lorraine Heath, author of *She Tempts the Duke*

"Refreshingly different, *Beauty and the Bounty Hunter* leaps off the page. You'll fall in love with the characters and the American West."

> —Susan Mallery, author of *Summer Days*

"Lori Austin knows how to build tension and keep the pages turning. With this action-packed tale of revenge and redemption, the reader is in for a wild ride."

> —Kaki Warner, author of *Bride of the High Country*

"From the first page, this book takes off like a horse tearing across the prairie—hang on and enjoy the ride!"

> —Claudia Dain, author of the Courtesan Chronicles

**The Once Upon a Time in the West Series
by Lori Austin**

*Beauty and the Bounty Hunter
An Outlaw in Wonderland*

AN OUTLAW IN WONDERLAND

ONCE UPON A TIME IN THE WEST

LORI AUSTIN

A SIGNET ECLIPSE BOOK

SIGNET ECLIPSE
Published by the Penguin Group
Penguin Group (USA) Inc., 375 Hudson Street,
New York, New York 10014, USA

USA | Canada | UK | Ireland | Australia
New Zealand | India | South Africa | China
Penguin Books Ltd., Registered Offices:
80 Strand, London WC2R 0RL, England
For more information about the Penguin Group visit penguin.com.

First published by Signet Eclipse, an imprint of New American Library,
a division of Penguin Group (USA) Inc.

First Printing, June 2013

ISBN 978-0-451-23952-5

Printed in the United States of America
10 9 8 7 6 5 4 3 2 1

ALWAYS LEARNING   PEARSON

ACKNOWLEDGMENTS

Thanks to the usual suspects: Robin Rue, Beth Miller, Claire Zion, Jhanteigh Kupihea, Kim Miller, Nancy Berland, Kim Castillo. Everything would be so much harder without you.

PART I

CHAPTER 1

Gettysburg, 1863

"Dammit." Ethan Walsh turned away from the bloody wreck that had so recently been an infantryman of the 69th Pennsylvania. "I didn't become a doctor to watch people die."

He lifted a hand to rub at his burning eyes, saw the blood dripping off his fingers, and lowered it again.

"Why *did* you become a doctor?"

Ethan was so tired and his ears were so abused from the rattle of artillery that had ebbed and flowed near Taneytown Road for hours upon days upon nights that he didn't respond. He wasn't sure if the question was real or imagined. Right then he wasn't certain if he was awake or asleep, alive or dead.

"Sir?"

Ethan lifted his gaze to the speaker. They were the only living, breathing, moving bodies in the makeshift Union hospital that had been set up at the Patterson Farm. Until now, the place had been full unto bursting. Their commander, Justin Dwinnell, estimated five hundred wounded soldiers had passed beneath the broad branches of the orchard and through the stone barn the first night.

How many had come wasn't as important as how many had left alive. Ethan didn't think it was anything close to the number he'd hoped.

"Who are you?" Ethan demanded. "And—" The chill deepened. "Where is everyone?"

Had a shell landed on the barn? Was he dead? His visitor certainly appeared to be.

The man was gray, and Ethan didn't mean Confederate, although it was impossible to distinguish the affiliation of the ash-covered uniform. The man had no hat. Perhaps he'd lost it crossing the River Styx.

Ethan coughed to cover the unseemly chuckle that threatened to escape. Of late, he'd found himself inordinately amused at situations that were far from amusing. Which was only fair, considering he also often fought tears that rose for no reason at all.

"You *are* Ethan Walsh?" The man shook his head, and particles of Lord knew what sprinkled the blood-dampened ground. His hair might be blond, or light brown when washed, but really, what did it matter?

"And who might be askin'?" Ethan fell back on his father's brogue, something he often did when overtired or just plain sad.

The fellow's smile cracked the dried paste of dirt and blood on his cheeks. He was younger than Ethan had first thought—perhaps closer to thirty than forty. "If you take a seat, I'll explain."

Frustrated, annoyed, and so damn tired, Ethan kicked over the nearest empty bucket, sat, and spread one bloody hand in a mocking "after you" gesture.

The man, unperturbed by the mockery or the blood, dipped his head. "At present my name is John Law."

At present? What did that mean? Ethan's confusion must have shown, for "John" continued.

"Last week I answered to Jonas Height. A month ago, Jacob Black." He winked. "I like my first name to begin with a *J*. I'm not sure why. I work for the government. The *Union* government," he clarified, smoothing his palms over a uniform that bore no distinguishing marks. "Though when traveling across battlefields, it's best not to be too specific."

Tired as he was, Ethan had a flicker of understanding. "You're a spy."

John winced. "Nasty word. Apt to get a man hung."

It had, in fact, done just that a year past. Despite an

unwritten agreement to exchange spies and not execute them, the Confederates had hung Timothy Webster in Richmond for his sins.

"I work for the Intelligence Service," Law continued.

"Never heard of it."

The smile reappeared. "Considering our occupation, gathering intelligence, that's good news."

Ethan's gaze was drawn to the dead boy on his table. "If intelligence could be gathered, there'd be a lot less stupidity in the world."

"Clever," John Law murmured. "That will help."

"Help with what?"

"We have a proposition. One we think will be instrumental in ending the conflict with less bloodshed."

"That ship has already sailed."

"This war could last a good while yet."

Ethan's attention moved from the dead body to the live one. "How long?"

"No one believed it would last this long."

Both the North and the South had rallied around the idea that the war would be over in weeks, certainly within months. No one could have ever been more wrong.

The North had the men, the munitions, the money. The South had Robert E. Lee and a cause. When Stonewall Jackson sent the larger Union force scurrying back to Washington after the first battle at Bull Run, the Yankees realized they were in for a fight and called for five hundred thousand additional troops. The Rebs realized they'd crossed a line they couldn't uncross and called for more troops as well.

That had been two years ago, and despite the apparent Union triumph in Gettysburg, Ethan didn't think a complete victory was imminent. The South had only just begun to fall. They weren't going to surrender until there weren't enough folks left to hold one another up.

"The Union lost Bull Run because of a spy," John continued. "First Manassas is what they call it."

Us. Them. North. South. Friend. Enemy. Ethan hated it all.

Shouts from the orchard caused Law to cut short his tale. "I'll get to my point. If we had someone at the center of the Confederacy, providing us with intelligence, we could put an end to . . ." He swept out his arm. "This."

"When you say the center—"

"Richmond."

Where Webster had died.

"When you say someone—"

Law's mouth curved. "I mean you."

"I can't just dance into their capital and start stealing secrets." While some days Ethan thought he'd have to die just to get some rest, he'd prefer not to do so at the end of a rope.

"Stealing is such an unpleasant word."

"Yet it fits so well with spying."

"Two different things. Stealing is taking what doesn't belong to you. Spying is merely listening, a little following, perhaps some light reading."

Still sounded like stealing to Ethan.

"Wouldn't you like to leave all this behind?" Law asked.

On any other day, Ethan might have said no. But today . . . His gaze returned to the dead soldier. Today was different. More shouts from the orchard made him realize the truth.

"I'm a doctor." He'd never wanted to be anything else.

Despite his mother having died in childbed bearing his brother, Ethan had still looked upon medicine as a kind of magic. He'd been fascinated with the potions and lotions, the shiny implements, even the blood. He'd followed Dr. Brookstone, the local physician, until, in exasperation, the man had snapped, "If you're going to be underfoot, you might as well make yourself useful."

So Ethan had fetched water, scrubbed floors and tables, mucked stables until he was old enough to become an apprentice. His brother had then taken over Ethan's duties, and instead of scrubbing dirt from beneath his nails each night, Ethan had scrubbed blood.

He had never felt such a sense of rightness, of completion, than when he healed someone. Which might be why he felt so wrong, so incomplete now. Ethan hadn't healed anyone in a very long time. Still . . .

"If I leave, people will die."

"They'll die anyway." Ethan winced. Law saw the opening and took it. "You'd continue to be a doctor. At one of the largest hospitals in the country." He shrugged one shoulder. "Just not *this* country."

Ethan added large hospital to Richmond and got— "Chimborazo." The other man smiled at the interest Ethan couldn't keep from his voice.

Chimborazo was indeed the largest hospital of its kind. Located near the convergence of five railroads, most of the Confederacy's wounded that survived field surgery were sent there for further treatment and recovery.

"The South might have wooed the best of West Point," Law continued, "but the North came out ahead on the doctors."

Ethan wasn't certain if that was meant to be flattery or merely a simple statement of fact. The North had bigger cities, larger universities, more money; it only followed that they'd have more physicians.

"I don't see what their lack of medical staff has to do with me."

"You said if you leave, people die. If you go, people would live. Do you really care if they wear the gray or the blue?"

Ethan couldn't and call himself a doctor.

"They need you there more than we need you here. *We* need you there more than we need you here. If you want to save lives, join the Intelligence Service. You'll be doing a damn sight more toward that end than you've been doing thus far."

And because he was tired, and sad, because his last patient had died despite everything he'd done, and because John Law had begun to make sense, Ethan sighed and said, "What do you want me to do?"

Law grinned. "I'll speak to your superior; we can leave straightaway."

"No." Law's smiled faded. "I can't leave in the middle of a battle. When this . . ." Ethan waved his hand; at least the blood had dried, and he didn't spray any of it about. "When this is done, I'll go with you. But not before."

"This *is* done." Law's gaze turned to the darkness outside the doorway. "The Rebs just don't know it yet."

"Nevertheless—"

"All right. While you finish trying to save the unsavable, I'll find a go-between."

"Not everyone is unsavable," Ethan muttered, though from the pile of bodies outside, he would have a hard time defending that statement. "What do you have to find?"

"Someone who can bring information from you without getting themselves caught or killed in the process."

"I know just the person."

Law lifted a filthy hand. "No offense, sir, but I'll recruit my own men."

Obviously accustomed to giving orders and having them obeyed, he left.

"No offense, *sir*," Ethan murmured, "but there's only one man I trust." Ethan kept his gaze on Law until, between one blink and the next, he disappeared. "And you aren't him."

Michael Walsh rode south in the wake of his brother.

From the moment Mikey could walk, he'd followed Ethan. He hadn't had much else to do. Their mother had gone to God; their father was a blacksmith, and the forge was no place for children. So Ethan and Mikey had spent all of their time together.

Ethan had gotten sick of his little brother being underfoot all the time. What big brother wouldn't? But he wasn't mean. He'd never thrown rocks or shouted. Instead he'd hidden and then snuck away. Which was how Mikey had learned to find him.

In truth, he'd always had a talent for it. If Da couldn't locate a tool or his belt or sometimes his shoes, Mikey would close his eyes, let his mind grow quiet, and the next instant he would go directly to the item, wherever it was. He did the same thing while tracking. Close his eyes, see the area in his mind; then, when he opened his eyes, the broken branch, the half footprint, the drop of blood would be so clear he couldn't understand why he was the only one who could see it.

Some folks thought Mikey was spooky. They avoided him, whispered and pointed. Until they needed something, or someone, found.

He waited until the two men were nearly fifty miles from Gettysburg. He watched them make camp, listened to them talk by the fire.

"If you walk into Richmond speaking like a Yankee, you're going to get hung."

"What do you suggest?" Ethan asked.

"How are you at Southern?"

"Well, I don't rightly know, sir. How's this?"

His companion winced. "God-awful. That'll get you hung even quicker." He tilted his head. "What about Irish?"

Ethan had often imitated their da's voice, though never in his hearing. He did so now, and the sound gave Mikey the shivers. It was as though Da were whispering from the grave.

"And would this be good enough fer ye, me boyo?"

"Better. Lots of Irish down South. It'll help you blend in."

Mikey remained in the shadows while they fell asleep. When he approached, not even the horses heard him coming. He gathered the weapons and hunkered down to wait.

Dawn flickered across the stranger's face. He opened his eyes, blinked, cursed, and reached for the rifle that was no longer there. Neither were his pistols. Mikey might be big, but he wasn't slow—in body or in mind.

"What is this?" Confusion darkened the fellow's gaze to the shade of a thunderstorm at midnight.

Ethan shoved back his bedroll and sat up. "You need a go-between, Law? I happen to have one."

"He's . . ." The fellow's mouth tightened, and his head tilted as he contemplated Mikey.

Mikey had hoped that someone known as an intelligence agent might have more brains than to repeat the same words everyone else said the first time they set eyes on him. However, instead of "huge" or any of its variations—"gigantic," "gargantuan," "massive"—the man blurted, "Twelve."

Mikey stiffened. "I am not!"

Law turned to Ethan. "You expect me to use this child as a go-between in sensitive intelligence operations?"

"Yes," Ethan said simply.

"No," Law returned.

"Did you hear him come into our camp?" The agent frowned. "Did you feel him take your holster and your rifle?" The frown deepened. "Did the horses snuffle, snort, or whinny? Did you have a single glimmer that we were being followed since Gettysburg?"

Law's mouth opened, then shut again, and he peered at Mikey with more interest. "How old *are* you?"

"Seventeen." The man cast Ethan an exasperated glance. "I was fifteen when I came to war with Ethan. No one thought I'd be any good, but I showed 'em."

He *had* to be allowed to enter the Intelligence Service with Ethan. His brother was smart about books and healing, but when it came to the world, Ethan was as blind as all the rest of them. Without Mikey to watch his back, bad things would happen.

"Mikey can find anything," Ethan said. "Sneak up on anyone. He's been that way since he could walk."

"And you know this how?"

"He's my brother."

Law's sharp gaze flicked back and forth between the two of them several times before he murmured, "No one more loyal than a brother."

The tight ball of fear in Mikey's chest loosened. Everything was going to be all right.

"Matron!"

Annabeth Phelan paused outside the surgery. Dr. Ethan Walsh was up to his elbows in a patient. Well, not literally, though from the blood coating his arms, it was very difficult to tell.

"Don't dally," he snapped. "I need ye over here."

She did as she was told, not only because he was a doctor and she was a matron, but because his Irish accent sounded exactly like her papa's. God rest his soul. And Mama's, too, along with those of nearly everyone else she knew.

Due to the Union advance toward Richmond, which had begun with the bloody battle in the Wilderness nearly two months past, Chimborazo Hospital possessed far more patients than the staff was capable of caring for. The surgeons were overworked, but at this point, who wasn't?

"Should I call a steward?" she asked.

The main occupations of a matron were to feed and comfort the soldiers. Thus far she'd held hands, written letters, and called a steward to remove the dead. Having nursed her parents, and many of their friends, through their final illnesses, Annabeth was capable of much more. Not that anyone had asked.

"Shove yer hands in that bucket," Walsh ordered.

Annabeth followed instructions, hissing as the liquid burned areas previously scrubbed raw. Dr. Walsh insisted on cleanliness in his surgery to the point that most of the other doctors sneered and whispered. However, fewer of his patients had died of gangrene and fevers than any of the others.

"The sting will pass. But it's necessary before you touch him, aye?" Annabeth nodded. "I know the others laugh, but cleansing everything with alcohol seems to help." He lifted one shoulder. "At the least, it won't hurt. Now, I need you to sew his wound. He's torn it open, thrashin' about."

"I'm not a nurse."

Walsh lifted his gaze. His light gray eyes shone brightly in his sun-darkened face. He was a striking man. The other matrons tittered whenever he walked past.

"That isn't true," he murmured.

Annabeth frowned, trying to remember what she'd said before his eyes had captured her. "I'm merely a matron, sir."

A status revealed by her dark gown and cap, along with the once-white apron. At Chimborazo, nursing duties were performed by detailed and disabled soldiers or slaves. Although at this point in the war, all able bodies were *in* the war. The assignment of soldiers to nursing had trickled to nearly none.

Walsh waved a hand dripping with blood. A few drops flecked Annabeth's bodice. She ignored them. She'd been flecked with worse. "I've seen ye work. You've nursed before, and blood"—he eyed what he'd tossed in her direction—"doesn't bother ye."

She wondered if he'd flecked her on purpose, then shrugged. Blood *didn't* bother her. Which, considering her life over the past few years, was a very lucky thing.

"What do you need me to do?"

Dr. Walsh smiled, and the expression made him appear younger than she'd believed him to be—nearer her own twenty-three instead of her eldest brother's thirty-two. Or the thirty-two he would have been if he hadn't died at Sharpsburg nearly two years past.

Annabeth pushed thoughts of Abner from her mind. If she didn't, she'd start thinking of how James had died at Ball's Bluff and Hoyt at New Bern, then Saul at Shiloh. But nearly as bad as their names on the death rolls had been the lack of any news at all of her youngest brother, Luke.

"If ye would sew the wound closed once more," Dr. Walsh said. "I'll be keepin' him still."

Annabeth lowered her gaze from the doctor to the patient. She'd heard they'd started handing guns to anyone who could hold on to them, but she hadn't realized exactly what that meant until now. This child didn't even have a beard.

"You'd do a much better job than me with the needle," Annabeth said.

"Doubtful. My samplers were never the rage."

For an instant Annabeth stared at him. Then she laughed. "Nor mine."

She was better at shooting than sewing. Not that it made any difference. Certainly she could have cut her hair, worn her brothers' clothes, and joined up, but she'd believed she would be of more help here. If anyone would actually allow her to help. So why was she hesitating now?

"If he comes about and thrashes," Dr. Walsh continued, "ye'd not be able to hold him still. He's stronger than ye'd think for one who's been gut shot. But that's often the case when the pain takes over."

Annabeth had held her brothers still often enough. But that had involved underhanded methods of pinching, hair pulling, and kicking areas no lady should know about, let alone kick. A lifetime with the Phelan brothers had taught Annabeth to fight dirty or lose. As she could not use those methods on a sick man, Annabeth retrieved the suture needle and thread from the instrument table.

"Silver suture wire is a thing of the past," the doctor said. "I've not seen such luxuries since just after Manassas."

"I've *never* seen suture wire." Annabeth pressed the gaping belly wound together and shoved the needle through the jagged edges.

"I miss it." Walsh wiped the welling blood away with a cloth drenched in the bucket of water that wasn't merely water. "Doesn't pull loose as easily as thread."

"Mmm," she murmured, concentrating on the wound, working quickly. The soldier stirred now and again but didn't awaken.

She finished the sutures, reached for scissors, and had Dr. Walsh slap them into her palm. Startled, Annabeth nearly dropped the instrument. Her gaze flicked to the doctor's, but his remained on the patient. Several days' growth of beard darkened his chin and cheeks. Had he been on duty that long? Or had he merely lost interest, as so many had, in things that did not matter?

Annabeth snipped the thread at the final knot and laid the scissors and needle on the tray. Walsh leaned close, studying her work. "Ye've done this before." His eerily pale eyes lifted. "Many times."

"I have brothers." *Had*, her mind echoed . . . but she ignored it.

"Ah." He straightened, his true height surprising her. Until now, she'd seen him only bent over someone. "That explains it, then."

Annabeth was considered tall for a woman. In truth, she was tall for a man. That, combined with her bright red hair and tendency to speak her mind—not to mention this hellish war, which had taken away all the boys and killed most of them before they'd had any chance to become men—might be the reason she was still Miss Phelan rather than Mrs. something else

For an instant she enjoyed looking into the eyes of a handsome fellow, imagining what it would be like if she weren't doing so over a bloody body, in a hospital full of many more. She couldn't quite manage it.

Annabeth stepped back. "If you don't need anything else . . ."

"I'm keeping ye from yer duties."

"This was more important." And the type of work she'd much rather be doing. "Good day, Doctor."

"I've watched ye," he murmured.

A trickle of unease made her pause only steps from escape. "Sir?"

"Yer talents are wasted writin' letters and stirrin' the soup."

Steeling herself, she faced him. "No one else agrees."

"Dinnae worry." He gave her that smile again, the one that made her breath catch and her cheeks flush. "They will."

CHAPTER 2

Ethan watched Annabeth Phelan hurry out the door. There was something about her that intrigued him.

"Fool," he muttered. He had no time for courting. Especially as he was living a lie. But she had healing hands that should be put to better use.

A sudden flash of the better uses he might have for them made Ethan grit his teeth and count out loud in Gaelic. *"A haon, a dó, a trí, a ceathair, a . . ."*

He struggled to recall the word for five, and instead remembered the fiery shade of her hair, the cream of her skin, the dot of freckles across her nose, and the scents of lavender and mint all around her. Perhaps he should count to one hundred, but he didn't know how.

He had been too long without a woman if the mere sight of one caused his body to stir and his mind to forget what was important. He could wind up hung for a spy if he wasn't careful. And a man thinking with his *bod* was far from careful.

Ethan's patient remained unconscious. While a good thing during the stitching, the boy's continued lack of awareness worried him.

Ethan sniffed the wound, caught no scent of bowel or rot. He would keep a close eye on the youth. Not that there was much he could do about a gangrenous belly wound, but he would not have the boy die alone.

The soldier still wore his trousers—homespun, not gray—but these days many of the Confederate forces were fresh out of uniforms and everything else. Ethan quickly searched the pockets, pulled out a small scrap of paper so stained with blood that whatever had been written on it was as gone as the lad's boots. This had been the case with nearly all of the scraps Ethan had discovered so far. However, delirious ramblings were often not as delirious as they seemed.

"Gotta cross," the youth muttered. "Cross the river."

Ethan, who'd had his hand in the boy's back pocket, took it out. "Yer fine," he soothed. The soldier's eyelids fluttered. "Not crossin' the river anytime soon."

"Rendezvous," he blurted, and Ethan stilled. "Rangers to Rectortown."

"Yer not speaking of the eternal river, are ye, now?" Ethan murmured. "Go on."

"Yes, sir, Colonel Mosby, sir." The boy groaned and reached for his wound. Ethan snatched his hand before it could find the mark. "I delivered the message. Rangers are a comin'."

Colonel John S. Mosby was one of the most wanted Confederates of the war. His 43rd Battalion of cavalry were partisans, guerillas in truth, harrying Union supply lines and disrupting transportation. They posed lightning strikes on their enemy, then rode off on some of the best horseflesh in the country and disappeared, blending in with the local folk.

Ethan chewed his lip as he frowned at his patient's homespun trousers, which now took on a whole new meaning. It was said that Mosby's Rangers wore no distinguishing uniform beyond a bit of gray on each man's clothes. He lifted the boy's discarded, bloody shirt and spotted a single gray pocket.

The tide of the war had turned after Gettysburg, but the conflict was still far from over. The end of Mosby's raids would have a twofold effect—bolstering Union morale even as it decimated Confederate confidence. Ethan had to get this information to Mikey. If they could use it to find Mosby, they could stop him.

The head matron bustled into the room, stopping short at the sight of Ethan. From her expression, the woman thought he was a lunatic. Most of the staff did. But they couldn't argue with his results—at least in his hearing.

Dr. Brookstone had believed in two things—the genius of Shakespeare and the necessity of cleanliness in the workplace. He'd come to understand, and Ethan had too, that putrefaction was a result of invisible particles in the air. If they entered an open wound, infection set in. The particles could travel on the instruments used, the sutures, even the surgeon's, the nurse's, or the patient's hands.

Brookstone had washed everything that touched a patient, including the doctor, with a mixture of alcohol and water. The practice had become second nature to Ethan. To those who didn't like it, he said, *Ag fuck tu,* though never out loud.

"Mrs. Dimmity," Ethan greeted. "How lovely to see ye, me dear."

Mrs. Dimmity had been a matron since the day of the hospital's inception nearly three years before. Chimborazo had begun life as a training ground for the Confederate forces. When the soldiers marched away, they'd left behind more than one hundred new wooden buildings, referred to as wards.

Dr. James B. McCaw had arrived with Mrs. Dimmity in tow and set to work turning those empty buildings into a hospital. Rumor had it that Mrs. Dimmity had served as the doctor's nursemaid. Ethan found this difficult to believe. McCaw was thirty-eight. If that rumor were true, Mrs. Dimmity would be nearing sixty.

Ethan did not doubt rumors of her age because she appeared young. She was as wrinkled as an apple dried by the sun, yet she marched across the room, her step as solid as Old Ironsides. Ethan doubted even a cannonball could make her retreat. She was on her feet before the sun rose and long after it fell. There'd been days when Ethan would have begged to sit down. If Mrs. Dimmity hadn't still been standing.

"I have a favor to ask of ye," Ethan began as Mrs. Dimmity reached for a cloth.

Ethan *tsk*ed and, though she scowled, the woman moved to the bucket and plunged her hands within. She even hunted for a fresh rag with which to wipe the patient's face instead of the already-bloody one she'd originally chosen.

Though Ethan would have preferred to finish what he'd begun with the boy, the soldier was in good hands— now that she'd washed them—and he had other duties.

"Return the private to the infirmary," he ordered. "If there's any sign of fever, send someone to fetch me."

"And where will you be, sir?"

"My quarters." The muscle beneath Ethan's eye fluttered, and he rubbed it absently. "Resting." Ethan headed for the door at the same nimble pace with which Mrs. Dimmity had arrived.

"You had a request, Doctor?"

He was so intent on getting where he needed to be and then back to his quarters before anyone knew he hadn't gone there, for an instant Ethan couldn't remember what it was. However, when he turned and saw the patient, he recalled those clever, healing hands.

"See that Miss Phelan is relieved of her duties as matron."

"Sir?" Her wrinkled face wrinkled even more. "She's one of my best."

"Aye," he agreed. "I'll have her as my nurse."

Mrs. Dimmity gasped. "That is not done!"

"'Tis now," he said, and left.

Despite his size, Mikey blended into the area around Richmond with ease—lots of trees, plenty of streams, hills that rolled on forever. He'd spent a lifetime tracking animals. If *they* hadn't seen him, people certainly wouldn't.

John Law's instructions were simple. Mikey stayed in an abandoned cabin not far from the Confederate capital. If anyone but the agent or Ethan arrived, he would pretend to be mute. Mikey had attempted both an Irish and a Southern accent. Neither had been convincing.

So far Mikey had always known folks were coming long before they arrived. He slipped into the trees, listened, looked, waited for them to leave, then returned.

He always knew Ethan was coming, too. Not that his

brother was overly loud or careless. Mikey just heard things no one else did—from farther away than he should.

Ethan dismounted, led the horse to the water trough, then joined Mikey on the porch. "Ye all right?"

Mikey nodded.

"Anyone been by?" Mikey shrugged, and Ethan sighed. "Ye can speak to *me*, ye know?"

Mikey had done so little talking of late, he'd gotten out of the habit. He cleared his throat; his first few words came out quite hoarse. "And you don't have to use Da's voice while you're here."

"I know." Ethan dropped the accent. "You get used to it."

Mikey was glad he didn't have to pretend to be someone he wasn't all the time. From Ethan's exhausted appearance, it wore on a man.

"John Law says he's gonna start giving me more to do."

Ethan frowned. "Law says a lot."

"He teaches me things."

"Like what?"

"Spy things. I can teach 'em to you."

For an instant Ethan seemed interested; then his frown returned. "What does he want you to do now?"

"He recruited a sniper. Fellow needs a spotter to keep an eye out while he has his to the gun."

"No," Ethan said.

"I can't just sit here all the time. I'd be good at watchin' his back. You know I would."

"What if I bring information and you aren't here?" Ethan asked.

"You leave a note, in that code of Law's. Like we talked about."

Ethan let out a long breath, and Mikey knew he'd won. Not that he'd planned to let Ethan tell him he couldn't work with that sniper. Or leastways, if Ethan told him no, he hadn't planned on listening. Mikey was almost eighteen—a man grown. Had been for a while now, and he'd do what he thought was best.

"I have to get back," Ethan said. "Before someone realizes that I've gone."

"What'll you say if they do?"

"I was out riding. I couldn't sleep. I needed air."

The lies tripped off Ethan's tongue like Gospel. Mikey wished he could lie like that.

"Tell Law that Mosby's called the Rangers to Rectortown."

Mikey nodded and stood. Law ranted a lot about Mosby.

"Where is he?" Ethan asked.

"Not tellin'."

"I'm your brother."

"Don't care."

"What if someone sees you?"

Mikey snorted. That wasn't going to happen.

"All right," Ethan agreed. "Just . . ." He set his hand on Mikey's arm. "Be careful." He started back the way he'd come. "If anything happened to you, I'd . . ." Ethan spoke again in their father's voice. "I'd kick yer ass so hard ye'd never let it happen again, me boyo."

Sometimes when Ethan spoke like that, Mikey felt as if ghostly fingers had trailed across his neck. Other times, like now, it made him laugh.

"Don't worry," he said. "What could happen?"

When Annabeth reported for her shift the following morning, Mrs. Dimmity awaited her.

"You're no longer a matron."

Annabeth blinked at the woman, whose usually placid face had gone frighteningly florid. "I . . . uh . . . What?"

"You helped the pretty doctor, didn't you?"

Mrs. Dimmity didn't have to explain which doctor she meant. There was none so lovely as Ethan Walsh.

"He told me to," she said simply. She'd do the same again. How could she peer into the man's pleading gray gaze and walk away?

But what if her behavior was cause for dismissal? At Chimborazo, women were maids and cooks, letter writers and hand holders. Nothing more. The idea of spending her days as she'd spent them before she'd come here—alone on the farm, waiting for the army—blue or gray, what did it matter?—to confiscate her remaining half bag of flour and the last scrawny chicken, if deserters didn't first do worse—terrified her.

She had a gun; she even had a few bullets, and she'd learned to shoot, ride, and hunt along with her brothers. But Annabeth was still a woman alone, and it was only a matter of time until something horrible happened.

She drew a breath. "I'll leave straightaway."

"You will not!"

"But—"

"You'll report to Dr. Walsh. You've been reassigned as his *personal* nurse."

Annabeth frowned at the woman's tone, which left no doubt what she thought Annabeth would truly be doing. She opened her mouth to deny the unvoiced accusation, then shut it again. Perhaps Mrs. Dimmity was right. They'd all seen women in Richmond who had once been ladies become something else in order to appease that annoying need to eat.

"We'll have more casualties soon." The older woman shooed her toward the door. "Another skirmish. Best be ready."

Annabeth backed into the hall and had the door firmly shut in her face. She had the feeling there would be many doors shut the same in her future. Unless—

She threw back her shoulders. She hadn't worked this hard to let some handsome Irish doctor ruin her. She would tell him no; then she would go home and do her best not to die.

Annabeth marched through the surgery ward, the infirmary, and the offices with no sight of her quarry. No one had seen the doctor since he'd left the night before. She could go to his quarters—if she knew where they were—however, that would serve only to prove to those who already cast her suspicious glances that the rumors about her and Dr. Walsh were true. Instead, she returned to the room where she'd met him. She did not have long to wait.

When he arrived, Ethan Walsh rushed to the bucket, washed his hands, face, and neck. He appeared a lot dirtier than he should be for a night spent resting. His dark trousers were damp, his once-white shirt sprinkled with dust.

His gaze lifted and he saw her. For an instant, she thought he might bolt—or maybe that was her—then he smiled and dried his hands on a clean cloth. "I'm glad yer here. We have wounded on the way."

When she continued to stand where she was, his smile faded. "Is somethin' amiss?"

"Everyone thinks I'm your whore."

He blinked at her crudity, but she'd always found it best to say what she meant straightaway. She blamed the war that she was alone, but in truth, she probably would have remained a spinster regardless. She'd have been a dismal failure at dancing and prancing and spouting pretty lies like a lady.

"I . . ." he began. "What?"

"Where are you from that you don't understand what a request like yours means?"

"Ireland," he murmured absently, then rubbed under his eye, which twitched as if something lived and jumped beneath the skin.

"You're tired," she said.

"I'm"—he dropped his hand—"not."

She nearly called him a liar, but she'd already insulted him enough. She could see from his confusion that he'd had no idea his request would be viewed as improper.

"How long have you *been* in this country?" She stepped closer and caught the scent of horse and dust. But if he'd been sleeping, then how—

Men poured into the room. They were so dirty, bloody, and rank with the smell of horse, she concluded she'd smelled them and not him. They carried a stretcher and they dumped an especially bloody, dirty, smelly soldier onto the table before leaving without a word. Really, what was there to say?

Annabeth stepped forward before the last man cleared the door. So intent was she on the fellow writhing on the table that she barely noticed the sting when she doused her hands in the bucket of more than water. By the time she'd dried those fingers, Dr. Walsh already had a scalpel in his.

"Where—" she began, and he slit the man's trousers up the side, revealing a long, deep gash in his thigh.

As he dipped his hand and the instrument back into the water, he snapped, "Bullet in or out?"

"In," the patient managed through clenched teeth.

A movement at the doorway caused all three of them to glance up as more soldiers entered with more wounded. The remainder of the day was drenched in blood and sweat. The sun went down; the moon rose. Annabeth's back ached. Her fingers cramped. Her eyes burned. She had never felt so good.

When the last patient lay in the infirmary and no more rested on the floor, in the hall, or outside on the ground, Annabeth plunged her fingers into clear, fresh water and relished that, for a change, she hadn't been the one bringing it.

She'd dug out bullets, stitched bayonet wounds, set broken bones. Most of the practices she had never performed before, yet with a few words from Ethan Walsh, she'd understood what was needed. She had saved lives, and her hands fairly shook with the wonder of it.

"I'll have a word with Mrs. Dimmity."

If she'd thought Dr. Walsh had looked tired that morning, she'd been wrong. Tired was how he looked now. Although something burned in his eyes that seemed to reflect the fiery sensation beneath her breast.

A sense of accomplishment? Of triumph? Or more?

"I didn't think. I just wanted . . ." He paused, and she heard the next word as if he'd spoken it aloud.

You.

Annabeth swallowed and ducked her head so he wouldn't see her flush. Unlike most women, when Annabeth's face heated, she did not appear lovely; rather, she looked blotchy and ill.

"I'll withdraw the request. Ye can go back to bein'—"

"No one," she interrupted. "Doing nothing."

If she hadn't been here and seen what had occurred, she might think they slaughtered hogs on a daily basis in this room. But she *had* been here, and she'd not only seen what was done, she'd been the one doing it.

A peace such as Annabeth had never known settled over her. There was nowhere else she would rather be.

"You will not withdraw your request, Dr. Walsh."

His eyebrows lifted, as did his lovely lips. She smiled in return as she realized something else.

There was no one else she'd rather be with.

CHAPTER 3

The intelligence on the Confederate Ranger Mosby led to Major Forbes being dispatched from Falls Church with one hundred and fifty Union men in pursuit of the partisans, which resulted in one hundred and six Union losses—twelve dead, thirty-seven wounded, and fifty-seven captured.

Mosby lost six men. Six.

Still, the information had been valuable enough to attract the attention of General Grant, who had given a commendation to Ethan through Law.

Men like you will win us this war.

Ethan only hoped it was soon. Each day brought more wounded, each night more dead. Ethan listened, looked, lurked, and discovered several more bits of information for Mikey. The last time they'd met, his brother related Law's newest plot to end the war.

"Losin' their leaders can make men retreat before they even start," Mikey said. "If we know where the battle's gonna be, me and the sniper will get there first. He'll eliminate the officers."

Ethan winced as if he'd heard the shots, but he couldn't argue with Law's logic. The removal of a few top men might, in the end, save the lives of many.

The sole bright spot in each day was Annabeth Phelan, and considering that Ethan saw her only across the bloody, broken bodies of young men, he shouldn't be so happy about it. However, his work was much easier now that she was part of it. She was intelligent, skilled, and devoted. He felt less alone every minute she was near.

He'd taken to thinking of her as *Beth* in his mind,

though he hadn't yet had the courage to call her so aloud. Would she think he was forward and crass? Or would she like it?

Ethan stepped from the surgery, then stood blinking at the sky. While buried in blood, he forgot how bright the stars were, how green the grass, how exquisite the flowers. As he lowered his gaze, he saw Miss Phelan—*Beth*, his mind whispered—speaking to a man he didn't recognize. Not that such was unusual. There were so many people at Chimborazo—personnel, patients, soldiers—in truth, he hardly knew any.

But there was something about this one that made Ethan uneasy. He kept his cap drawn low and his face tilted so shadows obscured his features. His clothes were baggy, dirty, and nondescript. Of course, at this point in the war, whose weren't? Everyone made do with what they had, found, or stole. Still, Ethan had learned enough since becoming a spy to suspect that anyone trying that hard to appear like everyone else wasn't.

He took a step in that direction, and the man murmured to Annabeth, ducked his head, and strode away. Ethan might have followed, perhaps called out, but she turned, and the moon cast a bluish hue across her open, honest, innocent face. She wasn't beautiful, perhaps not even pretty, but when she smiled at him, all Ethan saw was her.

"Was there something you needed, Doctor?"

You, his mind whispered.

"Not at the moment," he said, lifting his gaze to seek out the fellow she'd spoken with and determine where he'd gone.

Except he *was* gone. Considering all that lay before them was a long, flat expanse that led nowhere, Ethan's neck prickled. "Who was that ye were talkin' to?"

"A friend from childhood."

An unreasoning jealousy overcame him. She, no doubt, had friends all over this camp, all over this state. He wanted to be her friend.

Liar. He wanted to be so much more.

"You shouldn't be out here alone."

"I'm not alone." Her lips curved. "I have you."

He wanted her to have him, while he had her. His attraction for Annabeth Phelan was all consuming. He dreamed of her throughout the endless nights.

"Not all men are like me."

"None of them are."

She didn't know how right she was, and she never could.

"I'll walk ye to yer quarters."

She nodded and led him back the way he had come, past the surgery, in the opposite direction. He forgot about her friend—where he'd gone, who he was, and why, if he was a friend, he'd disappeared instead of shaking hands and introducing himself. It was only later Ethan thought of such things.

They didn't speak; they didn't touch, and that was all right. Whenever Ethan was with her, pretty much everything was.

"Here we are," she murmured.

Ethan had no excuse for what he did next. She wasn't his; she couldn't be. Yet when she lifted her face, he kissed her. Nothing was ever the same again.

She did not gasp; she did not cry out or push him away. She did not even stiffen; though he did. Down low, where such things occurred, he came immediately to rigid, relentless, and ready life.

He'd said she shouldn't be out alone because not all men were like him. But the way he felt now, he was very like the men he'd warned her about. He wanted to shove her against the wall right here, or perhaps drag her between the buildings over there. Haul up her skirts, skim a finger over the soft skin where thigh became buttock, fill his palms with that flesh as she gasped into his mouth, as she whispered his name.

"Ethan."

As she whispered it now, against his lips, their breath mingling. They stood so close, she would have felt the brush of his erection if not for the barrier of her skirts and crinoline. Then she would have been screaming, pushing, pointing. Telling him and everyone who would listen what he had done, how he had dared. He would find himself married to her by tomorrow, and that would be—

Her tongue touched his. How could she help it? His had somehow made its way into her mouth, and she tasted of dawn. Of new days and hope. Of sunshine pushing through darkness. Of life. And Ethan thought . . .

If he found himself married to her tomorrow, perhaps that wouldn't be so bad.

In the distance, cannons sounded, reminding him who he was, why he was here. He couldn't marry her while living a lie. He shouldn't kiss her while living one either.

Ethan stepped back. Her mouth glistened in the moonlight. Her tongue peeked out, as if she wanted to taste him again. He certainly wanted to taste her.

"Beth, I . . ." he began, uncertain what he meant to say, to do.

"Don't you *dare* say you're sorry!"

He snapped his mouth shut as she spun and went into the building. The slam of the door echoed almost as loudly as the artillery.

Had he meant to say that? Probably. It was what men like him did with women like her in situations like—

He glanced around. This situation was not one for which any etiquette existed. He was a physician with the blood of men—no, the blood of *boys*—beneath his fingernails. She was a nurse who no doubt had the same blood in the same place. They were not in a drawing room preparing to dance. The only music was that distant rumble of guns.

Yes, kissing her had been inappropriate. But here . . . What wasn't?

Annabeth's lips still tingled; she could taste Ethan on her tongue. Closing her eyes, she pressed her fingers to her mouth.

He'd called her Beth. No one else ever had, and the way he'd said her name in an accent that brought to mind emerald hills she hadn't seen yet somehow knew made her shiver despite the never-ending heat.

Were all kisses the same? Consuming. Inflaming. A promise to a world unexplored.

She had been kissed only once before, and at the first

touch of the boy's lips, she'd hauled back and broken his nose.

"You took long enough to get here."

Annabeth's lips tightened beneath her fingertips. She dropped her hand. "Speak of the devil"—Annabeth opened her eyes as Moses Farquhar stepped out of the gloom—"and he appears."

With golden hair and a gaze the shade of spring grass, Moze would have been too pretty if it weren't for the permanent crick she'd put in his slightly large nose when he was fourteen. Why he'd thought he could kiss her back then, she'd never quite figured out. At the time, she'd wanted to pound him into the dirt the way she had when she was eight. On the Phelan farm, Moze had just seemed like one more brother among many.

When Mrs. Farquhar died after scraping herself with a pitchfork used to shovel manure—her arm had first swelled, then oozed, then turned black—her husband was unable to care for three-year-old Moze and still manage the farm. Annabeth's mother, who already had six children underfoot, had shrugged and welcomed another.

As Moze and Luke were a few months apart in age, they'd been inseparable from the first. Even after his father remarried and Moze returned home, the two boys had spent all of their time together, doing their chores side by side, first at one farm, then at the other. For fun, they would harass Annabeth until she wanted nothing more than to smother them both.

"You're the one who ran off as if he had something to hide," Annabeth said.

"I do."

"Moze, what are you—?"

"I'm a spy, Annie Beth Lou." He called her by the name both he and Luke had used for her when they were children. She hadn't liked it much then either.

Silence reigned, broken only by the distant guns; then Annabeth laughed. "Sure you are."

"Did you ever wonder how I could stop in and check on you both at the farm and here? If I were attached to a regiment, I wouldn't be free to travel about."

He had a point. But his behavior tonight had her asking: "Who are you spying on?"

"Whom do you think?"

"The way you slipped off at the first sight of Dr. Walsh, I wonder."

He made a disgusted sound. "Only Yankees shorten names, *Beth*." The nickname, when spoken with a sarcastic Southern twist, no longer sounded like an endearment. "Haven't you ever noticed that?"

"As I don't know any Yankees, I haven't."

"You'll have to take my word on it."

"What are you trying to say?"

He sighed and reached into his pocket, withdrawing a paper and holding it out.

Annabeth put her hands behind her back; an unreasonable belief took hold of her. If she didn't look at that paper, whatever was written on it would not be true.

Moze tightened his lips at the same time he tightened his fingers, crumpling the sheet and dropping it to the floor. "Luke is missing."

"Missing?" she repeated. "What does that mean?"

"Captured. Wounded. Gone."

She didn't like any of those words, but at least they meant—

"Alive."

His gaze flicked to hers, then away. "Not always. Missing can mean dead but never found. Lying in a Yankee hospital. Unnamed in one of ours."

"Where did this happen?"

"Mount Zion Church."

"I didn't hear anything about a battle there."

"Not a battle." He let out a quick breath. "He's with Mosby. Or at least he was."

"He's a guerilla?"

"Partisan," Moze snapped.

"They were disbanded." The partisans were considered rogues, rebels even in a rebel army, and Lee had hated them.

"Mosby's Rangers were allowed to continue, as they possessed some form of military discipline."

"How long has Luke been with them?"

"From the beginning."

"And you didn't tell me?

"Luke didn't want you to worry."

"Luke? Or you?"

"Does it matter?"

"No." She *would* have worried; she *had* worried. "Thank you for letting me know."

"I didn't come for that."

"Then why?"

His hands clenched, released. "You shouldn't be kissing him."

"You're here to instruct me about whom I should kiss?"

He rubbed the bump in his nose. "Why didn't you hit him?"

"None of your business. Now, why are you here? Besides the desire to stick your crooked nose where it doesn't belong?"

"Someone at Chimborazo has been telling the Yankees everything he sees, hears, and reads."

Understanding dawned. "You can't—He isn't—Ethan's a doctor. A very good one."

"That doesn't mean he isn't a spy as well."

"Why would you think that?"

"One man came through this hospital who knew that Mosby was headed to Rectortown."

"Only one? I find that hard to believe."

"Believe it. He was sent to call the Rangers. He delivered the message, but he never returned to the rendezvous. I traced him here. Directly to Dr. Walsh's table."

"That means nothing."

"The only person with the knowledge of the Rangers' movements comes to Chimborazo; the last man he sees is Ethan Walsh. Then the Yankees arrive."

"You spoke with this messenger? He admitted telling Dr. Walsh the information? Who else was in the room?"

"When he's not unconscious, he's delirious. Even if he survives, he'll be lucky if he remembers his name, let alone what he said and to whom he talked."

Annabeth threw up her hands. "Which means you have no proof."

"I'm not done. There's a Yankee sniper killing officers."

"Isn't that what Yankee snipers do?"

"He arrives ahead of everyone, shoots before the armies even engage. Every single division that's lost their leaders reported sending wounded here. Wounded who were well aware in which direction they were marching. Next thing we know, their officers are shot in the head." Annabeth flinched as if she'd heard the report. "This man is the best marksman we've ever seen. We have to stop him."

"How do you plan to do that?"

"I'll need some help." His imploring gaze told her exactly whom he needed help from.

"Not me," she said.

"Luke may be dead because of intelligence that came from *this* hospital. Don't you want to know if Dr. Walsh is responsible before you kiss him again?"

"He isn't."

"You're so sure?" Moze asked, and she nodded. "Then prove it."

After a nearly sleepless night, Annabeth rolled out of bed at dawn and went to work. She stepped into the surgery ward and paused at the sight of Ethan Walsh.

He glanced up, saw her, and glanced back down. Her face heated, and she ducked her head. Would they forever be uncomfortable around each other now? He was no doubt mortified that he'd kissed his nurse and given the poor, plain girl ideas. And Annabeth? She couldn't stop thinking of what Moze had said last night.

Prove it.

"Beth," Ethan began, and she winced.

Only Yankees shorten names.

Would Moze *ever* shut up?

"I'll apologize fer me forwardness, *Miss* Phelan."

His voice had gone cool. He'd seen her reaction and believed she was offended because he'd overstepped.

She wanted to assure him that he hadn't, but it was probably for the best if they returned to formalities.

"What would you like me to do, sir?"

"Back to 'sir' and 'miss,' " he murmured, then gave a brisk nod. "Fresh dressing here—charcoal and yeast." He pointed. "Cool cloth there." He indicated another man. "Watch this one closely. The wound has swelled and gone red."

"Erysipelas?"

He studied her. "Ye never cease to impress, Miss Phelan. Aye. If he progresses to chills, yet he sweats, and his pulse is far too fast, find me." That condition, known as pyemia, followed the swelling and redness of erysipelas and was nearly always fatal. She could tell Dr. Walsh was disturbed by it. Very few of his patients contracted the disease.

"If that happens, sir, there isn't anything to be done but hold his hand."

He paused at the door. "As he's my patient, I'd like to be the one holdin' it." He left without looking back.

Annabeth did her best to keep the fellow at death's door from stepping through, but when the young man's eyes rolled back and he began to jerk with violent paroxysms, she waited at his side until he quieted; then she went to fetch Ethan. He wasn't anywhere in the building.

Seeing him that morning had unsettled her. Hearing him call her by the nickname she at turns loved and loathed had brought Moze's disturbing accusation to the forefront of her mind. She didn't believe Ethan was a spy any more in the light of day than she had in the dark of night. But still . . .

If you're so damn sure it isn't him, it won't hurt to prove it.

Had Moze known that planting the seed of doubt would make everything Ethan said or did suspect? Probably. Moze was a spy, after all.

She couldn't believe she hadn't suspected him of it before. That she hadn't made her feel gullible. If a man she'd known all her life had fooled her, couldn't one she'd known only a little while do the same?

Annabeth stopped a steward. "Where's Dr. Walsh?"

The white-haired fellow spread his one remaining hand. "If he ain't here . . ." She shook her head. "Try his quarters." Her confused expression brought forth a huff. "On this side of Georgia Hospital."

Chimborazo was so large, it had been divided into five sections, each with its own chief surgeon. In an attempt to impose order over the disorder, soldiers were assigned a section based on their state of origin. The first section, where Annabeth and Ethan worked, was known as Virginia Hospital. The other four were Georgia, North Carolina, Alabama, and South Carolina. Annabeth had no idea what they did with patients from Tennessee or Mississippi.

The steward sped away as glass broke in the infirmary. From the shouts, Annabeth deduced her patient was again jerking and spasming uncontrollably. She had to search out the good doctor wherever he might be before the end came and no further handholding was required. That Ethan felt such devotion to his patients gave her a tight, warm feeling in the center of her chest. None of the other doctors were half as dedicated.

Just outside the physicians' ward, which appeared exactly the same as the surgery ward—single story, long, and wide—she hesitated. Should she knock? Then it opened and one of the doctors stepped out. He blinked to find her hovering. "Miss?"

"One of Dr. Walsh's patients—"

He jerked a thumb over his shoulder. "Inside," he said before he hurried on.

The air within was still and stifling; the windows did little to help since there wasn't any breeze. Cots stood in a double row from front to back. All lay unoccupied save one.

"Sir?" she called. He didn't move. "Dr. Walsh?" He muttered and turned over.

Asleep. She hated to wake him, but she had to.

Annabeth approached. As she leaned over, hand outstretched, he said, "I'll see you soon."

With no accent at all.

CHAPTER 4

D r. Walsh!" Someone shook his shoulder.

"Mmm," he murmured, and burrowed deeper into the feather tick.

Except the lovely, soft bed he'd been dreaming of no longer felt so soft. In truth, it made a rickety squawk beneath him as a hand shook him again.

The scent of lavender and mint enveloped him, and he snatched the hand before it could escape. He opened his eyes, smiling into hers.

"Doctor." An odd expression darkened Annabeth's gaze and put a crease between her brows. Unease trickled down his spine, and he sat up, narrowly missing her chin with his head.

She stepped back, shoving her hands into her pockets. "Your patient is worse."

He stood, realized he'd taken off his boots, and sat again. "What happened?"

"Paroxysms."

"Hell." He stomped his heel into the right boot. When he glanced up, she was gone.

Moments later he entered the operating room as the man breathed his last. Neck wounds usually resulted in death on the field. Very few ever reached Chimborazo. The only injury more deadly was one to the head.

Still, his patient might have survived if he'd avoided pyemia, what Ethan referred to in his own mind as poisoning of the blood. As far as he knew, there was no cure once the condition took hold. Ethan believed his insistence on cleanliness was the reason so few of his patients died of it, but some still did. Each one tore at him, and though there was nothing he could do, he didn't like for them to die alone. He should have stayed here, but he'd been so damn tired.

He motioned for a steward. The quicker the dead were removed, the better. Not just for morale but for hygiene.

Not wishing to watch the man being carted away—the sight always made him feel a failure—Ethan turned and saw Annabeth. She laid her hand atop a pile of clothing, straightened a set of boots, hung her head. From her pensiveness, if not the blood on the material, he deduced the garments belonged to the deceased.

She glanced his way, then scurried off. He never should have kissed her. He'd ruined everything.

At a loss—no new casualties, and all his other patients had been tended to already—Ethan crossed to where she had stood. As was his habit, he slipped his fingers into the pockets of the dead soldier's shirt. Empty. Coat. Nothing. Trousers. The same. He nearly left before he remembered the boots. Shoving his hand inside, he found a wad of paper in one toe.

Perhaps the footwear had belonged to a soldier with bigger feet who'd died before this one, his boots then confiscated. But if that were the case, why wasn't there paper in both toes?

Ethan unfurled the stuffing. A chill went over him; he crumpled the missive once more and put it back. He set the boots where they'd been and strolled away as if he hadn't just read information that could put an end to the war.

Annabeth wanted to take back the note Moze had written the instant she shoved it into the dead man's boot. But Ethan arrived soon after, and she was afraid he'd see her do so.

As the only thing worse than setting a trap for a spy was being caught in that trap *by* the spy, she left the missive behind and ran away. If Ethan was innocent, nothing would come of this. The information would remain in the dead boy's boot; no one would arrive at the false rendezvous but Moze. Then she could say "I told you so" forever and ever more. That might almost make a day of shaking hands and nervous sweat worth it.

Later, she returned to the surgery ward and retrieved the dead soldier's clothes and boots. Before she consigned the blood-drenched clothing to the top of a pile of similar items that would be burned, she searched the pockets for personal items, found none.

Another man could use the boots. She would turn them over to a steward as soon as she—

Annabeth stuck her hand to the bottom and smiled when she found the crumpled paper precisely where she'd left it.

Annabeth and Ethan returned to the easy rapport of their working relationship, pretending, at least in each other's presence, that their kiss had never happened.

When she slept, however, Annabeth dreamed of a lot more than his kiss. She couldn't stop herself. He was brilliant and beautiful, and when he looked at her as if she were brilliant and beautiful, too, she couldn't help but fall in love with him.

Annabeth learned something new daily, sometimes hourly. Word spread of the physician at Chimborazo who saved more lives than he lost. Officers began to request his care. Soldiers arrived on stretchers with his name pinned to their bloody, torn uniforms.

And the war raged on.

The night of the false rendezvous detailed in the note came and went with no sign of Moses Farquhar. When Ethan asked her to accompany him on a picnic, she agreed with such enthusiasm, she embarrassed herself.

What if Ethan were exactly who he appeared to be? What if she were?

As she dressed in the only garment she'd brought from home—here she wore dark clothes like everyone else—a peach day dress with white sprigs dotted on the full skirt, she chided herself. Certainly she'd planted the note, but that didn't make her a spy. Especially if no one had found it. Which meant no one had gone to the meeting and nothing had happened. If it had, Moze would have arrived to arrest Ethan by now.

The clatter of a horse and buggy drew Annabeth to the door just as Ethan reined in. Seeing him arrive so grandly, she asked, "Is this yours?"

He jumped to the ground and offered her a polite hand up. "The horse is, aye. The buggy is a loan from a grateful patron."

Ethan joined her and clucked to the horse, which did not appear at all comfortable with the clattering carriage at its heels. Nevertheless, the animal drew them away from Chimborazo toward the flowing land beyond.

She'd often been dazzled by the beauty of the area that surrounded them. As Chimborazo was located on an elevated plain, they could see ships in the river harbor. To the west rose the spires of Richmond, and as they trotted east, once-lush farmlands surrounded them.

The armies had moved away for a spell, ending the distant thunder of artillery. Annabeth had become so accustomed to it that for the first few nights after the rattles and booms faded, she could not sleep.

"What do you mean by patron?" she asked.

"One of the boys we saved was from Richmond."

"A lot of them are." They worked in Virginia Hospital and the Confederacy's capital contained a large population.

"Not all of them have General Carstairs fer a papa. He asked what he could do fer me. I requested the use of a buggy. He sent one over directly."

"And the picnic?"

Ethan cast her a sidelong glance. "I have sewed a stitch or two in a cook's flesh. One was most happy to offer a basket."

They found the perfect spot in a grove of trees, a nearby brook providing water for the horse and a gentle music, along with the wind through the leaves. As he spread a blanket and she set out the food, they spoke of Chimborazo, of medicine and patients, of things that to others would be both boring and inappropriate but to them was fascinating.

They ate cold chicken and corn bread, drank from the brook, then lay on the blanket and watched the clouds float by. Annabeth had never been so content. Or so in love.

"You told me I shouldn't apologize fer kissing ye." His fingers curled around hers. "And I can't."

When he turned his head, she could not help but turn hers. Their noses nearly brushed. The blue of the sky caused his gray eyes to shimmer like a lake at dawn.

"I can't," he continued, "because all I want is to kiss ye again."

The next instant, she was in his arms. He tasted of sweet bread and cool water, with a hint of darkness just beneath. She wanted that darkness; she reached for it with her tongue, stroked his teeth, and he moaned.

He rose above her, and the sun winked out. She didn't mind. It had been so bright, she felt blinded. Or perhaps he had merely blinded her. She wanted to pull him closer, have him lay that long, lean body over hers and do things she'd only heard about in whispers.

He set his fingers in her hair; her pins sprinkled around them like hail; he rained kisses along her chin and jaw, pressed his lips to her neck, traced his tongue to the base of her bodice and tugged on it with his teeth.

Her breasts seemed to swell against her corset. She wriggled, then gasped as her nipples scraped the tight, hard material. She wanted his hands on her. His mouth. His tongue and teeth. She curled her palms around his neck and pulled him closer.

Sensations she'd never experienced, never imagined, rolled over and through her. Her skin was so sensitive, her stomach a jittery mess. And lower, where her legs met, she throbbed so uncomfortably, she couldn't help but arch and squirm.

The unexpected movement brushed his fingers against one breast. Before he could jerk away, she brought it back, laid his palm over the tingling swell. His thumb slid over the nipple, and her entire body tightened as her breath caught in her throat.

"Please," she whispered, and he pulled away, sitting up, moving back, not touching her any more at all.

Annabeth lay there staring at the sky and wishing it would fall on her so she wouldn't have to look at him. How mortifying to beg for more and have him deny her.

"Beth," he said, and her teeth ground together. "We can't."

"Why?"

His short, sharp exhale held a tinge of amusement.

Fury consumed her and she sat up, too. "You think I'm a child. That I don't know what I want."

"Ye are a child, and ye have no idea what yer askin' of me."

"Teach me." His gaze flicked to hers, then away. "Someone has to."

"Yer husband."

"Couldn't you—"

"No," he snapped, and she flinched. At least he didn't see her reaction, because he still couldn't meet her eyes. "The war, Beth. Our part in it. My part. I can't marry ye when I'm—" He paused. "I can't."

"You're already married."

"No!" His head jerked up. "It's not that attall."

"You're betrothed."

"No," he repeated.

"Then why? I thought you cared about me."

He didn't answer, and she began to doubt her own words. Why would he care for her? She was huge, gangling, red haired, and freckled. He was . . . Ethan—so brilliant and beautiful, he dazzled. She'd thought because they shared so much—medicine, helping others, the cause—that it might be enough. But it wasn't.

Annabeth began to put what was left of the food into the basket. It gave her something to do other than weep.

"I do care," he murmured. She ignored him. He was suddenly at her side, his hand on her wrist. "Look at me."

She shook her head. If she looked at him, she'd see all that she wanted and could never, ever have.

"I love ye, lass."

A sob stuck in her throat, choking her.

"I do! And because I do, I won't take yer virginity on a blanket beneath the sun while the war yet rages."

"What if the war never ends?"

"It will." He took a long breath and tangled their fingers together. "I'd do anything to make this war stop."

Annabeth felt a tingle of unease. However, wouldn't *she* do anything to make the war end? So boys would stop dying, armies would stop marching, she could find her brother, then marry and start a new life.

Ethan was right. Until the war ended, nothing else could begin.

She shut the top on the basket. "We should get back."

"I'm—"

"Shh." Annabeth laid a hand on his arm. "Don't."

Apologizing for touching her only made her feel as if they'd done something wrong, when in truth, nothing had ever felt so right.

He carried the basket to the buggy, helped her onto the seat, then clucked to the horse, but they did not head toward Richmond.

"There's a . . . a patient," he said in answer to her curious glance. "He lives up the road a pace." He lifted his chin to indicate a thicker area of trees. "I haven't seen him for a spell, and I'd like to make sure he's all right, if ye don't mind."

"Of course not."

No doubt her mother would say that traveling farther from Chimborazo and deeper into unknown territory with a man who was more mysterious than open was a fool's errand. But Annabeth had already established her penchant for foolishness where Ethan Walsh was concerned.

The trees thinned; a clearing appeared, with a dilapidated cabin to the rear of an equally decrepit barn. Nothing moved but the wind. Something wasn't right.

Annabeth knew it even before Ethan climbed from the buggy, lifting a hand to keep her in the seat.

He strode to the door. "Mikey?" he called in a tight, tense voice. Opening it, he stepped within.

Annabeth's gaze wandered to what was left of the barn. Age and rain, wind and sun had caused much of the roof to collapse; the structure possessed only three remaining walls, and they swayed so badly, Annabeth thought one or more would give way soon.

Ethan backed out of the cabin. The stiff set of his shoulders made her reach for the rifle under the seat.

As he emerged from the shadows and into the sun, a rifle seemed to sprout from his chest. The other end was held by a tall, broad man with tangled, dirty hair that obscured much of his face. He had the look of a deserter, desperate and dangerous with little left to lose. Annabeth straightened, keeping her own gun out of sight beneath her skirts.

"You come to see the gigantour who lives here?" the man asked.

"He's my patient."

"He's a spy."

Annabeth blinked. The person who lived here was a spy? Did that mean Ethan wasn't? Perhaps Moze had gotten confused. Although, how would a fellow who lived in the woods discover information from injured soldiers at Chimborazo?

"I have no idea about that," Ethan said. "I'm a doctor. He needed help."

"You're General Grant's spy. I suppose old U.S. told you to sneak behind the lines and keep sniffing until you find enough information to make the South surrender unconditionally, just the way he likes it."

Union newspapers had remarked that General Grant's initials—U.S.—were short for Unconditional Surrender, after the Battle of Fort Donelson when he'd told the fort's commanding officer that "no terms except unconditional and immediate surrender can be accepted." The nickname was so clever, even Abraham Lincoln had endorsed it.

Ethan didn't answer the man. Annabeth no longer thought the stranger a deserter. She almost wished he were.

"If your sniper pal had killed both Massa Jeff and Uncle Rob, Grant would have his wish. The Confederacy wouldn't survive without Davis and Lee."

Annabeth's fingers tightened around the gunstock as she remembered the words on the paper she'd stuffed into the dead man's boot.

Paris Ridge, Tuesday next. Midnight. Massa Jeff and Uncle Rob.

Uncle Rob was one of General Lee's nicknames. Everyone loved him. Massa Jeff referred to Jefferson Davis. Although the moniker had originally been spoken with affection, of late folks had begun to say it with a hint of scorn. Nevertheless, Moze certainly knew how to bait a trap.

"Where's Mikey?" Ethan demanded.

"Where do you think? There's one punishment for spies."

Ethan staggered, and for an instant Annabeth thought he might faint. His captor must have, too. He reached for Ethan's arm, lifting the gun away from Ethan's chest for just an instant.

Ethan pushed the barrel downward; his elbow jabbed up. The man's nose crunched, though the sound was forgotten in the roar of the rifle as a bullet plowed into the ground.

Ethan yanked the weapon from the fellow's hand, whirling on one leg, the other sweeping forward and knocking the stranger's feet out from under him. He landed on the ground with an "oof" and lay still.

Flustered, frightened, Annabeth fumbled with her own rifle. She was still trying to disentangle it from her skirt when Ethan landed next to her. He reached for the reins, then froze.

"Go!" she shouted.

"Too late."

Annabeth lifted her eyes. They were surrounded.

CHAPTER 5

Ethan didn't care for the look of the men who emerged from the trees. He specifically didn't care for the way they stared at Annabeth.

He'd thought they were safe. The armies had moved off, and if the intelligence he'd passed to Mikey proved useful, the war would soon be over.

He'd waited several days past the Tuesday next indicated in the note with no news. He couldn't wait any longer. As they'd been so close to the cabin, what could it hurt to stop in and ask what had happened?

Ethan should have known better. Questions such as that always turned out badly.

"Let the lady return to Richmond," he said as their weapons were confiscated and the bloody man on the porch was helped to his feet. "She's a nurse. They need her there."

"We need her here." The nearest fellow leered, revealing all four of his teeth.

"They're awaiting her at Chimborazo." The desperation in his voice only made them laugh. "She *must* be returned there."

The laughter died. "You aren't in charge here, spy."

"I'm not—"

"Shut up." The leader by virtue of his uniform epaulettes, dirty and torn, but still there, cast Ethan a glare. "We know who you are. We was headed to Chimborazo next."

"She isn't—"

"You're a spy; she's with you; she comes with us."

"I confess," he blurted. "Just let her go."

"No." The man reached over and took the reins of their horse.

The absence of Mikey was worrisome on several counts. His brother had yet to be surprised by man or beast. The fact that the Rebs knew about both him and the sniper, as well as the rendezvous and this cabin all led to one conclusion: Mikey had been captured or worse. As the common punishment for traitors was immediate death—hanging for spies, shooting for snipers—Ethan had a very bad feeling. Although . . .

They'd labeled *him* a spy, and he was still breathing.

The return trip to Richmond continued in silence. Annabeth wouldn't look at him; he didn't blame her. She was going . . . somewhere, and it would not be good because she'd been foolish enough to trust him. He'd come to Chimborazo to listen, to learn, to lie—hell, to spy. He'd do it again. The only thing he'd change was her.

He would never allow her near him. No smiles, no touches, no scent of lavender and mint, no working together, no laughter and light. Definitely not one single kiss.

"Oh, no," Annabeth whispered as if she'd heard his thoughts, and her voice shook.

She'd gone as pale as the clouds they'd so recently admired. Her deep blue eyes glittered. Her hands wrung. Her freckles flared. Ethan followed her gaze and cursed.

Richmond's Castle Thunder was one of the most notorious prisons of the Confederacy. It was comprised of three buildings that had once been warehouses and a tobacco factory. The majority of the captives were spies, political prisoners, and those accused of treason.

"Shove him in there." The leader pointed to Palmer's Factory. Two men dragged Ethan from the buggy.

"Palmer's is for Union deserters," Ethan said. He might be a lot of things, but he wasn't that.

"Was," the man who towed Ethan's right arm said. "Now it's for prisoners of war, too."

"And spies," the man on his left said. "Though you're the only one of those we got."

"The only one?"

The man grinned. *He* had all his teeth. Sadly, they were black as night. "Kilt all the rest."

The door opened, and they pushed him through. Ethan spun, but the door clanged shut before he could snatch one last, precious glance of Annabeth.

Ethan was a spy, just as Moze had suspected. The trap he had set, that she had, was sprung, and not only had Ethan been caught, but Annabeth had as well.

The gazes of her captors made her skin itch as if she'd rolled in filth. She had to clench her hands to keep from scratching at her hair, through which a hundred insects seemed to crawl.

Her gaze went to the now-closed door. She wanted Ethan back no matter who he was, no matter what he'd done. Better than being here, with them.

Alone.

If she'd learned one thing from living with five brothers, it was to bluff and bluff big. Fear only brought out the worst in both man and beast. These appeared a bit of both.

"I am a nurse at Chimborazo," she announced. "My brothers have all died for the cause. I am as much of a patriot as y'all."

No one answered. Annabeth was tempted to say that she'd been the one who set the trap. But something kept her silent.

The same men who'd dragged Ethan into the building led her toward Whitlock's Warehouse.

The Confederacy had begun to incarcerate women and negroes in this portion of Castle Thunder. How long would Annabeth be here before Moze discovered her missing? Would he think to search for her in prison? Would she ever get out?

She had no one to blame but herself. She'd planted the information to prove Moze wrong. Now that *she'd* been proven wrong instead, she wasn't sure what to think, how to feel, what to do.

Should she hate Ethan? His spying had not only

resulted in the disappearance of her little brother, but could easily have been the cause of the deaths of one or more of the others. She had no idea how long he'd been at his job or where he'd plied his trade before Chimborazo. He had certainly caused the deaths of innumerable Confederate soldiers. So why, instead of a desire to see him suffer, did she have to fight a sudden panic that she might never see him alive again?

I'd do anything to make this war stop.

When he'd said those words, she had wholeheartedly agreed. Of course he'd said them as a Confederate doctor.

Or had he? Ethan *wasn't* a Confederate doctor.

She thought of hearing him speak in his sleep without the accent. Was he even Irish? Was his name Walsh? Or Ethan for that matter? What else had he lied about?

I love ye, lass.

Her face heated as she remembered begging him to take her. Was his refusal that of a gentleman or merely because of a line he was not willing to cross? He'd said he didn't have a wife. But he'd said a lot things. Most of them untrue.

The door of Whitlock's Warehouse closed behind Annabeth with a final, fearsome thud. The smell within made her stagger. The shouts of women—half clothed, all filthy—made her flinch.

"I've done nothing," she began, then paused to clear the sudden tickle from her throat.

"But you will." The man on her right winked, or tried to; he was unable to close one eye without closing the other as well, making the motion more of an exaggerated squint. "You'll do a lot. For everyone." He jerked his head toward the unseen women in the rear. "Like they do."

"No," she whispered.

"You want to eat?"

Considering the stench, Annabeth wasn't sure she'd ever want to eat again. Would she ever want to eat badly enough to do things she could only imagine? She didn't think so, but she'd never been truly hungry either.

"Tell you what." The soldier on her left leaned close.

"You let me lick this"—he squeezed her breast—"I let you lick . . ." He grabbed his crotch, and his tongue snaked out.

"Me first." The other man jerked her right.

"No." She flew to the left.

A door opened; a gun cocked. "Mine," came a low, vicious voice.

The men dropped her arms and fled.

Annabeth stood in the dark hall, doing her best to ignore the distant screams and shouts. She tried to see into the shadowed room, to catch a glimpse of whoever had spoken, but she couldn't.

Somewhere outside, a whip cracked. Cries, then laughter. The whip sounded again. She rubbed her arms. Those men had left bruises. She doubted they'd be her last.

"Come," the voice whispered, and unease trickled over her. She didn't want to go in there, then again . . . She glanced toward the screams.

"Better mine than everyone's, don't you think?"

Though all she wanted was to be Ethan's, Annabeth straightened her shoulders, lifted her chin, and entered the room.

Hundreds of soldiers filled Palmer's Factory. Most were Union deserters, rough and violent men with no sense of morals or loyalty. But they bled red just like everyone else. Within an hour of his arrival, Ethan had stitched wounds and bound broken limbs. The conditions weren't ideal—hell they were disgusting—but he had to do something or go mad.

Where was Annabeth? What were they doing to her? Was Mikey dead? How was Ethan going to survive if either one of them died because of him?

He asked after Mikey, but no one had seen him. And if Michael Walsh were here, someone—everyone— would have.

The more Ethan helped people, the more people appeared in need of help. Within a few days, he'd claimed a section of the building as an infirmary—no one seemed to care—and did the best he could with what he had. However, without alcohol, soap, clean bandages, or instruments, he was unable to do more for most of his patients than watch them get worse and then die. But he couldn't just let them expire without doing something, even if what he did was mostly nothing.

Ethan was bent over a suppurating leg sore when a shadow blocked his light—what there was of it.

"Whatcha doin', Ethan?"

Ethan dropped the bowie knife, all he had with which to open the sore. He'd have to clean the blade again, but what difference did it make? He hadn't been able to clean it very well in the first place. He looked up into the grinning face of—

"Mikey."

A lump marked his brother's forehead, and his eye was swollen, the skin around it blue-black, but other than that, he appeared unharmed.

"I thought—" Ethan's voice broke.

"What?" Mikey sat on the other side of the patient, who glanced back and forth between the two of them with interest.

"I thought they hung you."

"Me?" Mikey laughed. "I'd break the tree."

"He would," the patient agreed.

Ethan ignored him. "I'm sure they could have found another way to execute you, if they'd wanted to."

That they hadn't was another curiosity to add to the ones he already had.

"Where have you been?" he asked. It had been a week since the rendezvous night. "What happened?"

"You think you could talk while you finish my leg?" The fellow on the cot grimaced. "Hurts somethin' awful."

"Of course." Ethan retrieved the knife, wiped off whatever muck it had accumulated on the floor with the least-filthy cloth available, then indicated Mikey should move back. Mikey, who'd learned the hard way not to argue with Ethan in situations like these, did.

"Went to the place you said," Mikey began. "Soon's me and the sniper arrived, we were surrounded. Rebs took their time gettin' us from there to here. Kept us in a barn for a few days while they waited for orders."

Ethan pinched his lips together and punctured the sore with the tip of the knife. The knife wasn't sharp enough, and he had to exert more pressure than he liked. The wound rose up on both sides of the blade, and Ethan considered what he would try next if this didn't work. Then the tight skin gave with a soft *pop,* and pestilence erupted as high as Mikey's shoulder.

"Ahh." The deserter sighed. "Thanks, Doc."

Ethan pressed a damp cloth to the mess. "Hold that a while."

Wouldn't do any good. The leg was infected so deeply, all Ethan could do was release the gore when it became too painful. But that was more than anyone else had done.

Ethan drew his brother aside. "I'm glad you're all right."

"Same here." Mikey slapped Ethan on the shoulder hard enough to make him step sideways. Ethan punched Mikey in the arm. His brother rubbed at the area as if Ethan had hurt him. Neither one of them could stop smiling.

They were Yankee spies in a Confederate prison, and heaven only knew if they'd survive, but for the moment, they were alive and they were together. At this point, it was probably the best they could hope for.

"I want you to meet Fedya."

"The sniper?"

Mikey nodded, beckoning Ethan to follow. "I like him."

As Mikey liked everyone, Ethan didn't comment. They were still a good distance from a group gathering at the opposite end of the warehouse when Mikey paused, head tilting.

"Hey, killer."

The words, low and vicious, seemed to echo around the suddenly silent room. Mikey strode ahead, shoving his way through a cluster of prisoners, Ethan at his heels.

A tall, dark-haired man sat on a cot in the center of the crowd. His fists clenched, he glared at the floor.

"Fedya," Mikey murmured, taking a step forward.

Ethan set a hand on his brother's arm as a man punched Fedya in the shoulder. "Hear you're quite the sniper."

Ethan recognized the voice even before Fedya shifted and revealed the speaker. Not a prisoner, but a guard, and the worst of the lot.

As wide as he was tall, which wasn't very, the man Ethan knew only as Beltrane possessed a squashed nose and protruding black eyes. He prodded Fedya in the stomach with the barrel of his Richmond rifle. "You must be the best if they sent you to kill the president and General Lee. We're gonna make you pay for that, boy. Pay long."

Fedya began to stand, and one of the other guards—all of them seemed to be here, which made Ethan wonder who was elsewhere—slammed a rifle into his head. When the sniper went to his knees, they began to kick him. The other inmates did not come to his aid. Instead they shouted encouragement and placed bets on how long until he lost consciousness. Or died.

It was most likely a mistake. One both he and Mikey would be sorry for, but Ethan couldn't just stand there and do nothing. As Mikey was already grabbing offenders and tossing them out of the way, Ethan waded in, too.

He was a doctor; he spent his time healing not hurting. But he also knew how to incapacitate a much larger foe with little but his hands and the knowledge of certain pressure points. He hadn't studied anatomy for nothing.

A jab to the kidneys. A thumb to the throat. A few other tricks he hoped no one saw. Within moments, the prisoners had retreated.

"I have enough folks in my infirmary," Ethan said. "I don't need any more."

Mikey growled; Beltrane glowered. But the guards left without any more violence.

Ethan wasn't so foolish as to believe that would be the end of it.

———

"Shut the door."

Annabeth complied. There was no one on the other side of it who would help her anyway.

The room was dark, the single window so dirty, the sunshine cast gray beams onto the floor. The speaker stood in the corner farthest from the light. She couldn't see his face, or much else beyond a man-shaped shadow.

"What in hell are you doing here, Annie Beth Lou?"

Annabeth blinked. "Moze?"

He stepped into the shallow light. He was so covered in filth, she wouldn't have recognized him if she hadn't known him nearly all of her days. Not recognizing his voice, she attributed to fear, panic, and exhaustion on her part, and also the fact that he sounded like a bullfrog with laryngitis.

"Of course, *Moze*," he snapped. "Who do you think?"

She resisted, barely, the urge to kick, to punch, to rain her fists on his chest and scream. "You scared me!"

"You should be scared." He glanced at the door. "Getting you out of here is going to take a goddamn miracle."

"I didn't *do* anything." She cleared her throat. Every time Moze moved, dust filled the air.

"Well, you did, but no one knows that." The dirt on his face cracked as he frowned. "And maybe . . . maybe they shouldn't."

Annabeth thought maybe they shouldn't either. It was bad enough that Ethan had been caught in her trap; having him learn the trap had been hers . . .

No, thank you.

"Walsh doesn't know you're a spy," Moze continued.

"I'm not."

Moze lifted his once-sandy brow, and Annabeth cursed. She was. Or at least she would be in Ethan's eyes.

If he ever learned the truth.

"He trusts you. You can discover more, if you stay."

"Discover what?" She threw up her hands. "Ethan's in prison. What's he going to learn there?"

"I won't know that until you do," Moze said in a perfectly reasonable voice that made her want to throttle him.

"I'm going back to Chimborazo," she said.

"Everyone here believes you're a traitor. Everyone there will as well."

He was right. Ethan had been proven a Yankee spy. As the woman who was considered his mistress, what would that make her?

She didn't want to know.

"Luke's at the Union prison in Rock Island, Illinois."

Annabeth gaped at the change in subject, then blurted, "Get him out."

"Hell, Annabeth, I can't get you out."

"Sure you can. You just don't want to." He scowled, but he didn't deny it. "Where's the sniper?"

Moze's scowl turned wary. "Why?"

"Tell me you didn't shoot him."

"Not yet." His gaze narrowed. "What are you thinking?"

"Prisoner exchange."

"That sniper's pretty important."

"So is Luke."

"To us."

"One of Mosby's Rangers should be worth as much as a sharpshooter."

"They might not know he's a Ranger. If they did, they would have hung him."

Grant *had* ordered immediate hanging for captured partisans.

"The Union is going to hand over just about anyone to get their sniper back," she said. "If they believe they're giving us only a lowly cavalryman, they'll do it even faster."

"My superiors won't agree."

"Then arrange the exchange on your own."

"Who the hell do you think I am? Bobby Lee?"

"I think you're a lot more than you're saying. You want me to spy for you, Moze? Get my brother back."

CHAPTER 6

Though Annabeth slept among the other female prisoners, she was not bothered by them or the guards. Which only added to her belief that Moze was a lot more powerful than he was letting on. Or maybe he was a lot more dangerous than he'd ever revealed. Either way, he managed to keep her safe during the time she spent in Whitlock's Warehouse, and he managed to get her permission to enter Palmer's Factory.

The joy that spread over Ethan's face the instant he saw Annabeth was echoed in the joy that burst to life within her at the sight of him. Whatever he'd held in his hand dropped to the floor forgotten as he crossed the room and crushed her into his embrace.

He was still a Yankee, a spy who'd betrayed her country, the man who might be responsible for one or more of her brothers' deaths. But she loved him.

"Beth," he murmured against her hair, saying the word for the first time without the Irish lilt. Lie though his accent had been, she missed it. "I'm sorry; I'm sorry."

She peered into his slate-gray eyes. "Me too."

"For what? I . . ." He released her, stepped back. She was suddenly cold despite the sweltering heat in Palmer's Factory. "You know what I did." She nodded. "I can't say I'm sorry for that. I believed—I *believe* I was saving lives." He lifted one shoulder. "A shorter war would be best for everyone."

After so many years of conflict, so many dead, she, too, wanted it over so they could all move on.

"I *am* sorry I lied to you," he continued. "That you were caught in my trap."

Annabeth managed not to wince. It had been *her* trap, and by not saying so, she was now the one lying. But telling him would do more harm than good.

"I can't believe they allowed you to say good-bye."

"Not good-bye. Not hardly. I'm your new nurse. Or maybe I'm your old nurse."

"No," he whispered. "You have to leave. You can't stay here."

"I was arrested, Ethan. I don't get to leave."

"I'll tell them you had nothing to do with it."

"Why didn't I think of that?"

"Where's a guard? The commandant?" He stepped past her, and she set her hand on his arm.

"They aren't going to believe you."

His mouth opened, closed. "Beth," he whispered, anguish chasing the joy from his face. She felt like muck on the bottom of a shoe.

"It doesn't matter," she said. "I have nowhere to go. I'd rather be here with you." And as those words were some of the truest she'd ever spoken, she smiled.

Ethan did not. "Go home."

"Can't." She coughed. Perhaps she'd swallowed a cobweb.

She crossed to the patient he'd been attending. The man was unconscious. Feverish and clammy. His leg appeared gangrenous. Considering the conditions, she wasn't surprised.

"Doctor?" she asked.

Ethan lifted his gaze.

"Will you join me?" She raised her brows.

He hesitated, but in the end he did.

She set her hand atop his. "I don't care what you've done."

It paled in comparison to what she had.

Mikey spent a lot of time scrounging for things that would help Ethan.

Clean shirts could become bandages. A single shot of whiskey might cleanse a wound just enough to allow someone to heal. Knives could become surgical instruments.

Stones, strings, pretty much anything might be useful. The trick was getting folks to part with what was often all they possessed.

The sniper Fedya proposed the idea of making people trade for medical attention. Ethan hadn't liked it.

"I'm a doctor. I can't take a man's last clean shirt before I sew his bloody arm."

"Then I will," Fedya said calmly. "Or, better yet . . ." He let his gaze travel over Mikey's large form and lifted a brow.

"I don't—" Ethan began.

"Precisely," Fedya interrupted. "You don't. You're trying to save people with spit and a rusty needle. I admire you for it, even if you are ten times a fool."

"Thanks," Ethan muttered.

"Dobro pozhalovat," Fedya returned, and Ethan frowned. "You're welcome," Fedya translated with a smirk.

For some reason, it annoyed Ethan when Fedya spoke in foreign tongues, which only made Fedya do it more often. Fedya had an ear for languages, and in Castle Thunder there were so many men from so many different countries, he sometimes spent hours learning from them.

Though Ethan and Fedya snarled and scowled at each other a lot, they also seemed to like being together. Some nights when Ethan sat up with a patient, Mikey would wake and see the two of them talking quietly together. Mikey thought Ethan needed a friend, and he couldn't find a better one than Fedya.

"I'll ask for payment, Ethan." Mikey didn't mind. Most times, all he had to do was ask.

"It isn't as though you're making the request for yourself, Doctor," Fedya said. "You're doing it for them."

He spread out his long-fingered hand, the gesture reminding Mikey of a man he'd seen once in a traveling show. That fellow had pulled a coin from behind someone's ear. Mikey had always wanted to do that. Maybe Fedya could teach him. He'd already taught Mikey a few Russian words, which Mikey whispered to himself each night before he slept. They sounded so pretty.

"Gentlemen." Miss Annabeth had arrived. Every morning a guard brought her from Whitlock's Warehouse to Palmer's Factory; she spent the day helping Ethan in the infirmary. At night they took her back.

"*Senorita.*" Fedya clicked his heels and bowed.

Annabeth rolled her eyes. She always treated Fedya like an annoying little brother. Mikey should know.

She patted Mikey's arm the way she did whenever she saw him—absently, but with love—or at least he thought it was love. No one had ever loved him but Ethan and their da, which wasn't the same thing as a woman's caring. However, when Annabeth looked at Ethan, love was all Mikey saw. She loved Ethan nearly as much as Ethan loved her. Seeing them together almost made being here all right.

Almost.

They were still in prison, and for Mikey, who was used to being out in the sun and the wind, to riding and tracking and hunting, prison hurt. Sometimes his stomach clenched from lack of food, his head ached from the stale air and dust, and he longed so much to stand beneath the sky, he thought he might cry.

If he'd been here alone, Mikey wasn't sure he'd have survived. But as long as he had his brother, who would never let anything truly bad happen to him, and Fedya, who was always good for a laugh or some sort of entertainment, Mikey managed. Along with the foreign words, which kept Mikey from being too bored, Fedya also taught Mikey and some of the other prisoners to imagine.

"Close your eyes," he'd say. "Think of a time when you were not here. Be there instead."

That helped. And as the days became weeks, then lengthened into months within the walls of Castle Thunder, Fedya organized games.

Not poker or checkers—they didn't have cards or a board. Instead they made believe that they were other people, in other places and times. Fedya was the best.

When he pretended to be someone else, he *became* them. It was almost scary. Mikey didn't often get to play—Ethan needed him—but when he did, he loved it.

The guards even watched their performances. Better than what those men would have done with their time otherwise. The guards had games, too. Ones no one wanted to play.

This was brought home to Mikey one afternoon when he went in search of Fedya and could not find him. They were in prison. Where could he be?

Shots erupted, closer than the distant artillery. These came from the brick enclosure between the buildings that was used for lashings and executions. Mikey had never been there.

He'd heard whispers of the games played with Fedya. Mikey had seen his friend perform incredible feats of marksmanship. He could understand why someone might want to see for themselves how spectacular Fedya was.

Mikey headed toward those shots. The door leading to the courtyard yawned wide. No need to worry that any prisoners might escape when there were several armed men standing just outside.

"Thought you were a killer."

Mikey didn't need to see the speaker to know who it was. Beltrane, the most vicious guard at Castle Thunder, carried a whip on his belt, which he used often and well.

It was no doubt because of Beltrane that the former commandant, George W. Alexander, had been called before the authorities to answer to charges of brutality. Though Alexander had been cleared, the cruelty continued even after Dennis Callahan replaced him.

"I . . ." Fedya's voice trailed off. Mikey didn't like what he heard in that single word. Fedya was not only confused but frightened. Mikey stepped into the doorway as Beltrane uncoiled his whip.

"You shot my cousin in the head, you fucking filth."

"I . . ." Fedya said again, then stopped.

The whip snapped, and Fedya jumped. So did Mikey. Beltrane laughed; the other guards did, too. "We gotta make this more interesting."

Fedya was near the far end of the enclosure. A kid who still wore the remnants of a gray uniform stood on the other side, shaking so badly, the can atop his head shimmied. The three holes through the tin revealed where the shots Mikey had heard moments ago had gone.

Beltrane chewed upon the last bit of a cigar and stared at Fedya; loathing spilled from his dark eyes.

"There you are." Mikey stepped into the courtyard. "What are you doin' out here?"

"It's not what you—" Fedya began.

"You don't know any of these folks." Beltrane bared his stained teeth. "So you don't really care if they die."

"Mikey," Fedya murmured. "Go back to the hospital."

Mikey would fetch Ethan. His brother would put a stop to whatever this was. He'd helped so many people in Castle Thunder—guards, prisoners, Yankee and Reb. Even Commandant Callahan liked Ethan. Ethan had cured the sores in the man's mouth.

Mikey turned; two guards blocked his path.

"He should return to his brother," Fedya said.

"He will." Beltrane chuckled. "Maybe."

"Just set another can on that deserter." Fedya took several steps closer to the far wall. "I'll move over here."

The gunshot was so loud, Fedya cried out and Mikey gasped. Blood bloomed on the Confederate kid's gray coat, and he collapsed to the ground.

"You don't need a new can." Beltrane's pistol was still smoking from the bullet he'd fired, but he tucked it into his belt next to the whip. "What you need is a new pedestal."

The guards marched Mikey toward the wall.

"No!" Fedya shouted.

Beltrane's whip cracked. Mikey tensed, prepared to pull free and save his friend. But the sharp sting of the lash erupted across his own back. He didn't mean to cry out, but he couldn't help himself.

"Don't budge," Beltrane said. Mikey didn't plan to. Every movement made the pain burn deeper.

"Or what?" Fedya asked. "You'll whip me?"

The guard laughed. "Of course not."

The sound of the lash came again; this time Mikey was prepared. It still hurt more than anything else ever had. He didn't mean to cry out again, but he did.

"Stop," Fedya said.

"No," Beltrane answered, and the whip cracked.

"What do you want?"

"The same thing I've always wanted," Beltrane said. "Some goddamn entertainment."

The guards shoved Mikey against the wall. They set a much smaller can upon his head.

"No," Fedya begged. "Please, just . . . No."

Beltrane flipped his hand as if swatting a bug. The men—four instead of the previous two in deference to Mikey's height and breadth—spun him around. The can flew sideways, bouncing against the brick wall with a tinny clack. The guards tore off his shirt. The air cooled the blood that ran from the open wounds on his back, making Mikey shiver.

"Either shoot the can," Beltrane said in a voice that chilled Mikey even more, "or I'll peel every last bit of skin from his bones. Your choice."

Fedya must have agreed, because the guards twirled Mikey around again. His back was to the wall, with the can perched atop his head once more. The man doing the perching had to stand on his tiptoes to manage it. Mikey was tempted to shake his head, toss the thing to the ground, and stomp on it. But his shoulders—burning, bleeding—reminded him of what would happen if he did. Besides, this was Fedya. He never missed. Even with the rifle they'd given him—a muzzleloader, so long and heavy—Mikey didn't believe Fedya would miss now.

Mikey met Fedya's eyes, trying to tell him without words that he trusted him; he could do this. Fedya paled and bobbled the gun.

Mikey stood taller and threw back his shoulders, holding steady. They handed Fedya a bullet; he loaded the gun. Were his fingers trembling? No. It didn't matter that the gun was not his own. Fedya was the best of the best.

Lifting the weapon, Fedya sighted down the barrel. Mikey held his breath. This would be over in an instant, and they could go back to Ethan with a new story to tell.

Mikey frowned. They should keep this one to themselves. Though Mikey didn't like to have secrets from Ethan, he didn't want him upset either. Maybe he and Fedya would make it their secret. It would bind them together like Alexi and Mikhail Romanov, the brothers they'd pretended to be in one of Fedya's recent make-believes.

"Shoot," Beltane ordered. "Now. Do it."

Still Fedya hesitated. Was he hoping that Ethan would come looking for Mikey? It was too soon for that. Even if he did, would Ethan be able to stop this?

The avid sparkle in the guards' eyes told the truth. Nothing would stop this. When the guards played their games, they played until *they* won. The longer Fedya succeeded, the longer he would have to play, until sooner or later one of his pedestals would—

The whip whistled. Sharp pain slashed Mikey's chest. He bit his lip, attempting to keep the moan from breaking free, but he couldn't.

"I won't hurt you," Fedya said. Mikey met his friend's gaze. "I promise. Everything will be all right."

Fedya pulled the trigger.

And the whole world changed.

When the guards crowded into Ethan's infirmary, shouting and laughing, carrying a litter on which lay a very bloody body, Ethan thought he'd gone mad. What could possibly be amusing about that? Then he saw the size of the body, the clothes that it wore, and he knew he *had* gone mad.

"Mikey?"

Annabeth, who'd been dispensing what medicine they had—mostly cold cloths and a kind word—lifted her head. Even with all the commotion and the noise, she sensed his distress and started toward him.

He should have stopped her, should have sent her

away right then, but he could think of nothing other than his brother lying on that stretcher, bleeding from the head.

"What happened?" He beckoned the guards to cross the open, looming space, dotted with the sick, the wounded, the dying.

He pointed to the table. As they lifted his brother onto it, he wanted to slap at their filthy fingers and order them not to touch. Instead he glanced at Annabeth; she was already gathering what he needed.

"The doctor asked what happened." She held a bowl of water. The scent of the alcohol that had been "donated" just that morning wafted upward. Ethan shoved his hands into it.

Someone sniggered. Ethan's gaze drifted over the men who'd brought his brother to him. "What did you do?" When no one responded, he shouted. "What?"

Annabeth laid a hand on his arm, but he pulled away, stepped toward his brother. There was so much blood, he couldn't see—

Then Annabeth was there, wiping Mikey's face, revealing the neat, round hole in his forehead. At least he was still breathing. Picking up a knife honed and sharpened into a scalpel, Ethan determined to keep him that way.

Another snigger. "Best goddamn sniper in the Union finally missed."

Annabeth's eyes met Ethan's, then flicked to the speaker, that brutal excuse for a human being named Beltrane. "Fedya did this?"

"Sure did." Beltrane fingered the blood- and flesh-flecked whip on his belt.

Ethan glanced at Mikey, but there was so much blood from the head wound, he couldn't determine if there were lash marks as well.

"Fedya doesn't miss," Ethan said.

Beltrane's grin revealed what was left of his tobacco-stained teeth. Though he appeared to be in his twenties, most of his thin brown hair was already gone.

"No one's perfect, Doctor. You oughta know that."

The guards enjoyed playing with the prisoners. The combination of viciousness and boredom meant their games were as evil as they were. For Ethan, they devised a simple torture—feed tainted food to Yankee prisoners, then watch while he tried to save them. He'd failed, of course; then they laughed and laughed and laughed. Was his brother's injury merely another torturous joke?

"You made Fedya do this."

"I *made* him pull the trigger? I *made* him miss? I think I'd have to break his fingers to get him to do that."

Something in Beltrane's voice caused Ethan to look up. "Where is he?"

The guard's cruel mouth curved. "Gone."

"You killed him?"

"'Course not. He's been released."

Annabeth's hands jerked so badly, water sloshed over the side of the bowl and onto her shoes. "Released?" she asked at the same time Ethan said, "Why?"

Beltrane's smirk widened. He lowered his eyes to Mikey, then raised them to Ethan's as if to say, *Isn't it obvious?* before he and his men walked out.

The next several hours passed in a rush of panic. Ethan had no idea what he was doing beyond digging for a bullet in very poor light, under terrible conditions.

He was a surgeon, but he'd never had to operate on someone's head. He'd never encountered anyone who'd been shot there and lived long enough to reach a field hospital.

"You need to stop," Annabeth said.

"He'll die if I don't remove the bullet."

"Ethan." She waited until he was able to tear his gaze from his brother and meet hers. "Neither of you can go on like this."

Ethan was so tired and scared and lost, he just blinked.

"The bullet's in too deep," she continued. "Who knows where it's lodged. If he hasn't died with it in there so far, maybe he won't."

Ethan knew better. "The body rejects foreign objects with suppuration. Infection." Which was often more deadly than the injury itself. Certainly he'd done his best to disinfect everything, but here his best was rarely good enough.

Ethan returned to work with a renewed fervor. He *had* to get the bullet out.

Minutes, hours, years later, Ethan found what he was searching for. He drew the obscenity from his brother's head and threw it across the room.

"Enough." Annabeth removed the scalpel from his hand, which ached almost as much as his eyes.

Mikey's face was unrecognizable due to the swelling and the wash of blood. Head wounds bled fiercely. Digging into them only made them bleed more so. Mikey was ice white, his hand, when Ethan touched it, too cool.

Annabeth held a needle and thread, which was all they had in this hellish place to close a wound. As she made tight, tiny stitches in the raw flesh of his brother's forehead, Ethan stood there, feeling helpless again.

"He's lost a lot of blood," she said. "His respiration has increased from far too slow to far too fast."

Head injuries led to slower breathing. Excessive loss of blood produced something akin to a pant. Right now, Mikey's large chest pumped like a stray dog that had run after a rabbit in July.

"You did all you could," she murmured. "Let him rest."

Ethan wasn't sure if Annabeth meant *rest* in the sense of eternal, or just for the night. Either way, she was right. Ethan had done all he could for the moment. He could barely stay on his feet; his fingers had cramped from holding the scalpel for so long; his eyes burned; his head ached.

"*You* should rest." Finished with her stitching, Annabeth pushed him toward the storeroom where he spent his nights. That small room was the one privilege he'd been given for all his hard work.

"I need . . ." His words drifted off. Ethan stared at his bloody hands, not quite sure what to do about them.

"I'll finish in here." She pushed him again. "You wash in there." He walked in the direction she'd urged him. "I may be gone when you come back."

Ethan turned. "What?"

"It's past the time when they usually put me out."

Every night before sundown, the guards escorted Annabeth to the women's section of the prison. Every morning at sunrise, they escorted her back to his. He still wasn't sure why.

"What time is it?" he asked.

"Nine? Ten?"

He should have known that by the flicker of the lanterns. Someone had lit them; it hadn't been him.

She spread hands as bloody as his. "Either they forgot, or they're being reprimanded."

Ethan laughed—just once, which was all he could manage. "For what?" She glanced at Mikey, whose only movement continued to be his puppylike panting. "This is Castle Thunder, Beth. One less Yankee prisoner is a good day."

She flinched. "I'm sorry."

"What do you have to be sorry about?"

She moved to Mikey's side. "They're Confederates. Like me."

Ethan thought of all *he* had to be sorry about. When he'd been shoved into Palmer's Factory, he'd thought he would never see her again, and that had bothered him almost as much as being here.

Ethan's chest went tight. Words of love trembled on the tip of his tongue. He almost allowed them to tumble free.

But not here.

His gaze went to his brother and stuck there.

Not now.

CHAPTER 7

For an instant, Annabeth thought Ethan might take her in his arms at last. Then he turned away and disappeared into the storeroom where he slept.

A foolish longing. He was a spy; she was a liar. That didn't mean she loved him any less. That didn't mean she didn't dream of his kiss, his touch, and more. Who knew what might happen. Just look at what had happened today.

Mikey dying on a makeshift table in a Confederate prison. Fedya forced to hurt his friend, most likely in as much agony as Ethan because of it. Ethan would be inconsolable if his brother died.

She should console him. Tomorrow was a mystery. But it appeared they, at least, had tonight.

After scrubbing the blood from her skin, she found a clean bowl and filled it with fresh water; she even managed to find a cloth that wasn't soiled. Then she quietly opened the door to the storeroom and slipped inside. A lantern swayed, casting golden sprays of light across the floor.

A cot sat behind several empty barrels. Before the barrel he'd fashioned into a washstand, Ethan scrubbed his chest. Annabeth had never seen a man's chest while he was conscious. Considering the way her body warmed and her hands itched to touch, her lips to taste, that was probably a very good thing.

He turned, saw her, and froze. "Is he—?"

"He's alive. Still breathing." She lifted a hand. "Slower. Better. But . . ."

"What?"

"There are lashes on his chest and back." The sight of them had made her want to bloody someone in exactly the same way.

"I doubted Mikey would agree to let Fedya shoot at him without encouragement." Awkward silence ensued. "Beth, I should—"

"Wash." She lifted the bowl.

She tried to keep her gaze on his face, but she was distracted by the beautiful, naked expanse just below. So much smooth, olive skin.

He reached for his stained shirt, grimaced, and dropped the garment back on the floor. He peered around for another.

"You traded it for some thread," she reminded him. The last of which they'd just used on his brother.

Annabeth crossed the room, set the bowl of clear water next to the bowl of red. After wetting the equally clean cloth, she turned. The back of her hand slid across his stomach.

He snatched her wrist—to pull her away or to pull her close, she didn't know. Neither one of them seemed able to breathe.

"Let me," she whispered.

Releasing her, he stepped back. She followed, pressing the cool, white cloth to his belly. The muscles beneath fluttered and danced. She stroked the material back and forth, back and forth. She wanted to make the same movements in the same place with her tongue. She traced her thumb there instead, and he tensed.

"Shh," she whispered.

He bit his lip as she washed his stomach, then his shoulders and arms, but he let her. What else might he let her do?

The hair on his chest appeared soft. Slowly, she reached out, tangling one finger in a curl, rubbing it between her fingertips. "It is"—she lifted her gaze—"soft."

He kissed her. Hard. She thought she might fall. She pressed both hands to his chest, wound her fingers into the softness, scratched her nails across his skin, and held on.

Her mouth opened; her tongue brushed his lips and slid, seeking, within. He tasted of heat and despair; she wanted to heal him as he had healed so many others, and this was the only way that she knew.

"Need . . . you," he whispered against her lips. "Need you, Beth. Hold me."

She wrapped her arms around his neck; he wrapped his around her waist as she pressed her body the length of his. The hardness at his center felt delicious, and she rubbed herself against it. He hissed in a surprised and somewhat pained breath.

She smiled, dazzled—his kiss, his touch, his face— so beautiful. "I'm dizzy." She laughed. She *sounded* crazy.

Concern flooded his eyes. "Sit."

He urged her to his cot, the only place in the room to sit. The rickety contraption teetered, creaked, held. That should have been enough to bring her to her senses, if her senses hadn't been full of him.

The taste of his skin—salt and spice. The scent of herbs, they soothed. His breath, harsh like hers, arousing. His hands both rough and strong, but with her, ever so gentle. The hands of a healer. She pulled one to her mouth and kissed the palm.

"Beth, you should—"

Her tongue snaked out and tasted where her lips had been. His eyes widened. He looked away, swallowed, then looked back.

She patted the cot at her side. He shook his head like a child who did not want his medicine. She merely patted it again. "You wanted me to hold you." She opened her arms.

He came into them with a sigh of surrender, kissing her with a desperation born of pain. She tangled her fingers in his hair, ran them across his shoulders, down his back, across naked, warm, smooth skin. She had never touched anyone like this, never wanted to. She couldn't think why.

She'd like to spend a lifetime learning every inch of him, but while they might have tonight, they also might not. Who knew when someone might remember her and come calling.

He freed the buttons of her bodice and everything else that needed freeing—her corset, his trousers, their shoes. Wherever he touched, she burned; wherever he kissed, she yearned. She welcomed his weight; they fit together just right. Though the night seemed theirs alone, the room a place far removed, they knew better.

"Please," she whispered, wanting him, needing him now.

He kissed her brow, began to lift himself away, and she clutched him tight. "Don't."

"This isn't a good idea. Not now. Not here. There'll be time enough—"

"Will there?" She locked her fingers at the base of his spine, pressed him ever nearer. "I could walk out the door and be hit by a cannonball."

He lifted a brow. "In Richmond?"

Despite the constant movement of the armies in the area, the city itself had remained relatively unscathed. Because it was the capital of the Confederacy, the troops protected Richmond as if it were made of gold.

She brushed her lips across his jaw, relishing the tingle brought about by his beard. Still nestled between her thighs, Ethan's hips moved forward on their own. Her head fell back, her neck arched, her breasts pressed into his chest, and he clenched his teeth.

"Don't," he managed.

She cupped her palm beneath the jaw she'd just kissed and left it there. "I don't want to die without knowing this. I don't want to live without loving you."

"Don't talk about dying."

"Death is all around us, Ethan. Not a cannonball? Fine. Then a runaway carriage. A stray bullet. A deserter."

"Don't," he said again, and his voice broke.

She understood. The idea of a life without him devastated her, too.

"Anything could happen to you," she whispered, leaving unsaid what they were both thinking.

Like it happened to Mikey.

"Make me yours, Ethan. So I can never be anyone else's."

She waited, holding her breath, hoping, praying, and when he closed his eyes, pressing his forehead to hers, whispering her name with anguish, she believed she had lost. She lifted her mouth for one final kiss, and when their lips touched, everything stilled.

Then he was kissing her as he never had before. As if she were already his, as if she always would be. His teeth scored her chin, tasted her neck; his lips closed on a breast and drew deep.

"Please." She begged again for the unknown.

She was so empty, she wept. When he filled her, something broke with a tiny ping of pain.

"Oh," she murmured, more fascinated than afraid. Understanding bloomed with her smile. "I'm yours."

"Yes." He kissed her brow as he began to move within her. "Mine."

She wanted to examine that statement further; she wanted to kiss and touch and cuddle, but what he was doing was so delicious. The rhythm of their bodies echoed the beat of their hearts. She'd never felt so enveloped, so loved, so chosen.

The emptiness was filled again and again. There was something special waiting for her just out of reach and only he could take her there.

"Ethan," she managed. "I—

He pulsed, and that tiny movement revealed all she needed to know. Like a cauldron set on too high a flame, she bubbled over. She could swear she heard a far-off sizzle. She clenched around him, holding him close both within and without. The waves, the heat, the sizzle continued. She never wanted them to stop. But, eventually, they did.

When Ethan collapsed at her side, he drew her into his arms, smoothed his hand over her hair, pressed his lips to her brow. She burrowed in close as his heart slowed, his breath evened out, and he slept. She had consoled him, and he had shown her a whole new world.

It wouldn't do for one of the guards to catch them like this. They'd never allow her to come back. But for just a moment, she imagined what it would be like to marry this man, to have his children, to live a life far away from here, leave the war and every last pain behind. To work at each other's sides saving lives.

"Heaven," she whispered. Too good to be true.

Carefully, she extricated herself from his embrace. He didn't resist; his eyelids never fluttered; he didn't even mumble. She was nearly dressed when she heard someone coming.

She blew out the lamp, shoved her last button through the buttonhole, and picked up her shoes. She managed to slip out the door before whoever was clomping through the infirmary reached the storeroom.

Once outside, however, she saw no one. Strange. Her gaze went to Mikey. She couldn't tell if he was still breathing, so she hurried across the room, set her hand on his chest. It rose—barely—then fell.

"Your bodice is buttoned wrong."

Annabeth jumped. Moze stood at her side. "I hate it when you do that."

"Your feet are bare."

She held up her shoes; her stockings were stuffed inside. "Anything else?"

"You smell like him."

Silence descended. Really, what was there to say?

Annabeth put on her stockings and shoes, then followed Moze out the door of Palmer's Factory and through the night to Whitlock's Warehouse. She started for her cot among the other women, but he stopped her, pointing to the room where they discussed things they wanted no one to hear.

He shut the door; Annabeth sat. She was so tired, the room spun.

"You can't go back."

Her head came up; the room spun faster. "I have to. He needs me."

"Everyone's going to need you."

"What?"

"Do you think no one else noticed your dishevel?" He flicked a finger at her yet-crooked bodice. "That they didn't see you go into the doctor's room and stay a while? Every man in Palmer's is going to want a taste. You think *he'll* be able to keep them from having one?" Moze shoved a hand through his golden hair. "Jesus, Annabeth, I thought you'd have more sense."

She had, too. But when she'd been in Ethan's arms, the only senses she'd had were filled with him.

"I'll be fine," she said.

"That's right, because you're going home."

"No."

"I'll tie you up, toss you in a wagon, and take you there myself. In fact, that sounds like the perfect plan." He pulled a length of rope from his belt. Annabeth whirled toward the door. "This is a prison. There's nowhere to run."

"No one will hurt me with Mikey—" Her voice broke. Mikey was unconscious. He'd be lucky if he lived one more day. Even if he woke, Lord only knew what he'd say, if he was capable of saying anything at all. It would be a long time before he could keep anyone from hurting himself, let alone her.

Annabeth's eyes burned. She continued to face away so Moze would not see. "I thought you couldn't get me out."

"You were right—I just didn't want to."

"Why do you want to now?"

"It's dangerous."

"It was always dangerous."

He sighed. "I need information, but it isn't worth your life."

"I never knew you cared," she muttered.

His silence made her arms prickle, and she faced him. She couldn't decipher his expression. "Moze—" she began.

"You said you'd spy if I arranged to exchange the sniper for Luke. Except you haven't found out anything worthwhile."

"There isn't anything to find out."

"Then it's time to go."

"Beltrane hinted that Fedya shot Mikey on purpose."

"You know better. It was an accident. But it's probably best to let that rumor stand."

"Why?" she asked.

He gave a growl of exasperation; she was stalling. "Better that the prisoners think Fedya was rewarded for being a traitor than that he was released to get your brother back."

"What difference does it make?"

"Everyone will want an exchange."

"Everyone isn't Fedya."

"Thank God," he muttered, then took her arm and tried to tow her out the door.

She yanked free. "I'm not going."

He bent and tossed her over his shoulder. "Yes, you are."

CHAPTER 8

Ethan woke alone. He couldn't think why that bothered him. When *didn't* he wake alone?

The scent of lavender rose from his pillow, and his usual morning erection went so rigid, he gasped.

"Hell," he muttered, and sat up. What had he done?

He threw back the blanket, saw a dark splotch of blood on the cot, and winced. Instead of taking Annabeth's virginity beneath the sun, he'd done so beneath the moon. Didn't make it any better.

He would have to marry her.

The weight on his chest lightened. Yes, he was in prison, but so was she. His fault, but she didn't blame him. She knew all his secrets, and still she had given herself to him.

He had to find her. This proved more difficult than ending the war.

At least Mikey still lived. That turned out to be the only good news of the day.

No one had seen Annabeth since last night. The prisoners knew nothing, the guards the same. His demands for information were met with a cuff on the head.

Day after day he sat at Mikey's side and stared at the door. Every time it opened, his heart lifted. Every time it closed without sight of her, it fell. He understood that the more desperate he became, the funnier the guards thought it was. Even if they'd known where she was, they wouldn't have told him. Tired of their laughter and jibes, their offhanded slaps and cuffs, Ethan stopped asking. The instant he was free, he would find her.

His main concern was Mikey. The injury suppurated at one point, oozing a foul-smelling discharge. He traded everything he had in the infirmary for some alcohol, opened the wound, cleansed it, and sewed it shut again.

His brother slept on.

Ethan spent every waking hour wetting Mikey's lips with a cloth, hoping some of the water went down his throat. He did not sleep on the cot that smelled of her, but rested his head next to Mikey's huge hand when he could no longer keep his eyes open.

One morning, he awoke. Someone had tapped his head. Ethan peered around. It was so early; the only thing up besides him was the sun. He scratched where the tap had occurred, thinking perhaps he had lice. It wouldn't be the first time. Then he turned his gaze to his brother. Mikey's eyes were open.

Ethan blinked. So did Mikey.

Ethan reached for a cup of water, nearly knocked it over, brought it to his brother's lips, and helped him to drink. That he could was very encouraging.

"Can you speak?" he asked.

Mikey nodded but didn't.

"Do you know your name?"

Mikey nodded again.

"Can you say it?"

"M-M—"

Joy filled Ethan. It was a miracle.

"Mikhail," his brother blurted.

"No," Ethan said. "You're Michael. Mikey. Walsh."

Mikey scowled, wincing when the expression pulled his stitches. "I'm Mikhail Romanov." He looked around. "Where's my brother?"

"I'm your brother."

Mikey returned his gray gaze to Ethan's. "Mister, I ain't never seen you before in my life."

Moze stood at the window, gun drawn, as horses approached the Phelan farm.

Annabeth had her father's Navy Colt out as well. She was glad she'd buried it in the orchard before she'd left. From the appearance of the place, both armies had been through here.

Several times.

Moze holstered his weapon. "It's them."

"Luke." Annabeth ran toward the door. Moze cursed, called her name, snatched at her skirt, but nothing was going to keep her from her brother. Not after all she'd done to find him.

Five men sat their horses in the yard. Four wore gray, the fifth a jumble of clothes that were far too large for him. He was dirty; he smelled. His hands were tied.

"Where's Luke?"

Someone shoved the smelly man off his horse. He landed with a thud that sent dust billowing across Annabeth's feet. "Luke Phelan, as ordered." But it wasn't her brother.

Annabeth turned to Moze. "I told you one of us should be at the exchange." Then, to her horror, she burst into tears.

She'd sacrificed the man she loved—she hadn't meant to, but the fact remained that she had—to get her brother back. That she hadn't was either poetic justice or perhaps the laughter of God at someone who believed she could orchestrate fate.

A half hour later, the strangers were gone, taking the man who wasn't her brother with them. His name was Luke Celan. An honest mistake, the leader said, though how anyone could confuse dirt-brown hair with Phelan red, Annabeth had no idea.

"You just exchanged the Union's greatest sniper for a farm boy who can't hit a tree with a shotgun from five yards away," Annabeth muttered.

"You don't know that. Maybe he can."

"I know he isn't Luke. Dammit, Moze. What a waste!"

"I'll keep looking."

"You've done a fine job so far."

He remained silent, and she felt bad. Moze loved Luke, too.

"Sorry," she said. "It's just . . . All that work. The lies. Ethan. Mikey. Castle Thunder, Moze. And we still don't have Luke. We aren't even sure if he was in that prison in the first place. What if he was hung for a partisan?"

"I think they might have mentioned that when we asked to get him back."

"I think they might not have," Annabeth murmured.

"I'll find him. I promise." Moze stood; his gaze flicked around the barren farmhouse. Only a few crates and the sofa, no doubt too big to drag off on a horse, remained. "Maybe you should come with me."

"Maybe you should—" Annabeth bit off the angry suggestion. She'd made quite a few since he'd carted her bodily away from Ethan and deposited her here. "I'm staying. Luke might wander down the lane tomorrow."

"I'm not a fool, Annie Beth Lou. It isn't Luke you're waiting for."

Ethan watched Mikey pace in front of the windows like a caged beast. Sometimes he even growled.

"Gotta find him," Mikey muttered.

"Mike—" Ethan paused as Mikey swung around, fists clenched. "Mikhail," he corrected. "Who are you looking for?"

"My brother, Alexi."

Ethan managed not to flinch. "I don't know anyone by that name."

Mikey rubbed at his head. Ethan fought not to yank his fingers away. Not only might that result in a punch to the face—his once-gentle brother had become inexplicably violent—but Mikey's injury was nearly healed—at least on the outside. Ethan doubted touching the scar would cause any further damage.

"Where am I?" Mikey asked.

He'd asked before, and Ethan had answered. Maybe one of these times the words would help Mikey remember the truth.

"Castle Thunder Prison."

"Prison." Mikey's nose wrinkled. "Don't like the smell."

"I know, Mikey."

"Don't call me that!" His fingers clenched again. "What kind of man lets hisself be called by that baby name? I'm Mikhail." He slammed his fist into his chest. "Mikhail Romanov."

"All right," Ethan agreed, though he doubted he'd ever be able to address Michael Walsh as Mikhail Romanov. "Maybe you could describe your brother. Maybe I just don't know him by name."

Mikey's fingers unfurled. "Dark hair, blue eyes. 'Bout the same height as you. Talks real purdy in all sorts of languages."

Fedya.

"His name isn't Alexi," Ethan began.

Mikey drove his fist into the wall. The plank cracked. A second blow caused the wood to splinter.

"Hey!" the nearest guard shouted. "Stop that! You want I should fetch Beltrane?"

Ethan lifted his hand. "It's all right. I'll—" He paused. What would he do? His brother not only didn't know him, but he didn't seem to like him much either.

"Gotta find him," Mikey repeated. "All we have is each other."

Ethan should have been happy that Mikey was alive and able to walk, talk, feed, and dress himself. Instead, he was furious. He missed Annabeth so much sometimes, he thought he might die. If anything happened to her—

His fingernails bit into his palms. If anything happened to her, he wouldn't know. Because he was in here, and she was . . . not. He felt so goddamn impotent.

"I'll see if I can discover anything in regard to your brother," Ethan said.

Perhaps he'd have more luck getting information about Fedya than he'd had when he tried to learn anything about Annabeth. But he doubted it.

"Gotta get out of here," Mikey muttered, then wandered away.

For the next few days, Ethan was occupied with an outbreak of fever, and without Annabeth's or Mikey's help, he fell onto his cot exhausted long after midnight.

He saw his brother here and there; he seemed to be making friends among the inmates.

One afternoon, a commotion at the front of the factory drew Ethan's attention. The guards shouted, shoving prisoners. The prisoners laughed and jeered.

Ethan wandered in that direction. "What happened?"

"Escape attempt."

"Again?" Escape attempts were common. Very few succeeded. They were in the middle of the Confederate capital with armies all around. Where would they go?

"One got away." The prisoner grinned. "Can't find him nowheres."

"Which one?" Ethan asked.

"That Russian feller." Ethan stilled as the man tapped his forehead. "One that done got shot in the head. Can't say's it slowed him down none."

Annabeth spent most of her time on the farm. Whenever she went to town, people whispered—*traitor, sympathizer, spy*. A few even spat. Richmond might be the capital of the Confederacy, but gossip traveled. What else did folks have to do but share the story of how the Chimborazo matron turned nurse had been carted off to Castle Thunder with a spy. That she'd been released eventually did not signify innocence. Instead it only inspired more tales of what she might have done to secure that freedom.

Annabeth laid her palm protectively over her still-flat stomach. As time went on, it was only going to get worse.

Moze brought food. She didn't tell him about the whispers or the spitting—or her stomach. What good would it do? He'd want her to leave, and she wasn't going to go. But she didn't sleep well. She started up at every rustle. One night, several weeks after she'd returned to the farm, she heard a lot more than that.

"Annabeth Phelan! Come on out here now. You make us come in, you might not like what happens."

She already knew she wasn't going to like what happened.

Her fingers tightened around her Colt as she went to the window. Six men. She didn't know them. So how in hell did they know her?

"Can't fraternize with the enemy and expect to walk free and easy now, can you?"

Wouldn't do any good to explain that she'd been working secretly for the South. No one would believe her.

Annabeth set down her daddy's Colt and went outside.

In the spring of 1865, the war ended at last. Once Ethan was released from prison, he was able to return to Chimborazo and retrieve his things. He'd had the wherewithal to sew some gold pieces, along with his father's watch and his mother's ring, into the cuff of a very old pair of trousers. Once he ripped them open, he bought a horse, asked a few questions about the Phelans, and then followed the provided directions to the farm on the outskirts of Richmond.

As he dismounted, the wind whistled through the empty barn. Was the place as deserted as it felt? If he called her name, would she answer? What if she'd disappeared from Richmond as she'd disappeared from Castle Thunder? What if she were dead?

Ethan swallowed and went to the front door. Did he knock or did he just go in? He lifted his hand, but before he could decide, the door flew open.

"Your hair!" he blurted.

Annabeth lifted a hand to her shaved head. "It'll grow back."

"How?" he asked. "Why?"

"It's a common punishment."

"Punishment?" he repeated. "For what?" Ethan couldn't think what she might have done to deserve this.

"Fraternizing with the enemy."

It took him an instant to realize she meant him. Certainly she was from Virginia; he'd only pretended to be. But they'd worked at each other's sides to save lives. Neither one of them had cared if those lives were Yankee or Reb.

"You were nursing soldiers," he said. "Just because you were helping me—"

"I was doing more than helping you, Ethan." Her gaze met his, and he remembered what they had done. The only thing that had kept him sane in the past three months was the hope that he could someday do it again.

"No one knew." Ethan considered her patchy scalp. Or at least he'd thought no one knew.

She turned, and her skirt tightened across her middle, revealing the slight rounding of her stomach beneath her dress.

"Beth," he whispered, and she lifted her gaze, smiling at the wonder in his.

"I'm with child."

Dizziness washed over him. He put out a hand, and she took it, hers tightening. What if the war had gone on? What if he'd died in prison? What if she'd died out here?

"I'm sorry," he said, and she yanked her hand away. He stumbled forward, trying to get it back.

"I'm not," she snapped. "This baby is the only good thing that's happened to me since—" Her voice broke.

"Since?"

"Since Fort Sumter."

He went silent. He remembered a lot of good things—the first day they'd met, the first time they'd kissed, the scent of her hair, the drift of her breath, the feel of her skin in the dark, the people they'd saved, the life they'd had—certainly it hadn't been easy, but it had been theirs.

"Why didn't you come to Castle Thunder and tell me?"

"It's a prison, Ethan. They weren't going to let me in."

"Why did they let you out?"

"They never had any proof I wasn't in the wrong place at the wrong time." She covered her mouth, coughed. Was she ill? He wanted to put his hand to her forehead, but she held herself just out of reach. "Whitlock's was overcrowded, so they released me. I was afraid if I came back, if I insisted on seeing you . . ." Her voice drifted off.

"They might not let you out again." He nodded. "I understand."

"Where's Mikey?" she asked. "Is he—"

"He's alive, but . . ." Quickly, he told her everything.

"He thinks his name is Mikhail and that Fedya is his brother," she repeated. "So he probably went and found Fedya after he escaped."

"Alexi," Ethan muttered.

She spread her hands. "Does it matter?"

"Honestly, Beth, I have no idea anymore." He ran his hand through his hair; he wanted to tear it out. "I need to find him, make sure that he's safe."

"If he's with Fedya—" Their eyes met. "If he's with *Alexi,* I'm sure he's fine."

"But I have to know; I have to see."

Silence fell like a stone between them. He had come to tell her how he felt, and now that he was here, he couldn't say a single one of the things he'd meant to.

"We're getting married," he blurted instead.

She folded her arms. "I don't recall saying yes."

He dropped to one knee. "Annabeth Phelan, will you marry me?" He pulled his mother's ring from his pocket.

Her eyes widened, then filled. "You—you—"

"Is that a yes?"

"You had that all along. . . . You were going to ask me even before . . ." She touched their child once more.

"You stood at my side, though I betrayed the cause you believed in. You gave yourself to me, your enemy."

"Ethan," she began, and choked.

"I lied. About everything. Who I was, what I believed, hell, how I spoke—and you forgave me. If I hadn't already loved you, I would have loved you for that alone. I'll always love you, Annabeth. Always."

She blinked, and tears flew off her eyelashes, rained onto his cheeks. "I . . ." She looked away, frowned, seemed to struggle with something; then her shoulders drooped. "I love you, too."

"Is that a yes?"

She met his gaze, smiling through her tears. "That's a yes."

CHAPTER 9

Ethan contacted the Intelligence Service and discovered that Fedya had been sent to instruct soldiers at Camp Astor, New York.

"You'll get there and back more quickly if you're alone," Annabeth said.

"I don't want to leave you, but—"

She watched everything that he thought, that he felt, flicker across his face. He was torn between wanting her at his side and agreeing that it would be easier if she wasn't. How had this man ever been a spy?

"Traveling isn't good for the baby," he murmured. "And you're going to be traveling enough just to reach Freedom."

Along with the information about Fedya, Ethan had received an offer to become the doctor in Freedom, Kansas. It would be a new start for them both.

Annabeth covered her stomach with one hand. For them all.

"Just go," she urged, so he did.

Two weeks later, he returned. One look into his eyes and she knew the visit had not gone well.

"What happened?"

"My brother tried to break my neck."

"Mikey wouldn't do that."

"*Mikey* wouldn't. Mikhail, on the other hand . . ." He shrugged. "To be fair, he thought I was hurting *his* brother."

"Why would he think that?"

Ethan glanced away. "I was."

"Oh, Ethan."

"I couldn't help it. Fedya's so damn smug. He made a comment—half of it was in Russian—and I . . ." He spread his fingers. "I put these around his throat. Making him stop talking felt so damn good."

Annabeth sighed. "Now what?"

"Now we go West." He smiled with his mouth but not his eyes. "Together."

They boarded the train in Virginia, got off in Kansas City, then walked to the nearest church. One glimpse of Annabeth's just-beginning-to-round stomach and the priest waived the banns.

Annabeth agonized all the way to Freedom. Should she tell Ethan the truth, or shouldn't she? It didn't seem fair or right that she knew all his secrets yet he knew none of hers. Then again, hers had led first to he and Mikey being imprisoned, then to his brother being shot in the head.

Ethan's continued anger at Fedya frightened her. He'd come to the conclusion, with a little help from the guards at Castle Thunder, that Fedya had been released as a reward for shooting Mikey. Fedya had not disabused him of the notion when they'd met in New York. Not that Ethan had given him the chance. Although even if the sniper had, she doubted Ethan would have believed him.

"What possible reason could anyone have for hurting your brother?" she asked.

"Not hurt. Kill. Mikey is dead. Fedya killed him. There is no more Michael Walsh."

"Ethan, you know that's not true."

"It is. You haven't looked into his eyes and seen a stranger staring back."

She had nothing to say to that, so she kept silent. She understood his anger was born of guilt. He hadn't protected Mikey, and now the little brother he had known was gone.

"Leave it alone, Beth." He took her hand, smiled that smile she loved, with both his eyes and his lips at last. "We'll leave the past in the East. We'll start new in the West. We'll be free of all the pain."

And because she wanted that, too, Annabeth decided to keep her secrets to herself.

Considering that Kansas was about as Yankee as could be, Annabeth worried that her accent might label her an outsider and that she would never be accepted in their new hometown.

However, the folks of Freedom wanted to leave the past in the past nearly as much as she did. They welcomed her as their doctor's wife. Certainly, there were those whose lips curled when she spoke, who whispered behind their hands when she came into the one mercantile in town, but as time passed, any lingering animosities faded.

It didn't hurt that she possessed nursing skills. From the day they arrived, she and Ethan worked side by side to heal their new neighbors. They were given a place of their own, a two-story structure in the center of town. The ground floor consisted of a waiting area, an examining room, and a kitchen. The second floor held two rooms—one for them and one for the child that grew steadily beneath her heart.

They bought furnishings, but Ethan insisted on making the crib himself. Sometimes she just stood in the doorway and watched him work. He would turn; he would smile. "You're so beautiful," he would murmur, though she knew she was anything but. The future was so bright, it blinded her.

Some nights Ethan would awaken shouting his brother's name. She held him and comforted him as she had in prison. Annabeth had nightmares, too, but she awoke with clenched teeth, as if, even in sleep, her mind and her body knew she had to swallow every secret she could not share.

But each morning she woke to another day as Ethan's wife. Each night she lay at his side and touched him as she'd always dreamed of, taking all the time she wanted.

Because she believed they had all the time in the world.

After riding to a neighboring farm to treat a nasty broken leg, Ethan returned to Freedom, stabled his horse, and hurried through the just-fallen night toward home. As he stepped inside, voices murmured in the next room.

"He doesn't know?" A stranger. A man.

"No." Annabeth, sounding tired, defeated, a little scared.

Ethan's fighting instincts, which he'd thought had gone into hibernation after Appomattox, awoke. He drew his gun.

"Have you found Luke?"

"Not yet."

Annabeth let out a long, discouraged breath. "What do you want, Moze?"

"If it weren't for you, we never would have caught that sniper."

Ethan's neck tingled. He began to get a very bad feeling.

"You saved a lot of lives, Annie Beth Lou."

Somehow, Ethan didn't think this Moze was referring to her nursing skills. He held his breath and clung to the shadows.

"Get to the point," Annabeth ordered. "Then get out."

"I work for Pinkerton."

"The enemy?"

Ethan winced. If Alan Pinkerton, once the head of the Union Secret Service, was the enemy . . . then what did that make him?

"He's not the enemy anymore, Annabeth. Besides . . . aren't you married to one?"

One? Ethan wondered. *One what?*

"Just say your piece."

"When I told Mr. Pinkerton all you'd done, he sent me to hire you."

"I'm otherwise engaged." The words were cool and dry.

"You didn't have to sleep with the guy."

Ethan was heartily sick of this conversation. Or perhaps he was just heartily sick. Was everything he'd believed about her, about them, a lie?

"I suppose a spy of his caliber wasn't going to tell you anything worthwhile just because you asked," the man muttered.

"If asking was the way you got your information, I'm surprised you're still breathing."

Moze chuckled. "Feeding him the news about the false meeting between Lee and Davis was best done in bed." He cleared his throat and murmured, "After. A man will believe anything then."

Ethan frowned. She hadn't told him about the meeting; he'd discovered it written on a scrap of paper stuffed into a patient's boot.

She was good.

His nausea was replaced by anger. Because of her, his brother was dead. Because of her, both Ethan, one of the Union's top spies, and Fedya, one of the Union's most gifted snipers, had spent months in Castle Thunder Prison. Because of her, he was married to the enemy.

But then so was she.

"You could have gotten in touch with me," Moze said. "If I'd known you were in trouble, I'd have . . ." His voice drifted off.

"I'm not in trouble," she said softly. "Or at least I wasn't until you showed up."

"Do you ever plan on telling him?"

"I don't think I'll have to."

The rustle of clothing followed the soft scuff of a boot. "If you need me, you know where I am."

"I do."

Ethan recalled her saying those words to him not so long ago. Words that had bound him to her and her to him forever. He'd been so happy.

How times changed.

The back door opened and closed. Cool blue silence settled over him. A match flared; the lamp came to life, spreading golden flickers across the floor.

"You can come out now," Annabeth said.

Ethan stepped into the room, gun still drawn. Her

gaze went to the weapon. "I wouldn't blame you." She flicked her eyes to the windows and then back to his. "But others might."

"You betrayed me."

"You betrayed yourself."

His hand tightened, and he put the pistol back in the holster, for an instant afraid of what he might do. "I think I'd remember that."

"It was a trap, Ethan."

"One that you set."

"I didn't think you'd jump into it. I was trying to prove you weren't a traitor."

"Were you ever going to tell me?"

"No." He blinked, surprised, and she threw up her hands. "What possible good could it do? You said you wanted to leave the past in the East, start new in the West."

"Your past seems to have followed us here."

"I didn't ask him to."

"You planned to live a lie forever?"

"It isn't a lie."

"It isn't the truth," he muttered. "What was?"

She laid a palm on her belly; his gaze lowered, and he swallowed as memories flickered. "You gave me your virginity to gain my trust?"

He didn't know her anymore. He'd never known her.

"It wasn't like that."

"What was it like? Tell me, please, because I don't understand."

"We were together that night, in Castle Thunder, after I set the trap."

"Your point?"

"I didn't need to gain your trust; I already had it."

"Then why? What did you think you could possibly learn from me in prison?"

"Nothing!" She swallowed as if her throat were desert dry. "It was a prison, Ethan, and I stayed there for you. Because I loved you. What was between us . . . this . . . ?" She pointed at him, at herself. "Is real."

He released a short burst of air through his nose.

Her hands clenched. "You think I'd—"

"I don't know what to think."

Unless it was that she'd fucked him for the cause, then had become pregnant and had little choice but to marry him. That sounded more truthful than anything she'd told him thus far.

"Maybe you should tell me what happened," he said. "From the beginning."

She nodded, rubbing her belly as if it ached. His chest certainly did.

"Someone at Chimborazo was notifying the Yankees of Confederate troop movements, plans, strengths."

"Me."

"I didn't know that. I didn't believe that."

"What gave me away?" He'd always wondered.

"Beth," she murmured, and he frowned. He didn't like how she kept rubbing her stomach.

"I don't—"

"Yankees shorten names," she explained. "Southerners make them longer."

Something that simple had been his undoing? Ethan almost laughed. "If I'd called you Annie Beth Lou"— he left out *like him*, but from her wince, she heard it just the same—"instead of Beth . . ."

"You also talk in your sleep," she muttered. "And you didn't have an accent."

"So you set a trap. But I wasn't the only one who fell in. You killed my brother."

Her lips tightened. "Only after you killed mine."

He shook his head, confused. "You said your brothers died at Sharpsburg, Ball's Bluff, New Bern, and Shiloh." All of those battles had occurred before Gettysburg. Before Ethan had watched so many die despite everything he did. Before he'd been asked to do more.

"My youngest brother, Luke, went missing at Mount Zion Church." Ethan couldn't control a slight twitch at the location. "One of Mosby's men was sent to rally the Rangers. They arrived. He didn't."

"I don't—"

"You *did*," she insisted. "He either babbled the information while delirious, or you found it in his things."

In truth, he couldn't recall. What did it matter?

Ethan had never allowed himself to consider the people his actions affected. He couldn't and continue to do what he'd promised. He had believed utterly that his efforts at espionage could shorten the war. But to someone whose entire family had died in it, he wasn't any kind of hero.

"What are we going to do?" he whispered.

"Do?" she repeated as if the word were foreign.

"About this? About us?"

"We're married, Ethan. For better or worse, as long as we live."

"It's a lie."

"I meant those vows."

"I took them with a woman I didn't know."

"You took them with me."

"Who are you?"

"Annabeth Phelan Walsh. My entire family is gone. All I have is you and—" She again set a hand over her stomach.

"My brother died because of your lies." He turned his palms up. "Sometimes I still see his blood."

She took his hands, squeezed them until he met her gaze. "He isn't dead, Ethan."

"He might as well be."

"I can't talk to you when you're like this." She tried to pull her hands free, but now he wouldn't let go. He yanked her close; her head snapped forward, narrowly missing his chin, and she stilled. "You're scaring me."

The monster inside of him was glad. How many young boys had been frightened, had been bloodied and died because of her?

Because of him.

Guilt blended with the anger, causing his fingers to tighten. "You were everything. The only bright light in so much darkness." She tore herself away at the same time as he released her. The momentum had her reeling back. She banged into the countertop as he turned away. "I loved you."

She didn't answer, didn't argue, and his chest tightened.

It *had* all been a lie.

Ethan strode toward the door through which Moze had left. He wasn't sure where he was going.

Somewhere. Anywhere but here.

"Too soon," Annabeth gasped. "Help me."

He spun, and the angry words died on his tongue.

She stood in a halo of light, clutching her stomach with one hand, reaching out the other to him.

The moon turned the spreading puddle of blood at her feet the shade of a storm at midnight.

Morning dawned and still Annabeth labored. Pain rippled across her stomach, settled in her back, tightened. She could smell death; she saw it hovering in the black spots that danced at the edges of her vision.

"Beth," Ethan whispered.

Just that. Her name. Nothing more. What more was there?

The baby, the only thing that might have bound them together amid so much deceit, was dying. Was this punishment for her sins? No child born this soon could live.

"Take me," she prayed, though she knew it was futile. God did not bargain. Most of the time, God did not even hear.

"You need to push," Ethan said in a voice as dead as her heart.

She'd curled in on herself, hunching her shoulders, drawing up her knees as she attempted to protect the life within. But her body had other plans. Her muscles bunched, and the sensation was such a relief after the hours of pain that she bore down. Then she couldn't stop.

Over and over again she tensed; she grunted; she pushed. Ethan tried to take her hands, and she swatted him away with weaker and weaker motions. Sweat poured down her face, and still she pressed on. The world wavered—coming into focus, then going back out. She almost passed out several times, but the pain always brought her around.

At last the baby slipped from her body. Annabeth strained her ears for a cry—even a weak, mewling kitten sound would have been better than the rasp of her own breath splitting the echoing silence. Ethan straightened, holding something far too small in his bloody hands. She turned her face so she couldn't see. "Take it away."

"Him," Ethan said in that same dead voice. "A boy. We should—"

"Out!" she shouted, or tried to. Her strength had died when he did; she couldn't manage much beyond a hoarse croak. "Get it away from me." If she looked upon that tiny, still face, she would shatter into a thousand bleeding shards.

Ethan's footsteps retreated upward. Almost immediately they came back down. Annabeth kept her eyes closed, her lips clenched as he cleansed and stitched, doing everything that needed to be done. She would have liked to order him out, too; she wanted to tell him she could take care of herself. But right now, she could do nothing but lie there and try not to think. If breathing had required any effort, she would have expired. Damn the ease of breathing.

"I'll carry you to bed."

"No!" She inched to the edge of the exam table and clung. The idea of going upstairs, where he'd taken "it," of sleeping in the bed where they'd shared so much, sickened her.

"Beth, you can't—"

"My name is Annabeth, you lying Yankee spy."

She waited for the guilt to flow over her, for the apology to tumble from her lips. But she felt nothing, certainly not guilt. And if her words made him leave her be, she couldn't be sorry for them. Her shoulders tensed against anything he might say. Instead, she heard him go.

"I wish you were dead," she whispered, uncertain if she were talking to Ethan or herself.

She must have slept, because the next time she opened her eyes, the sun was gone and the moon was back. For an instant, she wondered why she was lying on the table in the exam room in her night rail. Then she remembered, and a sob broke free.

She tried to snatch it back, but it was too late. She cried until her tears ran dry, and her breath clogged in her throat. Perhaps breathing wasn't so easy, after all.

When her sobs had faded, she heard how loud the silence was. Had Ethan returned? She wasn't going upstairs to find out. If he had, he didn't care about her tears. He'd said he didn't know her, that he'd married a stranger. She had no doubt he wished he'd never married her at all.

Annabeth sat up; then she stood up. She had to get out; she needed some air. But she couldn't walk around wearing nightclothes. Why didn't she keep an extra dress in the downstairs closet like Ethan kept extra—

She laughed, the sound a bit crazed and far too loud, then opened that closet.

"Thank you, Dr. Walsh," she murmured, and withdrew the clothing Ethan set aside in the office for emergencies. Children threw up; blood spattered all over. Ethan had taken to leaving a fresh shirt and clean trousers nearby.

Her shoes still resided at the back door where she'd left them. She snatched Ethan's hat from the nail on the wall as she went past. But she couldn't find any air on the streets of Freedom, no matter how long she walked them.

She discovered herself in the stable, staring at her horse. The stable boy was nowhere to be found. Visiting the outhouse or a woman—who knew? She certainly didn't care.

Annabeth hitched the animal to their buggy. She wasn't capable of riding astride—probably wouldn't be for over a month. But she had to find some air.

It wasn't until she crossed into Colorado that she was finally able to breathe.

Ethan went to the nearest saloon. What else did a man do when he needed to forget?

But he couldn't forget putting angry hands on his wife, wanting to shake her. Had he? He couldn't recall. He kept seeing, over and over, how she'd pulled away, banged into the counter. Then there'd been so much blood. The child so still and white, Annabeth the same.

He downed his whiskey and asked for more, though he knew he would never be able to erase the sight with mere alcohol. Just as he'd never stop hearing the words she'd whispered right before he'd left.

I wish you were dead.

At noon he stumbled to the house, opened the door, saw her lying where he'd left her, fast asleep. Her color was better; she was breathing just fine. He should have gone inside, woken her, made her eat and drink, carried her upstairs despite her protests, then buried their child. Instead he shut the door and went back to the saloon.

By the time he returned, the whole world was blurry. He came in the front door, climbed the steps, poured himself into bed. When he awoke, she was gone.

He waited for her to come back. Days turned into a week.

He sent a message to John Law through the Intelligence Service, asking for help in locating her. A week became a month.

He attempted to find Fedya and Mikey. They had disappeared as thoroughly as his wife.

And the month became years.

PART II

Five Years Later

CHAPTER 10

For most folks, a knock on their hotel room door meant little. For Annabeth, it could mean anything.

She drew her gun. Ellsworth was known as the rowdiest of rowdy cattle towns. Full of so many saloons, gambling halls, and whorehouses that most nights the sound of the music, the laughter, the gunshots was deafening.

"Who is it?"

A spate of indecipherable Spanish erupted, and Annabeth opened the door to a Mexican washerwoman. Figuring Lassiter Morant, the leader of the Morant Gang, had sent her to collect the filthy clothes he'd discarded in their room before donning clean ones and heading downstairs to play poker, Annabeth holstered her weapon and began to collect them.

The door closed. "Ethan's in trouble."

Every bit of cloth tumbled to the ground as Annabeth's hands went numb. Slowly, she turned. Even though she hadn't seen Fedya since they'd left Castle Thunder, she couldn't believe she'd missed that too-blue gaze.

"Are you crazy?" she asked.

"Are you?" Fedya waved a long-fingered hand, the movement causing his high-necked, black lace shirtwaist to swirl around breasts that appeared completely real. "This is not who you are, *moi drug*."

The Russian words clashed with . . . everything—this room, his skirt, her life.

"It's who I am right now. You, of all people, should understand that." She'd seen Fedya perform in prison. The way he could become someone else was uncanny. But she hadn't realized until this moment how very, very good at it he was. She eyed his face. Was he wearing makeup? He had to be, though she couldn't see any. "How the hell did you find me?"

The Morant Gang moved quickly from place to place. Lass never told anyone where they were going, just led them wherever that might be. He also made certain their faces were covered and that when any killing occurred in public, he wasn't the one doing it.

They rode into a town like thunder, stole as fast as lightning, and left behind the remnants of a hellish storm before disappearing into their secret hideout, leaving anyone in pursuit scratching their heads and eating dust.

"How do you think I found you?" Fedya asked.

Annabeth's sigh was as sad as her life. "Mikey."

"Mikhail," he corrected.

"How is he?"

"The same."

"Is he here?" If she could just borrow him for a day or two, she wouldn't have to—

"No. He's . . ." Fedya glanced out the window and frowned. "You need to get to Freedom as fast as you can. Ethan is . . ." A shadow flickered over his exquisite face. "He will die if you do not do something."

She followed his gaze, but all she saw was dust settling over the town of Ellsworth. When she looked back, Fedya was gone. She didn't bother to follow. Instead, she stood there, ignoring the music and the laughter from the saloon below, the shouts from outside. She was tempted to ignore Fedya, except . . .

There'd been something in his eyes that frightened her. He was not the type of man to exert himself for anyone except, perhaps, Mikey.

"Mikhail," she murmured.

That he'd gone to the trouble of finding her meant there was trouble. Big trouble. In Freedom.

She retrieved Ethan's old hat from the bed where she'd tossed it. The thing was filthy, sweat-stained; she needed a new one. But she hadn't been able to make herself throw it away. She gathered her hair and stuffed it beneath the crown.

A curse since childhood, that bright red hair. The freckles, too, though both had faded with age. Nevertheless, they marked her, made her memorable in ways and places she would rather not be.

Like here.

Certainly Ellsworth was large enough, busy enough, wild enough that the Morant Gang would go unnoticed if they didn't shoot up the place. What law there was—and there had been some pretty fancy lawmen who'd tried to tame Ellsworth—was too busy to take a second look at Lass or any of his followers as long as they did only what they'd come here to do. Drink. Gamble. Whore. And hopefully bathe. While Lassiter's men were dangerous, they weren't stupid. If they caused trouble, he killed them himself.

Annabeth descended the staircase, keeping her hat pulled low. She weaved her way to Lass's table. As usual, he was winning.

His chestnut hair had been freshly washed and shone like silk in the dim light. She'd consider him a handsome man if she didn't know that beneath the good looks lay a whole lot of crazy. She should leave and never come back, but she knew better. She was his woman, and Lass protected his property with a swift and certain violence.

He allowed her to ride with them because she was useful—both in private and in public. She did what she was told, and she didn't whine about it. Annabeth knew better. She also knew better than to turn up pregnant. There were ways to prevent such a thing if a woman listened to others, if she learned about herbs and cleansers, if she paid attention to the rhythms of her own body. Annabeth was no fool. If she couldn't be what Lass needed, she would be dead.

She hadn't been scared of much in her life, but she was scared of Lass. He owned one book, *Alice's Adventures in Wonderland*. Annabeth didn't know where he'd gotten it. He was not the kind of man to own a book; he wasn't the kind of man who could read. But he had read about Alice.

He'd dubbed his hideout Wonderland, and the place

was nearly as hard to find as the original. Perhaps because he let no one know its location whom he didn't trust completely. She wasn't among the lucky few. She thought the hideout was in Kansas, but where was anyone's guess.

He cast her a quick "what in hell are you doing here?" glance from eyes so dark, they seemed endless. She leaned close. "Gonna scout a few towns nearby."

Lass frowned, and she nearly held her breath, afraid he'd say no. Then what would she do? She managed to breathe in and out so her heart wouldn't thunder. He would hear; he would know, and then he would pounce.

"Five?" He tossed two cards toward the dealer.

He wasn't asking how many towns but how many days until he would meet her at the arroyo—the point where Lass blindfolded the untrustworthy before he led them to Wonderland. Folks left the same way—if they left at all.

"Better make it seven."

He glanced at her again. Again, she kept on breathing. She waited for him to ask how long it took to scout a few banks, ask a few questions about the stage or the train, listen to folks discuss the soon-to-arrive army, railroad, or coal-mining payroll. But he lifted his two new cards, saw he'd drawn a double belly buster, and she became a lot less interesting than the straight he now held in his hand. Annabeth headed for the door before his attention returned to her.

She wouldn't need seven days to do what she planned to do, but she'd take a little time away. She had to sometimes, or she would go mad as that damn Hatter.

Before dawn tinted the sky, Annabeth guided her horse down a street she'd sworn never to go down again. At this time of night, none of the townsfolk were about.

Annabeth dismounted. When the wind blew in from the prairie and whistled along the street, she was thankful she'd worn men's trousers rather than her split riding skirt. The yards of material would have billowed, perhaps spooked the horse.

In some towns, she might be jailed for dressing as a man. Hopefully the recent escapades of the legendary bounty hunter Cat O'Banyon, who was rumored to be a woman beneath the men's clothing, had put a stop to such threats. Annabeth doubted any lawman would have the grit to put Cat behind bars.

There'd been a lot of rumors about Cat of late. She'd been seen in Abilene, then in St. Louis. She'd been killed in Indian Territory. Then she'd just plain disappeared.

Annabeth paused outside the livery. Sometimes she wished she could disappear herself. Instead, Annabeth tossed a coin to the boy who'd been sleeping inside the stable door, handed him the reins, and moved on.

At the head of an alley that ran between the structures on Main Street and those to the north, she made her first mistake. She should have gone to the saloon and asked questions. Small town, someone would know something about the doctor. She would discover what had made Fedya behave so strangely and deal with it. How bad could things be?

Ethan might once have been a spy, but that was long ago and far away. Whatever problem there might be could be solved simply and quietly. He need never even know she was there. But he was so close, and it had been so long. What could it hurt to take a peek?

Thoughts like that always got her into trouble.

She palmed her daddy's Navy Colt. Most of Freedom was asleep; she was certain of it. But she'd been certain of a few things in the past that had turned out to be lies. Which had taught her to trust no one, believe nothing. And draw her weapon for any old reason at all.

She glanced through a back window, saw only darkness. She pressed her ear to the wood, heard nothing but crickets singing to the night. Turning the knob, she nearly stumbled inside when the thing swung wide. Why was she surprised? A good doctor never locked his door.

As she slipped quietly through the first floor, her gaze wandered over the medicine cabinet filled with colorful bottles—brown for cod liver, blue for laudanum, green for tincture of ginger—the exam table, several chairs, a desk. Everything appeared exactly the same, though hardly anything was.

Annabeth faced the staircase. She could slink and skulk a while longer, or she could do what she'd come to do. Tightening her grip on the gun, Annabeth began to climb.

She reached the landing and glanced through the open doorway. Moonlight filtered across the empty bed. She swallowed, the sound crackling through a pulsing silence broken only by those damnable crickets. Why were they so loud?

Her gaze went to the window—nothing but a gaping hole where glass had once been. Her heart, which had already been beating far too fast, beat faster. What had happened here?

She backed out of the room, glanced toward the next, tensed. He wasn't in there. There was no reason for her to be. Nevertheless, Annabeth headed in that direction.

The first door had been open; the second was closed. She stood for several seconds, staring at the knob, unable to make herself reach for it.

It's only a room, she told herself. *Probably empty. Gathering dust. The doctor's not even here. He's gone to help some poor soul. Or maybe just gone.*

But she didn't believe it. She wasn't that lucky.

Annabeth ignored the tremble of her fingers as they wrapped around the knob and pushed.

The moon cast an eerie light across the man slouched against the far wall. His black hair tumbled over his brow, curled around his neck. Several days' beard darkened his jaw, making his olive skin appear pale.

Long legs stretched in her direction; the bottoms of his bare feet were filthy. He smelled like a saloon the morning after any night. But Ethan Walsh was still one of the handsomest men Annabeth had ever seen.

She retreated a step and saw the crib in the corner. She tried to snatch back her pained gasp and failed.

His eyes opened, caught the gleam of the moon and shone silver.

CHAPTER 11

At first Ethan believed he was dreaming. He always was whenever he saw her. But in his dreams, she never held a gun; she wasn't wearing—

What in hell was she wearing?

Ethan sat up, rubbing his jaw, grimacing at the stubble and the spit. This wasn't the way he'd wanted to see her again. Of course, he'd never thought he *would* see her again.

"Beth?" he asked. He still wasn't sure she was real. Lately, he wasn't sure a lot of things were real.

Her eyes narrowed. "What is wrong with you?"

For an instant, he panicked, wondering how many empty bottles lay around him. But he was more adept than that. He always disposed of the empties as soon as they became that way. One never knew when a patient might happen in. It wouldn't do for the doctor to be found unconscious amid the evidence.

He didn't care for how she towered over him, so he got to his feet; he managed not to sway. He desperately wanted to scratch the itch that never seemed to go away. But he'd had plenty of practice pretending. He was probably better at it now than he'd been before.

He didn't tower over her, never had, which was one of the things he'd loved about her. She could almost look him in the eye. Back when she'd still been able to look at him.

As if to illustrate his thought, she glanced at the ceiling. There wasn't much either of them could stomach the sight of in this room.

"What's wrong with me?" he repeated, and her gaze

lowered, fixing resolutely on his throat, not his face. "Why on earth would there be anything wrong?" He waited a beat, then murmured, "Darlin'," in the brogue she'd once adored.

She stiffened, and her gaze flicked up, then back down. "Don't call me that."

"No?" He walked toward her, slow, like a cat through the tall grass. And like that cat, he quivered in anticipation. "What name are ye usin' these days? I'll bet me da's last gold eagle it isn't Walsh."

She winced, and he had his answer. Why it hurt so much, he couldn't say.

"You know my name," she said.

"Beth."

"No." She lifted her chin. "Annabeth."

How could he forget? His shortening of her name had been one of the mistakes that had given him away. He should have lengthened it, drawing her name out, making it last, putting all that he'd felt back then into the words. Annabeth Louise. Miss Annabeth. Annabeth Louise Phelan. Miss Phelan. Annabeth Lou.

"And so on," he murmured. She cast him another quick, worried glance. "Did you come to make yourself a widow?"

She blinked. "What?"

He flicked a finger at the gun. He'd never seen her with one in her hand, although the way she held it, he could tell she knew how to use it. Was that something she'd learned since leaving him? Or something she'd known all along? There were so many things about her he hadn't known.

She frowned as if she weren't quite sure how the weapon had gotten into her hand, then shoved it into the holster that rode low on her hips. "You think I'd hurt you?"

"Honey," he murmured, and even in the silver-tinged darkness, he saw her shudder—with disgust or desire, he didn't know, didn't care. "Just seeing you makes me hurt so deep, I want to die."

She released an impatient huff. "I didn't come here

to listen to your blarney. I had my fill of that—" She paused, and Ethan heard her thoughts as clearly as if she'd said them aloud. *I had my fill of you.* "Long before I left."

Suddenly Ethan was so tired and sad, he wanted to sink back onto the floor and find another blue bottle. But first he had to get rid of her.

"You don't have to listen to me. You don't have to look at me or live with me."

Or touch me, or kiss me, or love me. He tightened his mouth lest those words slip out. He might be pathetic, but he didn't want to be that pathetic.

"You left," he said, "and I moved on." He stared her up and down. "Apparently, you did, as well." Though to what, where, when, why . . . ? He pushed aside those thoughts. They'd haunted him enough. "I never heard from you. Not a word to let me know if you were alive or dead."

After a year—or had it been two?—with no whisper of his wife, Ethan couldn't bear to sit in this house one more instant—listening, waiting, hoping, hating. So he'd left.

He'd heard about a physician in Glasgow who'd employed techniques to keep putrefaction at bay with carbolic acid instead of alcohol. Ethan had spent six months studying with Dr. Lister. He could have remained, but he'd started to wonder: Had she come back? Was she waiting in Freedom? Would she leave again if he stayed away too long?

He'd returned to a house full of dust. No letters. No wires. No wife.

Silence settled over them. The years apart had made him angry. What had they made her? He had no idea where she'd been, what she'd done, who she was. But why should now be any different from then?

Annabeth walked out. Ethan gaped. He'd wanted her to go; now she had and—

He hurried to the doorway, catching his toe on a loose board and nearly falling on his face. Reaching the hall, he cast his gaze to the stairs, listened for the clatter of steps downward. He heard nothing, saw the same, and suddenly he understood where she'd gone.

Four strides and he reached his room. She'd looped the gun belt over one bedpost, tossed her hat over the other. Her hair—that glorious red hair he used to bury his face in as he buried himself in her—tumbled down her back, brushing the swell of her rear. The trousers left little to the imagination. No wonder she carried a gun. Any man who saw that would want to—

She turned, and he jerked his gaze upward. He meant to meet her indigo eyes, but he got caught on the fine line of her throat revealed by the buttons she'd already released.

"Wh-what are you doing?" He was dry mouthed, not from need for the bottle but need for her, something he'd thought long dead.

"It's late. I'm tired."

The thought of her climbing into his bed, laying her head on his pillow, rubbing her scent all over the sheets, made him hard in an instant. He couldn't remember the last time he'd gotten an erection without a whole lot of effort.

Then, suddenly, he did. Because it had been right here. In this room. With her.

Her fingers released another button, revealing the swell of her breasts. She wasn't wearing a corset. Why would she? How could she beneath a man's shirt and pants?

He couldn't pull his gaze away; his mouth became drier and drier as more and more flesh appeared. Her ribs. Her belly. Her navel. He had a sudden recollection of running his tongue along its edge. She'd laughed and tangled her fingers in his hair.

When she dropped the shirt and reached for the waistband of her jeans, Ethan spun, but not before he saw everything he'd once touched and tasted, everything that had once been his.

Her boots thudded to the floor.

"Get out of my bed."

"It's my bed, too."

His shoulders drew in, an involuntary flinch. "Where am I supposed to go?"

Instead of remanding him to hell, her sigh was long and just a bit sad. "You were sleeping on the floor when I got here."

"I wasn't asleep." He'd been passed out, but he wasn't going to tell her that.

She didn't comment; he wasn't sure if that was good or bad. He wanted to look at her, then again, he didn't. What if she was sitting up in bed, the covers pooled at her waist, her breasts shimmering in the dying light of the moon?

"You'll leave in the morning?" He'd meant the words to be an order, but they came out a question instead. Soft, just above a whisper, more a plea than a command. If she stayed, she'd discover every secret, as she had before, and this time those secrets would ruin him.

He risked a glance. She was asleep, cheek on his pillow, the sheets at her waist as he'd imagined, her breasts bared to the night and to him.

And just as he'd feared, he wanted her as much now as he had the first time he'd touched her.

For an instant after Annabeth awoke she thought everything that had happened in the past five years had been a dream. She'd never left Freedom. She hadn't done things that would make Ethan hate her. Then she remembered.

Why she had left. What she had done. Why she was back.

"Hell," Annabeth muttered.

She rubbed her face against the pillow; the aroma of herbs and strong soap billowed around her. The scent of a healer, she wished it could heal her. She'd never felt safer than when she'd been in Ethan's arms. Amid the lies, love had been their only truth.

But love couldn't conquer the grief, the blood, the betrayal, the death. Nothing could.

Annabeth tugged the other pillow over her face.

Immediately she sat up, and it tumbled to her lap along with the sheet. She lifted the bolster again, took a tentative sniff. Her gaze narrowed on the open doorway.

She knew a woman when she smelled one.

After climbing out of bed, she crossed to the armoire and then stood in front of the large wooden structure for several seconds before yanking open the door on the right. Ethan's shirts hung side by side with his trousers. She pulled on the left. All she found were more of the same.

Annabeth rubbed her roiling belly. She hadn't discovered another woman's clothes, but she hadn't discovered her own either. What had he done with them?

Her saddlebags, which she'd left with her horse, sat just inside the door. Uncertain what, exactly, their presence meant beyond the ability to don slightly fresher clothes, Annabeth removed her dress, a shift, some drawers from the bag. She'd tossed her corset long ago, hadn't missed it even once.

She used the water in the pitcher and the soap next to it to wash as best she could before dressing. After a quick glance into the spare room—no Ethan, not a sign of her things—she trotted downstairs.

He stood in the exam room, using a pestle to savagely mash whatever lay at the bottom of a mortar.

"I think it's dead."

He started, nearly dropping the bowl, then tossed a scowl over his shoulder.

"What did you do with my clothes?" she asked.

He went back to mutilating whatever he had in the bowl—something that smelled both red and spicy. "Burned them."

The front door opened and a man came in. The sun was at his back, and she couldn't see his face. Had Lass sent someone after her already?

Then he stepped out of the light, removing his sweat-stained Stetson. His hair was gray, his eyes were blue, his hands large, scarred, and capable. The guns at his hips were the same. "Mrs. Walsh?"

She opened her mouth; nothing came out. Legally, that name was hers, but she hadn't used it in . . . forever.

"Can I help you?"

Annabeth shivered as Ethan's breath stirred her hair; at the same time, his heat warmed her from shoulders to shins.

"Dr. Walsh?" Ethan must have nodded, because the man extended his hand. "I'm Ren Eversleigh, U.S. Marshal."

Ethan stiffened, or maybe Annabeth did. The lawman didn't seem to notice. He shook Ethan's hand; Annabeth moved closer to the door.

"I have some questions about the sheriff. I'm told he fell from the upstairs window."

Only someone who knew Ethan as well as Annabeth did, who had thought about every minute they'd spent together over the hundreds of nights since she'd left him, would have seen the slight flutter of the muscle beneath his right eye and known what it meant.

Ethan Walsh was getting ready to lie.

"He did," Ethan agreed.

Annabeth coughed. Ethan kept his gaze on the marshal, but his hands clenched.

"How?" the lawman asked.

"I wasn't here."

"Hmm," Annabeth murmured. No twitch there.

Ethan cast her a glare that very clearly said he wished she would go away—preferably the same way the sheriff had—before returning his attention to the lawman. "Since when do federal marshals investigate the accidental deaths of small-town sheriffs?"

"When they aren't accidental?" Annabeth asked. It appeared fairly obvious to her. It also made her wonder if the sheriff's death was in some way related to the danger to Ethan.

Ethan put his hands behind his back, no doubt to keep himself from throttling her. She shouldn't bait him, but she found that sometimes—like when he lied—she just couldn't help herself.

"Why would you say that, Mrs. Walsh?" The marshal tilted his head. "You *are* Mrs. Walsh?"

"I . . ." Her eyes met Ethan's, and her desire to bait him faded. "Am."

His lips thinned. His shoulders hunched. Pretty soon his fingernails were going to puncture his palms.

"You believe the sheriff's death wasn't accidental?" Eversleigh continued.

She tugged her gaze from Ethan's. It wasn't easy. "I have no idea if it was or it wasn't. I was . . . away."

"Was *anyone* here when he died?" the man snapped.

Ethan rubbed beneath his eye. "No."

"How well did you know the sheriff, Dr. Walsh?"

"Well enough to say hello."

"Yet he fell to his death from your bedroom window?"

Ethan dropped his hand. "What are you trying to say?"

"Apparently something you don't like."

"I can't decide if you're accusing me of killing him or fucking him."

Annabeth choked. The marshal cast her a quick glance, then went back to his interrogation. "Is either one the truth?"

"No."

Ethan refused to look away, as did Eversleigh. Annabeth feared they might bump chests and growl. "My husband saves lives, Marshal; he doesn't take them."

Ethan frowned, obviously wondering why she was defending him. She kind of wondered that herself.

"I don't think you know as much about him as you think you do, ma'am."

"You're wrong."

She knew everything; she only wished that she didn't.

CHAPTER 12

"Your husband was a spy," Eversleigh said flatly.

"I know," Annabeth returned. "I'm the spy who caught him."

Ethan sighed. "Beth."

He wasn't sure if the glare she shot his way was because he'd spoken, or because he'd again shortened her name. He couldn't help himself. To him she was Beth, and she always would be. If she didn't like it, she could leave.

Ethan scratched his wrist. He really needed them both to leave.

"Is that the South I hear in your voice, Mrs. Walsh?"

"Virginia," she agreed. "Richmond."

"As Ethan Walsh is listed as a surgeon at Chimborazo Hospital, I'll assume that's where you met."

"Yes."

"How?"

Annabeth frowned. "I was a matron."

"You just said you were a spy."

"I was both."

"Like him?"

"Yes," she said again, then quickly, "No! We weren't on the same side."

"You worked against each other, yet you're married," the marshal clarified.

Her gaze met Ethan's; he lifted his brows. Hers crashed down, and she faced the marshal. "That's in the past—over and done with." She cleared her throat. "You've obviously investigated Ethan. I want to know why."

Ethan did, too.

"Someone wrote the marshal service in Wichita. Said the sheriff died here 'bout a month or so back under suspicious circumstances."

"Sheriffs die every day," Ethan said.

"Not too many fall out of windows."

"Accidents happen."

"Whoever sent the letter seemed to think he was pushed."

"Who sent it?"

"No signature."

"Obviously the letter writer is the person who tossed the sheriff from the window," Annabeth said. "Why get the law involved at all unless it's to turn suspicion away from oneself?"

"According to your husband, no one was here to toss the man. He fell."

"Someone's lying," Annabeth said.

"Always," the marshal agreed. "But who?"

"I'd tend to believe the fellow standing in front of me as if he has nothing to hide over a person who writes anonymous letters. But I'm funny that way."

"Somethin's funny," Eversleigh muttered, turning to Ethan. "I heard that not long before the 'accident' you had visitors."

"Not visitors. A patient," Ethan clarified.

"And the giant who joined them?"

Annabeth cast Ethan a glance. She knew exactly who that was.

"I don't remember any giant."

"Dark hair. Light eyes. Nasty scar right about here." Eversleigh pointed to his forehead.

"Ah." Ethan rubbed his eye. "The brother of my patient's husband."

Annabeth shifted her weight to one hip, then fidgeted it back to the other. She wanted to ask questions, discover the truth about his visitors. But she knew that if Ethan was skirting the inquiries, there had to be a reason. He doubted she would care if he were arrested, but she'd make sure Mikey wasn't.

"Thank you for your interest, Marshal." Annabeth crossed to the door. "Have a safe trip back to Wichita."

Eversleigh didn't move. "Something smells here."

"That's the medicines we make in the back room." Annabeth opened the door.

The man peered at Ethan, then at Annabeth. He knew they were lying, but he wasn't sure about what.

"If he lied then . . ." the marshal began.

"He did," Annabeth agreed. "I did. That was *what* we did."

"Then why should I believe him now?"

"As I told you before, Ethan isn't a killer."

"He's never killed anyone? Not even during the war? Not before or after?"

Ethan waited for her to deny him, to say that he had killed the most precious thing in their world.

"Never," she said. She always had been a far better liar than he.

The marshal loosed a short, sharp, annoyed yet defeated sigh, and turned to Ethan. "Where did your visitors go?"

"They told me they were from Texas."

"Whereabouts?"

"Didn't say." Probably because they weren't actually from Texas.

"You didn't ask?"

"Didn't care. I was more concerned with my patient."

"What was the matter with her?"

"Fever." Which often occurred in poorly treated gunshot wounds.

"Which you doctored and then—"

"They said they were returning to Texas."

"Yet they were seen headed north."

The marshal *had* been busy.

"I'm not responsible for their poor sense of direction."

Eversleigh's lips tightened. "I'd like to speak with them."

"Look in Texas." That should keep the man occupied for the next several years.

At last the marshal stepped onto the porch. His suspicious gaze met Ethan's. "I'll find out what happened."

"We'll enjoy hearing about it." Annabeth shut the door in his face.

"We will?" Ethan asked.

She waited until the clomps of the marshal's boots faded before she faced him. "I'd like to know what in hell happened. But I doubt he'll be the one telling me."

"No?"

"Giant? Had to be Mikey. And since he's always with Fedya . . ." She spread her hands. "Who was the woman?"

"According to Fedya, 'no one.' "

Annabeth snorted. Ethan agreed. Fedya wouldn't have ridden his horse until it almost dropped dead on Main Street, with the woman both he and Mikey had called "Cathy" in his arms, all the way from Indian Territory if she'd been *no one.* Fedya had loved that woman.

Whoever she was.

"Who threw the sheriff out the window?" Annabeth asked.

Ethan shrugged. "I wasn't here."

"So it had nothing to do with you," she murmured.

"Me? No. Why would it?"

Fedya had insisted he had done it; the woman insisted she had. Ethan had lost a few nights' sleep over the lawman's demise, but the fact remained . . . The sheriff *was* dead, and Ethan would probably never know the why of it.

Fedya Kondrashchenko could call himself Alexi Romanov and pretend pretty much anything, but he would always be the slickest confidence man both east and west of the Mississippi, and if he didn't want anyone to know the truth of what had happened in Ethan's room, no one ever would. Besides, Ethan had enough sins of his own to agonize over. He didn't need to add someone else's.

Annabeth peered at the street, brow furrowed, thinking hard, though about what, he couldn't determine.

"Do you need money?" he asked.

She blinked. "What?"

"Is that why you came? I have some. I'll give it to you; then you can go."

The flush of fury began at the neck of her dress—frayed, faded, the garment hung on her as if it had been made for someone else. "You think I came back for your money?" Her mouth twisted on the last word, as if he'd offered her his latest crop of armpit hair.

"You certainly didn't come back for me."

"No?"

"Don't." He held up one hand, saw it was trembling, and put it back down.

"Don't what?"

"Lie."

She sighed, staring out at the town called Freedom, which was anything but. "Is your brother—?"

Ethan's chest went tight. He couldn't breathe. He spun, palming a blue bottle from the counter, then tucking the glass into his pocket before heading upstairs where there were locks on the doors.

Mikey was still Mikhail, which meant that, for Ethan, his brother was dead.

A door slammed, and several thuds followed. Annabeth continued to gaze out the window. Ethan could say what he liked; he could do what he wanted. But she wasn't leaving.

Not yet.

She smoothed her hand over her skirt and grimaced. The garment was tired and pale—ruined—like her. She had no idea where Lass had gotten it; she hadn't asked. Questions like that yielded troubling answers.

She'd always hated this dress, but she didn't have another, nor occasion to wear one if she did. But suddenly, she wanted a different garment—one she'd purchased herself, one that hadn't been tossed at her like payment.

Annabeth stepped outside, closing the door behind her. If Ethan decided to lock it before her return, he'd discover she'd learned quite a bit in the past five years. She could pick any lock ever made.

Folks milled about on the streets, more than she remembered milling about when she'd left. When she'd lived here before, the town was just big enough to afford a doctor, though it *had* boasted three saloons. Now she counted six, plus two mercantiles, three restaurants, a dressmaker, cobbler, milliner, and whorehouse. The sheriff's office stood right next to Ethan's place. Though it appeared deserted, the rest of Freedom was booming.

Since Lewis's Sewing and Sundry stood closer than either of the mercantiles, she went there first. Inside, a familiar scent washed over her, and she sniffed, wondering what it was.

"Good morning." A woman emerged from the rear of the building, her low, husky voice completely at odds with her small stature and doll-like beauty. The voice was that of someone who'd spent a lifetime in smoky saloons, singing—or worse—for her supper. But her face was unlined, youthful, her blue eyes honest and sweet, her hair the shade of daffodils, worn loose and caught at the nape with a pink ribbon. "I'm Mrs. Lewis."

"I . . . uh, yes." The woman lifted a brow at Annabeth's discomfiture. "Good morning." She felt huge and awkward. A redheaded troll in the presence of a princess.

"What can I do for you?"

"I need . . ." Annabeth indicated her faded gown.

"Of course." Mrs. Lewis hurried forward, pulling a measurement cord from around her neck. "I can get started right away."

"Do you . . . uh . . . have anything ready-made?"

"In your size?" Mrs. Lewis managed not to laugh in Annabeth's face. Most likely because she was far too small to see into Annabeth's face. "I don't—" She paused, frowning; then just as suddenly, she smiled. "I do!" She clapped her tiny hands and hurried off on tiny feet.

She returned almost immediately, holding a light green day dress. Annabeth stifled a grimace. Pale green was not her color. Mrs. Lewis did not seem to notice. She attempted to place the bodice where Annabeth's bodice resided, but she couldn't quite manage it.

Annabeth took the gown and positioned the neck where the neck would go. The hem ended two inches higher than it should. The cuffs stopped an inch above her wrists.

"Don't worry." Mrs. Lewis tugged on the skirt, and Annabeth let go. "I can let down the hem and add longer cuffs. Won't take me but an hour."

"I assume you made this for someone." She doubted Mrs. Lewis sewed clothes the size of an Amazon for her own amusement.

"I did. However, the lady left town without paying for it."

"Won't she be back?"

"Doubtful. But I can always stitch another. Would you like me to make those changes?"

As Annabeth had nothing but the dress on her back and the trousers in her saddlebags, she nodded. "Please." The color would make Annabeth resemble a holly berry, but she didn't have much choice. "Could I order more of the same? In my size but different material?"

"How many?"

"Three more." She planned to burn the one she was wearing. "And the colors . . ." She lifted her hand to her hair, which also hung loose, but as it had been shoved beneath a sweaty hat for days did not look half as lovely as her companion's.

"Of course." The woman began to pull out bolts of cloth in browns, golds, and deeper greens. Annabeth pointed to one of each shade.

"I'll need undergarments, stockings. Pretty much everything."

"What happened to your clothes?"

Revealing that her husband had burned them was probably not a good idea. "Flood." Annabeth cleared her throat.

"Oh!" Mrs. Lewis set her slim white hands on her rosy cheeks. "How horrible."

"Yes. You'll have the dress modified in an hour?"

"I will."

The door opened. Annabeth recognized Sadie

Cantrell as soon as she walked in. They had been friendly before Annabeth left. The former frontier schoolteacher had done everything she could to make the young doctor's wife feel welcome.

Sadie and her husband, Jeb, were old enough to have been the first settlers of the great state of Kansas. They were certainly among the first settlers of Freedom, or at least there was no one left alive to contradict the claim.

At the sight of Annabeth, Sadie's one remaining good eye widened. "Hello, Sadie," Annabeth began. "I'm—"

"Dead," Sadie interrupted.

"Excuse me?"

"You're dead."

Annabeth opened her mouth, shut it again, then glanced at Mrs. Lewis, who spread her hands. Although the past twenty-four hours had been slightly hellish, Annabeth was fairly certain Freedom wasn't purgatory.

"I assure you I'm not."

"Ye better tell yer husband that, 'cause he's been mournin' ye somethin' fierce."

"Mourning?" she repeated.

Sadie eyed Mrs. Lewis. "Ye didn't come to have a catfight with yonder sewin' woman, did ye?"

Yonder sewing woman drew in a sharp breath. "What's your name?"

"Annabeth."

"Beth?"

Annabeth got a chill. "How did you—"

"Surname?" Mrs. Lewis snapped, and Annabeth, who'd been known for the past five years, and for many before that, as Annabeth Phelan nevertheless answered, "Walsh."

The woman, who'd already paled as if Annabeth were the ghost Sadie claimed, gave a wordless cry. Her eyes fluttered, and she slid out of sight behind the countertop.

Annabeth hurried around the edge to discover Mrs. Lewis in a heap on the floor. She knelt next to her and caught again that familiar scent.

Mrs. Lewis smelled just like Ethan's spare pillow.

The indentation of his wife's head still marred the bolster. Though Ethan knew it was a mistake, he sipped at the bottle, staring at the curve in the white fabric, and the next thing he knew, he'd placed his own cheek right where hers had been.

He could have sworn the material was still warm from her skin, which was just foolish. It was the tail end of summer in Kansas. What wasn't warm?

But the damn thing smelled like her. Also foolish. She'd been riding for days, weeks . . . who knew? She had smelled—of horse, sweat, and that disgusting old hat she'd pulled over her exquisite hair. So why, then, did he drift into the deepest sleep he'd enjoyed since she'd left with the scent of lavender soap filling his nose?

Because he was crazy. But he'd known that for a long time.

"Ethan!"

Her voice was further proof of his insanity, because he heard her calling his name as if she were right in the room. He swore she shook his arm, but that couldn't be. He'd locked the door. Therefore he was dreaming again.

And since he was, he reached for her, tangling his fingers in her hair, cupping the back of her head with his palm, tugging her lips ever closer to his. He caught the scent of mint—she'd often chewed the leaves to freshen her breath, not that he'd ever found it anything but sweet.

She resisted at first; she always did. She'd left him; she hated him. But no matter the hate, the pain, the past, they'd always had this.

Their lips met, and she gasped, the reaction opening her mouth to his tongue, rubbing her breasts—no corset, how odd—along his chest. The friction—her clothes, his, nothing more—caused her nipples to harden. He tilted her head, delved deeper, and after an instant when he thought she might pull away—something that never, ever happened in a dream and therefore did not happen now—she kissed him back.

She tasted the same—the flare of whiskey in the dead

of winter, mint juleps at the height of summer, intoxication of the very best kind.

The buttons of her bodice opened with barely a touch, and he slipped within. Cupping the warm, familiar weight, he ran a thumb across the tip. Ripe, round, and rigid, she groaned as he rolled the bud, the sound vibrating against his mouth, his chest, making him ache. She wasn't the only one ripe and rigid right now.

In all his dreams, she'd been young, the way she'd been at Chimborazo, wearing a drab dress, a stained apron, and a horrid cap over her incredible hair.

He'd never seen anything quite like Annabeth Phelan's hair. Not red, not really. Not orange either. But a brilliant hue in between that should have been unfortunate but wasn't.

"Ahem!"

Ethan kissed his wife more thoroughly, running his hand from her neck, down her back to her buttocks, pressing her tightly against his larger-than-lately erection.

"Ethan," she murmured.

"Beth," he returned.

"Dr. Walsh?" someone said.

He opened his eyes at the same time Annabeth opened hers. For an instant he saw the self he wished he still was reflected there. Doctor. Husband. Lover. The man she'd believed him to be, because he'd pretended so well. Then he remembered the bottle in his pocket, the spare room nearby, and the reasons for what he kept in both.

He yanked his hand from her bodice. Something tore; a button came loose and hit him in the eye. That small pain was nothing compared to the shock when she scrambled off of him, sliding a knee down his manhood with just enough pressure to make him gasp.

He took one look at her face and understood it hadn't been an accident. Annabeth knew exactly what she was doing. Always. So why in hell had she been kissing him?

He struggled to his feet, and a second bout of throat clearing had him spinning toward the door through which Sadie Cantrell peeked. "How did you get that open?"

Sadie pointed at Annabeth, who was trying, to no avail, to button a bodice sadly lacking a button right where a button was needed the most. The pale, beautiful curve of her breasts taunted him.

"It was locked," he said.

Annabeth rolled her eyes. "Please."

What did that mean? He nearly asked, but Sadie butted in. "Doc, ye gotta come quick. Thought yer wife was gonna bring ye."

"Come where?" he asked, though he was already following Sadie toward the stairs—slower than usual, with more of a limp than he liked, but he was following.

"Miz Lewis's place."

He froze. "What happened?"

"Cora done fainted dead away."

Ethan got a very bad feeling. "What does my wife have to do with it?"

"They was talkin'. Then Miz Walsh said her name, and Miz Lewis swooned."

A helpless, frustrated sensation swamped him. He should have done something to prevent this. But what? If he'd told Annabeth not to go to Cora's shop, she'd have gone there straightaway.

He glanced at his wife. "Why did you—"

"I needed clothes." She stopped fussing with the rent bodice and threw up her hands, casting Sadie an exasperated glance. "He burned mine."

Sadie's white eyebrows shot toward what remained of her white hair.

"I was going to ask why you came for me," Ethan said. "You're perfectly capable of handling a fainting spell on your own." She'd handled far worse.

"I wanted to give you this." She crossed the floor in three quick steps and punched him in the stomach.

He doubled over. On the way down, he saw a movement and twisted his head to the left, narrowly avoiding a knee to the nose.

One girl, five boys? Annabeth Phelan had learned young to fight dirty.

He could have sworn Sadie laughed, or maybe she choked. Although, when he glanced her way—after he made certain Annabeth wasn't going to hit him again—the old woman's face held only concern. "Ye all right, Doc?"

He nodded, rubbing his gut. "What the hell, Beth?"

"You slept with that woman." He blinked. "In our bed!"

"Did she tell you that?" He couldn't imagine Cora discussing such a thing with anyone. Ever.

"She didn't have to." Annabeth snatched a pillow off the floor. "You could have at least laundered the sheets, Ethan." He frowned, confused, and she made a disgusted, infuriated sound before she threw the pillow at him. It bounced off his chest and fell to the floor. "The thing reeks of her."

He glanced at Sadie. "We should probably have this discussion later. Cora needs—"

"She done woke up just after yer missus left," Sadie interrupted. "But she does wanna talk t' ye."

"No doubt," Annabeth muttered.

Ethan ignored her. "Would you tell Mrs. Lewis I'll be along directly?"

Sadie nodded and, after a curious glance at his wife, left.

"What did you think would happen?" Ethan lifted his gaze from the pillow that lay next to his foot. Annabeth still appeared furious, but now he was, too. "Did you think you could disappear for five years, then return, and I'd be sitting right where you'd left me?"

"You are where I left you."

She was more correct in that statement than she knew. He was exactly where she'd left him in every way. Same house, same job, same town—in agony, full of hate, afraid of love, trusting no one.

Especially her.

"You mean to tell me no other man has touched you since you left?"

She turned toward the window, and his belly burned. He'd asked her what she'd expected, but what had he? From the first, everything between them had been a lie. Unfortunately, he hadn't discovered that until after he'd married her.

"Why did you come back?" he asked.

"Why do you think?" She continued to stare outside.

"Honestly, Beth, I have no idea."

"Neither do I."

CHAPTER 13

Annabeth started when a door closed downstairs. Ethan appeared on the street below, carrying his medical bag, hurrying toward Lewis's Sewing and Sundry. Annabeth hadn't heard him leave the room. She hadn't even heard him on the stairs. She was slipping.

But Ethan had always known how to move without making a sound; he was very good at sneaking, lying, spying. The only reason he'd ever been caught was her.

He went into the shop; Sadie came out. Annabeth's lips tightened. Was Ethan kissing the tiny, blond, perfect Cora? Had he told her he was sorry? That everything would be all right?

How could it be? His dead wife wasn't quite so dead.

Annabeth turned away. Why torment herself? As Ethan had asked: *What did you expect?*

Strangely, she hadn't expected this.

She retrieved her saddlebags, her gun. But before she could sling them over her shoulder, she remembered her torn dress.

She drew out the clothes she'd been wearing last night. They were filthy; they smelled. She tossed them onto the floor; they were all she had, thanks to Ethan's pyre.

She considered going to the Sewing and Sundry and taking the dress she'd been promised. She could wear a skirt that was a bit short. It wasn't as if she hadn't done so before. All her life she'd outgrown clothes faster than her mother could sew them or her father could pay for them. At least her breasts wouldn't be showing and she wouldn't smell like a pig in wallow.

However, she might do something she'd regret—like

gouge out her own eyes, or perhaps Cora's—if she walked in on Ethan and the lovely Mrs. Lewis tangled in each other's arms. Instead she stepped to the armoire, selected one of Ethan's shirts. While she was there, she stole a pair of his trousers and one of his coats, too. Wasn't the first time.

As she walked toward the livery, folks stared and pointed. It would just be her luck that dressing as a man would get her thrown in jail when riding with outlaws hadn't. Then she heard the whispers.

"Where's she been?"

"Thought she was dead."

"Poor Miz Lewis."

"Poor Doc. Woman's a giant and that hair . . ."

Annabeth's fingers clenched.

"They were gonna be married."

Married?

"Uh-oh."

The last was uttered in a cacophony of voices when she stalked to the door of the shop and went in.

Ethan held Cora's hand. He wasn't certain what else to do. She kept crying, and nothing he could say would stop her. He'd never been much good with crying women. Probably because he hadn't known very many.

His mother had died giving birth to his brother. He had no sisters. His wife was not the crying type. He'd never seen Annabeth shed a single tear during the war. Certainly, at the worst point of their lives, there'd been tears. But, mostly, they'd been his.

He patted Cora's hand, making noncommittal noises as she continued to sob. How long did such outbursts last?

"Y-y-your w-wife," Cora stammered.

"Mmm-hmm."

"She's n-n-n—" Cora paused, breath hitching, large blue eyes beseeching Ethan for help. The only word he could think to suggest was "nice," and he was fairly certain that wasn't it. So he made more noises and patted faster.

"Not," Cora finally managed. "Not dead."

"No," he agreed. Really, what more could he say about that?

"You said she was dead."

Had he? His recollections since returning from Scotland had been fuzzy at best.

As time passed, he'd started to tell people she was "gone." Everyone assumed "gone" meant "dead," and as more years passed, he had begun to believe it, at least in the light of day. In the night, when he was alone, he'd known she was out there somewhere.

Out there choosing not to be with him. Which had led to the empty blue bottles.

"Ethan!"

He couldn't recall Cora ever being so shrill before. Until now, her voice had brought to mind fog and smoke, not skinned cats. Of course, she hadn't been committing adultery before.

Well, she had been. She just hadn't known it.

"Yes?" he managed, though his head had begun to ache and his mouth was so damn dry.

"What are you going to do?"

"Do?"

Her bottom lip pouted. "About her?"

"I don't understand." Annabeth was his wife—for better or worse—and though there'd been so much more worse than there'd been better, he didn't really see how that mattered.

"Aren't you going to . . . ?"

He waited, once again trying to fill in the blank and coming up short. Cora's expectant smile gave way to annoyance, and she let out a huff. "Divorce her!"

The thought had never occurred to him.

"She abandoned you, Ethan. She can't just walk back into town and become Mrs. Walsh again."

"She doesn't have to become Mrs. Walsh; she is." Although Ethan didn't think that she wanted to be.

Maybe divorce was the reason Annabeth had returned. But if she'd wanted to be free of him, she should have just stayed . . . free.

"What about us?" Cora whispered.

Ethan brought his attention back to the woman before him. He cared for her. How could he not? She'd given herself to him when he was desperately in need of something, someone, to hold on to. She'd believed they would marry; he had heard enough hints to that effect both from her and from the folks of Freedom. He hadn't discouraged those expectations. It had felt too good knowing someone loved him, someone wanted him, when the only woman he loved and wanted didn't.

Would he have married Cora eventually? He wasn't sure. He only knew that he couldn't now. She needed to know that, too.

Ethan took Cora's small, soft hands in his. "My wife isn't dead. I don't know where she's been, or why she was gone for so long, but she's back." He kissed her knuckles.

When he lifted his head, she wasn't looking at him but behind him. She wasn't crying; she didn't appear ready to scream. Instead, her face had turned white; her rosy lips had taken on a hint of blue. Alarmed, Ethan tightened his grip, and her gaze flicked to his.

"I'm with child," she said.

The whole world shimmied. He couldn't speak; he couldn't breathe. Someone behind him choked.

Ethan spun. His wife stood in the doorway. "Beth," he began. "I—"

She ran.

Ethan's skin went clammy; sweat beaded his brow. He swallowed several times and managed to keep himself from puking. Could life get any worse?

He took one step toward the gaping door, and Cora cried out. He glanced at her just in time to see her eyes flutter; he caught her before she hit the floor.

"Jesus," he muttered, gaze flicking to the exit and then back to her. He wanted so badly to follow Annabeth, but what would he say?

Oops?

The laugh that escaped sounded slightly hysterical. Ethan pursed his lips. If he continued to laugh like that, he might not stop. Instead, he concentrated on the only thing he'd ever been good at. Doctoring. He certainly wasn't much of a man.

Not true. By any "man's" standards, he was quite the specimen. How many women would he impregnate before he was through?

Ethan retrieved his bag, dug inside, and found the smelling salts. One wave beneath her nose and Cora choked, then opened her eyes. She shoved the bottle away. "What are you trying to do to me?"

"Hasn't anyone ever used smelling salts when you fainted?"

"I've never fainted." She set her hand on her stomach. "Must be the baby."

Ethan glanced toward the still-open doorway and sighed. "Must be."

"Aren't you happy?"

Ethan was a lot of things, but happy wasn't one of them. Happy hadn't been one of them for so long, he couldn't recall what happy felt like.

He returned his gaze to Cora. "Can you sit up?"

"If you help me." He helped; she clung. "Tell me that you love me." Her indrawn breath quavered, jiggling her breasts against his arm. Ethan wanted to tear away, to get away. "That you love *us*."

Should he lie? Or should he break her heart?

The impossible choice was postponed when Sadie reappeared. "Doc!" Cora released an annoyed huff, and her fingers tightened on Ethan's arm. "Yer wife."

Ethan stood, the movement tearing Cora's hold free. "What's wrong?"

"You should probably run," Sadie said.

Folks continued to stare and mutter as Annabeth stumbled up the street. She ignored them as she headed for the livery. She'd been on her way out of town. She wished she'd just left and not decided to confront her husband and his mistress about their bigamous plans. Now she had a new painful memory to add to the old.

I'm with child.

She leaned against the corner of the nearest building; her chest rebelled at the lack of air. She took another gulp, which sounded too much like a sob. She

AN OUTLAW IN WONDERLAND   129

hadn't cried since she'd left Freedom; she wasn't going to start again now.

Annabeth glanced behind her, afraid Ethan might have followed. But why would he? He'd just been given everything he'd ever wanted.

Her fingers curled until her nails bit into her palms. The tiny, sharp pain brought some clarity. She couldn't leave. Not quite yet.

She retraced her steps to the office. No one spoke; everyone moved out of the way. Shoving open the front door so hard, it banged against the wall, her gaze circled the room. Cold stove, nearly empty wood box.

An ax.

Her fingers closed around the handle. Slowly, she climbed the stairs and went into the spare room. What had seemed like a good idea five minutes ago didn't any longer. She couldn't lift the ax; she wanted to sink onto the floor and die.

The footsteps pounding up the stairs caused her to tighten her grip. The sound of her name being called in a desperate, frightened voice made her want to laugh. What did Ethan think she was going to do?

He appeared in the doorway, his face as white as it had been at Cora's. He was sweating; he appeared ready to vomit. That made two of them.

Make that three. Or would it be four? She was fairly certain Cora wanted to vomit right now as well, and did she count as one person, or two? Annabeth shook her head. Was she losing her mind? It wasn't the first time she'd wondered.

"Beth?" Ethan stepped into the room. Hands open to show he held nothing in them, he stared at her as if she were a wild thing. "What are you doing?"

"What you should have done." She tightened her grip. "Long ago."

"Honey," he began.

"Shut. Up." Annabeth swung the ax.

The crib shattered into several large chunks. She continued to hack away at it until the thing lay in several dozen small ones. When she finished, she tossed the blade in the center of the room and peered out the window. She needed to leave—this room, this house, this town, this life—but right now it was all she could do to stay on her feet.

"Why did you keep it?" she whispered.

"I . . ." he began, then sighed. "I don't know."

On the street below, a few people still paused and pointed, but most of Freedom had gone about their business. No doubt the doctor and his no-longer-dead wife would be a topic of conversation on street corners for weeks to come, but folks had work to do and only so much time in which to do it.

Annabeth's gaze went to Lewis's Sewing and Sundry. At least Cora had the sense not to stand outside and stare, although she might have been doing just that behind the windows. The sun glanced off of them bright enough to blind.

Ethan came up beside her. He didn't speak; she had told him to shut up. Annabeth still couldn't look at him.

"Why?" he murmured. She wasn't sure which "why" he meant. Why was she here? Why had she left? Why had she lied, spied? Why had they even tried?

Or maybe just why had she used his ax on their dead child's crib? At least for that question she had an answer.

"You might have put Cora Lewis in our bed," she said, "but you aren't putting her child in the one you made for ours."

"I wouldn't," he began.

She had no idea anymore what he would or wouldn't do, but she knew one thing for certain. "Now you can't."

They continued to peer outside. Did Ethan see the streets, the buildings, the people? Or had his vision blurred with memories, too?

Standing in this room all those years ago, the town below them dustier and smaller—but back then wasn't everything? Laughing together, her belly round and taut. When he'd laid his palm against it, everything in the world had seemed so right. How could it have gone so quickly, and so totally, wrong?

Lies.

His. Hers. She still wasn't sure where one began and the other ended. She probably never would be.

A flash of light drew Annabeth's attention to the sewing shop; the sun had moved just enough to take the bright flare off the windows and reveal that Cora was not standing behind the glass.

The sparkle came again farther down, near the edge of town. She'd seen sparkles like it before.

Annabeth shoved Ethan aside as the window shattered all over them. They bounced off the wall, landing on the floor in a heap of limbs and glass and crib chunks as the echo of a gunshot rang in her ears.

Ignoring the spike of glass and wood against her knees and palms, the tiny cuts across her face and throat, Annabeth crawled to the door where she'd dropped her possessions. She slid her Colt from the holster, muttering a few curses that she'd left the rifle in her saddle's scabbard. A pistol was going to be of no use unless whoever was shooting at them decided to approach the house. And if they were going to do that, they would have done it in the first place rather than snipe at them from afar.

Annabeth thought about what she'd seen in that instant before she'd pushed Ethan out of the way. A glint of sun off metal at the edge of Freedom, where few people roamed, in a place where whoever wanted them dead could slip back into town during the commotion, or jump on a horse and disappear during the same. Although, around here, there wasn't much cover.

She doubted the culprit was still out there. Nevertheless, she peeked over the edge of a window that now matched the empty one in Ethan's room—very quick, just in case—but no more shots were fired.

A cloud of dust had marred the horizon. A horse and rider? Or just dust? She couldn't tell. Fleetingly, she thought of Lassiter Morant. But if he'd been shooting at them, someone would be dead.

"I think they're gone, but . . ." She paused. The words "stay away from the window"—one never knew just how gone 'gone' was—remained unspoken.

Ethan didn't move, didn't speak. She considered he

might be frightened, but as he'd once spent time as a field surgeon in the middle of a war, shots had come closer to him than this.

"Ethan?" She sat on her heels and glanced over her shoulder.

She'd been wrong. No shot had ever come closer than this.

One minute Ethan stood at Annabeth's side, remembering the day he'd built the crib that lay in pieces behind them. The next, a sharp pain in his temple preceded images flashing through his mind so quickly, he could barely grasp them.

His mother—so young, Mikey still in her belly.

His da—so old and dying.

John Law grinning through the gray ash on his face.

Fedya's smirk.

Mikey's laughter.

Annabeth tugging at the shorn ends of her hair. *It'll grow back.* Then the wonder on her face as she'd laid her palm on her stomach and murmured, *I'm with child.*

Pain dragged Ethan from the past, and he moaned, batting at whoever was poking his temple; his brain felt on fire.

"Stop that!" His hand was grasped, then shoved to his side.

Ethan opened his eyes. Annabeth's face swam into view. Her hair *had* grown back.

His vision went hazy. He blinked, and his left eye burned. He began to swipe at it again, and she growled. His arm fell to his side.

He heard footsteps on the stairs, saw movement in the doorway. But Annabeth didn't even glance in that direction. All her attention was for Ethan.

"What happened?" A man with gray hair and blue eyes knelt on Ethan's other side. Memory flickered— there, gone, and then . . . just gone.

"If you can't decipher that, you aren't much of a lawman," Annabeth muttered.

Lawman. The sheriff? Except he didn't resemble the sheriff of Freedom at all.

"I heard the shot," the man said.

"Didn't everyone?" Annabeth stood, and memory glimmered again. Another place, another time. So much blood, but the face beneath it was not his own.

Ethan caught the cuff of Annabeth's trousers—why was she wearing them? They looked like his—and tried to draw her back. She yanked the material from his fingers and headed for the door.

"Baby," he managed, and she stopped so fast, her boots slid in the broken glass and slivers of wood.

"I need supplies." Her voice was hoarse. "Make sure he doesn't get up or touch that wound."

Footsteps clattered downward; Ethan waited for the door to open and close. When it didn't, he relaxed. Although, knowing Annabeth, she could leave without him ever hearing her go.

He tried to remember—when had she left? Why had she gone? When had she come back?—but he couldn't, and the fact that he couldn't bothered him.

"Seems like more happened here than a gunshot through your window," the man observed.

"I dinnae recall," Ethan said.

The lawman, who'd been frowning at the room, now frowned at Ethan. "Since when do you speak with an Irish accent?"

"I dinnae—"

"Recall. I suspect getting shot in the head can do that."

He'd been shot in the head? No. That hadn't been him; it had been—

"Mikey," he said.

A sharp intake of breath had Ethan glancing toward the door where Annabeth stood, one arm full of medical supplies, a bucket dangling from the other, face as white as the clouds drifting past the open window.

"This isn't like Mikey." She bustled inside, setting what she held in her arms onto the ground and busying herself with them. "A flesh wound. You'll be fine."

"Who's Mikey?" the unknown lawman asked.

Annabeth, a large bottle in her hands, glanced at Ethan as if waiting for him to speak. When he didn't, she dumped the contents into the bucket she'd carried upstairs. The two liquids merged, and a strong medicinal scent filled the room.

"Someone from the war." She shoved her hands inside. Her indrawn breath made memory flicker again. An operating room, another bucket, the same pained hiss.

"Alcohol," Ethan said.

"That's right," she agreed. It wasn't, but he couldn't think why.

Annabeth lifted her chin in the other man's direction. "You'll need to wash yours, as well."

"In alcohol?" He stared at his hands, which no doubt had several raw patches from his horse's reins, if not cuts from Lord knew what. Most folks' did. "I don't think I will."

"Then get out." Annabeth doused a clean cloth and lifted it toward Ethan's face. "Nothing touches him that hasn't been in that solution."

Ethan yelped when the cloth met his head. "*Mac soith*," he snapped, and jerked away.

"Why is he suddenly speaking Irish?" the lawman asked.

"I have no idea."

She pushed the bucket in the man's direction. He sighed and shoved his hands in. His mouth tightened, but he didn't curse or hiss. "Why alcohol?"

Annabeth submerged a length of sparkling thread, along with a needle. "During the war, Ethan used alcohol to clean everything that touched his patients. More of his lived than anyone else's."

"Lister," Ethan said. "Scotland."

Annabeth's eyes grew concerned again; the lawman appeared only more confused. "I could swear he's talkin' Irish."

Annabeth stuck the needle into Ethan's head.

Ethan talked a lot of Irish after that. Luckily, no one could understand it but him.

CHAPTER 14

The gash required five stitches. It was a glancing slice. The bullet had embedded itself in the far wall of the room and not Ethan's head.

As Annabeth drew his flesh closed with silver suture wire, she recalled his telling her how he missed it, using the same accent he was cursing in now.

I've not seen such luxuries since just after Manassas.

How she'd loved that accent. It had given her shivers in the night. Until she'd heard him speaking without it.

Had that been the beginning of the end for them? Or had it been only the beginning? Even after she'd learned the truth, she'd loved him. She should have known that a love born of lies could only end badly.

"Done." Annabeth cut the wire with scissors that had been dunked in the bucket. She lifted her gaze to the marshal's. "You can go."

Eversleigh smiled. He still had all his teeth, which made him appear younger than she'd first thought—maybe forty, instead of fifty. The gray hair and deep lines on his face aged him, but the war had aged them all.

"I don't think I will," he repeated. "There's still the little matter of the bullet that nearly went into his brain."

Annabeth's mind shied away from the thought of how close Ethan had come to death. Although maybe, like Mikey, he wouldn't have died but merely been changed. Right now, she wasn't so certain he hadn't been. The Irish accent was making her nervous.

"It didn't." She couldn't help herself; she brushed her fingers through Ethan's hair. They came away speckled with blood.

"And why was that?"

Annabeth rinsed her hands in the bucket, soaked another cloth, and wiped Ethan's face. Every now and then, his eyes opened, fixed on hers as if to ascertain she was still there, then closed again.

"I pushed him out of the way."

"Why?"

"I didn't want him dead."

The marshal cast her an exasperated glance. "I meant, how did you know a shot was coming?"

"The sun flashed off the barrel."

"Where?" he asked.

"Past the last building on the right at the edge of town." Seeing the marshal get to his feet, she added, "Don't bother."

The man's gaze turned suspicious. Certainly her assertion that she'd been a spy during the war might account for her knowing a few things about sneaky behavior, but how did she explain knowing the flash of sun had been off a rifle barrel and not someone's spectacles?

She couldn't. Or maybe she just wouldn't.

"You're not the law here," she said. "This isn't your concern."

"As there *is* no law here"—he frowned at Ethan, and she could almost hear him wonder if that was a problem Ethan had caused—"it's become my concern."

"Don't you have somewhere else to be?"

Now he frowned at her. "I'd think you'd want to know who took a shot at your husband."

"Once I do, I'll just have to find them and kill them." And right now she didn't have the time.

Eversleigh's scowl deepened. "You hadn't ought to say a thing like that in front of a lawman, even if you don't mean it."

She had meant it, but she did see his point.

"Could you help me get him into the bedroom?" she asked.

The marshal stared at her for several seconds, then touched Ethan's shoulder. "Doc?" Ethan opened one eye. "Can you get up on your own?"

"Some days, aye. Other days, nay."

He was still using the damn brogue.

"What about today?" the marshal asked.

Ethan lifted his arms, then his head, then his shoulders until he was sitting. He tried to stand and nearly fell. Eversleigh and Annabeth caught him by the elbows and hauled him upright.

"I'd say that was both an aye and a nay, wouldn't ye, darlin'?"

Annabeth ground her teeth at the endearment and towed him toward the door. Moments later, they lowered him onto the bed. Annabeth tugged on his boots to get them off.

"You have no idea why anyone would want your husband dead?" the marshal asked.

"No," she said. "Ethan *heals* people."

"We've had this conversation before." Eversleigh's gaze went to the empty window in Ethan's room. "Or close enough."

"Your point?" Annabeth stumbled when one of the boots popped off.

"He was a spy. I'm sure someone wants him dead."

He was right. There were probably quite a few someones. But why now? After all these years?

"Then again . . . you were a spy, too." Slowly Annabeth nodded. "You sure they were shooting at him?"

"No one ever knew about me." Annabeth dropped the first boot to the floor and yanked on the second. "Except Ethan." And Moze. But he didn't count.

She'd didn't think Fedya had ever learned the truth, but with him, one never could tell. However, if the Union's best sniper had been shooting at her, Annabeth would be dead. Besides, if Fedya had wanted her that way, all he would have had to do was kill her in Ellsworth where he'd found her. Instead, he had sent her here.

"You plan to stick with that story?" the marshal asked.

Annabeth cleared her throat. "I have no idea what you mean."

Eversleigh snorted and left.

The morning faded to afternoon, and Annabeth sat at Ethan's side. He shifted, moaned. She touched his face. No fever. Not yet.

"You're all right," she said.

"Hurts," he murmured.

She lifted his head and pressed the rim of the medicine bottle to his lips. "Drink," she urged, and he did.

"The bairn," Ethan muttered. "Poor little lad."

Annabeth swallowed. She hadn't thought of the baby in a very long time.

Liar!

Ethan's voice. Always was.

He slurred a few more indistinguishable words, then slept.

Not long after, she heard footsteps on the stairs. Sadie Cantrell appeared in the doorway. "How is he?"

"I . . ." Annabeth paused, realizing she had no idea how he was. She hoped when Ethan awoke, he would remember everything, including that his blasted Irish accent was fake. Every time he used it, Annabeth wanted to both kiss and kill him. He thought she was a liar? Who'd lied first?

"Glass houses," she murmured, and Sadie tilted her head, birdlike.

"You okay, missus? I can sit with him so's you can rest."

"No." She had to be at his side when he opened his eyes. Would he remember her? His medical training? The past? The war? This town? Its people?

His mistress?

"Where is everyone?" Annabeth asked. The only person who'd barged in after the gunshot was the marshal. Considering there'd been a gunshot, she had expected half the town to come by.

"The marshal asked Jeb and some of the others to stand outside and make sure no one disturbs ye." She rolled her good eye. "Especially that ninny Cora."

"She was here?"

"Whining. Begging." Sadie crossed her arms over her chest. "I sent her packin'."

Annabeth hesitated. What if Ethan wanted to see the woman? Did Annabeth have a right to keep her out?

Sadie patted her hand. "His wife belongs at his side."

Annabeth hadn't been at his side for a long, long time.

Sadie saw more with one eye than most saw with two. "Yer here now. That's what counts."

"Is it?" Annabeth murmured.

"Yes'm. Without ye . . ." She shook her head. "He was pitiful."

"Not too pitiful for Cora Lewis."

"He's a doctor; she's a widow. Everyone thought he was a widower. Including him." Sadie's eyebrows lifted; she waited for Annabeth to elaborate. When Annabeth didn't, the old woman shrugged. "Now yer back; she'll have t' move on."

Cora wasn't going to move on with Ethan's child inside of her. Ethan wouldn't let her.

Tears threatened. Annabeth had never been so happy as when she'd had a life growing within. She'd never been so miserable once it had stopped. She'd never felt so loved as she had when Ethan had claimed her— claimed them—as his. And she'd never felt so alone as when he'd denied her.

She would be the one moving on, not Cora. But Sadie didn't know that, and Annabeth wasn't going to tell her.

"Why'd someone shoot atcha?"

That was the question. Had the shot been meant for Ethan or for Annabeth? Because of the past? Or the present?

"No idea," Annabeth answered, and coughed.

"Strange how the windows of this place are suddenly gettin' broke so violentlike."

Annabeth didn't think it was strange at all. Around her, things got broken "violentlike" a lot.

When she'd left Freedom, she'd gone to Moze and accepted his offer of a job with Pinkerton. At the least it gave her the means and the opportunity to search for her brother.

She hadn't had any more luck at the task than Moze had. Over time, she'd become one of the agency's most daring operatives. She went places no woman would go; she did things no lady would contemplate. At first because she hadn't cared if she lived or died. But as time went on, and she'd seen the good that had come from her actions, she'd been seduced by the promise of justice. When she captured or killed someone who deserved it, the world—which had been all wrong—became just a little more right.

Her latest assignment, join the Lassiter Gang and discover the whereabouts of Wonderland so Moze could arrest every last one of them, had been more difficult than usual due to Lass's paranoia, but she would manage.

Annabeth was a spy—plain and simple—and she was damn good at it because she did whatever she had to do to get the job done.

For the past five years, the job was all that she'd had.

By the time Sadie returned with venison stew, night had fallen and Annabeth had changed out of her bloody clothes. She'd washed and treated the tiny cuts on her face and hands while Ethan murmured Gaelic and nonsense.

Annabeth thanked the woman and set the plate aside. "I'll eat when he does."

"Now." The woman forked up a mouthful and held it to Annabeth's lips. "It'll do him no good if ye faint like that other fool."

Annabeth's mouth curved, and Sadie shoved the stew inside. Her stomach snarled for more. She couldn't remember the last time she'd eaten, but it hadn't been in Freedom. Which meant it had been more than a day. She was lucky she hadn't fainted like that "other fool."

If she had any mortification left, Annabeth might have been embarrassed at how quickly she finished the meal.

"I set the pot in the kitchen." Sadie took Annabeth's empty plate. "For when the doc wakes up."

Annabeth ignored the persistent whisper of "ifffff." He *would* wake up. She would not let him escape that easily.

"The marshal has a watch posted," Sadie continued. "Seems to have made himself right at home."

"Ye don't like him?"

"I don't know him." Annabeth frowned as a thought slid through her mind. "He could be anyone."

Sadie laughed. "Why would he come to town and pretend to be a marshal?"

"Why would anyone pretend to be anything?" Annabeth murmured. She could think of so many reasons.

As soon as Sadie left, Annabeth retrieved her pistol from the spare room where she'd dropped it and placed the weapon on the nightstand. She remained at Ethan's side for hours, leaving only once for more cool water. Her concern for him made it impossible for her to sleep, and that was all right. Certainly there was a guard downstairs, but no one would protect him the way she would.

In the depths of the night, Ethan groaned, reaching for his head. Annabeth grabbed his hand before he could touch the stitches. "That'll hurt more than leaving it alone."

He stilled. "Beth?"

Joy shot through her. He knew who she was. The accent had fled. He was fine.

"I had a dream." His voice shook as he tangled his fingers with hers. She couldn't see him in the dark, but she knew his touch better than anyone's on the earth. "There was so much blood."

"Hush," she murmured.

"There was a man."

She made more soothing noises, rubbing her thumb along his. There'd been a lot of men—at the hospital, in the war, in prison, and ever since.

"In our house."

Her thumb stopped moving, and she glanced over her shoulder at the darkened doorway. Now or then? Real or imagined?

"You and I argued." His fingers clenched. "The baby."

Annabeth extricated herself from his grasp; it wasn't easy. "I need to light the lamp."

Her hands shook as she struck the match, but she managed to put the flame to the wick, and a golden glow spread over the room, over him.

Pale, sweating, his hands shook as badly as hers. The silver suture wire sparkled between the crusted blood of his wound. He blinked several times; confusion flickered. "What happened?"

Annabeth opened her mouth, shut it. She wasn't sure if he was asking about the past or the present.

"Why are you wearing my clothes? And your hair . . . it's long." Ethan closed his eyes, his black lashes stark against the waxy pallor of his face. "Was it a dream?"

"Yes." Not a lie. Even if he'd dreamed the truth, he *had* dreamed it. What he was talking about—the night he'd learned her secret—had happened five years ago.

"The baby's fine," he murmured. "You're fine. We're fine."

"What year is it, Ethan?"

He opened his eyes and his smile was woozy; he appeared a little drunk. Her gaze flicked to the laudanum bottle on the nightstand, but she couldn't remember how full it had been when she'd brought it up.

"Shhh-ummer. Eighteeeeen." His eyes slid closed. She didn't think he was going to finish before he fell asleep, but he did. "Shhh-ixty-five."

Annabeth spent the rest of the night reading Ethan's medical books. Many of them dealt with brain injuries. Understandable, considering Mikey.

Sometimes Annabeth thought Mikey had come out of the war the least scathed of any of them, despite that damn bullet. Because Mikhail Romanov had never been a Union scout; he'd never gone to prison; he'd never been shot.

Annabeth's gaze touched on the stitches she'd set in Ethan's flesh. How strange that both he and his brother would have similar injuries, with both similar and dissimilar results. Ethan had lost time, but he hadn't lost himself. If he had, he wouldn't know Annabeth.

She wished that shot had hit her and not Ethan.

There was quite a bit of the last five years she would like to forget.

The sun had begun to lighten the distant horizon, spreading fingers of red, gold, pink, and orange across the flat Kansas landscape when she shut the text in her lap. Until recently, she'd spent much of her time in Colorado, where anyone or anything could be hiding behind the next mountain or tree. Because of that, she appreciated the ability to see in any direction for miles.

As the shadows waned, Annabeth considered what she had read. It wasn't much help. The brain was unexplored territory. No one knew how it worked or had any proven idea how to fix what didn't. In several of the books, she'd found nothing under the heading "brain trauma" beyond a platitude she'd heard a hundred times before.

"Time heals," she whispered. A greater load of shit had never been shoveled. If she wasn't adequate proof of that, Mikey certainly was.

"Beth?"

The pain, the wariness that had been born in his eyes the night he'd learned the truth about her and continued to live there after she'd returned, was gone. For Ethan it was 1865, and they'd just been married. The war was over; they'd survived. They were expecting a child. He knew that she loved him. He still loved her. He seemed to have forgotten his earlier questions about her clothes, her hair. He never had asked why her belly was flat.

Annabeth gulped. She had to tell him. "You were hurt, Ethan."

He smiled the smile she'd fallen in love with back when she thought he was who he said he was—a brilliant young doctor of the Confederacy. That smile had pulled her in. And the truth?

The truth had changed little but his affiliation.

"What happened?" he asked.

"You were shot."

His smile faded. He lifted his hand before she could stop him and rubbed his fingers along what would probably be a scar. "Who?"

"We don't know. The marshal—"

"Where's the sheriff?"

"According to you, he fell out the window." His gaze went to the hole in the wall; his frown deepened. "Do you remember any of this?" He shook his head, wincing when he jarred the wound. "What do you remember?"

"One of the hands at Moriarty's farm broke his leg. Could have used you there. But no riding until the baby's born."

Annabeth had to clench her fingers to keep from brushing her too-empty belly.

"The house was dark. You were talking to someone. Then—" Ethan tore at his hair and moaned.

She was reaching for his medicine when he dropped his hands. "Better?" she asked.

"A little." He blinked away tears the pain had brought to his eyes. "What were you saying?"

"There are things you don't remember, Ethan. About me, the baby, the past few years."

"The past few years?" he repeated. "How could I forget the war?"

"The war's been over a long time."

"That's impossible. We just came to Freedom."

"We didn't."

His gaze lit on her saddlebags near the door. "They're still packed. We did just come here."

He ignored the gaping wardrobe that held only his clothes, a room that was obviously masculine, not a hint of her anywhere. "I just came back."

"Where were you?"

Should she tell him? What would be the point?

"I had to go away."

"You aren't supposed to ride. The baby."

"The baby d—"

Ethan cried out and grasped his temples, writhing against the tumbled sheets. Annabeth reached for him, trying to see why he was suddenly in so much agony. She waited for blood to pour through his fingers, but it didn't. Wounds did not open and gush spontaneously.

Ethan's fingers went white as he pressed them to his

head. Annabeth gave up trying to pry them loose and snatched the blue bottle. She put the edge to his lips. Amazingly, he stopped thrashing and drank like the baby he couldn't stop asking about. When she pulled it away, he reached for it. At least he no longer cradled his head.

"Better?" she repeated.

His eyes opened; the haunted expression was back. "You're scaring me."

No more than he was scaring her. "Sleep." Maybe it would help. Or maybe when he awoke again, he'd have lost another five years.

Which would eliminate memories of the war, prison, Mikey's injury—and her. But maybe, considering everything, that would be for the best.

Ethan's eyes slid closed; his breathing evened out. Annabeth waited until her heart stopped thundering and she could think again. Then she picked up one of his books and paged through until she found the section that reflected Ethan's recent behavior.

Any wound to the brain is a trauma, those inflicted accidentally or through violence even more so. The mind is not prepared. It rebels just like the body. Where the injury may emit a foul-smelling seepage in protest, the mind may block out memories. This is called amnesia.

In some cases, the patient may, contrary to any evidence of reality, see only what he wishes to. Do not insist the afflicted believe what he does not or remind him of things he has forgotten. The patient must be kept calm. Only in this way will the brain heal, allowing the memories to return on their own.

Annabeth shut the book and hurried downstairs, opening drawers until she found the scissors. Then she gathered her hair into a tail and sliced it off at the jaw.

She contemplated the handful of bright red locks. She wouldn't miss them, wasn't quite sure why she'd allowed the length to reach to her waist. In her line of work, long red tresses were a hindrance. Cutting them was overdue. In Freedom, shorter hair would be one less thing to lie about. When she left, she'd have one less thing to hide.

She couldn't do anything to disguise a flat belly that should be round beyond continuing to wear loose clothes. If the pages she'd just read were accurate, Ethan would see what he wanted to anyway.

Guilt weighed her down, and she climbed the stairs with feet that felt dredged in mud. So many mistakes, so many bad choices. She couldn't make another and leave Ethan like this. She'd have to stay until he remembered everything.

Except . . .

Mikey never had.

Ethan woke as the sun slanted across the foot of his bed. Afternoon. He couldn't remember the last time he'd slept this late.

He moved his head, and pain flickered. The hand he lifted shook badly. He was thirsty, and his skin itched.

On the bedside table sat a blue bottle. He thought he should drink from it; then again, he thought he should not. But why would it be there if he wasn't meant to partake?

He managed to wrap his fingers around the glass, managed not to spill it as he drew the opening to his lips. The taste was familiar, one he remembered and adored. He drank deeply—until the shakes, the itching, the pain faded. Then he was able to sit up, set his feet on the floor, cross to the washstand, and peer into the mirror.

The stitches sparkled against his pale skin. Interesting. He hadn't seen silver suture wire since just after Bull Run.

No. That wasn't true. He'd stocked it here. In Freedom.

He examined the wound. No sign of infection. Certainly the area was red, but that was to be expected.

A shuffle from behind had him shifting his gaze to meet that of his wife's in the mirror. As always, the sight of her much-shorter hair caused guilt to flicker; this time the guilt was so sharp, his belly roiled.

"Did I do something wrong?" she asked.

Pain shafted through Ethan's head. She had. He just couldn't remember what.

"Ethan?"

He grasped the washstand so tightly, his fingers ached. He made himself release the edge, though he continued to lean upon it. His legs weren't as steady as he'd like. "Your stitches are as good as the day I met you."

Her smile seemed sad, although it might just have been the mirror. There was something about the reflections in it that bothered him. Her stomach didn't appear as large as it should, but as she was wearing his clothes, who could tell?

He'd been hurt; he'd had bad dreams. Everything, right now, seemed fuzzy.

"As I recall," she said, "that seam was as crooked as this one."

"I've always preferred those who can make stitches in bleeding flesh to those who make them in cloth."

"Not lately," she muttered.

"What?" He turned too fast, nearly fell down.

She hurried to his side. "Why did you get up?"

"I . . ." Despite her tugging in one direction, Ethan turned in the other and gazed into the mirror again. "I couldn't remember what happened. I wanted to see."

Her face swam into view at his shoulder. Not only did she appear sad but worried. "Do you remember now?"

"Not really. But . . ." His gaze met hers in the glass. "Why do I look so old?"

CHAPTER 15

Old?" Annabeth repeated. "You're—"

She bit her lip to keep the word *thirty* from tumbling out. In his mind, he was still twenty-five.

"A few years older than me," she said instead.

The five years he was "missing" had been hard on both of them. Until Ethan had mentioned it, she hadn't noticed that he'd aged. She'd been too damn glad to see him.

Right now, she could see all of him. As he couldn't rest properly wearing trousers and a shirt, she'd removed everything after the marshal left.

However, she'd done so with her gaze averted. It hadn't seemed right to stare at his body when he was unconscious. But it had been so much work getting him out of the clothing, she hadn't bothered to put anything on him but a sheet. As Ethan didn't seem disturbed by his nakedness, she shouldn't be.

Except she was. And not because of any inappropriate lust, but by the visible proof of how the years had changed him. He'd always been slim and tall. He would become busy with his work and forget to eat unless she reminded him. He'd started to fill out during the time they'd spent together.

Now she could see each of his ribs and the bony spike of his hip beneath his skin. His knees and feet appeared especially knobby. She was happy the mirror was large enough to reveal only his face.

The years had taken their toll in the creases around his eyes. Not laugh lines, not hardly. But squinting into the sun, being whipped by the wind, lack of sleep, worrying had all left their mark.

Annabeth moved out of the reflection before Ethan noticed her new lines. They weren't laugh lines either.

"When was the last time you preened in a mirror, Doctor?" Annabeth tugged again, and this time he followed, allowing her to tuck him into the bed.

His frown deepened the latest furrows about his mouth. "When I shaved?" He lifted his palm to his chin, rubbing at several days of stubble. "Not long enough to add all those years."

"You were injured. Ill." She smoothed her palm over the sheets. The same rasping sound came from the contact of her skin with the material that had come from his palm to his chin. Running, hiding, spying, lying wreaked havoc on the hands. "That puts lines all over the place."

"How long have I been unwell?"

As a day or two would not explain the five years on his face, she hesitated. She was going to have to break that mirror. After what she'd seen of herself in it, she couldn't wait.

"You haven't eaten since yesterday," she said. "Sadie brought stew."

Her words distracted him from his question. "I'm not hungry."

"A little?" she coaxed. "With me?"

"All right." His gaze narrowed on her. "You seem thin, Beth."

Being on the run from the last person she'd betrayed, or on the road to the next, had left little time for food, not that being who and what she was left her with any appetite.

"Maybe it's just those clothes," he continued. "Why are you wearing them?"

"I'm having some larger dresses made." The lie tripped off her tongue without thought. She cleared the tickle from her throat. "I don't fit in mine anymore."

He nodded, accepting her tale despite the fact that if

she had been with child, she would have thought to purchase new dresses long before she needed them.

"I'll fetch the stew," she said.

He could also use something for the pain that haunted his eyes and tightened his mouth. Her gaze flicked to the bedside table, but it was empty except for the lamp. "Wasn't there . . . ?" She paused. He wouldn't remember a bottle even if there'd been one. "Close your eyes for a spell. I'll be back."

Annabeth descended to the first floor, reheated the stew, offering some to the guard at the door—a man she did not know. After five years, there were probably a lot of them.

He accepted in a hurry, but then paused in his eating. "Mrs. Lewis has been by already," he said around a mouthful of meat. "She seemed awful upset not to be able to see the doc. The marshal said to keep everyone out, but . . . Should I let her in?"

"No!" Annabeth said the word so loudly, the man bobbled his plate. "Sorry." She took a breath, searched for a lie. She couldn't tell a stranger that she didn't want her husband's pregnant mistress upsetting him. "He's not well enough to receive anyone yet."

The guard glanced up the street, his uncertainty plainly visible. "She's gonna be back."

"I'll pay her a visit directly."

Now his uncertainty focused on Annabeth. News of her last visit must have been shared all over town.

"Just keep her out," Annabeth said. "And everyone else, too."

She stopped at the medicine cabinet, pocketed another blue bottle, then headed upstairs, balancing two plates of food. Ethan sat up in bed, rubbing the side of his head.

"Here." She set the meals on the nightstand and reached into her pocket. "Damn."

He lowered his arm, the red imprint of his fingertips stark on his too-pale skin. "What's the matter?"

Considering the sunlight through the window, his pupils seemed exceedingly large. Annabeth leaned close, comparing the two. Head injuries could cause one pupil to become larger than the other. However, his were the same size. Huge. She didn't like it.

Annabeth straightened. "I forgot a spoon."

"Never stopped me before," he muttered, and held out his hand. She placed the bottle into it.

He took several sips, wiped his nose across his arm, and took several more, then held it out to her. "I always forget a spoon. Folks in agony don't mind drinking from the rim."

She set the glass container on the table and handed him a plate. "You're in agony?"

"Not agony. Not anymore. But I do ache everywhere."

She put her hand on his cheek but, considering the already climbing heat of the late-summer day, he wasn't any warmer than he should be. "If you start to shiver . . ." she began.

"I won't."

"How do you know?"

"I'm a doctor."

Doctors were the worst patients. They knew too much, which either made them obsess over every little symptom, or ignore the symptoms altogether.

Ethan continued to hold the plate but made no move to eat, instead rubbing his thumb along his belly. The white sheet pooled in his lap, and despite his being thinner than she liked, the sight of his chest covered in a light dusting of black hair, his flat stomach with a trail of the same leading down to—

She jerked her gaze to his face, hers flaming. He stared, grimacing, out the window at the sun, which appeared to have been doused by a rain cloud.

"Does your stomach hurt?"

"A little."

"Hunger." Her own cramped, and she picked up her plate. "Eat."

For the next several minutes, they did just that. She finished every bite; he managed only a third before he shoved the fork into what was left and shook his head. "I better stop."

"Maybe later." She took the plate. His pupils had shrunk. That should make her feel better, but for some reason, it didn't. Now they seemed exceedingly small, which bothered her as much as when they'd been large.

"Lie down," she ordered.

He did, barely managing to place his head on the pillow before his eyelids closed. She remained until his breathing evened out. His dark beard and nearly black hair only emphasized the paleness of his skin. He was still one of the most beautiful men she'd ever seen.

"Ethan?" When he didn't respond, she leaned over and pressed a kiss to the unmarred side of his brow. His hair brushed her lip; he still smelled the same. Like summer herbs and fresh laundry on the line.

Straightening, she let her tongue slide over her mouth. He tasted the same, too. Promises in the dark. Secrets without lies. A life she'd wanted so damn badly, she'd have done anything to keep it. But she'd never had the chance.

She carried the dirty plates and forks downstairs, taking a few moments to wash and put them away. Then she straightened some things that didn't need straightening. The house was pristine, cleaner than when she'd lived in it. Annabeth had always been distracted by patients, by Ethan. The least of her concerns had been the house. But, apparently, that was not the case for whoever had been keeping it. She had a pretty good idea who that was.

The back door had been locked from the inside, marshal's orders, so Annabeth marched to the front. "No one in, no one out," she told the guard, another man she did not know.

As he tugged on the brim of his hat and murmured, "Yes'm," Annabeth assumed her command echoed Eversleigh's.

Annabeth hurried to Lewis's Sewing and Sundry, nodding when folks greeted her but not stopping to chat, even though many of them did, their gazes widening when she continued past. She had no time for chatter. She had business with her husband's—

Annabeth stopped outside the door. Her husband's what? As all of the labels that ran through her mind were uncharitable, she settled on the only one that mattered: Cora Lewis was the mother of Ethan's child.

Annabeth tightened her lips to keep the sob from breaking free. If she let it out, she would not stop, and then where would she be? Standing outside the Sewing and Sundry, weeping until she melted into a puddle of tears and pain.

Which was why she'd left Freedom in the first place. If she'd stayed, she would have melted, and she didn't think she would ever have been able to put herself back together again.

She wasn't completely healed, but she wasn't completely broken anymore, either. Not like Ethan.

Annabeth set her hand on the door. She was here to discuss Ethan's injury with Mrs. Lewis. She had to make the woman understand that Ethan needed to be handled with care until he remembered everything he'd forgotten.

If he remembered.

For just an instant, Annabeth wondered what that would be like. An Ethan who didn't remember all that she'd done, all that he had. Who thought their marriage was intact, that their child was.

However, while that Ethan and that Annabeth might be nice to think about, they wouldn't last. Would he eventually demand to know why her belly wasn't growing? Or would someone let slip the reason Cora's was?

Annabeth stepped inside. She just managed to duck before something hit her in the head. The dish shattered against the wall and rained crockery shards into what was left of her hair. Crouching, she shuffled to the right. Luckily, she was still wearing breeches; attempting the maneuver in a dress would have caused her to fall on her face. Nevertheless, Cora Lewis nearly crowned her with a second crockery plate.

"Stop that!"

Cora threw another. She had incredibly bad aim. Which could have something to do with the tightness of the sleeves on her sky-blue day dress, or perhaps the restriction of the bustle. Annabeth was able to dodge the next missile, too, and when Cora paused to retrieve a fresh stack of plates, she hurried forward and snatched them away. "Have you lost your mind?"

Cora narrowed her eyes. "Have you?"

"I'm not throwing crockery."

"He says your name in his sleep. Never mine. Not once." Cora let out a long breath. "Why couldn't you stay dead?"

Annabeth wasn't sure what to say. She probably should have.

"Did someone hack your hair off with a knife?" Cora eyed Annabeth's attire, and her lip curled. "I suppose it doesn't matter, considering."

She was right. Annabeth had bigger concerns than the state of her hair and clothes.

"I didn't come to argue with you." Annabeth set the stack of dishes on a low table, well out of Cora's reach. "Or to discuss my toilet, or to get my head smashed by a plate." Although the way Cora threw them, that hadn't been likely.

"Why did you come?" Cora gasped, setting a dainty, white hand against a perfectly corseted and laced breast. "Is Ethan—?"

"He's fine." Annabeth swallowed an impatient huff—although she wasn't certain if her annoyance was for her own lie, or Cora's dramatics.

"If he's fine, then why can't I see him?"

Annabeth was usually good at reading people; she had to be. But she couldn't quite read Cora. Was the seamstress pretending to be foolish, childish, and needy when, in fact, she wasn't? Or did Annabeth just want her to be a treacherous, manipulative—

"What's wrong?" Cora must have seen something in Annabeth's expression that frightened her. Probably the nearly overwhelming temptation to throttle the woman.

"Stop that," Annabeth repeated, this time because

Cora was breathing too fast and shallow. "You'll get the vapors."

"But—" Pant. Pant. "But—"

Annabeth lost patience. She came around the counter, and before the woman could even cringe, shoved her into a chair. "Breathe," she snapped. "Deeply. Slowly."

Breathing deeply was damn near impossible in a corset, but Cora did her best. Eventually, her color returned, her breathing evened out, and Annabeth stepped back, though she remained close enough to rescue the woman if she fainted. Annabeth didn't want Cora to land on her face. All she needed was for Mrs. Lewis to walk out of here with a broken nose or a black eye. Too many people had seen Annabeth walk in.

"Someone shot at Ethan," Annabeth began.

A sneer marred Cora's pretty face. "The entire town knows that. What we don't know is why."

"Neither do I."

"He needs me." Cora stood. "I'll nurse him."

"No."

The woman's huge blue eyes widened, then blinked. Her mouth opened; nothing came out.

Annabeth had known women like Cora before, during, and after the war. Their beauty ensured that they rarely heard the word *no*. Whenever they did, it seemed to only confuse them.

"He doesn't remember you."

Cora blinked again; then laughter spilled from her still-open mouth. "Of course he does." She set her hands over her stomach. "I'm the mother of his child."

Annabeth gulped as her own stomach rebelled. "The bullet creased his temple. I sewed the wound. He'll have a nice scar."

Cora gasped and lifted her hands to her mouth. Annabeth ignored her. A scar was the least of Ethan's worries.

"When he awoke, he thought we were still . . ." Annabeth paused. They *were* still married. "He thinks it's 1865, and the war just ended."

"That's silly."

Annabeth thought it was a lot of things. Silly wasn't one of them.

"The brain is a mystery," she said. "Ethan could remember everything tomorrow." Or not. "The best way for him to heal is for him to remain calm. If he's upset, he might get worse."

"Might?" Cora tilted her head. "You don't know that for sure. You're not a doctor."

"Right now, I'm the closest thing to a doctor Freedom has."

Fury sparked in the other woman's eyes. "You're just being mean."

"Mrs. Lewis, you have no idea how mean I can be." Or how mean she would like to be.

"You don't want me to see him."

"He doesn't remember you."

"He would if he saw me." Her eyes filled with large, limpid tears. She put her hands over her face and sobbed.

Annabeth wasn't sure what to do. Leave Cora alone? Pat her on the back? Stuff a wad of cloth in her mouth and shove her in the closet? She clenched her hands to keep herself from doing just that.

The woman spun and raced from the room. Annabeth listened for the tap of tiny feet on the stairs to the living quarters. When she didn't hear any, she assumed Mrs. Lewis was composing herself in private and wandered around the store.

She found her dress—or rather, the dress of whoever had left town in too big a hurry to retrieve it—thrust beneath the counter. Cora hadn't adjusted the hem or added new cuffs. Annabeth didn't think she was going to. Nevertheless, Annabeth needed something to wear besides trousers or a garment with a gaping bodice. She tucked the light green gown beneath her arm. She'd deliver the money later.

Releasing an impatient huff, she glanced at the empty doorway. If Cora got herself under control and came back with questions, Annabeth should be here to answer. But how long must she wait?

Maybe she should fetch Sadie. The older woman would be better at calming a hysterical Cora Lewis than Annabeth could ever be.

She opened the front door, glanced up the street toward the sign that read DOCTER—obviously fashioned by the same hand that had lettered SHERRIF—and caught a flash of blue silk as it disappeared inside the doorway underneath it.

CHAPTER 16

You shouldn't be out here alone.
I'm not alone. I have you.
"Ethan!"

He'd been dreaming of the night he first kissed Annabeth, beneath the moon at Chimborazo, when a woman's voice, followed by the staccato beat of footsteps, pulled him away.

The sharp, panicked panting didn't sound at all like Annabeth. His wife never panicked. At least not until—

The agony in his head yanked him awake so quickly, he was left gasping, blinking into the sun that was so different from the moon he'd left behind. As much as the woman in front of him now was different from the one who'd been in front of him then.

"Hello," he began, then realized he was naked beneath the sheet, which had fallen to his waist. Completely inappropriate to appear so in front of a lady, though what "lady" would burst into a man's room?

However, his chest wasn't the largest issue. No, that would be the area below his waist, where his member stood at attention, no doubt brought there by the recollection of that kiss. The sheet fell away from it like the canvas flaps of a revival tent from a pole.

The woman's gaze lowered and stuck there. Ethan lifted a hand, thinking to cover it, then paused. If he did that, he'd only appear to be pleasuring himself. She'd probably scream. He couldn't believe she hadn't already. Instead, he tugged a pillow into his lap and tried not to groan as he laid his arms over the snow-white material and pressed. Her gaze lifted. Memory shimmied. There was something about her that—

"I knew that you loved me."

"I beg your pardon?"

She pointed at his erection. "You were thinking of me."

He had no idea what to say to that beyond, "Who *are* you?"

At that, the woman began to scream.

Annabeth appeared in the doorway, red-faced and sweating. Exasperation flashed in her dark blue eyes. The same tightened her delectable lips. She slapped the visitor across the cheek. The resultant crack echoed loudly in the sudden silence. Ethan discovered his mouth hung open and closed it.

"Annabeth," he began.

"You snuck out the back?" she demanded. "You kicked the guard in the balls?"

The woman—a pretty little thing, blond, petite, so pale, the imprint of Annabeth's hand shone livid on her skin—gasped. Whether from Annabeth's use of the word *balls* or from a return of breath to her lungs, Ethan wasn't sure. He had no idea what was going on, but he was transfixed.

"Then you come into my husband's sickroom—" The stranger opened impossibly pink lips, and Annabeth lowered her voice to just above a whisper. "Speak and I will make you stop."

Those lips closed.

"The doctor is unwell," Annabeth continued. "He is not to be disturbed. What is there about that you don't understand, Mrs. Lewis?"

Mrs. Lewis? That seemed familiar. Was she a patient? Why couldn't he recall?

She blinked a few times, confusion flowing over her face.

"You told her not to speak," Ethan pointed out. Gratitude replaced confusion, and Mrs. Lewis gifted Ethan with a smile that would have dazzled, if he were a man to be dazzled by such things.

Annabeth sidestepped, blocking the lady from his view. "Get out," she said.

"If Mrs. Lewis needs medical attention, I can—"

"You've done enough for Mrs. Lewis." Her voice was choked—was it anger or anguish?—he wasn't sure. Why would she feel either? He couldn't remember that any more than he could remember Mrs. Lewis.

Ethan lifted his hand toward the pain in his temple. Annabeth snapped, "If you touch those sutures, I will break your fingers."

She still wasn't looking at him. How did she know what he was doing? Ethan lowered his arm. She was going to make an incredible mother.

The thought made his head ache so badly, he almost threw up.

"You can't talk to him like that," Mrs. Lewis said.

"I just did." Annabeth grasped the smaller woman's elbow and headed for the door. "Remember, *I'm* his wife."

As the two of them descended the stairs, he could have sworn he heard Mrs. Lewis mutter, "Not for long."

How dare she?

Annabeth was tempted to send Cora Lewis down the steps the hard way.

Not for long? Although she was probably right.

In the wake of the despair that followed the thought, Annabeth tightened her grip on the woman's arm. Cora gasped and tried to pull away, which only made Annabeth increase the pressure. "You will not tumble down the stairs and lose that baby."

Cora stilled. "I'd think you'd want me to."

They began to descend—slowly, carefully. Annabeth did not let go of Cora's arm, though she did loosen her fingers a bit. "Then you don't know anything about me at all."

They reached the ground floor, and Annabeth glanced through the front window, where Jeb Cantrell now stood in place of the guard Cora had assaulted. If she hadn't wanted to throttle the woman, she might be impressed by her ingenuity.

"I know you ran out on him as if he didn't matter at all."

Annabeth returned her gaze to Cora. "Is that what he told you?"

The woman peered up the stairs, obviously weighing her chances of being caught in a lie. Then her shoulders sagged. "I asked folks about you."

Of course she had. What woman wouldn't?

"Then you know I didn't leave because I didn't care." She'd left because she cared too much.

"How could you do it? When he needed you the most, you rode away, and you didn't come back."

"But I did come back," Annabeth murmured.

"Too late. He loves me now." The words were said with a tinge of desperation. Perhaps if Cora said them enough, they would come true. Had she learned that from Ethan?

My wife is dead. Say it enough times, and maybe it'll be true.

"He doesn't know you," Annabeth pointed out.

"He will."

"Until he does, you'll stay away." Cora's chest shook with outrage, which Annabeth didn't give her a chance to voice. "If I catch you upsetting him again, you'll be sorry I'm not dead."

"I'm already sorry."

Annabeth narrowed her eyes, and the woman lowered hers. Again, Annabeth wondered if Cora was smarter than she let on. Or perhaps she just possessed an animal instinct. One that prompted submission to a bigger, meaner bear.

"I won't be leaving until I'm certain he's in his right mind," Annabeth continued. "So it's in your best interest to do as I say."

Cora pouted. "How do I know that what you're saying is true?"

"You don't. But as he still thinks I'm his wife—hell, I *am* his wife—you don't have much choice."

"I could tell him the truth."

"That isn't going to change the facts. I'm married to him; you are not."

Cora's eyes flicked to Annabeth's. "I—"

"I know," Annabeth interrupted. "You're pregnant."

Cora's mouth pinched at the crass term. "With child."

"Which puts you in a bad position."

"Bad?" she repeated.

"What if Ethan never remembers you? He'll deny the child is his. In his mind, he's never met you."

"But everyone knows—" She paused, and Annabeth pounced.

"They know you were keeping company. If you'd gotten married, and the baby arrived early . . ." Annabeth shrugged. It happened all the time. It had happened to her—or would have. "But to be the unmarried seamstress whose belly is slowly expanding . . ."

Cora lifted her chin. "He's as much to blame as me."

"More so," Annabeth agreed. "You thought I was dead; he only hoped I was. Unfortunately, no one will see it that way."

Confusion crinkled Cora's face. "Why?

"The woman always pays the price for these things." Annabeth certainly had.

"You're just trying to get me to leave."

She hadn't even thought of that. What an appealing idea. However, Annabeth didn't want Ethan alone again when she departed; she would not deprive him of his child. She'd done that enough for one lifetime.

"Give him the opportunity to remember on his own. In the meantime, I'll see what I can do about the marriage. Is there a lawyer in town?"

"Pryce Mortimer. But . . ." The woman nibbled on her dewy pink lips. "The more I think about it, the less I want to be married to a divorced man."

Annabeth sighed and rubbed her forehead. "You can't be married to him at all unless he is."

"If you hadn't barged back into town, we would have been."

"If I'm not really dead, you're not really married."

Somehow the two of them had leaned in to each other until they were toe-to-toe, nearly nose-to-nose. Considering Annabeth was a good eight inches taller, she had to bend over a mite to get there. At least they'd kept their voices lowered to a vicious, nasty whisper.

Cora Lewis appeared as if she wanted to kick Annabeth in the knee. Considering what she'd done to the guard, she might. Annabeth stepped back, straightening just as Marshal Eversleigh opened the door.

He glanced between them and lifted a brow. "Problem?"

"No," they both answered at once, though anyone who knew anything about women would have been able to tell that such a *no* really meant *yes*.

The marshal snorted. "You don't wanna tell me, that's fine." He pointed a finger at Annabeth. "I need to talk to you." He flicked his ice-blue glaze at Cora. "Alone. Now."

"I was just leaving." Cora went to the door.

"Remember what I said," Annabeth murmured. Her answer was a resounding slam.

"She's awful little to have kicked my guard's privates up near his throat." The marshal watched as Cora stomped across the street, sending up puffs of dust that billowed and dirtied her skirt. She didn't seem to notice.

"She was riled," Annabeth said.

He returned his attention to her. "She got reason to be?"

"Being riled isn't going to change anything."

The marshal lifted his eyes to the ceiling. "He's still confused?" Annabeth nodded. "Doesn't remember . . . ?"

"Much," Annabeth finished.

"Apparently, he doesn't remember her."

Annabeth let out an exasperated huff. "If you know who she is and why she's riled, why are you fishing around?"

His lips quirked. "I could say for my own amusement, but that might get me kicked like my guard."

"Might," Annabeth agreed. "When did they become *your* guards?"

"When I asked them to watch your door and they agreed."

Annabeth thought the townsfolk had agreed more on Ethan's behalf than the marshal's, but she kept that to herself. "What did you want?"

He glanced upward again. "Should we—?"

"No." His gaze lowered. "First you tell me. Then, if I think he needs to know, I'll tell him."

"When did you become his keeper?"

"When I said *I do*."

He lifted a brow. "Mrs. Lewis isn't going to like that."

"From what I've seen, she doesn't like much." *Except my husband.* "Until he remembers that it isn't 1865, he needs to be kept calm. Upsetting him might just . . ." She paused.

"Might just what?"

"Tell him too many things that make his head ache, and something in there could snap. I can't sew up a hole in his brain."

Even if she could, Annabeth doubted it would do any good. Ethan had tried with Mikey. But like Humpty Dumpty, there was no putting his brother back together again.

"Why does he think it's 1865?" the marshal asked.

Annabeth spread her hands and shrugged. "Happier times?"

"Not for me." Sadness flickered across his face before Eversleigh noticed her noticing and straightened. "We all have our crosses to bear. I suspect some are heavier than others."

Annabeth suspected the crosses weren't heavier, but rather, some folks were better able to heft them and keep walking.

"I rode out to the edge of town, where you said you saw the flash of the sun off a barrel."

"And?"

"Nothing."

"No tracks?"

"Plenty. Horse tracks, dog tracks, boot prints. Headed

both into and out of Freedom." Annabeth cursed. "Maybe if I had an experienced scout. Know anyone?"

She knew Mikey, but she had no idea where he was now. Ethan might have had some idea, but asking him today would provide information too out of date to be of any use.

"No," she said.

The marshal lifted a brow. He was either very good at reading faces, or she'd become extremely bad at hiding things. Considering how long she'd had to practice deception . . . he was good at reading faces.

"As I'm sure you know," she began, "I've been away."

"Where?"

"Not here."

"Why?"

"I'm sure you know that, too."

"You had some trouble. A sadness."

Annabeth didn't answer. What could she say?

"You'd think folks would come together over that instead of fall apart."

"You'd think."

"You disappeared for five years. No one could find you."

"No one tried." Moze would have mentioned it.

"If they had, would they have been able to?"

"No."

"You know what, Mrs. Walsh?" The marshal rubbed his thumb along the grip of his gun. "The more I find out about you, the more I think that shot wasn't meant for him."

CHAPTER 17

Annabeth managed to herd the marshal out the door without answering any more questions. Most folks weren't even aware that they'd asked and she hadn't answered. Unfortunately, she didn't think Marshal Eversleigh was most folks. He knew she was evading him.

But she doubted he suspected the truth, that she rode with an outlaw gang and was considered—almost—one of them. That she'd done things that haunted her. She'd had little choice.

She considered the marshal's words. Had the shot been meant for her? She'd think so, except for that visit from Fedya.

Ethan's in trouble.

What had Fedya seen, heard, sensed? If someone had threatened Ethan, wouldn't the sniper have killed them himself? Certainly there was no love lost between the two men, but she doubted Fedya would stand back and watch Ethan be killed if he could stop it. His guilt over Mikey wouldn't allow that. His trip to Ellsworth to warn Annabeth of impending doom proved it.

But what if Fedya had thrown the sheriff out the window and then had to make a run for it before he could do anything to help Ethan? Though why would he have done that, she had no idea. If she ever saw Fedya again, she'd ask, but chances of that were slim.

Still, if there were trouble, why send Annabeth? Why not send Mikey?

Annabeth had no idea. All she knew was that Ethan was in danger, and she couldn't leave until she found out why and then eliminated the threat. She just needed to do it before her other life caught up to her.

The distant breaking of glass caused Annabeth to hurry upstairs. The laudanum bottle she'd left on the bedside table had shattered on the floor; what was left inside had seeped into the planks. Ethan lay with an arm thrown over his eyes.

"Ethan?"

"Aye."

Irish again. Damn.

"Are you . . . ?" She paused. He wasn't all right. He might never be all right again. "Does your head ache?"

"A bit." The accent was suddenly gone. He was making her dizzy. "I dropped the bottle before I managed to drink any. Would you get me another?"

"Of course." She scurried downstairs, snatched up one more, and shoved it into her pocket. On her way out, she also grabbed the carbolic acid—during her night with the medical texts, she'd come across a paper written by Joseph Lister, which explained the rows of carbolic acid in the exam room—as well as a bucket with water and a clean cloth.

She returned to the bedroom, set the bucket on the floor, and tossed the cloth into it. Eyes still closed—no doubt the sun felt like stabbing needles—Ethan lifted his arm from his face and offered his hand. She placed the bottle into it, and he twisted free the top, took several swallows, and gave it back.

Annabeth set the container within reach but not too near the edge of the table. Her gaze went to the broken glass, and she frowned. There was something about it that—

"Was Fedya here?"

"I . . . uh . . ."

"I dreamed he threw the sheriff out the window, but that can't be right."

Annabeth kept silent. What else had he dreamed?

"Mikey was with him. He still didn't know me."

I'm sorry, she thought. She said nothing.

"They left. I told Fedya that I'd kill him if I saw him again."

Which might be why Fedya hadn't hung around to deal with whatever trouble remained. Although she'd never known the man to be scared of much; he certainly wasn't scared of Ethan.

"Ethan . . ." she began, and his eyes opened.

"He murdered my brother."

"You know that's not true."

"My little brother who trusted me to take care of him."

"You did."

"I led him straight into hell."

"You went there together." And if anyone had been leading, it had been Mikey. Scouts always went first.

"He did what I told him."

"He did what he was ordered to do, same as you."

"Where are they now?" he asked.

"I don't know."

"They were here?"

Annabeth hesitated, unsure if telling him that would hurt or help. He seemed to be remembering the past in his dreams.

"They were," he murmured, his voice beginning to slur. "But you weren't. And that . . . doesn't make sense."

"Hush," she said.

"My head . . ." He reached for his stitches, and she grasped his wrist.

"I'm going to clean your wound." His fingers were spotted with dried flakes of blood. "These, too."

"'kay."

She dumped the carbolic acid into the water, plunged her hands into it, then wrung out the cloth so that the solution didn't drip into his eyes. She pressed the rag to his head.

She didn't swipe at the wound or dab; she didn't want to start it bleeding again. Instead, she continued to swirl the cloth in the solution, then wring it out and press it to the flesh around the wound until all the dried blood had dissolved. She did the same a few more times for good measure.

"Don't dislodge the antiseptic crust," he murmured.

"The what?"

He opened one eye. "A scab forms over the wound. If you use carbolic acid at the start, the crust that results will keep the miasma out."

That he was discussing carbolic acid was encouraging. He hadn't been using it when she'd left, which meant he'd learned about it during the time he had forgotten.

"Interesting." She lifted his hand to wash it.

He closed his eye, frowned. "There was a man."

Her fingers clenched, sliding across his damp flesh. Real or imagined? Dangerous or harmless?

"He had a brogue."

The Scottish Dr. Lister? Ethan's Irish father? Or someone else? Who knew? Not her and probably not Ethan.

"So did you at one time," she muttered before she could stop herself.

"I've apologized for that, lass," he murmured in the very same brogue. "Ye know why."

"I do," she whispered.

But he didn't hear her; he'd fallen back to sleep.

Annabeth cleaned up the remains of the bottle from the floor and carried everything downstairs. The dress she'd appropriated sat on the counter where she'd tossed it when she'd run in after Cora.

Quickly she put it on, then nearly took it off again. Too small in some places, too large in others, the garment had obviously not been made with her in mind. However, the extra material around her middle seemed to disguise her lack *of* a middle, and right now . . .

She lifted her gaze to the ceiling. Right now that was for the best.

Annabeth considered strolling through town, asking folks what she'd come to ask in the first place. What kind of trouble was Ethan in?

The only difficulty she'd uncovered thus far had been

Cora Lewis, and the woman hadn't been a problem until Annabeth turned up alive and not dead. But if there'd been something worse than a mistress threatening Ethan, wouldn't someone—anyone—have mentioned it by now?

Life had been a little chaotic since she'd gotten back to Freedom. It wasn't every day that a sheriff fell out the window, a federal marshal arrived asking questions, Annabeth returned from the dead, and the local doctor was shot in the head.

The front door opened. "Missus?"

She stepped out of the kitchen. Jeb Cantrell and a much younger man stood in the front hall. The stranger appeared ill.

"This here's Major Tarkenton," Jeb shouted.

Annabeth put a finger to her lips, and Jeb winced, shrugged sheepishly, and stepped onto the porch. She wasn't sure a half-deaf old man would be any kind of guard, but she didn't have the heart to tell him. At least he could see, unlike his wife. Perhaps the two of them together would make a single decent sentinel.

Annabeth turned her attention to the major. Where was his uniform? She couldn't believe he was out of the schoolroom, let alone in the army with the rank of major.

Then again Custer, the boy general, had been twenty-three at his promotion. Considering the staggering loss of men during that damnable war, she shouldn't be surprised to discover a major this young. In Richmond, she'd seen boys who hadn't shaved yet toting a gun.

"Major?" she began, letting her gaze sweep his dirty, civilian clothes. "Is there a problem at Fort Dodge?"

The closest fort to Freedom, Fort Dodge was located on the Santa Fe Trail. At the intersection of the dry route, also known as the *Hornado de Muerti*, or Journey of Death, and the wet, which followed the river, the army base had been established during the war to protect the wagon trains that often rested there during their journey.

It hadn't taken the Indians long to discover that the groups camping in the area were weakened after navigating a trail that often had no water for the entire distance—hence the name. They attacked with great regularity until the army arrived; then they found other places to raid.

Annabeth couldn't blame them. The white man not only traipsed across their home, putting huge ruts in the ground so that more white men could follow, but they laid rails, built towns, and slaughtered buffalo as if they owned every blade of grass in the world.

"Problem?" the man repeated.

"The fort, Major?" Annabeth hoped the Comanche and the Kiowa, who'd once fought each other but had now joined together to destroy their common enemy, hadn't grown bored elsewhere and obliterated the place. "Did something happen?"

"Uh, no. Yes. I mean . . . no." He took a breath and tried again. "I'm not in the army; I'm not *a* major. My grandfather distinguished himself in the Second War for Independence, and my mother named me after him. So, there's no problem at the fort." He frowned. "That I know of."

"What *is* the problem?"

"My wife's havin' a baby. But it ain't . . ." His lips tightened; his gaze fell; his shoulders hunched.

"How long has she been in labor?"

"Two days," Major said.

Annabeth snatched Ethan's bag from the floor and went out the door. She'd climbed into the buckboard that waited out front before she realized Major had followed only as far as the porch.

"I . . . uh . . . came for the doc."

"You've got me. If you want your wife to live, we need to hurry." Two days of labor usually meant one day from death.

"But the doc—"

"Is unwell." Her gaze met Jeb's.

"I'll fetch Sadie to sit with him," he said.

Jeb probably hadn't heard the majority of the conversation, but it wasn't hard to decipher that Annabeth was leaving with Major and therefore Ethan was alone.

The old man turned his attention to the younger one. "Miz Walsh was a nurse in the war. Afore she . . ."

Jeb paused, and Annabeth waited for him to say: *Afore she ran off like a thief in the night and left the man she'd promised to honor and obey, for better or worse, as long as they both lived, alone with his pain and his past and his demons.*

But he didn't.

"Sometimes she done took care of the birthin's herself when the doc was busy. It'll be all right." He took the boy's arm and led him to the wagon, urging him to climb up beside her. "You'll see."

The clip-clop of horses' hooves and the rattle of a buckboard drifted through the open window. As Ethan had heard the same a hundred times before, he waited for a door to open, a shout to follow. The speed of the hooves and the intensity of the rattle meant someone needed him quick.

When the door remained closed, his name uncalled, and the rattle-clop had faded, Ethan climbed out of bed, ignoring the distant thrum of pain in his head, and dressed.

He'd dreamed of Gettysburg and John Law. Even when he opened his eyes, the memory of the blood, the death, the despair remained with him, and he had a hard time letting it go.

"War's over," he murmured. He lived in Freedom now. With his wife. Their soon-to-be-child. A whole new life awaited them.

"Beth?" he called. When she didn't answer, he experienced a moment of confusion at the thought she wasn't here, that his memories of her return—

"Return?" He rubbed at his head. "Where did she *go*?"

Somewhere that made him sad and also a bit mad. Anger roiled in his belly, mixing with an inexplicable sense of fear.

"Beth!" he called more loudly, then started down the stairs.

The waiting area was empty; no one stood on the porch, though why they should, he couldn't quite recall. He stepped into the exam room. Also empty.

His hands had begun to shake, palms gone clammy, and the backs felt as if ants crawled over the surface. He scratched at them absently. His head hurt so badly, he couldn't think.

Ethan crossed to the cabinet, took out a blue bottle, and sipped until the shakes and the itching and the pain went away. He had just picked up another when the door opened. He slipped both it and what remained of the first into his pocket.

A tiny blond woman crept across the vestibule and toward the stairs. Shoulders hunched as if to make herself smaller than she already was, she tiptoed, glancing behind her every few seconds.

"May I help you?"

Her indrawn breath was so loud, Ethan's head ached again. Her big blue eyes turned his way, and he remembered. "Mrs. Lewis?" Her pretty mouth pinched; the line between her eyes deepened. "Are you in pain?"

She stared at him for several ticks of the clock; then her expression smoothed. "A bit."

Her voice—low and a bit hoarse—was such a contrast to her petite, ethereal beauty, it beguiled. Or would have, if he were a man to be beguiled by anyone other than his wife.

"Perhaps I can help."

The brilliance of her smile made something shimmer, just out of reach, but when she stepped into the exam room, pulling the curtain that hung in the doorway across the opening, it fled. Her smile might be as beautiful as she was, but there was something in her eyes that reminded him of a snake. Cold and hungry, ready to snap and strike with little warning. Danger hung in the air, and he wasn't sure why.

"We should leave the curtain open," he suggested. "Your reputation."

Her loud, abrupt laughter made him start as if he had been bitten. "No need to worry about that."

Perhaps she was the local madam. Why couldn't he recall? Because he'd never had occasion to visit such an establishment, in Freedom or anywhere else.

"Should I lie down?" she asked.

Ethan opened his mouth, shut it again. Why did he feel as if he'd heard her say those words before?

Without waiting for his answer, she clambered onto the exam table. "What, exactly, is wrong, Mrs. Lewis?"

Instead of speaking, she captured his hand and drew it to her stomach. Yards of material lay between his palm and her skin, but for an instant Ethan could have sworn he had touched her before. He tried to pull away, but she held on.

"Can't you feel it?" she whispered.

He swallowed, and his throat clicked loudly in the silence. "What?"

"The baby."

He stopped trying to pull away as everything—or at least one thing—became clear. Mrs. Lewis was with child. She merely wanted him to make sure that the child was all right. Tell her when she could expect the birth, how far along she was. Why she made him so uncomfortable, as if he wanted to leap right out of his skin, he wasn't certain.

"Congratulations." He pressed her belly as low as was proper. She released him so he could continue the examination. He tapped high, then right, left. His gaze flicked to hers. She stared at him so intently, his unease returned. He cleared his throat. "Any symptoms?"

"I fainted!" she exclaimed.

"I'm sorry."

Her eyes narrowed, as if he'd annoyed her, though he wasn't sure how.

"Sickness in the morning?" She seemed to be asking rather than telling. Her eyebrows lifted as she waited for his comment.

"That happens," he agreed, and she released a breath, her stomach deflating beneath his fingers. He pressed again.

"My . . ." Her hand went to her breast, and she cupped

the weight; one thumb brushed over the place where her nipple must be. She moaned, and his shocked gaze lifted to hers. "They ache," she whispered.

Ethan snatched his hand away from her stomach. There was something going on here he didn't understand.

"Ethan?" She sat up. Why was she calling him by his given name and not—

"Doc!" The curtain flew back, and Sadie peered in. She took one look at Mrs. Lewis and snapped, "Get out."

"Sadie," Ethan began. "Mrs. Lewis is . . ." He paused. He wasn't sure what was the matter with Mrs. Lewis, but it wasn't Sadie Cantrell's concern.

"We all know what she is," Sadie muttered, making Ethan think he'd been right in his assumption of the woman's profession. "And she knows she ain't supposed to be here." Sadie's lip curled as she glared at Mrs. Lewis. "What'd ye do? Wait until Jeb come t' get me, then sneak in?"

Mrs. Lewis *had* been sneaking. But why?

"I have as much right to be here as you." The blonde jumped off the table, then lifted her chin. "More."

"What'd she say, Doc?"

"None of your business!" Mrs. Lewis balled her fists and took a step in Sadie's direction.

Ethan took the older woman's arm and led her into the waiting area. "Have you seen my wife?" he murmured. "I thought she might examine Mrs. Lewis." Maybe Annabeth could figure out what was going on.

Sadie choked, and Ethan pounded her on the back until she stopped. By the time she could breathe again, Mrs. Lewis had disappeared.

"That woman didn't make yer head ache with her yammerin'?" Sadie's good eye narrowed on Ethan's face.

"No," he said. Though there was something about Cora Lewis that made his brain itch. Especially after he'd examined her. "My wife—" he began.

"Done gone to the Tarkenton place."

"Tarkenton," he repeated. The name meant nothing to him.

"That's right." Sadie snapped her fingers as if she'd forgotten, too. "They weren't here in 1865."

She spoke as if it wasn't 1865, and now his head did hurt. He reached to rub it.

"Don't do that." She pulled his hand away from the pain. "Josie Tarkenton's been in labor for two days."

Ethan started for the door. It wasn't until he reached down to snatch a bag that wasn't there that he heard what Sadie had said about his wife. "Annabeth went to help?"

"Major took her in his buckboard."

Well, at least she hadn't ridden, though a buckboard could be as jarring to a pregnant woman as the back of a horse, especially if it were being driven hell-bent like the one he'd heard earlier.

"I'm gonna ride out."

"Missus won't like that." Ethan was already striding for the back door, which was closer to the stable. Sadie scurried after. "Marshal won't neither."

"Who's Marshal?" Ethan asked.

"The lawman that done posted guards at yonder door." Sadie grabbed his elbow, and Ethan paused, more out of respect than because she had enough strength to stop him. "Someone shot at ye, Doc. No one knows who or why."

Ethan didn't either. Unless it had something to do with the war and his role in it. The thought, which should have made him stay where he was, instead made him even more desperate to follow his wife. "She needs me."

"She does," Sadie agreed, still holding on to his elbow. "Ye aren't gonna do her a damn bit of good dead."

Gently, Ethan removed himself from the woman's grasp. "If Josie Tarkenton has been in labor that long, there's a problem. I can't just leave her there."

He wasn't sure if he was talking about Josie or Beth or both. It didn't really matter.

Sadie's hands fell to her sides. "Don't say I didn't warn ye. If ye get yerself dead, don't come whinin' to me."

Ethan's lips twitched. "No, ma'am."

As Annabeth had taken his bag, Ethan needed to bring nothing to the Tarkentons' but himself.

He didn't recognize the stable boy, though the fellow greeted Ethan with, "Hey, Doc!" and brought the correct horse without being told. He also knew the Tarkentons and was able to give Ethan directions, along with a curious frown that Ethan could not decipher.

He was the recipient of many curious frowns, both on the way to the stable and on the way out of town. He wished he could recall what he'd done to deserve them.

CHAPTER 18

By the time Ethan reached the dugout that was the Tarkentons' home, the sun had moved halfway to the horizon and the heat was intense. He allowed the horse to drink from a pathetic late-summer flow nearby. At least it was something; he'd seen creeks this small become nothing at this time of year.

Ethan drank, too, splashed his face, dunked his hat beneath the surface—the brim scraped rocks—then set it on his head, letting the water trickle over him.

The buckboard sat abandoned before the earthen home. The horses had been unhitched and stood with their heads down, clustered in the meager shade of one lonely tree.

Ethan's gaze returned to the open doorway. "Hello?"

Since the incident at Sand Creek, when the Colorado militia had massacred a band of Cheyenne—the majority of whom were women and children—the Cheyenne, Kiowa, and Sioux had been troublesome. Every white man in Kansas was understandably nervous.

Ethan thought the Cheyenne, Kiowa, and Sioux were understandably furious. Regardless, walking into someone's home without warning was a good way to get shot, and Ethan had been shot enough for one week.

A young man appeared in the opening. Ethan had never seen him before in his life.

"Doc!" The boy's mouth tilted into a tired smile. Apparently, the fellow had seen him. He beckoned.

"My horse," Ethan began.

The man, Major Tarkenton, Ethan surmised, reached into the dugout and came out with his rifle. "I'll take care of him. You go in." As Ethan handed over the reins, the boy murmured, "She can't bear much more of this."

The home had been dug out of a hill. The walls were earth, the ceiling, too. Ethan stepped inside, then stood, blinking, waiting for his eyes to adjust to the shadows. Dirt showered down, sprinkling over the black pools of blood like salt over soup.

The woman lying atop the straw tick on the floor was so pale, her skin glowed even in the small amount of light that filtered through the door. Annabeth knelt between her feet. She glanced over her shoulder, and the flicker of the lamp across her face reminded him of another room—hot and dark—blood on the floor. On her hands. On his.

"Too soon," Annabeth gasped. *"Help me."*

"Ethan?"

He shook off the strange sensation of the past and the present merging. He'd never seen Annabeth bleeding, crying as his own heart thundered until he thought it might burst free of his chest.

"Help me," she ordered.

The pain in his head caused Ethan to stagger. He set his hand against the wall, ground his teeth, and refused to let it consume him. He focused on *this* room, *this* woman. The other one—

"Later," he murmured.

"Now," Annabeth snapped.

"Yes." Now was all that mattered. All he could allow to matter. Because then was kind of fuzzy.

A bucket of water sat at Annabeth's side. Ethan shoved his hands into it, relishing the familiar sting. "What's wrong?"

"She was pushing when I arrived. According to Major, she had been for quite a while." Annabeth's expression crumpled. "Poor thing."

"Let me look."

Annabeth moved aside; Ethan took her place, but he couldn't see a thing in this light. He'd have to use his hands. He was glad the woman was unconscious. Most didn't much care for an internal examination, especially in an area that probably felt as if it had been pounded from the inside with a hammer. He immediately discerned the source of the problem and sat back.

"What?" Annabeth asked.

"That's not a head."

"Hell."

"I'm going to need more light."

"Out of candles; lantern's dry." Her lips tightened. "You think I'd work in these conditions if I didn't have to? It's too much like—" She broke off, and her shoulders slumped.

For an instant he thought she remembered what he did, but that was impossible. The images of her ice white and gasping, tears on her cheeks, blood on his hands . . . they were merely a bad dream. They had to be. Annabeth was talking about the war. Or rather about—

"Castle Thunder."

"Yes," she said. "We never had enough light."

They'd never had enough anything. But it *had* been a prison.

"Should we bring her outside?" Annabeth asked.

Usually, inside was better than outside, less miasma blowing around. But in here . . . Ethan frowned as more dirt rained onto the already blood-soaked straw. He shoved his arms beneath Josie's shoulders, her knees, and rose.

"Find something clean. Quilt, sheets, even fresh straw would be an improvement." Ethan ducked into the sun as Annabeth ransacked the dugout.

The buckboard still sat nearby, throwing a large shadow, which was exactly what Ethan was looking for. He knelt in its shade as Annabeth joined him with what appeared to be the newest item in the house—a basket quilt, all white except for the appliqués in several lively shades.

The husband arrived, flushed and breathless. "What are you doing?"

"The doctor brought her outside where the light is better," Annabeth said. "All right?" She nodded until the young man nodded, too. "Can you fetch fresh water, please?"

"What are you doing with that?" His gaze went to the quilt. "Her ma made it for our wedding. Took her the better part of a year. We've never even—" His voice broke. "We wanted to save it for a house that wasn't dirt."

Annabeth spread the quilt on the ground. "It's good that you saved it. There's nothing more important than having a place for your child to be born."

Major's mouth opened; Annabeth gestured sharply to Ethan, and he set the woman on top, settling the issue.

"The water?" she repeated, her tone brooking no argument. Major set his rifle against the dirt wall, grabbed a second bucket from inside, and trotted toward the creek.

"We'd best do whatever you plan before he gets back," she murmured.

In Ethan's experience, fathers were the most squeamish during childbirth. Which was why they were usually relegated to the other side of a door. When there was one.

The woman moaned; her eyelids fluttered. "We should do it before *she* comes back," Ethan said.

Concern flickered in Annabeth's eyes. "Do you know what to do?"

"Why wouldn't I?"

"There weren't a lot of babies born at Chimborazo."

"Nor any at Castle Thunder. But I—"

He paused as another flicker of a past that couldn't be filtered through his mind. A cabin on the prairie—a snow-covered Kansas prairie from what he could see through the window. A woman he didn't recognize crying, bleeding, pushing to no avail.

Ethan shook his head. The vision was merely another dream. It was summer. They'd just arrived. He'd never delivered a baby in Kansas, especially in the winter. Though he had done so elsewhere.

"I assisted at plenty of births while I apprenticed with Dr. Brookstone."

Though Pennsylvania did not resemble Kansas, that had to be where the memory came from. Ethan did not have the time right now, nor the inclination, considering the way his head throbbed, to ferret out where, why, or how he knew what to do. He needed to do it.

"Hold her," he ordered.

Josie's eyelids fluttered. "Maj—" she mumbled. Her hands, though weak, reached for those of her husband, but they fell back to the quilt before she was able to lift them very far.

"I should have brought something for the pain," Annabeth said.

Ethan reached into his pocket and pulled out the half-empty laudanum bottle. His wife's expression brightened. "You think of everything."

When Ethan had put the bottles in his pants, he'd known nothing of Josie Tarkenton. He'd done so without thought, as if the act were familiar, one he'd done a hundred times before. Another behavior he didn't know the why of.

Annabeth lifted the woman's head. "Just a few sips." Josie swallowed, and her eyes closed.

Ethan glanced toward the creek and Major Tarkenton. "Rinse that bucket!" he called. "At least twenty times."

Major, who'd been poised to return, turned back and knelt again on the bank. Ethan lifted his gaze to his wife's. "Hold her." Annabeth bore down on Josie's shoulders. "Not like that. Under the arms, so she doesn't slide toward me."

Annabeth's mouth tilted down; her forehead creased, but she didn't ask what he planned to do; she just did as she'd been told.

Ethan followed the memory that wasn't with hands that seemed to know well what to do. He inserted two fingers on each side, slid them past the baby's buttocks— round and smooth like a baby's head, easily mistakable to anyone who had not felt the same before—then hooked them around the hips. His biceps flexed; his legs tensed as his toes dug into the dirt. The woman's eyes snapped open; she drew a long, deep breath and screamed.

Ethan had heard worse—both in the war, in prison, and . . .

For an instant the world went blurry. Day became night. This woman became another. He was dizzy, nauseated, but he continued to pull. Hesitation only prolonged the pain.

The mother screamed one last time, then went silent as her child burst into the world. The infant was silent; then suddenly he screamed.

"Josie?" Annabeth slapped the woman's cheeks lightly as her husband scrambled up the riverbank and hurried toward them.

Ethan continued to work, dealing with all that had to be dealt with after a birth. His patient's chest still rose and fell. She'd fainted. He didn't blame her.

Ethan rose, holding the squalling child in front of him. His eyes met Annabeth's. Her face was so pale, the slash of blood across her cheek looked like a wound. The world shimmied again as the past merged with the present.

A bloody child in his hands. Annabeth as white as the moon through the window. Fear and confusion, panic and pain.

Then and now broke apart, revealing every difference. The sun not the moon. Squirming and squalling instead of lying ever so still.

This child was breathing.

Theirs never had.

"I . . . uh . . ." Ethan stared at the baby. A boy.

Yes, it had been.

He staggered, and Annabeth leaped to her feet, snatching the child before Ethan dropped him.

"Sit," she ordered, and he did, sinking into the dirt as if his legs had been kicked aside.

Major, who'd been standing as though frozen, staring at his wife, uncertain what to do, set the bucket down, sloshing quite a bit over the side in his haste.

"Kiss your wife," Annabeth ordered.

The man complied. When Annabeth used that tone, pretty much everyone did.

Ethan couldn't look away from the woman on the ground. What was it about her, about this, that made him shove his hand into his pocket, finger the bottle he found there, fight the urge to take it out and drink every last drop?

Fingers snapped in front of his nose. He lifted his gaze. Reddish brown streaks marred his wife's face. Just like last time.

The hair on Ethan's neck, his arms lifted as if a breeze had trilled across his skin. But the single tree in the yard remained still. Not wind. Merely the whisper of a ghost.

"Is he . . . ours?" Ethan asked.

Annabeth bobbled the baby. Ethan reached out to catch him, but she gathered the boy against her, as if she didn't want Ethan to touch him. Was she afraid that he'd . . . what?

Bury this child as he'd buried the last?

The chill wind that wasn't blew over him again. His gaze flicked to his wife's stomach, but it was hidden by the baby and the ruined, bloody folds of a very ugly dress.

"You need to make sure Josie's all right," Annabeth said. "Deliver the afterbirth; if she's—"

"I know what to do," he interrupted. Although ever since he'd held that baby in his hands, his mind hadn't felt like his own.

She peered at him for several seconds—seeking, searching—then nodded and disappeared into the dugout. An instant later, she marched out with a basket of clothes, diapers, and blankets. As she passed, she dropped his bag at his side.

Considering the trauma, Josie wasn't bleeding too badly. If she avoided childbed fever, the most common cause of death after birth, she'd be fine. She had a better chance of this since Annabeth had done her best to keep everything clean, but Lord only knew what had been going on in the two days before his wife had arrived.

Feeling steadier, saner after completing the familiar tasks of bathing and stitching, Ethan climbed to his feet. The cries of the baby sliced along his skin like a January wind. Those cries shouldn't bother him; they sounded healthy. Still, he wanted to turn away, to run away. Instead, he approached the creek. His wife had washed the boy and laid him atop a fresh blanket beneath the sun.

"Poor little fellow," she cooed, diapering his bruised behind. His back legs lifted toward his ears even after she gently pressed them down.

In contrast to most, this child's head wasn't misshapen; his face wasn't red or blotchy. All the pressure of the birth had been applied to the opposite end.

Annabeth finished swaddling the child, then carried him to his mother. Ethan followed, feeling a little lost. What day was it? Hell, what year was it?

Annabeth set the baby in Josie's waiting arms. In seconds, he nursed loudly. His wife turned her face, blinking as if the sun were far too bright. She snatched up dirty cloths with fingers that trembled.

Ethan took a step toward her, planning to tell her that everything would be all right, that this would not happen to her, but even if it did, he would be there; he would save them both.

The sudden pain behind his eyes made him curse. It wasn't until he saw his wife's face that he realized he'd cursed in Gaelic, like his da. Though why she would appear so worried, almost terrified, at hearing that, he had no idea. It wasn't as if he hadn't cursed in Gaelic before.

"Mo mhíle stór," he murmured, reaching out. She stepped back just as Major stood.

"Thank you, Doctor," he said. "And you, too, Missus."

Annabeth didn't respond, staring at Ethan with wide eyes. They needed to talk. Alone. But first . . .

"Everything that comes into contact with your wife and child must be as clean as possible," Ethan instructed. "Any sign of a fever, fetch me right away. Do you have any alcohol?"

"Whiskey."

"Mix it with water—half and half. She should use that to bathe her private area, as well as the child's umbilicus until it falls off."

"All riiii-ght," Major agreed skeptically. "Is the baby—?"

"Marbh," Ethan muttered, and blinked. Why had he said the child was dead?

Major's eyes narrowed, as Annabeth's widened. "I'm sorry, Doc. I don't—"

"He'll be fine," Ethan blurted. "Keep him swaddled. Place him on his belly to sleep so his legs get used to being straight and not up by his ears."

"Will he walk?"

"He might have a bit of trouble at first. Might not." Ethan set his hand on the young man's shoulder. "But there's nothing wrong with him that time won't heal."

Annabeth choked and ran for the creek.

"Women," Major muttered. "Babies always make 'em cry."

"Apparently," Ethan agreed. When Major joined his wife, Ethan did the same.

Annabeth kept her gaze on the gurgling water. "I hate that platitude."

"There isn't anything wrong," he said. "Not like there could be." She laughed, and the sound was full of tears. "Beth—"

"Don't call me that!"

Memory fluttered, like a ribbon from a tree, waving to him from high and away.

"Only Yankees shorten names," he murmured.

She spun, and as she did, her ruined dress pulled tight across her flat, empty stomach.

The world shimmied once, and he vomited, narrowly missing her shoes.

CHAPTER 19

I'll take you back to town," Major said.

"You'll tend your wife," Annabeth snapped. "I've dealt with men in far worse condition than this."

"I'm all right," Ethan insisted, and except for his pale face, set jaw, damp brow, and the fact that he'd deposited everything he'd eaten in the last decade on the ground, he seemed to be.

When she attempted to clamber up behind him so she could hold him in the saddle if need be, he glared and refused to allow her to mount anywhere but in front. Then he put his arms around her as if she required help and protection.

When Annabeth tried to question him about what had made him so ill, he growled, "Not now." From then on, nothing but the clop of the horse's hooves and Ethan's own harsh breathing echoed in the descending night.

Once in Freedom, he tossed the reins to the stable boy and headed home. Annabeth had to hurry so she wouldn't be left behind.

She stepped inside and knew they weren't alone. Her hand went to her hip. The smooth cotton of the ruined dress was all that met her grasping fingers. She'd left her Colt upstairs and, occupied with the Tarkentons and Ethan, hadn't missed it until now.

A shadow separated from the darkness, and in the instant before the face appeared in the tiny glow of moonlight, Annabeth relaxed. There'd been no guard on the porch because the guard was within.

"Would you like to explain why two of you were needed to deliver one child?"

"Difficult birth," Annabeth said.

The marshal's gaze cut to Ethan. "Everything okay?"

Annabeth moved between them. "Fine. Now, if you don't mind—"

"As the two of you were out wandering the countryside, begging for a bullet in the brain, something I've been trying to prevent, I do mind."

"Sorry," she said, though she wasn't. Not about that. She hadn't even considered the danger; she'd been too concerned with getting to Josie Tarkenton before she died and then with Ethan's odd behavior. However . . .

"As no one took a shot at us while we were very easy to shoot, I'd say whoever wanted to is long gone. You can probably stop posting a guard."

They were starting to annoy her. He was starting to annoy her. If any guarding needed to be done, she would be the one doing it.

Eversleigh's lips pursed. "I don't—"

"It's not as if the guards are much good. I left; then Ethan did."

"I wouldn't call the Cantrells any kind of guards."

"Who is?" Annabeth threw up her hands. "The best ones for the job are the ones you've got the townspeople guarding. Ethan and I will be all right, Marshal."

"Why is there a marshal?" Ethan asked.

Annabeth's heart took one hard thud against her chest. She'd hoped his behavior at the Tarkentons' had meant he was beginning to remember.

"The sheriff died," she said.

Ethan tilted his head, as if he'd heard distant glass breaking. Then he pulled the laudanum bottle from his pocket, took a few sips, and set it on the counter.

"Don't disappear again," Eversleigh said.

Annabeth urged him to the door. "We can't hide in the house when someone needs help."

"Then don't blame me if you get shot." He stepped onto the porch.

"I won't. You gonna remove those guards?"

Eversleigh glanced at Ethan, shrugged, nodded. She

shut the door, but she didn't turn. She was tired; she was sad. She needed a few minutes to herself. "I'm going to wash in the bedroom. You can wash down here."

She ran up the stairs before Ethan could agree or disagree. As she reached the landing, the medicine cabinet opened, bottles clinked, and the cabinet closed. She felt an instant of guilt that she'd left Ethan to put away the supplies alone, but she just wasn't up to helping him.

Annabeth slid the ruined dress from her shoulders. Too large, it slithered straight to the floor. The moon shone so brightly, she had no need of a lamp to determine her chemise was ruined, too.

Standing in nothing but her drawers, Annabeth drew a damp cloth over her neck and arms. She was bone tired; she ached so deeply, she wasn't sure where the pain ended and she began. She hadn't felt this way since—

A snuffle escaped. She caught her breath, pursed her lips, and refused to let another break free.

Downstairs, nothing but silence. It wasn't until Annabeth's chest grew tight and her face hot that she realized she still held her breath. She let it out on a rush. The air she drew in hitched a little, and the next thing she knew, she was sobbing. She covered her mouth, her nose, pressing hard, trying to keep the sound, the pain within. But tears flowed over her fingers, dripping off her wrists like rain.

The birth. That child. Ethan.

So much blood.

She dropped her hands, lifted her brimming eyes, and saw him in the doorway. He was naked to the waist, his usually bronzed skin gleaming silver in the light of the moon.

He crossed to her, one dusty boot landing atop the pile of equally dusty clothes. "What's wrong?"

"Oh, Ethan," she whispered. "What isn't?"

Confusion flickered in his gray eyes, and she shook her head. One of her tears struck his belly. He jerked as if the drop were scalding, and his gasp split the night.

They stood so close that when he leaned in, her unfettered breasts, still damp from her ablutions, brushed his chest. His lips touched first one cheek, then the other.

Though she meant to hold him away, to tell him to stop, her hands curled around his biceps, and she was just holding him, not telling him anything at all.

His muscles bulged against her palms as he took her mouth. She tasted tears. Hers? His? Did it matter? This was a mistake. There'd been so many lies, other people, secret lives, responsibilities that did not include each other, as well as shared pain, guilt, and sorrow that had never truly been put behind. She should stop this. She nearly did. But she needed him too badly.

Yes, touching him was a mistake, but it wasn't one she hadn't made before.

She slid her hands across his shoulders, her thumbs trailing his prominent collarbone before locking behind his neck. Her breasts crushed to his chest; she rubbed herself against him, and together they moaned.

He tore his mouth free, and she feared he would speak, stop, run. Instead, he walked his lips to her neck, suckled the curve, licked her own prominent collarbone, and then nipped her shoulder. She tangled her fingers in his hair.

He carried her to the bed, depositing her in a pool of moonlight. She should have felt exposed, embarrassed. She hadn't seen this man for five years. She'd left him with no intention of ever coming back. She didn't know him anymore; he certainly didn't know her.

But he remembered none of that. He remembered his wife—whom he still loved—not a woman who had torn out his soul and spit on it.

"You're so beautiful," he said, and she smiled.

She was no beauty. Her hair was too red, her freckles too many, her body too large to be anything but awkward. However, Ethan had always insisted she was the most beautiful woman in the world. Or at least the most beautiful woman in his world. He'd always been the most beautiful man in hers. Ethan Walsh would be the most beautiful man in any world.

He might be thinner, paler, but he was still Ethan—so

handsome, he turned heads. His dark hair made his light eyes gleam; his sharp cheekbones gave him an exotic appearance. His long legs, taut chest and stomach were an unexpected surprise in a man who made his living as a healer.

The moon turned his skin to alabaster—smooth and sleek. Would he be cool to the touch, or would he feel on fire as she did?

Annabeth sat up and placed her hand against his belly. The muscles fluttered like the gentle lap of a creek against the bank. Fascinated, she traced their path with her fingers, then with her tongue.

He tasted of saltwater—both hot and cool. She used her teeth on the jut of his hip, and he groaned. Leaning back, her gaze caught on the ridge beneath his trousers. She brushed a palm over it, and he grasped her wrist.

"You'll unman me."

"Wouldn't want that." What she wanted was him.

She tugged on her wrist. He released her, and she unbuttoned his trousers, not an easy task considering the pressure from the other side. When she finished with the last button, he sprang free.

Falling back on the bed, she opened her arms, and after kicking off his boots and pants, he dealt with hers. Her boots hit the floor. Then he slid her drawers from her hips, down her legs, off her feet. After an open-mouthed kiss to the arch, he drew his tongue across the opposite ankle. Several nibbles at the calf, a long scrape of teeth to the thigh, his tongue at her hip. He hovered at her center, blowing on the already-damp, swollen flesh. Desire caused her to shift and squirm.

He grasped her waist, and she waited for him to taste her as he had only a single time before. Instead he kissed her stomach, traced his lips across the expanse, pressed his cheek against her skin.

He'd done that many, many times. Then he would whisper: *Hello. I love you. I'm here.*

Annabeth's eyes burned again with tears. "Ethan—"

"Shh."

He followed the ripples caused by the hush with his

tongue, using his teeth along the ladder of her ribs. He spent an inordinate amount of time on her belly—mouth, lips, teeth, tongue, fingertips, thumb, and palm. At first she had to fight not to push him away. If he continued, he would know how empty she was.

But his ministrations took her back to a time when the only thing good had been this, the only thing right had been them. She tangled her fingers in his too-long hair and rubbed her thumb along his ear until he shuddered.

She should put a stop to this, but how would she explain? Modern medicine advised her not to tell him the truth, and if there was one thing Annabeth was very good at, it was not telling the truth.

She was selfish; it was wrong. Nevertheless, she tightened her lips and said nothing.

Until he nuzzled her breast with his cheek, licked the underside, then latched on to her nipple. The press of his tongue, the draw of his lips made her gasp, then tug on his hair as one word slipped free. "Now."

His eyes shone like the moon on the water; his smile was like the sun emerging from the clouds. "You always were impatient." He flicked her nipple with the tip of his tongue.

When he entered her, she shattered like the windows of a house—of this house, lately—into a hundred shiny shards.

"Impatient," he repeated, then began to move, in and out, friction and heat, a familiar rhythm—both as old as time and as new as . . .

"Now," she repeated.

As if in answer, he drove deep and pulsed, his head thrown back, the line of his neck, his chest, shimmering white. She ran a fingertip down that line, using her nail, tracing his bones, wishing she could be part of him like this forever.

He buried his face in her neck; his hair brushed her cheek. His weight was both heavy and welcome. She stroked his back, marveling that while she'd seemed to shatter instead, she felt almost . . . whole.

"It's been so long," he whispered as he rolled his weight to the side.

The steady rasp of his breath and the beat of his heart soothed her toward sleep in his wake. It *had* been so long.

Her eyes opened. What had he meant by that?

A noise downstairs had Annabeth sitting straight up in bed, her feet already meeting the floor as her ears strained to identify the sound. She wasn't sure what it was, but she didn't like it.

The marshal's down there, she thought. *Or some other poor soul assigned to watch the door.*

Except the marshal had walked away after agreeing to remove the guards. Why on earth had she asked him to do that? Now she had to investigate for herself.

Ethan hadn't moved. In the past, any sound would have brought him as awake as she was. But his injury, followed by the journey to the Tarkentons', the birthing, the trip home, and then this had exhausted him.

Annabeth donned another of Ethan's shirts and shoved her legs into a pair of his pants. She left her boots but picked up her Colt from the nightstand and quickly, silently navigated the stairs.

The porch lay empty, the silhouette of Marshal Eversleigh, or anyone else, no longer framed in the window. If a patient had arrived, they'd not only be standing in plain view but they would have shouted for help.

The scuffle of a shoe had Annabeth spinning to the right, finger tightening on the trigger. She didn't shoot; she wasn't sure why. Perhaps because she'd known before she even came down here whom she would find.

"Moze," she said.

Moses Farquhar leaned against the counter in the examining room. "You were expecting someone else?"

Annabeth joined him. "I wasn't expecting you. What the hell are you doing here?"

"A better question might be, what are you?"

The moon gave Annabeth enough light to see his face. She didn't need to answer; he already knew. Or thought he did.

Knowing was his business. It was how he'd stayed alive throughout the war; it was how he'd continued to stay alive this long after it despite his seemingly irresistible attraction to danger. Moze made it his mission to discover everything about everyone, and therefore he could never be surprised.

For a spy, being surprised was a very bad idea. Annabeth had learned that the hard way when Ethan had fallen into her trap.

Surprise!

"What happened to your hair?"

"I cut it," she snapped. "Better me than someone else." Though she'd survived being marked as a Union sympathizer, she'd never quite gotten over it.

"You shouldn't be here, Annie Beth Lou."

The moon sparked off his sea-green eyes. He was lucky he hadn't been born a Phelan. Those eyes would clash with the bright red hair.

"What if someone recognizes you?"

"Everyone's recognized me."

"I meant as an outlaw."

"I'm not wanted," she said.

"Not for lack of trying," he muttered. "I've had to stifle reports of a red-haired woman robbing a stage in Missouri, a bank in Iowa, and a train in Colorado."

"Only one of those was me."

"Which one?"

"Does it matter? Lass isn't going to trust me unless I prove myself trustworthy."

"By stealing?"

"Among other things."

She could feel Moze's gaze on her, waiting for her to say what "other" entailed. She wasn't going to. He was a smart guy; he'd figure it out. If he thought a man like Lassiter Morant allowed a woman into his gang just because she'd asked, he was dumber than dirt. Moze knew she'd slept with Lass; he just didn't want to hear it out loud any more than she wanted to say it.

Moze had many talents, and when she'd left here and taken the job for Pinkerton, he'd taught most of them to her. Or rather, he'd refined what she'd already learned as the only girl among so many boys about riding and weapons, stealth and skullduggery. He'd even taught her how to pick locks, a skill that had been useful more often than she cared to count.

"You need to leave," Moze said. "Before Lass comes looking."

As she'd had the same thought, Annabeth didn't contradict him. She'd told Lassiter she'd be gone a week, half of which was already gone.

"Any idea yet where his hideout is?"

"Besides down a rabbit hole?" she muttered. "I wish you'd just shoot him."

"Bring him where I can see him and I will."

She'd tried, but Lassiter was the most careful outlaw Annabeth had ever had the misfortune to meet. Not only was he paranoid about the location of his hideout, but he went nowhere without a posse; he avoided areas that might be a trap with the instinct of a hunted wolf. His men were loyal, or they were dead.

A fate that awaited her if he ever found out who she really was.

Ethan woke from a dream of whispers in the night to more of the same. His wife was gone. The murmur of her voice from downstairs explained why.

Ethan found his clothes and followed that murmur as he had once before. And as he had once before, Ethan hovered outside the examining room and listened to things he did not want to hear.

"I wish you'd just shoot him."

"Bring him where I can see him and I will."

Rubbing his forehead, Ethan frowned. Were they talking about him?

"He still doesn't trust me."

"You know how to fix that."

Annabeth sighed. "Yeah."

"That isn't a problem, is it?" Annabeth didn't answer. "Considering where I found you tonight, I can't see how it would be."

"He's my husband, Moze."

"You haven't been his wife in five years. Why now?"

Five years?

Images tumbled through Ethan's mind. *Annabeth crying. Blood on her hands. On his. A baby's squalls beneath the sun. Another too still beneath the moon.*

"You left him, Annabeth. You never gave any hint you planned to return."

"I didn't."

"Then why did I find you in his bed?"

The silence that followed the question was so complete, and Ethan was listening so hard for his wife's response that he started when the latch clicked. He hadn't heard the door close. He didn't hear anything but crickets until Annabeth said, "You can come out now."

The past and the present snapped together with a louder click than the latch had made. Ethan stepped into the exam room. Annabeth stood alone, staring at her bare toes.

"You're still a spy," he said.

Her head came up, her eyes wide. "You remember?" Ethan nodded, and she cast a frown at the door and then back at him. "Just now?"

"I've been having flashes since . . ." He swallowed; his mouth was so damn dry. His gaze went to the cabinet, and he had to use all of his will not to open it.

"Since the Tarkenton baby," she finished. "I could tell something wasn't right."

"Isn't it right that I remember? It's 1870. Our child is dead. I killed him and you left me."

"Killed him," she echoed, her voice faint. "Oh, Ethan, is that what you thought?"

"It's the truth."

"You didn't kill our son. He just . . ." She swallowed, too.

"I was angry. I put my hands on you. I wanted to do more." He felt again the fury that had come over him when he'd discovered everything was a lie.

"I don't blame you," she said.

"You don't have to."

"That whole day, I didn't feel well. I had cramps." She rubbed at her stomach, then shifted her back.

A memory of her doing the same on that long ago and horrible night teased at the back of his mind.

"Blood spots, too."

His fingers tightened. "Why didn't you tell me?"

"You were gone, and then . . ." She sighed. "So was he."

Silence settled over them like the night. "I still shouldn't have . . ." His voice trailed off.

"We both shouldn't."

"Why did you leave?"

She rubbed at her forehead as if her head ached as much as his did. "There were too many lies, Ethan. How were we ever going to get past them?"

"You got past them well enough an hour ago," he muttered.

"An hour ago, you didn't recall them." She dropped her hand and shot him a glare. "Or at least I thought you didn't."

"You did."

Her lips tightened; her fingers curled into fists. "What do you want me to say?"

"The truth, if you're capable of it."

"I needed you."

He wasn't sure what he'd expected, but not that.

"Just because I remembered everything that happened to us doesn't mean I allowed myself to think about it. Today, at the Tarkentons', I saw you with that baby, and all I could do was—" Her voice broke.

"Me too," he murmured.

She stiffened. "You touched me even though you remembered?"

"Not everything. Not then."

"When?"

He had a flash of his mouth on her belly, the ripples beneath the flesh that had brought about another memory, and he'd touched and pressed and poked in the guise of . . . what?

Love? Perhaps. But what he'd discovered while kissing

his wife's stomach was that there was nothing within but her. The same thing he'd discovered earlier.

With Cora.

Which was something he wasn't going to share with Annabeth. Not until he talked to Cora Lewis. Perhaps the woman truly thought she was expecting. As her physician and her lover, he owed her the courtesy of speaking with her about it first.

"I heard you down here," he murmured. "With him. Just like the last time." Then she'd called the man "Moze," but beyond that, Ethan knew nothing more. "Who is he? You never said."

"You never asked."

They both went silent as they remembered why that was. Blood and tears, anger, fury, accusations.

And that too-still body.

"Who is he?" Ethan repeated.

"Moses Farquhar."

"Never heard of him. And why is that?"

"He's the one who asked me to spy at Chimborazo."

"How did he know you and that you'd be any good at espionage?"

Her lips curved. "We were raised together after his mother died. He was Luke's best friend."

Ethan didn't like that smile. He thought Moze might have been her best friend, too. Or perhaps even more.

"Why didn't he do his own dirty work?"

"They needed ears at Chimborazo, and Moze is little more than worthless around blood. Besides, I was already there."

Ethan frowned. "Why were you there?"

"I had nowhere else to go. My parents were dead, as were all of my brothers but one. I'd nursed my mother and father along with several neighbors. I was good at it."

"Who suggested Chimborazo?"

"Moze. But he wanted me safe, not alone at the farm."

"He wanted you *there*. He planned to recruit you from the beginning." She didn't appear convinced, but she didn't argue. "It was a dangerous game he asked you to play." No matter when he'd decided to ask her to play it. "I understand why you agreed to help him at Chimborazo, but why did you agree to help him again?"

She let out a short, sharp laugh. "What was I supposed to do? Sell myself in the streets?"

"You're a nurse and a good one."

"Unfortunately, without a nice, bloody war, there isn't a lot of work for nurses."

"Instead you're spying for . . ." He paused as another part of that long-ago overheard conversation resurfaced. "Pinkerton."

"Yes."

"Farquhar came here tonight to get you to return to . . ." Ethan paused. "What?"

"Have you ever heard of the Morant Gang?" Ethan shook his head. "They started robbing banks and trains and stages back when everyone else was occupied killing one another out East. They ride in fast, take what they want, shoot any resistance, and disappear."

"Disappear? In Kansas?"

"The leader, Lassiter Morant, has a hideout no one's been able to find. Several Pinkerton detectives have tried to become part of the gang. The next time we saw them, they were dead."

"So Moze sent you." Annabeth shrugged. "It's dangerous."

"No more so than anything else I've done in the last five years."

"What else have you done?"

Her gaze met his. "You don't want to know."

She was probably right, and since he didn't relish her asking what he'd been doing—his gaze flicked to the cabinet, then away—he moved on. "Have you ridden and robbed along with them?"

"I wouldn't have lasted very long if I hadn't."

"There's a federal marshal in town." His gaze touched on her bright red hair. "Why hasn't he recognized you?"

"Moze has made sure that every wanted poster of me looks like someone else, if he didn't get any mention of me omitted altogether."

"Sooner or later, Lassiter's going to get suspicious about all your good luck," he said.

"Let's hope it's later," Annabeth muttered. "I need him to trust me."

"He doesn't?"

"You don't," she muttered.

"If you're supposed to be riding with this gang, then why are you here?"

She was silent so long, Ethan thought she might not answer. Then she blurted, "Fedya found me."

"How?" She didn't answer; they both knew how. "Why?"

"He said you were in trouble, that you might die."

Damn Fedya. He'd always seen too much.

"So you thought you'd ride in under cover of darkness and make everything all right?"

"If you'd tell me what's wrong, maybe I could."

"Fedya was mistaken," Ethan said stiffly, blinking as his eyelid fluttered. "There's nothing wrong."

"Yet I wasn't in town a day before someone took a shot at you."

"As no one ever took a shot at me until you returned, I'm starting to think, more and more, the shot was meant for you."

Her lips tightened. "I have to get back."

"Back?" he echoed before he could stop himself.

She threw up her hands. "What did you think I'd do, Ethan? Stay?"

He'd thought that what they'd just shared had meant something. But why should now be any different from then?

CHAPTER 20

Ethan didn't answer, then again, what would he say that hadn't been said before? Annabeth should never have come anywhere near him. She should never have hinted that she still cared.

She never should have done a lot of things, including sleep with him. Both now and back then.

"Did you ever find your brother?" he asked.

"Not yet."

"You're still looking?"

"I won't stop."

"I'm sorry."

Ethan stood in the shadows. The moon had shifted, and she could no longer see his face. "Wasn't your fault."

"I seem to remember you saying that it was."

"I said a lot of things." So had he.

"He was missing," Ethan continued. "You never heard anything else?"

She'd heard plenty; she just hadn't wanted to share it with him.

"Didn't you ever wonder why Fedya was kept alive and not executed?"

Understanding dawned. "You exchanged Fedya for your brother." He blew an impatient burst of air through his nose. "All this time, I believed Fedya shot Mikey on purpose and you knew he hadn't?"

"I told you he hadn't, but you wouldn't believe me. Think, Ethan. Why would anyone want to hurt Mikey? What would Fedya's shooting him gain?"

"We'll never know because Mikey isn't Mikey anymore."

She wasn't going to have that argument again. "With a prize like Fedya, I could have ransomed Jefferson Davis. The Union was happy to turn over my brother."

"Then where is he?"

Annabeth had spent a good portion of the past five years trying to find out.

"Have you heard of Galvanized Yankees?" she asked.

"Confederates who changed sides." From his tone, Annabeth understood Ethan's low opinion of the practice.

"Most were prisoners, like you, in terrible places with too many others, starving, sick, dying. When given a chance to get out, they took it. Wouldn't you?"

"I refused," he said quietly.

"You what?"

"I was offered the chance to leave Castle Thunder, to pledge allegiance to the Confederacy and become a field surgeon. I said no."

"Why?" What difference did it make if he operated on Rebels or Yankees as long as he was saving someone? He'd said as much to her a half dozen times before.

"You saw how bad it was in Castle Thunder. How could I leave people to suffer and die if I could help? I couldn't leave Mikey either; I couldn't leave—" He broke off, swallowed, looked away.

Had he been going to say he couldn't leave her? Most likely. At that time, he'd still believed she was who she said she was—a Southern farm girl who'd volunteered her nursing skills for the good of the cause.

"If Fedya was exchanged for your brother, why are you still searching for him?"

"Fedya was taken to an agreed-upon location and exchanged for a man said to be Luke Phelan. It wasn't until they brought him to me that I was able to tell them he wasn't Luke at all."

"How underhanded of them," Ethan murmured, and startled a burst of laughter from Annabeth.

She'd never been certain if what happened then was the misunderstanding the Yankees said it was or the lie she still believed it to be. Illinois was a long way from

Virginia, and there'd been a war going on. Communications went awry all the time.

"Two opposing groups, whose job it was to lie, worked out an exchange and one of them . . ." She spread her hands. "Lied. Shocking."

"What happened to your brother?"

For a while, she'd believed Luke had died in prison and been buried in an unmarked grave, or worse.

"They said he swore allegiance to the Union before leaving prison and then he came West to fight Indians. But Moze found no record of him at Fort Dodge or Fort Zarah, where most of the Galvanized Yankees landed." Not that the records kept of rebel prisoners were very accurate.

"Fort Dodge, Kansas?" Ethan asked.

"Is there another one? Why don't you just ask what you want to ask? Did I marry you to get closer to where I thought my brother had gone?" Ethan didn't answer, didn't need to. "I didn't find out about him being galvanized until recently. But even if I'd known back then, I could have traveled to Kansas on my own if I'd wanted to. I certainly didn't need you."

"Thanks," he murmured, and she felt bad. Would they ever stop hurting each other?

"I loved you, Ethan. That's why I married you."

"Not because you were pregnant and alone and scared?"

"Well, that too," she agreed.

Now he laughed, and Annabeth found herself smiling in return, until he spoke again. "You could have gotten out of Castle Thunder anytime you wanted. Why didn't you?"

The anger she'd banked suddenly roared to life, and she crossed the few steps that separated them. She had to tilt her head only a bit to glare into his eyes. "I told you once before, Ethan. I stayed there for you."

Regret flickered in his eyes. For an instant, she thought he might lean close, kiss her brow or maybe her mouth.

Speaking of Castle Thunder brought back memories

of their first time. Their coupling had been fast, desperate. They hadn't known how long they would have before someone—a guard, a prisoner—returned. But there'd been so much pain and so much death. The two of them had wanted nothing more than to find some joy, to reaffirm life.

Moving together, coming apart, their eyes meeting, their bodies straining. The way her breath had caught, not from the pain of her first time, but from the beauty, the utter rightness, the completeness she'd felt only in his arms.

"Ethan," she murmured, and her breasts bumped his chest.

He hissed as if she had scalded him. Then he stepped back, face averted; he would not look at her as he turned away. She was left alone, fists clenched, anger and agony pulsing so strong, she felt feverish. She had to get out of this room, this house, this town, his life.

Annabeth spun and ran up the stairs.

Ethan took another bottle from the cabinet—hell, he took two—then he slipped out the back door. By the time the sun lightened the horizon, he'd downed a good portion of the first. His chest still hurt, but it always did when he came here.

Ethan traced the name carved on the tombstone. "Michael," he whispered. "Michael Walsh."

Not his brother, but his son.

Annabeth didn't know about the grave. She'd disappeared before it had been dug.

Everyone dealt with tragedy in his or her own way. Ethan lifted the laudanum bottle in a toast to the grave. "Yer mother runs away and spies on people, me darlin'." He took a sip. "Apparently, it helps." Or maybe not. Annabeth didn't seem any more over their tragedy than Ethan was.

His horse, tied to the oak tree that lent shade to the solitary grave, huffed and shuffled. The grave site wasn't that far from town. Certainly, it was a bit of a walk, but he hadn't needed to bring the horse. However, Ethan knew from past experience that ascending the hill sober was a damn sight easier than descending it when he wasn't.

From his vantage point on the small hill—were there large hills anywhere in Kansas?—Ethan watched Cora step onto her porch and shake out a rug. Just the sight of her made Ethan want to—

A growl rumbled in his chest, and his hand tightened around the bottle so hard, he nearly broke it. He loosened his hold, but he couldn't stop glaring at the woman. She was as much of a liar as his wife.

Ethan lay on the grass and stared at the bright summer sky. Why had he suddenly remembered everything he'd forgotten? It was a mystery. One he'd like to solve. Because if he could remember, then . . .

Couldn't Mikey?

Hope fluttered—or at least he thought it might be hope. He couldn't quite recall what hope felt like.

The last thing Ethan remembered clearly was standing in the spare bedroom as his wife took an ax to their child's crib. He'd been amazed, frightened, a little aroused. Which was pretty much the effect his wife always had on him. She was an amazing, frightening, arousing woman.

From that point on, his thoughts were hazy—dreams and reality blended together, the past and the present jumbled. People would appear familiar, but he couldn't decipher why. Or they would seem to know him, but he would not remember them at all. His waking hours had taken on a dreamlike quality, while his dreams . . .

His dreams had seemed more like the truth.

Was that why the sound of Moses Farquhar's voice had caused the wall in his mind to tumble down? He'd dreamed of the first time he'd heard it, then woken and heard it again? Same place, same person, similar words.

"No," he murmured, and his horse pawed the grass once and then stilled. "I started to remember at the Tarkentons'."

Because of the baby.

Difficult delivery. A sea of blood. Panic. Cries. Screams.

"Similar situation." Ethan shuddered. "Different results."

Alive not dead. So why had he seen that child and remembered his own?

He traced the gravestone again. "Head trauma can cause memory loss." He hadn't needed to read a dozen books to know that. He'd had to only look at Mikey.

Ethan lifted the bottle to his lips—a single swallow and it was empty. Hell, he'd been in such a hurry to leave, he'd grabbed one of the bottles he'd taken to the Tarkentons'. He lifted the second, saw that it was only half full, too, shrugged, drank. He wasn't going to be here long. He'd be back in his surgery before he needed more.

All the texts advised keeping the patient calm because upsetting him or her could make the situation worse. But had any of those patients gotten better? Ethan thought not or the books would have mentioned it.

Considering what had happened to him—head injury, memory loss, repetition of similar trauma to trauma he'd endured before, followed by the return of his memories—Ethan had a new hypothesis.

If trauma could cause memory loss, perhaps trauma could bring those memories back.

"What if it does?" He sat up. His horse lifted its head, snuffled, then returned to munching on grass. "Does that mean I should set a can on my brother's head and have Fedya shoot it off?"

Was Ethan willing to risk his brother's life on a theory? What if, instead of making him better, the experiment made Mikey worse? Or what if, just like last time, Fedya missed? His brother would not survive two bullets to the head.

So Mikey thought his name was Mikhail Romanov. So he believed Fedya was his brother, Alexi, and that the two of them had many adventures. So what?

Ethan had a sneaking suspicion that Fedya/Alexi was involved in some shady undertakings and that he'd drawn Mikey into them, too. Why else would Fedya have shown up with a woman who'd been shot?

Then there was the matter of the dead sheriff. About both situations, as well as what they'd been doing since the war, Fedya had remained tight-lipped.

Mikey had followed Fedya's orders like a hired henchman. He wouldn't even look at Ethan, let alone talk to him. The three of them had behaved as if they were on the run from something or someone and as if they had plenty to hide.

But was Ethan any better? He'd been a spy, and he'd used his brother to take information he'd stolen from the sick and the dying to what most people in the area would label the enemy. Mikey had been thrown into prison. Ethan had blamed Annabeth for what had happened, but she was right. She'd only set the trap.

Ethan was the one who'd jumped into it.

The door opened and then closed downstairs. As no voices followed, Annabeth concluded that Ethan had left rather than that someone had arrived. She leaned over, hand outstretched to snatch her saddlebags; then she straightened and kicked them instead. Dust puffed upward.

"Idiot," she muttered.

Now that she'd revealed to everyone in town that she wasn't dead, Ethan would have a helluva time saying she was. Before she left forever, she had to visit the lawyer—what had been his name?—and request a divorce. Then Ethan could have the life he'd always wanted. With Cora not Annabeth, but what choice did she have? Even if Cora hadn't carried Ethan's child, Annabeth doubted he would want Annabeth back once he knew the truth of the past five years. If she stayed, she would have to tell him everything, and she wasn't sure she could bear to watch Ethan's face reflect disappointment and disgust.

Unfortunately, the sun wasn't yet up, and she doubted the lawyer would be available until it was.

She listened to the house creak as the horizon lightened to gray and then pink. She must have dozed, because the next time she looked, the sky blazed gold and people bustled about on the streets. She slung her saddlebags over her shoulder and left.

Two doors beyond Lewis's Sewing and Sundry, a sign proclaimed: LOYER.

"Someone really needs to paint new signs."

Annabeth hoped to slip past Cora's place without being seen. Hell, she hoped to slip out of town without having to talk to anyone besides the "loyer." Of course, what she hoped rarely happened. She was three steps from success when a door opened behind her.

"Missus—" An exasperated huff followed. Annabeth reached for the doorknob, hoping she might still escape. "Don't you dare!"

Annabeth turned. Cora Lewis had two bright spots of color high on her cheeks, which caused her blue eyes to shine bluer. The effect made her appear both ethereal and insane.

"You stole that dress!" she shouted.

Annabeth glanced down at Ethan's trousers and shirt, then at the crazy woman.

"You know what I mean."

She did, and she hadn't stolen it. Of course, she also hadn't paid for it; nor could she return it in its current condition.

The stares of the townsfolk bored into Annabeth's back; her own cheeks heated. "Could we step into your shop?"

She preferred not to have a private conversation involving money—and name-calling, no doubt—in front of everyone.

Cora lifted her pretty, pointed chin. "No."

Annabeth's hands clenched, and she moved closer, crowding the woman back. "I have the money; I'll give it to you inside."

"And if I refuse?" The woman raised her voice so everyone could hear. "Will you hit me again?"

"When did I hit you?"

"You slapped me in the face."

Understanding dawned. "You were hysterical."

Cora sniffed. "So you say." Then she spun and stalked into the shop.

Annabeth risked a glance at their audience. A few discovered fascinating particles of dust just above their heads. The rest stared at Annabeth with accusing, disappointed expressions. She saw how the situation appeared. The tiny, petite, and lovely seamstress threatened and abused by the looming, large, unlovely woman who'd deserted their beloved doctor.

As there was nothing she could say to disabuse that opinion—it was largely the truth—Annabeth followed Cora inside. She placed the greenbacks on the counter. "That should be more than enough."

"You're unfamiliar with what dresses cost these days." Cora let her gaze wander over Annabeth from hat to boot, and her lip curled. "Obviously."

"You didn't adjust it as promised," Annabeth said. She didn't bother to add that the dress was ready for the ragbag after a single wearing. Though she'd like to blame the woman for everything, Annabeth's wearing it to a birthing had not been the fault of Cora Lewis.

"You think I'd work for you?"

Annabeth slapped a few more dollars onto the counter and stepped toward the door. She paused with her hand on the knob. "Tell Ethan . . ." Her throat closed, and she had to swallow several times before she could speak again. "Tell him I'm filing for divorce. He should see the lawyer."

"He remembers?"

"Yes." Annabeth waited for a cry of joy; when it didn't come, she glanced over her shoulder to discover Cora's face wreathed in a frown.

"Everything?" she asked.

"I assume so."

"How?"

Annabeth wasn't going to explain. She wasn't sure she could explain. All she knew was that Ethan was himself again, or close enough, which meant she had to leave.

She'd warned him of danger; he'd denied there was any. He believed the shot that had hit him had been meant for her. So did the marshal. As there'd been no further incidents, despite plenty of opportunity, she was inclined to agree. Maybe the bullet through the window had even been an accident. Someone's gun had misfired and the culprit did not want to admit it. She certainly wouldn't.

Annabeth was beginning to wonder if Fedya's warning had merely been a means to an end. He thought she should return to her husband. Which didn't sound like the man she knew, but little she'd heard of Fedya since coming back to Freedom did.

Perhaps, if it hadn't been for Cora and her child—and Lassiter Morant—Annabeth might have stayed and tried to make their marriage work. As it was, she needed to go.

Pryce Mortimer sat behind a wooden table in the center of his office. Hunched over and scribbling madly, he was nearly obscured by the stacks of books and papers all around him. He didn't glance up when Annabeth stepped inside. After several silent moments broken only by the sound of his pen on paper, Annabeth cleared her throat.

Mortimer lifted his dark head; Annabeth blinked, but she did not flinch or look away from the man's ravaged face. She'd seen enough smallpox victims to recognize the cause of the damage. During the war, the army had tried to vaccinate the soldiers; however, the vaccines were not always effective. Most regular folks had no idea what a vaccine was, not to mention the Indian populations, which had been decimated by the disease. That Mortimer had survived the horrible, murderous illness revealed a lot about the man without him ever saying a word.

"I would like to engage your services." Annabeth took the chair on the other side of the table without being asked.

"In what capacity?" Annabeth blinked again. Pryce

Mortimer had the deepest, most commanding and beautiful voice she had ever heard.

"I need a divorce."

Mortimer frowned, though the expression was merely a downward twitch of his lips. His face had been damaged too deeply to move much at all. "Divorce," he repeated. "I don't think—"

"I do."

"You must have a reason, Missus . . . ?"

"And here I thought I was the main topic of conversation in Freedom these days."

The expression in his dark eyes turned wry. "I don't leave this building. I talk to no one unless they first talk to me. You can see why."

"No, I can't."

"You don't appear blind."

"And you don't appear stupid."

Mortimer stared at her for a few seconds, and then he laughed. His laugh was as beautiful as his voice. "Why don't you tell me who you are, who you want to divorce, and why."

"I'm Annabeth Phe—" She paused. "Annabeth Walsh."

"The doctor's wife. Everyone thought you were dead."

"Thinking doesn't make it so." Neither did hoping.

Too bad for Cora Lewis.

"No," he agreed, and something in his voice made Annabeth believe he had firsthand experience with the situation. Poor man.

"Why do I need a reason?" she asked. Annabeth knew little about divorce except that she'd be going to hell for it. But since she'd already been there, what was one more trip?

"Although divorces are more easily granted in the West, fault is required. In layman's terms . . ." He spread his equally damaged hands. "A reason."

"What kind?"

"Why don't you tell me yours, and I'll decide if it's good enough?"

"How about you list what's acceptable, and I'll pick one?"

Everyone would know soon enough about Cora and Ethan's child. Annabeth planned to be far away before that news circulated. However, as she was doing this to ensure Ethan's future happiness, she didn't intend to spread reputation-ruining rumors along the way.

Mortimer studied her for several seconds. Annabeth studied him right back. Eventually, he gave in. "Adultery, bigamy, cruelty, desertion, habitual drunkenness, impotency, and failure to provide."

"Desertion." Everyone knew that she had.

Mortimer scribbled a few words, then folded his hands atop the table. "You're certain?"

"That I deserted him? Yes."

"But you're back."

She glanced out the window. "Not for long."

"You'll need to sign some papers."

"When?" She could always slip into town and out again, unseen, as she should have done in the first place.

"An hour?"

Annabeth's lips tightened. She wanted to leave *now*, but if waiting an hour meant she wouldn't have to return, she'd wait a damn hour.

"Fine," she agreed.

"And your husband? Where is he?"

"No idea."

"He's probably at the grave. I'll—"

Annabeth reached out and snatched Pryce Mortimer's high-collared shirt. "What grave?"

CHAPTER 21

The hill wasn't that far out of town, so Annabeth walked, even though she could see that Ethan had taken his horse. Maybe he just liked his horse.

As she hadn't observed any evidence of life beyond that, perhaps Ethan wasn't even there. Though who else would be at the grave of their child so early in the morning? Or ever, for that matter?

The sun beat down on the brim of her hat, hot enough to make sweat dampen the hair she'd stuffed beneath. Thunderclouds danced on the horizon. She was glad she'd asked Pryce Mortimer to keep her saddlebags until she returned. Dragging everything she owned up the slope would have made her more uncomfortable than she already was, and a summer storm would drench all of it.

Annabeth crested the rise as a breeze stirred the leaves of the huge oak tree. Removing her hat, she sighed as the wind cooled her. The air today was so thick, she could hardly breathe.

"Goway." Ethan lay flat on his back. He didn't even lift his head.

Annabeth knelt and traced the name on the headstone. "Michael," she whispered; her voice broke.

"Don't." Ethan snatched her wrist.

Don't touch? Speak? Cry? Stay? It didn't matter.

"You should have told me he was here."

"He isn't."

She tugged on her wrist, and he let go; then she brushed his brow as the wind blew through the leaves and whispered like a ghost in the night. "Are you sure?"

He kept his gaze on the clouds and not on her. "The dead don't come back."

"I did."

He made an odd sound—half snort, half laugh—and laid his arm over his face. "Goway," he repeated.

He slurred the word, and concern sparked. Had his wound become infected? What she could see of it appeared fine. Of course, who knew what was happening beneath the surface?

"What year is it, Ethan?"

"Ag fuck tú," he muttered, though there was no heat to the words. "That means—"

"I know what it means." Just because he'd spoken Gaelic didn't mean he hadn't been quite clear.

"I haven't relapsed. If I had, I certainly wouldn't remember our dead son beneath this tree."

He had a point.

"You named him Michael," she said.

"Someone had to."

Annabeth had refused to name their child. She'd refused to look at him, to touch him, or be in the same room with him. She couldn't bear it.

"Ethan," she began as she got to her feet. He sat up so quickly, she stepped back.

The bullet whizzed past her chest and smashed into the tree, spraying bits of bark onto the grass. She dropped flat on the ground, shoving Ethan flat, too.

"Beth!" He lifted his head; she pushed it back down.

"Stay there." She crept forward on her belly until she could peer over the edge of the hill at Freedom. Folks milled about. She didn't see anyone on the streets that shouldn't be.

If the shot had come from town, people would have run inside. They hadn't. No one even glanced in their direction. Probably because the wind blew against her face, carrying sound toward her and away from them. Then Annabeth caught movement in the swaying prairie grass.

Someone was coming. Perhaps several someones.

"We have to go." Annabeth scooted backward on her belly.

"Who is it?"

"I assume the same person who shot at you . . . me . . . us before." She tugged on Ethan's boot; he yanked his foot out of her reach and craned his neck so he could see her face.

"Why do you think this is the same person?"

"Because if it's someone else, we have more problems than I thought."

"We can't just leave."

Annabeth let her forehead fall to the ground. Tempted to bang it against the hard summer earth a few times, she refrained. In the distance, thunder rumbled. "We can. We should. We have a horse; they don't. Considering our position and my lack of ammunition . . ." She should never have left her saddlebags with the "loyer." "We have to."

Ethan must have heard the panic in her voice, because he crawled backward, too. They slithered along the ground until they reached the horse, which shuffled and huffed at their behavior.

"Mount up," she said. "I'm right behind you."

"*You* mount up."

Annabeth's fists tightened. She wanted him in front of her, protected. He obviously wanted the same thing. In reverse.

"I don't know where we're going," he said.

"Right now, just away from here." When he continued to hesitate, she shrugged and reached for her gun. "If you'd rather I shoot until my bullets run out . . .

He gave a growl of frustration and climbed into the saddle. She could have sworn he swayed a bit. He offered his hand, and she took it, swinging up behind him as he urged the animal into a run.

An hour later, Ethan reined in his horse. "Anyone following?"

"No."

"You're sure?"

She shrugged, rubbing her breasts against his back. Ethan ground his teeth together and closed his aching eyes.

The sun blazed down; he didn't have a hat. They were both drenched in sweat, as was the horse. The blessed breeze that had rustled the leaves of the tree earlier had died, leaving behind an eerie stillness.

They couldn't go on much longer. Ethan didn't have a bottle that wasn't empty, which was soon going to be a bigger problem than the heat or the gunfire.

"When can we turn around?"

"I don't—" She tensed, the movement removing the soft weight of her breasts and slamming her gun belt into his spine.

"Hey." His gaze followed hers; he stilled at the sight of the big, whirling, dirty cloud on the horizon.

"That's enough dust for an entire posse," Annabeth murmured.

"That's not a posse." And he'd thought lack of a full bottle was his biggest worry. "That's a twister."

Ethan faced forward and allowed their mount, which had begun to sidestep and fight the bit, its head. Annabeth wrapped her arms around his waist and held on.

He'd seen tornados before. This was Kansas; they were common. However, Ethan had never been out on the range, on a horse, with nowhere to run or hide as a killer storm bore down.

The wind picked up; the sky went dark. Though no rain fell, Ethan could smell it somewhere, along with the lightning. The distant thunder became one long, low, rumbling snarl. The earth shook as though a train approached, though the nearest track lay twenty miles' distant.

Annabeth shouted, but he couldn't make out the words. Debris flew past them, picking up speed. Ahead, several tumbleweeds fell into space.

Gully. Ethan headed right for it.

He pulled the horse to a stop several feet way—wasn't easy—the animal wanted to get gone. Annabeth slid off, tugging Ethan's leg so hard, he nearly fell on top of her. He risked a glance west. The cloud had turned black and seemed to fill the horizon from north to south.

As soon as Ethan leaped free, Annabeth towed him

toward the hollowed-out ditch created by spring runoff. He attempted to bring the horse, but the animal reared, yanking the reins from his hands before sprinting east.

Ethan jumped into the long, narrow crevice; his wife landed next to him. She shoved him beneath the slight overhang on the far side, then pressed her belly to the ground beneath the one opposite. Above them, the wind screamed.

Unless that was his horse.

Ethan rose onto his knees. His mount was gone. He didn't think the animal could have run fast enough to be out of sight by now, but he certainly hoped that was the case.

Annabeth slammed into him, pushing him back where he'd been and then shielding his body with hers. She said something, but he couldn't hear it above the gale. His ears crackled and popped; the air seemed to snap and buzz. She wrapped her hands around his neck. His arms circled her waist as the storm tried to pull her away.

Ethan tugged Annabeth close—hip to hip, chest to breast—he hooked his ankle over hers. She pressed her face into his neck. Her breath tickled his collarbone. He curled himself around her and murmured, "Don't let go."

Considering the trill of the wind, the thud of his heart, the sudden torrent that beat down, turning the dry gully into a river of mud, she should not have been able to hear. Just as he should not have been able to hear her answer: "Never." But he did.

Ethan kept his eyes closed against the slap of grit and rain. He clasped Annabeth with every ounce of strength he had so she would not be whirled away like his horse. His fingers were slick; they kept slipping. He feared he would not be able to outlast the ferocity of the gale, but he would not lose her again.

His ears rang so loudly, he first became aware of the passing of the storm more by the lessening of the pull on his wife than by the lessening of noise. Cautiously, Ethan opened one eye, then the other. A shaft of sunlight blazed between slate clouds.

"Beth." His voice sounded far away. His wife's ears

must have been equally beleaguered because she didn't answer; she didn't move. "Beth!"

This time he shouted, or thought he did, and shook her a bit. Her head came up so fast, she nearly knocked him in the chin. He reared back and knocked his head on the earth overhang. Grass and dirt and rocks rained down.

Her deep blue eyes appeared black, huge in her pale face. She seemed to have more freckles than he remembered.

"Is it gone?" she asked.

His gaze went again to the shaft of sun, which had become wider, pushing against the clouds on either side. "From here."

"So fast?"

"Fast?" To him, the time he'd held her, afraid his strength would not be enough to save them, had been an eternity.

"Was that five minutes? Ten?"

"All right," he agreed, still dazed or perhaps just dazzled. She was so damn pretty.

A crease appeared between her brows. "What's wrong?"

"Wrong?" He still held her as if the storm might take her away. He didn't want to let her go.

Annabeth laid her palm to his cheek. "No fever." She brushed her fingertip along his stitches. "Do they hurt?"

He shook his head. He wanted her to touch them again, touch him again.

"I should take those out."

"Okay." He tilted his face toward her, and she laughed.

"Not now. The only thing I have that might be sharp enough to do the job is my teeth."

The thought of her using her teeth on his forehead was unappealing. However, the idea of her using her teeth elsewhere . . .

Annabeth stilled. She had felt his response. This close, how could she not? Ethan kissed her; he couldn't help himself.

For an instant, he thought she might pull away, roll away, stand up and run away. Then she seemed to melt—into him, through him. She became part of him. She still tasted like dawn, like hope. And oh, how he needed it.

He traced her lips with his tongue, rubbed his thumbs along the lowest ridge of her ribs, learned again the contours of her mouth, her teeth, discovered anew the flavor of her skin. Drinking her sigh, he marveled at the sweetness of her breath. His must bring to mind month-old milk.

She didn't seem to notice; in fact, she breathed in deeply, as if trying to draw him within, to memorize his scent as he longed to memorize hers.

When he lifted his head, her eyes remained closed; her tongue darted out and ran over her lower lip. "You still taste like . . ."

"What?" he whispered, and her eyes opened.

For an instant, a smile trembled, threatening to break across her face like dawn broke the night. Then she drew back, released him, and the moment was gone. He could have held on, but why? The harder he tugged in one direction, the faster she would run in the other.

Annabeth rolled onto her back, plopping into the mud at the lowest point of the gully. She didn't appear to care; she was too intent on getting away.

She hauled herself upright and then took a giant step onto the prairie, shading her eyes from the now-abundant sunshine. Somewhere along the way, she'd lost her hat. "Is that . . . ?"

Ethan had planned to remain where he was, at least until his erection went away, maybe longer—he wasn't feeling too well. The shiver he'd experienced at the image of her teeth tasting him, her tongue taunting him, had become a full-blown shudder, so deep his bones ached. Yet his skin had broken out with a light sweat. But her words had him rolling free and standing, too.

He swayed a bit, forced himself to stop before he asked, "What?"

Annabeth dropped her hand; those lips he'd so recently and thoroughly kissed at last spreading into a smile. "I think it's your horse."

He looked where she had. "It's *a* horse," he allowed.

"Good enough." She started to walk, stepping over bits and pieces of debris that lay here and there or, in some cases, tumbled past. Dry leaves. Sticks. A tree limb from which hung a bit of cloth. Her boot heel clipped something that sounded like a tin cup.

Ethan was dizzy and hot; his stomach churned. His bowels gurgled like the muddy water in the ditch behind them. He didn't want to walk to the horse, which he knew from previous experience was a lot farther away than it appeared, but he also didn't want to walk back to Freedom, which was even farther.

Annabeth turned. "What's wrong?"

Ethan stroked his thumb over the empty blue bottles in his pocket. He ducked his head as his eye began to twitch. "Nothing," he said, and joined her.

"We should find a place to stay for the night."

Ethan's heart jerked. He rubbed the empties again. If he rubbed them enough, would a genie grant his wish that they might suddenly become full?

Ethan snorted. Those were the kinds of fantasies he had after he'd drunk more laudanum than he had today.

"No," he said.

Annabeth cast him a confused, concerned glance and continued walking. "I don't think we'll make it to Freedom before dark." She pointed at the horizon. "Even if we manage to catch that horse."

As expected, the animal appeared farther away now than when they'd started out. Was it a mirage? The silhouette *had* started to waver. "I have to get back. Tonight."

"I suppose Cora will worry."

He stopped walking, rubbed his aching eyes, then scratched at the invisible ants crawling up his arm. "About Cora," he began.

The sun flickered, as if a great hand had waved before it—over and back, over and back. Sweat dripped to the end of Ethan's nose; his shivering caused it to fly right off.

"Ethan?" Annabeth's frowning face appeared in front of him an instant before the great hand closed around the sun, squeezing until his whole world went black.

CHAPTER 22

Ethan's eyes rolled back. Annabeth caught him in her arms.

They were nearly the same height, and he was so thin, he couldn't weigh much more than she did. However, dead weight was a helluva lot heavier than live weight. Her legs gave out. They landed atop the muddy grass in a tangle.

Someone was keening, "No, no, no," and it was her. Annabeth hunched over Ethan, protecting him from . . .

She wasn't sure. At first she thought he'd been shot again. But there'd been no report; there wasn't any blood. Had a lethal infection crept into his brain? What would she do? Out here, she had no way to help him.

A watery, slightly hysterical laugh erupted. She had no way to help a brain infection anywhere. No one did.

Annabeth lifted her head, let her gaze wander the horizon. The only living thing in any direction was the two of them and the horse. If anyone were out there shooting, they'd be dead. The sniper wouldn't need a quarter of Fedya's skill with a gun to put an end to them sitting in the middle of a great big nothing just waiting to die.

Annabeth laid Ethan on the ground. His breath came far too fast, too shallow, and he was pale, sweating, yet he shuddered as if a blue norther had followed the storm. Gently, she slapped his cheeks, received no response. Even if he woke, she doubted he'd be able to walk very far. She needed that horse.

She glanced again toward the horizon, hoping the

animal might have begun to wander in their direction. But luck had never been on her side.

Annabeth set her lips to Ethan's ear. "I'll be back as fast as I can." Her only response was another shudder that racked him from head to toe.

She left Ethan alone in the mud and the wet grass, the sun blazing on his damp face. It was one of the hardest things she'd ever done.

Annabeth was tempted to run. But in this heat, without water, she'd be exhausted before she got there. Besides, a fast approach might frighten the animal. She wished for a grove of trees, not just for the shade but for the cover. However, if wishes were horses, then—

"I wouldn't need that horse," Annabeth muttered, and fought another hysterical bubble of laughter.

The sun had moved past the apex before she came close enough to see that the horse wore a saddle—at least it wasn't wild—though she couldn't tell if it was the horse they'd rode in on.

Didn't matter. She just hoped the animal was past spooked and moving toward thirsty, hungry, lonely, or anything else that might make it stand still and not run away.

She approached slowly, murmuring nonsense. Perhaps her luck had changed, because it walked toward her with a lowered, docile head and allowed her to scratch between its ears, then swing into what appeared to be Ethan's saddle.

She couldn't believe their mount hadn't been whirled away with the wind. But twisters were strange. She'd seen them take a house and leave a barn, uproot this tree and leave that one untouched—no rhyme or reason to the destruction at all. Was there ever a rhyme or reason to destruction?

Her gaze went to where she'd left Ethan, and her heart thudded once before lodging at the base of her throat. He no longer lay on the grass. Instead he stumbled, nearly falling, before dragging himself up to zigzag some more.

Annabeth urged the exhausted horse into a gallop.

The animal shied as they approached, and Ethan veered into their path, then out again.

"Whoa," she said. The animal listened; Ethan did not. He muttered unintelligible words as he continued to make his awkward way toward Lord knew what.

Annabeth leaped to the ground, keeping a firm hand on the reins. Ethan swung toward her. His eyes were wild; he smelled the same. Sweat glistened on his face, his neck, and dampened his shirt.

"Find," he muttered. "Find!"

"Hush." She wasn't certain if she was talking to man or beast, or if Ethan, at this moment, was a little of both.

The horse snorted, spraying snot across Annabeth's shoulder. Ethan tilted his head like a dog that had heard a voice it just might recognize.

"You want to ride, Ethan?"

His head tilted the other way when she said his name. But he didn't answer, and her concern deepened.

"You're sick," she continued. "We need to get out of the sun."

"Find," he said, and stumbled on. Was he talking about Annabeth? Cora? The baby? Freedom?

Who knew? Did it matter?

"It'll be easier to search on the horse."

He didn't answer, didn't even glance her way. Annabeth tugged on his arm, but he yanked himself free and continued. She couldn't *make* him take the saddle. But if he fell, she doubted she could lift him into it either.

Annabeth chewed her lip and followed her husband across the prairie.

Ethan was hot; he was cold. Sweat ran down his back, even as he shivered and shook. His teeth chattered. But up ahead was something he had to find. He couldn't stop. He needed . . .

He wasn't quite sure.

His mouth was dry. His skin itched. His stomach rumbled, though not with hunger. He hoped he didn't disgrace himself. But who would know?

The woman who trailed behind him along with the

horse might look and sound like Annabeth; however, he knew a hallucination when he saw one. He'd been seeing them for a long time. He should climb on that horse and leave her behind. Although perhaps the animal was as much a delusion as the wife.

There'd be no getting rid of her. Not when he slept, not when he woke, not when he drank another bottle dry. She was there—always—unto the end of his life.

And that was all right. That was what he had craved all along. If he hadn't wanted to see his missing, possibly dead wife, he wouldn't have bothered with the cursed blue bottles. Not only did they take away the pain, but they brought back her.

"Ethan?"

He glanced over his shoulder, and the agony in his head faded a bit at the sight of her.

"Let's ride the horse," she said, as if he were an imbecile.

He was tired; he was hot; he was dizzy and nauseated. He was an imbecile. Why not ride the horse? Even if he rode only in his mind.

Ethan swung into the saddle. Before he could direct the animal forward, Annabeth climbed on behind. Her breasts pressed into his back; her thighs slid along his; her hair brushed his neck; her arms circled his waist. He waited for his body to respond as it always did to her touch, be she real or imagined. When it didn't, he began to suspect that he was sicker than he'd ever been before. Maybe this time, at last, he would die.

"Where are we go—?"

Ethan urged the horse into a gallop, and the rest of her words flew away with the wind. He ignored every question she asked after that. Even when they slowed to a brisk walk, making conversation a possibility, he did not speak. He didn't have the strength.

He skirted the gully that had saved their lives. Eventually, the crack in the earth widened to a stream, then a river.

"I'm thirsty," Annabeth said, her voice vibrating

against his back, causing the shivers he'd thought gone to return. "Aren't you?"

He clucked to the horse, which began to trot. The black dots that had been dancing across the bright blue sky increased in number until they nearly obscured his vision. He gritted his teeth; he would not allow them to collide. If that happened, he might not wake for days.

At last they rounded a bend, and Ethan reined in. Annabeth's fingers clenched on his hips. Memory shimmered—of another place, another time, another life.

"We should go," she whispered.

Instead, Ethan slid to the ground and strode inside the tepee.

Annabeth held her breath, waiting for Ethan to come back out. She only hoped he did so alone.

She had seen such structures before, though less and less in the past few years since the Kansa Indians had been relegated to the reservation at Council Grove. Before that, they had lived in villages of round, earthen lodges. The men used tepees for hunting—back when they'd been allowed to hunt.

Whenever she'd seen the tepees, Annabeth had given them a wide berth. Still, for hours afterward she would be nervous, twitchy, expecting the Indians to appear as if from the earth in front of her, or perhaps sneak up behind. Annabeth had the same feeling now. She even looked over her shoulder, but nothing was there.

As no Kansa brave had burst free of the lodge carrying her husband's head, or even his scalp, she breathed a little easier. Of course, they could have killed him and left him where he fell.

The horse had lowered its head and begun to drink from the river. Annabeth ground tied the animal and followed Ethan.

Approaching the tepee, she drew her gun. "Hello?"

When nothing answered but the wind, she drew back the flap. No outcry was raised, no weapon discharged. She peeked inside. The tepee appeared empty.

"Ethan!"

What did she expect? What did she fear? That he'd found a bottle that said, DRINK ME, shrunk like Alice, then slid down the rabbit hole into Wonderland?

Another hysterical burble of laughter escaped her dry, brittle lips. If she wasn't careful, she'd be chattering in the corner like a lunatic.

The tepee was shaded by the riverbank, and the air inside was cooler than she would have thought. She cast a glance at the rear of the enclosure, wondering if Ethan had slipped in this side and out the other, but the only openings in the conical structure were the one behind her and another high above to release smoke.

The mats and blankets on the ground began to move. Annabeth pointed her gun at the shivering, shaking mass. Ethan's dark head emerged.

She went to her knees, set aside the weapon. At first she thought he'd fainted again, until the violent movements, the rigid set of his neck and jaw brought a different diagnosis.

"Paroxysms." She hadn't seen those since the war. She hadn't liked them much then, either.

Quickly, she turned her husband on his side so he wouldn't choke. She made sure there was nothing anywhere near him on which he might hit his head. His head had been hit enough.

She considered running to the river and retrieving cool water to bathe his fiery skin, but until the paroxysms ceased, she could not leave his side. What if he stopped breathing? She'd seen it happen before. Often the result of a high fever, or a head injury, there was little to be done for the condition but treat the symptoms.

Cool water. Rest. If those didn't work . . . an early grave.

"No," Annabeth murmured. "Please, no."

Whom she was talking to, she wasn't sure. God hadn't listened to her in . . .

"Forever." Then again, she hadn't spoken to him in nearly that long.

Ethan's violent movements slowed, although his legs

continued to twitch as if he were running. He was drenched in sweat. She removed his clothes so he wouldn't be chilled when night fell. After tossing the soaked clothing outside, she settled him on the woven mats. He still shuddered, but the movements became more natural, the result of cooler air brushing his damp skin.

Annabeth stroked his brow. "Hush your cries," she whispered. "Close your eyes." Her mother had sung those words whenever Annabeth was ill. There was more, but she couldn't remember it. "Something about ponies."

He quieted, pulling in on himself. Curling his legs toward his chest, his chest toward his knees, cradling his belly as if it hurt. The position was the one she'd taken the night their child died—first protecting what lived within and later mourning what lived there no longer.

Annabeth's eyes burned; she got to her feet. Snatching an earthen bowl that hung from the center pole, she stepped into the blazing Kansas sun.

Except the sun wasn't blazing, at least not on her. Instead, the glare was blocked by the shadows of four men.

CHAPTER 23

Annabeth stumbled back, reaching for her gun, but it was gone. She'd dropped the Colt to help Ethan and then forgotten it completely.

The Indians stared at her with no expression in their dark, endless eyes. One had hair standing straight up along the center of his head, while the rest of his scalp had been shaved. The other three bore only a single long lock that fell past their shoulders. Every one of them had been tattooed.

They made no move to touch her. Their weapons—bows, arrows, a rifle or two that resembled those carried by the army—remained slung over their bare shoulders. One of them held the reins of Ethan's horse.

"That's mine." She pointed to the animal.

No one moved; no one spoke. Hell, no one blinked. They seemed to be staring at her hair. Even chopped at the shoulders, no longer hanging to her waist, it was hard to miss.

Annabeth stepped toward the horse, and the largest Indian—still not as tall as her, but taller than any other she'd ever seen—shifted. Just a tilt of his hips, his shoulders, and he blocked her way.

"That's mine," he repeated, but he pointed to the tepee.

"Oh. Yes. I apologize, but we . . . he . . . Ethan, he's—"

"E-tan?" The tall man, the only one who'd spoken thus far, strode toward her so fast, she stepped out of the way lest she be plowed over. He stuck his head into the opening and then pulled it back out. "*Nika*," he said.

Annabeth stared at him blankly and spread her hands.

"E-tan." His thick, dark arm shot into the tepee. "Doc."

"Yes. He's a doctor."

"*Ni.*" He pointed to the river with his other arm, then to his head. "*Wexli.*"

From that she assumed he wanted her to put water on Ethan's head. What *nika* meant, she had no idea.

Nodding, she sidled toward the river. The three braves who'd barred her path separated. They continued to stare at her hair; she thought one even reached out as she passed and touched it, murmuring something that sounded like *zhu'je,* but when she turned, their hands remained at their sides, their lips compressed into identical flat lines.

Annabeth hurried to the water's edge, dunked the bowl beneath the surface, and hurried back. Only three people and five horses remained outside the tepee. Terrified at what the Kansa leader might do—even though he had appeared to know "E-tan," it didn't mean he liked him—she rushed inside.

The man sat on the ground next to her husband, blowing sweet-smelling smoke from his pipe into Ethan's face. Ethan remained unconscious, but he seemed less ill. He'd straightened from his curled-in, defensive position and lay on his back, his breathing almost normal.

She caught the glint of her gun half buried beneath a woven mat and dropped down in easy reach of both Ethan and the weapon. She didn't think the Kansa were going to turn violent, but one never could tell.

"*Wak'o.*" The Indian pointed at Annabeth. "*Ni.*" The bowl. "*Wexli.*" He tapped Ethan's head.

Annabeth tore off the least muddy, sweaty portion of her shirttail, dipped it into the water, and bathed Ethan's face. She didn't care for the puckered look of his stitches. If she didn't cut them free soon, Ethan's body would begin to reject the foreign matter with an infection.

She wished for some alcohol to clean them. While she was at it, she wished for scissors and Freedom, a world where her child wasn't dead and Ethan didn't blame himself for it. She also wished she'd never seen Lassiter Morant or Moses Farquhar, for that matter.

"If wishes were horses," she murmured.

Then it wouldn't matter that the Kansa had taken theirs.

Ethan swam toward the surface. The water was thick and dark and hot, like nothing he'd ever experienced.

His thirst, the aches were familiar. But his pulse raced, fast enough to concern him, and his belly cramped, hard enough to embarrass him.

He came awake retching. A bowl beneath his mouth caught the tiny amount of liquid that spouted free. His bowels loosened, but there was little left to lose. He couldn't recall the last time he'd eaten, or when he'd drunk anything but—

His hand went to his pocket, except he had no pocket. His clothes were gone.

"Better?" Annabeth asked.

He opened his eyes; however, the face that filled his vision was not his wife's but—"Joe?"

The Indian's lips twitched, his version of a smile.

A curse drew Ethan's attention to Annabeth as she placed her palm on his forehead. *Her* lips frowned. "What year is it?" she asked.

"I'm not out of my head." Though he wished that he was. If he was delirious, he wouldn't be so mortified.

"You called him Joe."

Joe grunted at the mention of his name and muttered, *"Wak'o,"* with the manner of every man who'd been exasperated with a *woman* in his life.

"I think his name is *Wak'o,*" she said.

"Wak'o means woman."

Annabeth's frown deepened. "Then I don't much care for his tone."

Ethan laughed, but the movement jarred his belly and bowels, so he stopped. "His name is long and unpronounceable, except for *Wasabe,* which means bear. I assume he's called Big Man Who Kills Bears, or Black Bear, Brown Bear, Crazy Bear Who Kills Anything. I just call him Joe. Saves time, and he doesn't seem to mind."

"How can you tell?" Annabeth asked, eyeing the Indian, who couldn't stop eyeing her hair.

"He hasn't scalped me yet."

"He seems more interested in scalping me."

"Hair like yours is unusual in his world."

"In any world unless you're a Phelan," she said.

Ethan had never seen anyone with hair quite like it, and no doubt Joe felt the same. Ethan couldn't resist teasing her. "I'm sure a scalp in Phelan red would be an incredible prize."

Instead of inching closer for protection, her hand crept beneath the mat she knelt upon. Ethan caught the flash of a gun barrel.

"No," he snapped, and she froze. "He wouldn't hurt you even if he weren't my friend. The Kaw, which means People of the South Wind, is what the Kansa call themselves, and they're peaceful. Most of them are on the reservation."

"And that isn't anywhere close." She kept her hand on the gun and her gaze on Joe.

"Every so often, Joe and his friends go off to hunt."

"The army must love that."

"Which is why Joe comes here. This isn't—*wasn't*—their territory. It belonged to the Wichita."

At least as much as land could "belong" to an Indian. They believed the earth belonged to everyone—a conviction the white man had made good use of.

"The Wichita have been confined in Indian Territory since the war," she said.

"How do you know so much about Indians?" Had Moze told her? Perhaps Lassiter Morant? Or some other man she'd spied on and lied to in the past five years?

"When riding about, it's best to know who you might encounter and how friendly they're apt to be. I've seen Kans—" She paused. "I mean Kaw tepees before but not Wichita."

Joe growled at the final word.

"I don't think he cares for them," Annabeth said.

"His people usually fought with the Cheyenne," Ethan began.

Joe snarled. Ethan ignored him. The Cheyenne had been sent to a reservation in Indian Territory, but they hadn't stayed on it any better than Joe stayed on his.

"The Kaw also skirmished with any other band that got in their way," he said.

"Like the Wichita."

Ethan nodded, then wished that he hadn't when the sudden pain in his head made his stomach roil. He breathed in and out as he had a stern talk with his belly. If there'd been anything in it, he might have lost the argument, but for now he managed not to dissolve into another pathetic bout of retching. Though he couldn't say how long that would last.

"With the Wichita on the reservation," he continued, "and actually staying on it, unlike most other bands, their territory is open."

"And their territory was here."

"When Joe and his friends leave the reservation, the army looks for them in Kaw territory." The army wasn't exactly known for its ingenuity. To be fair, they weren't expected to be.

"How do you know all this?" she asked.

"Joe told me."

"You speak Kaw?"

"Enough."

"Enough for what? You've obviously been here before. You know each other. How? Why?"

"I treated one of his men."

"You just happened across a band of Indians as you were strolling across the prairie?"

"Something like that."

He wasn't going to tell his wife the whole story. Which involved his getting on a horse half conscious, planning to . . . he couldn't quite remember what. Die, most likely—back then that had always been his plan. He'd just never been very good at it.

He'd fallen off his horse. Only his sorry state had

kept him from breaking his neck. As his father always said: God watched over fools and lunatics. Most days Ethan was both.

Joe had found him, brought him to this tepee. Joe and his men had sat around the fire staring at Ethan; Ethan had stared back. He'd figured they would kill him eventually, and since he'd been trying to die anyway, he didn't care.

"One of the braves had a cut on his hand that had putrefied," he said. "I drained, cleaned, and stitched it. After that, I returned every month around the full moon."

"Why?"

"Because a few weeks later, Joe walked into Freedom. The only reason he left alive was that he was holding a feverish Kaw child. From then on, we met here."

"Androcles," his wife murmured.

Joe snorted. Both Ethan and Annabeth glanced at the Indian as if a dog had sat up and spoken.

"Do you think he—?" Annabeth began.

"No," Ethan said, but he wondered. Sometimes he thought Joe understood a lot more English than Ethan understood Kaw.

"Do you know the fable?" she asked.

"I do."

"My mother used to tell us stories at night." Her face went soft at the memory. "Sometimes it was the only way to get so many of us to sleep."

Ethan had not had a mother to read to him. Instead he'd read to Mikey. *Aesop's Fables* had been one of his brother's favorites.

"Joe followed you like the lion in the story," Annabeth continued.

There *were* times Ethan felt like a slave. And other times he wished to be devoured by wild animals.

"Joe isn't tame."

"Most lions aren't, even when they pretend to be."

Ethan wasn't sure whom they were talking about anymore. He didn't think it was Joe.

"Why the full moon?"

"It's a time he understands." Days, weeks, months, hours meant nothing to the Kaw.

"If he meets you every full moon, then why is here now?"

"Just because he meets me under the full moon doesn't mean he doesn't come here at other times. It's *his* tepee."

"There's no doctor at the reservation?" she asked.

"Joe prefers me."

"Mmm," Annabeth murmured, gaze on the half-naked man. "Just don't stick your head between his jaws."

"I don't plan to."

"I don't trust him."

"I don't care." Ethan liked Joe. The man was quiet and still—the perfect companion. They'd shared many friendly fires. Joe smoking, Ethan sipping.

"Could I have some water?" Ethan asked.

"Can you keep it down?"

"Doubtful."

"Then no."

"I might get paroxysms."

"You already did."

Ethan frowned. He was a lot worse off than he'd thought. "We should get back to Freedom."

"After you rest."

"No." He struggled upright. "I have to go."

She pushed him down. Ethan was so weak, she didn't even need Joe's help, though he gave it. "Deliriums," she muttered.

"I am not delirious." But he would be.

"It's nearly night." Annabeth stood and went through the opening in the tepee. Her words drifted back. "We'll see how you feel in the morning."

When darkness descended, the Kaw built two fires— one in front of the tepee and one within. They hunkered around the flames of outdoor fire and cooked a few rabbits.

Except during the time he retrieved a bit of meat for himself and Annabeth, Joe remained nearby. He pointed a greasy finger at a fitfully sleeping Ethan, lifted the meat, and shook his head.

"No food for him," Annabeth agreed.

Concerned with how sunken Ethan's eyes appeared, she'd relented and had given him the requested water. He'd thrown up almost immediately, and her concern had deepened to fear. A man could live a long time without food. Water was another matter.

She bathed his face, his neck, and his chest, his entire body. Perhaps some of the liquid would seep through his skin. She knew better—even if it did, he was emitting more through sweat and vomit than she could ever rub in. Still she kept trying. She had no idea what was wrong with him, and therefore no idea what to do. But she had to do something. If he died . . .

Her mind faltered; her heart stuttered; her hands began to shake. A world without Ethan Walsh was not a world she could even bear thinking about.

Joe continued to sit and smoke and stare. She wanted to ask what it was that he smoked and if it would help Ethan. But even if he understood her question, she would not understand his answer.

In the darkest part of the night, Ethan spasmed and jerked. His harsh, rasping breaths frightened her. Until they stopped. Then terror paralyzed her.

"Iha!" Joe pointed to his lips, to hers, to Ethan's. When Annabeth didn't respond, he banged his fist against Ethan's chest—once, twice, again.

"Stop." Annabeth reached for his hand. Joe pulled it back and pointed once more to his mouth. *"Iha,"* he said, then blew out. When she continued to stare, he leaned over as if he might kiss Ethan, and suddenly she understood. If Ethan could not breathe, then she would breathe for him.

She placed her lips on her husband's and blew. The air rustled her hair as it came through his nose. Two long, dark fingers pinched Ethan's nostrils shut. Annabeth tried again. This time Ethan's chest lifted and then lowered. She did this several times. She had no idea if it would work, but she felt less hysterical doing something.

Joe smacked Ethan in the chest again, and this time Ethan gasped and then began to breathe on his own. Annabeth laid her cheek against her husband's. His was damp. Or maybe hers was.

As she lay there breathing in the scent of him—not the most pleasant right now, but still *him*—she understood that she would always love Ethan Walsh. No matter what he'd done, no matter what she had. Even if he'd died, she would have loved him every second until she did. She would still leave—he deserved the life he'd always wanted, and he could have that with Cora—but for her there would never be anyone else in the way that there was Ethan.

"Beth?"

She peered into his pale, damp face. "I don't know what to do. I don't know what's wrong." Something flickered in his eyes. "Do you?"

He glanced in Joe's direction and stiffened, so she turned her head, too, expecting to see the Kaw with a knife. Instead the man stood, hands empty but clenched, his gaze captured by Ethan's. For one so stoic, his expression now reflected uncertainty. He was torn, though about what, Annabeth had no idea.

"Don't," Ethan said.

While Joe had been out retrieving rabbit, Annabeth had retrieved her gun from beneath the mat, and replaced it in her holster. She set her hand on the grip. The two men continued to stare at each other until Joe sighed and headed for the door. Annabeth's fingers almost slid free. Joe was leaving; that was all. Ethan didn't want him to, but she wouldn't mind.

The Kaw brushed back the tent flap, reaching outside and returning with Ethan's trousers in one hand. She'd meant to take his clothes to the river and wash them, but she hadn't had time. She doubted Joe was going to.

"Joe." Ethan's voice was urgent. Why was he so worried about his muddy, sweaty pants?

Annabeth turned her gaze from the Kaw to her husband. Ethan was not only worried but afraid.

She drew her gun just as Joe drew his hand from

Ethan's pocket. The sound of the weapon being cocked sliced through the silence.

"No," Ethan murmured, though whether he was talking to her or Joe, she couldn't say.

The Indian extended his arm, a blue bottle balanced upon his palm. Annabeth accepted the container. As it had no cork, she deduced it was empty. She turned it upside down. Not a single drop fell out.

Confused, she lifted her eyes. Joe handed her a second bottle.

That one didn't have a cork either.

CHAPTER 24

The truth dawned on his wife's face as she stared at the empty bottles.

"Your pupils," she murmured. "Sometimes they're small, other times huge. But not when they should be. I thought I was crazy." Her laugh sounded that way. "You kept scratching." She shrugged. "Could have been anything."

"Beth," he began, though what could he say? He didn't think she wanted to hear that when he had "enough" laudanum, his pupils became too small, and when he didn't, they grew.

"You're too thin, but so am I. Pale. I thought you worked too much. Depressed." She spread her hands, still holding the empty blue bottles. "Who isn't? How could I have been so stupid?" Now Ethan laughed, and she glared. "What could possibly be funny?"

"I have an unquenchable thirst for laudanum, yet you're the one who's stupid?"

"How long?" she asked.

"Long?" he repeated. She lifted a bottle, tilted her head. "Oh." Ethan considered. His mind was fuzzy, had been for about . . . "A year?" Definitely hadn't been two.

"Why?"

"I don't—"

"You do." She threw a bottle at the wall. Unfortunately, or perhaps fortunately, the wall was made of skin, and it only bounced off and landed harmlessly on the jumble of mats and blankets.

Ethan cast a quick glance at Joe, but he was gone. Smart man. He returned his gaze to his wife. Her hair seemed to crackle like fire, standing up here and there around her head. Her eyes had gone dark, her face white. She both broke his heart and made it whole. He'd lost, then found her. Now he was about to lose her all over again.

"Why laudanum?" he asked. "Or why then?"

"Yes."

He shrugged. Both questions had the same answer. "Alcohol wasn't enough." When her frown deepened, he elaborated. "To make me forget."

She lifted her hand, examining the bottle with sudden interest. "This made you forget?"

"Yes." At least until it wore off. He tried not to let it.

Annabeth tilted the bottle to her lips, sucked on the opening, ran her tongue around the edge. If Ethan hadn't been half dead, those actions might have brought him to life. As it was, they worried him.

She threw the second bottle at the wall. This one, too, fell harmlessly to the ground. "You drank every drop and left none for me?"

Memory flickered. Dr. Brookstone had adored Shakespeare. He'd quoted the bard often.

"Drunk all," Ethan murmured, "and left no friendly drop to help me after."

A chill trailed over him despite the excessive heat from the fire in so small a space. *Romeo and Juliet.* Doomed if anyone ever had been.

"Where did you get it?" Annabeth demanded, ignoring his soliloquy.

"Shakespeare."

Her eyes narrowed. "The laudanum."

"I made it." He made all his medicines. He certainly didn't buy them from a traveling show. Lord knew what those people put in their bottles.

When she continued to scowl, Ethan elaborated. "Poppies. Dried and crushed. Boiled with alcohol. Some sugar and water."

"Where did you learn that?" She jerked her thumb at the tepee flap. "Them?"

"The Kaw?" he repeated, incredulous.

"They know more than you think. When you stopped breathing, Joe showed me how to bring you back."

There was no way that Ethan knew of to bring someone back if they weren't breathing. "What are you talking about?"

She let out an impatient huff and explained tersely what had been done.

"Fascinating," he murmured. "I'd heard of something similar in France, but how would—"

"Not now," she snapped.

He nodded, regretted it instantly as pain exploded in his head, but he soldiered on. He certainly couldn't ask for any laudanum.

Where had he been? Ah, yes. How he'd learned to turn poppies into peace. "Dr. Brookstone taught me how to make laudanum."

"The physician you apprenticed with."

He'd told her about the man shortly after they'd met, one of the few times, back then, he'd ever divulged the truth. "He was an apothecary, as well as a physician."

"Men were dying in agony at Chimborazo. Dying *from* agony." Her eyes darkened with the memory. Ethan could have sworn he heard the screams, and he wasn't even asleep. "If you knew how to make laudanum, why didn't you?"

"You think I purposely withheld the knowledge so that Confederates would suffer? You know me better than that."

"Do I?" She bent and picked up one of the empty bottles.

Anger flared. "There weren't any poppies." Her gaze lifted. "Hell, Beth, there was barely any corn, or wheat, or cows. If I'd had poppies, I'd have made laudanum."

"Now you do, so you did."

He didn't answer what hadn't been a question.

Silence descended, broken only by the crackle of the flames. He hadn't wanted her to know. He hadn't wanted anyone to know. But, lately, he couldn't seem to keep secrets like he used to.

"What on earth possessed you, Ethan?"

"Despair," he said simply, and she released a sigh so full of the same, his chest ached.

She turned the bottle in her hand, and the firelight played across the glass. "You feel like you're drowning," she said. "You can't breathe. It hurts."

"What?" he whispered.

"Everything."

"Yes." Sometimes he swore his blood hurt, his skin, his hair. Not to mention what was left of his soul.

"You want to die." She paused, swallowed, closed her eyes, and her fingers clenched on the bottle. "Like he did."

She had put his feelings into words. His pain was her pain. She understood. She was the only one who ever could.

If they'd talked like this then, shared more of themselves than their bodies, maybe everything would have been all right.

Ethan sighed. Nothing was right—not now, not then. He wasn't sure it ever could be.

"Alcohol wasn't enough," she murmured.

"You don't drink."

"I didn't," she corrected. "I couldn't afford to. What if I let something slip?" She lifted the bottle to the light, turned it this way and that. "Drink me," she whispered.

Ethan's mouth watered. Would he ever stop craving oblivion?

"I'd have done anything to forget." Annabeth continued to stare at the bottle, as if all the answers lay within. If it hadn't been empty, they might. He'd certainly found answers there, or at least an end to the infernal questions.

"There were times I rode until I could barely stay on the horse," she murmured. "It was the only way I could sleep."

Until Ethan had tried laudanum, he would work, read, help everyone in town, even lend a hand on the outlying ranches for the same reason.

"Whiskey until I passed out," she continued. "But it gave me . . ."

"Nightmares," he finished, and she at last stopped looking at the bottle and looked at him.

"Yes. Worse than anything that had truly happened."

He wasn't certain that was possible.

She glanced away, swallowed as if she might vomit, then stood and left. Naked beneath the blankets, he was so light-headed, he didn't think he could stand. He definitely couldn't run after her.

He didn't blame her for going. Not now. Hell, not even then. Still, he thought he might cry when he heard her speak to the Kaw, followed by thuds, rustles, grumbles, and finally, the thunder of hoofbeats fading to a silence so deep, it was unearthly. He'd never felt so weak, so useless, so discarded, disgraced, or deserted.

The tent flap lifted.

"You didn't leave."

Her brow wrinkled as she placed a bowl of fresh water at his side. "Where would I go?"

"After what you've seen, heard, learned?" He blew out a long, disgusted breath. "Anywhere but here."

"What have I seen or heard or learned that's worse than what I've seen and heard and learned before?"

"Your husband enjoys a nice bottle of laudanum."

"That is new," she agreed, and pulled a large, lethal blade from her pocket.

"You don't need to kill me over it."

"I'm going to take out your stitches before they grow into your brain."

"With that?" The blade sparkled in the firelight.

"Yes." The tip lowered toward his head.

Ethan tried to pull back, but he was already flat on the ground. "Disinfected?" he asked.

"Used Joe's whiskey."

"Where the hell did he get whiskey?" The army frowned on the Indians having alcohol. "He could get into trouble."

"He doesn't have it anymore."

Joe was a good man, but he was not what Ethan would call a charitable fellow. "What did you give him for it?"

"Your horse." She flicked her wrist. A stitch popped. Didn't hurt, but he didn't much like it, either.

"How will we get back?"

Flick. Pop.

She shrugged.

Flick. Pop. Flick. Pop.

"Wait." He shifted his head to the side, lifted a trembling hand to stop her. He couldn't think when she was doing that.

Her mouth twisted; her fingers tightened on the knife, which she continued to hold poised over his face. "We aren't going anywhere until you're better."

Flick. Pop.

"I'm not sure I'll ever be . . . better." The word came off his tongue as if it were foreign. "I'm weak."

Her eyes found his. Already dark blue, in the firelight they shone like night. "If I'd had a way to make the pain stop, to forget . . ." She paused, but Ethan heard her thoughts as clearly as if she'd spoken them.

Forget him. Forget you. Forget us.

"I would have."

"I don't—" he began.

"The lies, the pain, the things we saw."

She laid down the knife, soaked a bit of cloth in the water, then pressed it to his forehead. From the sting, there was more than water in the bowl.

"The things I did," she whispered.

"What did you do?"

Annabeth shoved the cloth into the bowl, became inordinately fascinated with rinsing it out. "Things I never want anyone to know."

"Me too." He set his hand on her knee, waited until her gaze returned to his. "But you do."

"This?" She reached into her pocket and withdrew an empty blue bottle. "Oh, Ethan." Her eyes left his, and the expression that cast over her face was infinitely sad. "This is nothing."

The night passed—slowly, as nights often did.

Though Ethan slept, his eyelids twitched. His hands

moved restlessly; his legs jerked. Annabeth tugged the blanket over his ankles. He would only kick it off again, but she needed something to do.

Just like a broken heart, the only treatment for laudanum dependency was time. Would the cure actually work in his case?

Annabeth bathed Ethan with cool, fresh water. He thrashed and muttered and called her name. If she hadn't understood why Cora hated her before, she certainly could now. If Ethan had spoken the other woman's name, she wasn't sure what she might have done.

As it was, she whispered, "I'm here," and "It's all right," even though she wouldn't remain and it wasn't all right. She had to swallow the tickle of tears at the lies, but they were what she did best, so she used them.

In the darkest hour that preceded dawn, Ethan stiffened and jerked; his eyes rolled back as his jaw and neck tightened. Fearful that he might again have paroxysms, Annabeth slapped his cheeks and shouted, "Ethan!"

"Beth," he answered, but he didn't seem to know she was there. "Thunder," he said.

She listened, heard nothing, not even the rain.

"Mikey." She stilled. "Need . . . you. Need you, Beth. Hold me."

She shivered as if a cool storm wind had blown across the prairie, across her. He was delirious or dreaming, perhaps both. When he reached for her, his eyes still closed, she wanted to skitter back, but she was frozen—the past and present shimmering together, coming apart. Like them.

His fingers circled her wrist. He was so damn cold, he made her shudder. Her other hand landed on top of his. Could her warmth seep into him? Heal him? Comfort him?

Comfort her?

She removed her clothes—heat was best imparted skin to skin—then gathered him close and pulled the blanket over them both. But he was still so damn cold. She tightened her arms and held on.

He muttered and moaned; she could only understand

a word here and there. But she didn't need many to piece together what he dreamed. She'd been there, too.

That night they had made their son.

In the dark, with only the shadow of the moon visible through the smoke hole above, Annabeth listened to Ethan ramble. But eventually, he warmed and then quieted.

Together, they slept, and she dreamed of a past she had tried to forget and a future that had never been. She awoke when he kissed her. Like the girl in the fairy tale—which one was it?

All of them, or at least the ones her mother had shared. Mama had recounted fables—"Androcles and the Lion," "The Goose with the Golden Egg," "The Wolf in Sheep's Clothing"—to all of the Phelan children. But the boys had not been interested in any tales of girls, so Mama had shared those with her daughter alone. In every one, the princess, the pauper, the girl in rags who swept the fireplace would fall asleep, or worse, then be awoken by the kiss of her one true love. In the stories, true love solved everything. In life, the same could not be said.

As Ethan's mouth took Annabeth's, the past, the present, the dreams merged. When he slipped inside of her, she had a moment to wonder. Was she still dreaming? Was Ethan even here? Was she?

Though she was tempted to open her eyes, to make certain the tepee still ranged above them, instead she squeezed them shut. What if she saw the stars, a campfire, herself alone? Or worse, what if she saw a cave, a cabin, a rock face behind the outline of a man who was not him?

But she tasted Ethan, smelled him, too. Her palms stroked a back as familiar as her own. The body above and within her was the first one she'd ever known. The only one she wanted to know.

Maybe she was dreaming. If so, she never wanted to wake up, and therefore she opened her mouth, welcomed him in, just as she wrapped her legs around his and held on.

He moved slowly. No rush as there'd been that first time. Even then, he'd been gentle and sweet. After the initial pain—not much, not really, as pain went—the world had narrowed to the place where they'd become one.

As it did now. In. Out. Deep. Shallow. Slide. Retreat. Never, never end. Because when it did, she would have to remember. And remembering always, *always* hurt.

Tears seeped from her eyes, dampened her hair. Not from pain or sadness, but from the beauty of what they shared—a pure and eternal rightness she had once believed in with all of her heart. She had been such a fool. Nothing was pure or right. Least of all her. Not then. Not now. Not ever.

But she would worry about purity and rightness, truth, lies, reality, dreams later. Now she gave herself over to the wonder of Ethan. His kiss, his touch, his body within and above her—both familiar and new. Her husband. The man she'd loved, lost, and found again. The man she would love and leave once more.

She clenched around him, pulled him close, surrounded him as he surrounded her. He kissed her freckles the way he always used to, sipped her tears, nuzzled her neck, then her breast. Her fingers stroked his back, his buttocks, his arms, tracing the bones, the muscles—relearning, remembering. His hair so soft, his chest so hard, everything about him fascinated her.

He stilled, and she at last opened her eyes. Did the wonder in his mirror the wonder in hers? She felt as if they were in a room made of glass, reflecting the past into the present. Joining them forever, even as they shattered apart.

Later, when they lay side by side, legs tangled, fingers too, she stared at the conical twist of the hides into the tepee above them as she realized what she hadn't before.

She never had been anyone else's. Not the way that she'd been his.

CHAPTER 25

Time passed in the manner that time often did. Slow when she wanted it to be fast.

Ethan trembled, delirious. He spewed out whatever he took in. He spoke of Mikey, of Michael, of Fedya. The war. His patients. The dying. The dead. His eyes rolled back, and he jerked, choked, breathed too fast, then didn't breathe at all. She smacked him in the chest, demanded that he awaken, then kissed him like the prince kissed the princess, breathed her own life into him and, at last, he gasped.

And time moved fast when she wanted it to move slow.

The days connecting their isolation, their place out of time on the prairie—away from Freedom, from Moze, from Lassiter and Cora and everyone who would keep them apart—to the night of the full moon when Joe would return sped along as if the entire world rolled downhill. She'd been away from the Lassiter Gang longer than she'd promised. Had anyone come looking for her in Freedom during their absence? If they had, what would they do to find her gone?

After the first day, Ethan managed water. On the second he took the broth she made from the rabbits Joe left behind.

God bless Joe.

On the third he managed, with help, to walk to the creek so he could wash. He fell in. Annabeth dragged him out. They made love on the muddy riverbank in the sun, then washed each other as the steadily rounding moon rose in the sky.

Every day Ethan became stronger; every night Annabeth fought tears. She was living the life they would have had, could have had, the life she'd wanted.

Minus the tepee.

When he was better, he wouldn't need her anymore. When they returned to Freedom, she would leave. He would marry Cora and have the life he wanted. It was the least she could do.

For now, she enjoyed their idyll. She cooked; Ethan kept the fire burning. He even fished a bit. He wasn't very good at it.

"You have other strengths," she said when he returned carrying only the pole she had fashioned from a soft sapling branch.

"I am very good at taking laudanum," he muttered.

"Not anymore."

Something flickered in his eyes, and she set down the potato she'd been cutting into a pot with the last of the rabbit. She'd found all sorts of things stored inside the tepee. The place didn't seem temporary to her. She supposed the Kaw couldn't carry a hunting lodge around when they weren't allowed to hunt. Which meant they had to leave the structure behind, along with all they kept inside.

"You miss it," she said.

He flicked a glance at her, then crouched on the other side of the fire. "Not yet."

"You think you will?"

"I know I will."

Disappointment fluttered. She'd wanted to heal him. But she didn't think she had.

"Don't look at me like that," he said.

"Like what?"

"As if I've broken your heart."

Annabeth tightened her lips to keep the truth from coming out. He had broken her heart. But it was only fair since she'd broken his.

She picked up the potato again. "We aren't going back until you're better."

"I don't know if I'll ever be better, Beth."

"You're getting better already. You don't shake or sweat. Your eyes . . ." She paused.

His pupils were no longer large when they should be small and vice versa, but his eyes weren't the eyes of the man she'd fallen in love with. They were the eyes of the man he had become. Dark even though their shade was light. Sad even when he smiled. Old even though he wasn't. Did she appear the same?

"What happened, happened," he said. "I'll always remember and mourn. I'll try not to use laudanum to forget, but I can't promise that I won't. All I can promise is that I'll try."

Once he had his child in his arms, she thought trying would be a whole lot easier.

"Joe will be back tonight."

"Tonight?" he repeated.

"You said he meets you here every full moon. Which is tonight, remember?" His frown said he did not. Time was strange out here. "He'll bring the horse."

"Didn't you trade the horse for the whiskey?"

"More of a rental. Until the full moon."

Understanding dawned across his face. "You had Joe take the horse away so I wouldn't bolt."

"You weren't yourself."

"I'm not sure who that is anymore."

"You're the same man you always were."

"Spy, murderer, liar, and thief."

Is that what he thought? Why shouldn't he? It was what she had.

"We've both done things we regret. In a lifetime, everyone does."

"Do you?"

"Of course." Right now she was having a hard time remembering something she didn't.

Unless it was him.

"I guess neither one of us can throw stones," he said.

If he knew what she'd done, he might.

"Do you regret this?" he asked.

"I could never regret helping you heal."

"Is that what you were doing?"

She'd thought so. Now she wondered. Had she been trying to heal him? Or herself?

Annabeth tore her gaze from Ethan's, set it on the western horizon, which was starting to blaze pink and orange and red. Tomorrow they could return to Freedom unless—

"You said you weren't healed. We could stay until you are."

"Forever?" he asked.

The joy that burst within her at the thought caused a flush to rise. She ducked her head. They couldn't stay forever, no matter how much she might want to. He had a new life waiting in Freedom; her old life awaited her elsewhere. She still hadn't found her brother; she still hadn't made sure Lassiter Morant paid for his crimes. Perhaps, if it hadn't been for Cora and the baby, she might have—

No. Even if she stopped searching for Luke, and she wasn't certain she could, she'd never allow Lass to roam free. The brief time she'd spent away from him, living among decent people, had only emphasized how indecent he was. She knew what Lass was capable of. While her job with Pinkerton had begun as nothing more than a job—something to fill the time, pay for food, enable her to look for Luke, keep her sane—it had become so much more. She'd done a lot of good, and in doing so had not only helped others but also herself. At her lowest point, the job had saved her, and she couldn't turn her back on it now. She had to return and finish what she had started. She couldn't live with herself otherwise.

"Not forever," she said. "Just until you're more . . ."

"What?" he snapped when she didn't finish.

She glanced up, then quickly back down. She'd been going to say "more yourself." But in light of their conversation, she understood how foolish the words would be. Neither one of them were the people they'd been. They never would be again.

"I have to return," Ethan said, though he didn't

sound happy about it. "Folks depend on me. What if someone's sick? What if someone died?"

"You were sick. You almost died."

Annabeth didn't want to go back. She didn't want to go forward either. But she couldn't stay here; nor should she go back there.

"Maybe Joe will have an extra horse for me."

Ethan's forehead creased. "We rode here on one. Why do we need another?"

"It'll only complicate things if I return to Freedom." His forehead creased. "I can't stay, Ethan, so why go?"

"You're my wife."

Not for long, she thought, then had to breathe through the pain. She would never love anyone the way that she loved him. She didn't want to.

"You're going to be a father."

"No," he said. "I'm not."

Had the fever and the paroxysms caused him to forget again? She'd seen no indication of it before now.

"You remember Cora Lewis?"

"Of course." A flush crept up his face, proving he remembered everything.

"Which means I have to leave." He didn't really think she could stay and watch another woman bear his child? The very idea made her ill.

Ethan straightened, then stepped around the fire and sat at her side. "Cora's a bigger liar than I am."

She dropped the last chunk of potato into the pot. Water rose up and over the rim, causing the flames to hiss and jump. "I don't—"

He took her hands, rubbed his thumbs over hers until she met his gaze. "She isn't carrying my child."

"How can you say that?" She tried to pull away, but he wouldn't let her.

"It's the truth." He tightened his fingers until she stopped squirming. "I wasn't going to say anything until I spoke with her. She's a patient as well as . . ." His lips tightened . "I thought I owed her the chance to explain. But now . . ." He shook his head. "You deserve to know what I found when I examined her."

"When did you examine her?" She'd told the woman not to go near him—several times. Not that Cora had listened.

"I . . ." Ethan paused, frowning. "You'd gone to help the Tarkentons."

"I left instructions that no one was to talk to you. Especially her."

"You can't expect the Cantrells to be very good guards."

"Or anyone else, apparently." She'd been living with outlaws for the past several months. If someone was a bad guard, everyone got dead.

"She wanted me to examine her," he said.

"I bet she did," Annabeth muttered.

The idea of Ethan's hands on the woman, even as a doctor, made Annabeth want to commit murder. Though he'd obviously had more than his hands on her in the past.

"What did you find?"

"Nothing." He released her to scrape his fingers through his hair. A cowlick stood up on the side, making Annabeth's own fingers itch to smooth it down. Would their child have had the same cowlick? They would never know.

He dropped his hands into his lap, where he began to wring them as he pursed his mouth, and memory shimmered as elusive as the moon.

His lips on her stomach. His murmurs to their child. His breath, so warm, brushing her skin. His fingers pressing—right, left, high, low. Both back then and—

"You wondered when I truly remembered?" he asked. "When I touched you and realized the child was gone, that you were . . ." He swallowed.

"Empty," she said. And, apparently, so was Cora Lewis. That now-familiar urge toward murder returned.

"From the first, a woman changes." Ethan continued to stare at his hands. "She hadn't."

"What did she say when you told her there was no child."

"I didn't."

"Why the hell not?"

"I didn't remember her. I wasn't sure what to do."

"All right," she allowed. "But you'll have to."

His fingers clenched—frustration and fury—and when he lifted his eyes, she pitied Cora Lewis.

"I know."

"I still can't go back."

"What?" Confusion replaced the fury. "Why?"

"No one leaves the Morant Gang. At least not alive."

"Let Moze deal with them."

"If he could have, he would have. I need to finish what I started with them; then I need to find my brother and . . ." She attempted to clear her throat of the sudden tickle, but swallowing only made her cough. "Then I can come back."

The inevitability of night had often led Ethan to partake from the blue bottle. Because in the night, what dreams may come. His had always been of her.

Now she was here, and in the night he held her, he touched her and loved her. He didn't crave oblivion; he craved only her.

He gorged himself on the taste of her lips, the scent of her skin, the rich, smooth drift of her hair across his chest. She rose above him, took him within, and as the treacherous moon shone through the smoke hole of the tepee, he lifted a hand, cupped her face, rubbed a thumb across her cheek. "Look at me."

Her eyes opened, shining like onyx at midnight. She leaned back, her body rocking against his, like a slow, leisurely ride at dusk.

He was not such a fool as to believe that his revelations about Cora and the child that wasn't might suddenly pave the way for reconciliation—even without Annabeth's sudden urge to cough right in the middle of her promise to return.

No one would know from his wife's face or voice that she was lying. Unless they'd known her as long as Ethan had, heard her lie before and deduced, after many months and a lot more lies, that they seemed to make her cough.

Years apart, hours spent with only memories, combined with her return, a few more lies—and coughs—then voilà, Ethan saw the truth. He couldn't believe that he hadn't before. It might have saved them all a lot of heartache.

He clasped her hips, held her still, gritted his teeth so he would not move, even when she tried to. "See me," he managed.

Those eyes, which had gone dewy with the promise of release, sharpened. "Ethan," she said. "All I've ever seen is you."

His fingers loosened, from capture to caress, and she began to move again, her breasts catching the silver sheen and glowing like that moon across the water. When he touched them, kissed them, they cooled his heated palms, soothed his fiery lips. She was a balm to every ache that he owned.

His teeth worried her nipples to stone, and when she rocked her hips one final time, tightening, milking, making him come, as she did, he suckled, drawing from her, even as she drew from him.

Satisfied, replete, her breathing softened, smoothing out, coasting toward sleep and drawing him there, too. All was peaceful and right. What would happen when she left?

He would go back to the nightmare he'd lived before her return, and he couldn't let that happen.

Annabeth lay pressed to Ethan's side, cheek to his chest, leg insinuated between his. He didn't want to move, but he had to. The instant he did, she stirred and then mumbled his name.

"Shh." He brushed her hair from her brow as her leg thudded limply to the ground. "I have to relieve myself."

"'kay."

He stepped outside, then into his clothes. He didn't have long to wait before Joe and several of his friends appeared on the other side of the river. Ethan indicated only Joe should cross. As the man was very good at understanding pantomime, he complied, though he did bring along Ethan's horse and one other.

Joe leaped to the ground, slapped Ethan on the shoulder. The Kaw unleashed a stream of his own language, very little of which Ethan understood. From the softening of his usually stoic features, Ethan assumed the man was pleased with how much better he appeared than when the Kaw had left.

Joe attempted to hand Ethan the reins of two horses. Ethan refused, taking only his own. Joe tried again. Again Ethan refused. If he and his wife possessed only one horse, she would have to return to Freedom with him. He'd worry about getting her to stay once they got there. He was fairly certain that if she went back to Lassiter Morant, he would never see her again.

Joe let out an exasperated huff; then he pointed at the full moon, the ground, Ethan, and himself.

"I'll be here," Ethan said.

Joe leaped on his mount and, trailing the spare, crossed the creek. He and his friends rode west without looking back.

The next morning, Annabeth frowned suspiciously at Ethan's horse. "What do you mean Joe was here and gone?"

"When I stepped out to relieve myself, there he was."

"Just him?"

"And my horse."

Annabeth's gaze narrowed. "Your eye is twitching."

He touched a finger to the pulsing muscle. "So?"

She merely snorted and put out the fire.

As they didn't have much to pack beyond each other, Ethan and Annabeth were on the trail within fifteen minutes. Getting back to Freedom took a lot longer.

Annabeth hadn't realized they'd strayed so far, although she should have. If they'd been closer, someone would have found them. She didn't believe that the folks of Freedom would allow their doctor to disappear without ever searching for him. She was certain Cora wouldn't.

As the sun fell toward the horizon behind them and Freedom appeared before them, Annabeth reined in.

"What's wrong?"

She fought a shiver as Ethan's breath stirred her hair. The sight of town reminded her why they'd ridden out in the first place. As she still had no idea who had fired at them or why, riding into Freedom in the daylight made them an easy target.

"Maybe we should wait until dark," she said. "Less attention, less trouble, fewer questions—"

"Too late," Ethan murmured.

Annabeth had been twisting the horse's mane around her fingers. Now she glanced up. A posse headed their way, Marshal Eversleigh in the lead.

"Why would they ride out to meet us?" he wondered.

"I doubt it's because they can't wait to extend a welcome home."

They could do that in town.

"Marshal," Annabeth greeted as the posse reined in. She nodded to the townsfolk; she didn't know most of their names. That Jeb wasn't among them concerned her.

"Ma'am." Eversleigh pulled on the brim of his hat. "Doc. We didn't think you'd come back."

"Where would we go?" Ethan asked, obviously confused.

"Anywhere but here."

The marshal's gaze flicked to Annabeth's, and she frowned. Something wasn't right.

"Cora Lewis is dead," he continued.

Ethan straightened so fast, his chest slammed into Annabeth's back. She set a hand on his thigh and squeezed. Eversleigh lowered his eyes to Ethan's leg then back to her face.

"How?" she asked.

Before he even spoke, she knew. If Cora had died from natural causes, there'd be no need for a posse. She'd have been buried, and they would have learned about her death in gossip—as it should be.

The same would be true if she'd been killed by a known culprit, even herself. She'd be buried—either outside the churchyard if she'd died by her own hand, or within—before her murderer swung from the gallows. Which left only one reason Annabeth and Ethan would be met out here by a federal marshal and a group of armed men.

"I did it," she said at the same time Ethan blurted, "It was me."

CHAPTER 26

Y ou wanna hand that over?" The marshal indicated Annabeth's gun with a tilt of his head.

"No," Annabeth said.

The members of the posse murmured; their horses shifted, revealing their unease. They were townsfolk, not lawmen, and they weren't sure what to do.

"Beth," Ethan murmured.

"I didn't say I wouldn't hand it over. Just that I didn't want to."

If things went badly—and considering the posse, she wasn't sure how things wouldn't—she'd do whatever she had to do to save Ethan. Without her pistol, that was going to be more difficult than she liked, but she didn't see any way to keep it.

Annabeth reached for her Colt.

"Easy," the marshal cautioned, laying a hand on his own weapon.

Did he really think she'd risk a shoot-out on the prairie with Ethan in the way? The posse might be made up of amateurs, but even Sadie would be able to hit them out here where the only cover was the town of Freedom, which lay too far away.

She tossed the gun to the ground, and a young man she'd never seen before, which only made him the same as the rest of the group, dismounted, snatched up the Colt, and carried it to the marshal.

"You're gonna come back with us; then we'll talk." Eversleigh urged his horse toward Freedom.

Annabeth considered kicking their mount into a run, but that would leave Ethan exposed to over half a dozen guns. She couldn't do it. Then the posse surrounded them, and the opportunity was lost.

Ethan's breath brushed her ear. "You did not kill Cora."

"How would you know?" she whispered.

"Because I did."

"Stop saying that!" She glanced between the men on their right and those on the left. No one was close enough to hear them over the movements of the horses.

"I'll say whatever I have to say to keep you safe," he murmured.

"So will I."

They remained silent the rest of the way to town. The marshal stopped in front of the building marked SHER-RIF, dismounted and indicated they do the same. Annabeth glanced longingly at the building labeled DOCTER. Would she ever step foot in it again?

The posse dispersed, taking Ethan's horse with them. Eversleigh swept his hand in an exaggerated flourish toward the door.

"Made yourself right at home, I see." Annabeth turned the knob and walked in.

Ethan followed, Eversleigh on his heels. "I couldn't leave with people dying all over the place."

"Sure you could." Annabeth took the chair in front of the desk. Ethan stood behind her and rested his hands on her shoulders.

The marshal leaned against the desk, boots only inches from Annabeth's own. His gaze touched on Ethan's hands, then Annabeth's face. He removed his hat, tossed it onto the desktop, lifted a brow. "I'll assume, Doctor, that you've remembered . . ." He paused, waiting.

"I have," Ethan agreed.

"Where have you been?"

"We were on the hill . . ." Annabeth's quick glance at the lawman revealed he knew what else was there. "Someone shot at us again."

Eversleigh frowned. "Did you see who it was?"

"Didn't wait for them to come out of the high grass;

just got on the horse and left. How about you? Didn't anyone hear shots?"

"Shots on the prairie?" He shrugged. "Hunters. Outlaws. Indians. No one goes looking. Maybe if you'd come back right away, we might have found something. Why didn't you?"

"Because, apparently, I murdered Cora Lewis," Annabeth muttered at the same time Ethan blurted, "Twister. Came between us and Freedom."

"We were lucky it missed town," the marshal said. "But that was days ago. Pert near a week."

"We were lost."

Eversleigh snorted. "Gossip around town is that Mrs. Lewis was in a family way." Neither Annabeth nor Ethan said a word. "Did that come as a shock to you, Mrs. Walsh?"

"Why would it?"

"As your husband is rumored to be the father, I'd say it might."

"Rumors? Gossip? I don't listen to either one."

"Then why were you and Mrs. Lewis arguing on the street? Why did she say you'd struck her?"

"Because we were and I did."

"Why?" the marshal persisted.

"I don't like her."

"Did you dislike her enough to kill her?"

"She didn't do anything," Ethan said. "It was me."

Annabeth lost patience. "I filed for divorce. You can check with Pryce Mortimer. There was no reason for Ethan to kill her. I was going to free him so he could have everything he wanted."

Ethan's sigh brushed the top of her head. She could have sworn he whispered her name in a voice that made her ache.

"But what if what he wanted, Mrs. Walsh, was you and not her?"

Annabeth frowned. "He didn't kill her. I did."

"If you were divorcing him so he could be with her, why would you?"

"She didn't." Ethan lifted his hands from Annabeth's shoulders. She had to clench her own to keep from snatching them back. "I did."

"You expect me to believe that you—a man described by everyone as a healer, the saver of lives and not the taker of them—killed both the mother of your child and that child?"

"There was no child."

Eversleigh's expression sharpened. "What's that?"

"Cora lied."

"Ethan," Annabeth murmured. Both men ignored her.

"How do you know?" Eversleigh asked.

"I examined her. I've done the same for many women who were with child. She wasn't."

"So the woman was trying to ruin you." The marshal's eyes narrowed. "I suspect that made you angry."

"He examined her days before she turned up dead," Annabeth interjected. "If he was going to kill her in a rage, he'd have done it then."

"When he examined her, he didn't remember who she was," Eversleigh pointed out.

Hell.

"Once I remembered," Ethan murmured, "I wasn't happy."

"Hush," Annabeth said. "I wasn't very happy when I found out, either. I was furious."

"You didn't find out until I told you," Ethan snapped. "Out on the prairie. After I'd already killed her."

"I saw her alive before we left town," Annabeth returned. "We were arguing in plain view of dozens of others. You were already on the hill. I killed her, came to you, and we ran."

"I thought you ran because someone was shooting at you," the marshal murmured.

"I lied." Annabeth cleared her throat before the cough broke free. Ever since they'd started discussing this, her throat had tickled so badly, it hurt.

Eversleigh straightened away from the desk, looming over Annabeth. Ethan made a movement as if he would come around the chair and step between the two of them, so she stood, sweeping out her arms, a barrier to keep Ethan back.

"It wasn't him," she repeated. "It was me."

"She lies." Ethan shoved past. "She just admitted as much. And about this she definitely did, since I killed Cora Lewis."

"Enough," Eversleigh snapped. "I'll solve this argument. How did she die?"

Annabeth glanced to her right, where Ethan hovered. His forehead creased, and he glanced at her. "Shot," he said, at the same time she chose, "Strangled."

They turned to the marshal. His gaze narrowed on Ethan. "Shot where?"

Damn! She should have picked shot, but strangled— considering Cora Lewis—was so damn appealing.

"In the . . ." Ethan drew out the words, narrowing his own gaze on the marshal. But Eversleigh was smart. He gave away nothing, merely waited for Ethan to finish. "Head?" Ethan frowned. "Um, chest. Neck?"

"Neither one of you did it."

Relief flowed through Annabeth, and she reached for Ethan's hand just as he reached for hers. Their fingers tangled; their palms met, held.

"You rode out because someone shot at you, stayed away because of the storm, and then didn't come back because you were lost. That about right?"

"Yes." Annabeth squeezed Ethan's hand. It would not do for the marshal, or anyone else, to discover Ethan's penchant for laudanum. Lord knew what he'd be accused of then.

"Convenient that you would disappear when the woman who's made your life hell is killed."

"I thought we'd just established that neither one of us did it."

"If you were smart, you'd work together. Spy and a . . ." He shrugged. "Spy. You could lie right to my face, and I'd probably never know."

He was right, but Annabeth wasn't going to say so.

"You might purposely tell me the wrong thing, confuse the issue."

"We might," Ethan agreed. "However, being a spy and a . . . spy, as well as a physician and a nurse, we certainly wouldn't kill anyone in a way that could be construed as murder. If we were smart."

Eversleigh lifted a brow. "Go on."

"If I wanted to kill someone, there are ways to do it that wouldn't get me hung."

"For instance?"

"Don't answer that," Annabeth snapped. The marshal thought they were shifty; he was the same. "How did she die?"

Eversleigh contemplated Annabeth for several seconds, then stepped behind the desk. He pulled a rifle from beneath. "Ever seen this?"

"May I?" Ethan held out his hand.

The marshal passed over the weapon, and Ethan lifted it to his shoulder. "This is a sniper rifle."

Annabeth frowned. Had Fedya left it behind? That didn't sound like Fedya. She peered at the rifle more closely.

"That's an Enfield," she said, the weapon of choice for most Union sharpshooters. However, the Union's most dangerous sniper had used a Confederate rifle—a Whitworth, the best of the best, no doubt stolen off one of his victims.

"Where'd you find it?" Ethan asked.

"Come with me."

When they got back onto the street, folks scurried out of their way as they followed the marshal to Lewis's Sewing and Sundry. No one greeted them; everyone stared. Annabeth was happy to duck inside, though she could still feel the brush of curious gazes through the window.

Eversleigh strode behind the counter and pointed beneath. "I think it was right about here."

"Here?" Ethan echoed.

"Next to some buttons."

"Walking around town with an Enfield would be suspicious," Annabeth murmured.

"Mrs. Lewis wasn't shot," Eversleigh said. "She was stabbed."

"Then why did you show us the rifle?"

"I thought you might recognize it."

Annabeth didn't understand what difference it could make if they'd seen it or not. Cora hadn't been shot.

"Woman alone," the marshal mussed, "with a business. If she hadn't had a weapon beneath the countertop, I'd have wondered. But there was the little matter of a sniper rifle under this counter and the shot through your upstairs window."

"Cora loved Ethan," Annabeth said.

"Enough to lie to keep him," Eversleigh agreed. "Enough to kill for the same?"

"It makes no sense for her to kill him," Annabeth insisted.

"She wasn't trying to kill him, Mrs. Walsh. She was trying to kill you."

"Well," Annabeth said, "that makes sense."

Ethan rubbed a hand over his face. "I don't see the connection between a rifle under the counter to a shot through my window. If there were, the majority of the town would be suspect."

"The majority of the town wasn't carrying your child."

"Neither was she."

"I see your point," the marshal allowed. "And I wouldn't have thought any more about it except for her husband."

"What husband?" Annabeth asked.

"*Mrs.* Lewis? Doesn't that mean there was once a mister?"

"Not necessarily." Annabeth spread her hands. "People come West for a lot of reasons. Change their names, change their pasts, invent a husband."

"She didn't."

"How can you be sure?"

"I looked into it."

"Why?" Ethan asked. "How?"

"It's my job." The single sentence answered both questions; nevertheless, the marshal elaborated. "I've discovered that the motive for a murder can often be found in a person's past." He lifted a brow in Annabeth's direction. "Mrs. Cantrell informed me that Cora Lewis hailed from Cleveland, Ohio."

"She did," Ethan agreed. "Or . . . at least that's what she said."

Anyone could say anything out here. Unless they were murdered and a federal marshal with a brain happened to be in town, no one would ever know the truth. It was how Annabeth had made her way the past five years. She became who she had to be, said whatever was required. As she'd been dealing with criminals who did the same, no one had been the wiser.

"I sent a telegram," Eversleigh continued. "Asked for information about Mrs. Lewis and her husband. Hiram Lewis trained sharpshooters during the war. His prize possession was an Enfield. The only people allowed to touch it were he and his wife. The two of them practiced marksmanship together. I hear that, for a woman, she was damn good."

"Yet she couldn't hit me in the head with a plate," Annabeth muttered.

"What plate?" Ethan asked.

"You said my name in your sleep. She tried to crown me with crockery; she missed."

"Strong feelings can make the hands shake like leaves in a winter wind," the marshal observed.

"True."

Something in Ethan's voice made Annabeth glance his way. She could tell by his expression, he was thinking of Mikey. Had he accepted, at last, that his brother had been injured due to excess emotion and trembling hands rather than a conspiracy no one knew the why of? She hoped so.

"She was angry when I left that day," Annabeth murmured. "I said I was filing for divorce, but she didn't want to marry a divorced man."

"She couldn't have it both ways," Ethan began, then uttered a soft, "Oh."

"Exactly." Annabeth's fingers clenched; she still wished she could put them around Cora's neck just once. "No need for a divorce if I was dead." The woman had said as much several times. "The first shot, through the upstairs window, occurred right after she found out her widowed doctor wasn't so widowed."

Why hadn't Annabeth connected the dots? Because the idea of the petite and helpless Mrs. Lewis wielding a rifle was laughable. Until it was proved the truth.

"What did Cora's rifle have to do with her death?"

"Nothing, if neither one of you killed her."

Annabeth followed his logic. The rifle was only important if they'd known Cora was using it. Either one of them might have killed the woman to keep her from killing them or in retaliation for having tried.

"I thought we'd established that we didn't."

Eversleigh shrugged. Apparently, he liked to keep an open mind.

"Are you going to arrest me?" Annabeth asked. "Ethan? Both of us?"

"Not today."

Annabeth stared at him for several seconds. "I can't tell if you're kidding or not."

"Neither can I," Eversleigh said.

"If she was stabbed, where's the blood?" Ethan murmured.

He was right. The floor was as pristine now as it had been the last time Annabeth had been in the room.

"She wasn't killed here."

"Where?" Ethan asked; at the same time Annabeth muttered, "Hell."

The marshal beckoned, and they followed him out of Lewis's Sewing and Sundry, down the boardwalk, into their house, then up the stairs. Once in Ethan's bedroom, Eversleigh lit a lamp against the encroaching night. The golden glow shone off the dark splotch in the center of the bedroom floor.

"Where is she?" Ethan whispered, horror haunting his face.

How anyone could believe that a man who was overcome by the blood of a woman who'd lied, cheated, and attempted murder could kill was beyond Annabeth's understanding.

"We buried her," the marshal said.

It was summer. They'd had to.

"Your house, your bedroom." Eversleigh indicated the stain. "The two of you are nowhere to be found. You can imagine what I thought."

"Lover's quarrel," Ethan suggested.

"Or I caught the two of you together," Annabeth countered.

The marshal's sigh sounded as exhausted as Annabeth felt. "Either you killed her or you didn't. Pick one."

"Didn't," Annabeth snapped. "Who found her?"

"Mrs. Cantrell."

"I hope she wasn't too upset."

"You'd have to do a damn sight more than toss a dead woman in her path to upset Sadie Cantrell."

As Sadie had taught school on the frontier for a long, long time, Annabeth had to agree.

"Why was Cora here?" Annabeth wondered. "Looking for me? Or maybe for Ethan?" She paused. "Probably for Ethan." When the two men glanced at her, she shrugged. "She didn't have her rifle."

Eversleigh snorted, then started for the door. He paused, reaching for his back pocket a little too fast. Annabeth's palm slapped her empty holster. The marshal lifted a brow as he offered the knife he'd withdrawn hilt first. "Ever seen this?"

The blade was long and wide—a bowie. Common enough. What wasn't were the intricate vines and flowers carved into the golden-brown wood.

"Never seen it before in my life," Annabeth said.

And then she coughed.

CHAPTER 27

"Doc?"

Ethan turned his narrowed gaze from his wife to the lawman. The marshal still held the knife in his palm. Flowers and vines trailed along the hilt.

"Nice work." Ethan traced a fingertip over the one flower he recognized among all the others. "Roses?" How had the creator managed to shade them red?

He drew back at the realization that the red "shade" had been produced by spatters of blood.

"They are roses," Eversleigh agreed. "Got no idea what all the others are. Could be they're made up."

Annabeth coughed again. Ethan resisted the urge to pound her between the shoulders until she stopped.

Coughing? Or lying? He wasn't sure.

"So?" The marshal waggled the knife.

"Never seen anything like it," Ethan said. He turned his gaze to his wife, who peered through the empty window.

But she had.

"You two look tuckered out." Eversleigh shoved the weapon into his pocket and once more headed for the door. "I don't have to tell you not to disappear again, now, do I?"

"No," Annabeth said. "You certainly don't have to tell us."

Had the marshal noticed that she hadn't agreed not to disappear, only that the man didn't have to tell them that? Doubtful. Answering questions without really answering was one of her gifts.

"We'll talk tomorrow." The marshal's boot heels

clattered down the stairs. The door thudded lightly as he left. Annabeth continued to stand at the window.

"Whose knife is that?" Ethan asked.

"Never seen it before." Her throat clicked when she swallowed.

"You can cough," he said. "I know you're lying."

She spun, eyes wide before she narrowed them. "I'm not." She cleared her throat.

"You cough when you lie."

"If I had a tell like that, I'd be dead by now."

"I doubt anyone's been around you as much as I have. Or been lied to as extensively. Folks would have to know that you lied to connect the two. And if they knew that, you'd be dead anyway."

"Your eye twitches," she muttered. "But I doubt anyone's noticed but me."

If anyone had, he wouldn't have lived through the war.

"Is the knife yours?" he asked.

"No."

She didn't cough or swallow or even clear her throat. Wasn't hers, but still . . .

Her chin went up. "I'm not lying."

"Oh, you're lying." Ethan stepped past her and gripped the edge of the bed. "But I know better than to think you'll tell me the whole truth until you're ready." He yanked and the mattress thumped onto the floor.

"What are you doing?"

He set the thing upright and dragged it toward the door. "Maybe you can sleep in a room with that . . ." He indicated the stain with a lift of his chin. "But I can't."

"I'm not sleeping in the baby's room."

Ethan's hands slipped, and the mattress listed to the right. Annabeth snatched the other end. "I hadn't planned on it either," he said.

Their eyes met, and they shared a moment of silence for the child they had lost.

"It wasn't your fault, Ethan."

"If not mine, then whose?"

"I've learned over the past few years that things

happen with no fault and for no reason at all. Fate? God? Bad luck? Pick one. I don't think it would have mattered what we did. I think . . ." She paused, then blurted, "He wasn't meant to live. Sometimes they aren't. No matter what you do, there's no saving them. Him," she clarified. "Michael. Our son."

Her eyes shone in the soft dusky light, and she reached for him. Ethan took her hand, and his chest, which had contained a tight, hard ball of pain for years, suddenly loosened. He could breathe deeply for the first time since his son died.

They should have talked back then, shared their fears, their feelings. But they were both too young, too angry, too damn stupid to try.

"Downstairs?" she suggested.

"Downstairs," he agreed.

They managed, through a series of shoves, grunts, and curses, to pull, push, and carry the mattress down the steps. They nearly lost their grip in the front hall. Ethan was sweating so profusely in the close, heated air, even his fingers were slippery. They shoved it into the exam room, where it fell to the floor with a thump.

"If anyone bursts in here during the night, needing the doctor, we'll have to move it again," Annabeth said.

"Better than the alternative." Sleeping in the room where Cora had died.

"Are you all right?" she asked.

"Are you?"

"A question isn't an answer, Ethan."

"No?"

She snorted. She knew all his tricks; they'd been her tricks, too.

"Someone I . . ." Her lips twisted. " 'Knew' wasn't murdered in my bedroom."

"You knew her," Ethan pointed out. "And that was—*is*—your bedroom." He thought of the divorce. Did she still want it?

"You know what I mean," she said, as she wandered back into the foyer and he followed. "I feel like I should say I'm sorry, but—"

"You're not."

"I didn't want her dead." She rubbed her throat.

"I'd understand if you did. There were times I . . ." He paused.

"You wanted her dead, too."

"That seems harsh, especially now. I didn't really want her dead, just—"

"Gone," she finished. "Like magic."

"I've wished a lot of people would be gone like that."

She lifted her gaze to the new-fallen darkness beyond the windows. "Me too."

"Stay," Ethan whispered, then wished he could snatch the word back. She'd already told him she had to go. "I'll help you find Luke. Let Moze deal with Lassiter. Don't go, Annabeth. Please."

"All right," she said, and he blinked. "Yes. Of course I'll stay."

He stepped toward her, and she stumbled back. "I'm going to wash."

She hurried into the next room and drew the curtain behind her.

Annabeth plunged her hand into the bucket of tepid water that stood near the back door and lifted some to her mouth, swallowed, then lifted more. Eventually the telltale tickle went away.

She'd sat at Lassiter Morant's side while he carved the flowers from *Alice's Adventures in Wonderland*—tiger lily, larkspur, violet, daisy, and rose—into the knife's handle. His workmanship was incredible. Lass could make an honest living if he tried. The knife was his prized possession. The only reason he would have left the weapon behind was as the threat she knew it to be.

Return to me before I return to you.

She hadn't needed the reminder. She'd known all along he would never let her go. And she couldn't let the outlaw roam free. She had to make certain Lassiter Morant either hung for this crime or spent a lifetime in prison for any of his others. To do that, she had to leave, and she had to make certain the man she loved, and always would, didn't follow. She had a pretty good idea how to do that. She'd been doing it for the past five years.

Lie with her mouth and then with her body.

She unbuttoned her shirt, stepped to the curtain, and drew it back. Her husband stared out at the night. "Ethan?"

He turned, and she offered her hand. He put his into it with all the trust of a child, and she almost felt bad. She would have felt bad if she weren't doing this for his own good.

If he knew what she planned, he would want to join her, to help her. Ethan might once have been a spy. He might once have done things that gave him nightmares. But that had been long ago and far away. He was no longer that man, and she didn't want him to be. Wouldn't let him be.

The water in the basin was tepid but clean. The room was shadowed, dark, but she ignored the lamp. What she planned on doing was not something she wanted illuminated in the window.

"Take off your clothes," she murmured. "Or would you rather I did?"

His swallow was audible, her smile hidden by the night. With a shift of her shoulders, the loosened shirt slid free, landing on the floor with a whisper. His followed.

Annabeth dampened a cloth, washed his face, his neck. She would have continued with his chest, but he stared at her so intently, she couldn't think.

"Turn," she murmured. For an instant, she thought he would refuse. Then he spun, and the slight ruffle the movement made through the air caused her nipples to pucker. She couldn't help herself; she leaned forward and rubbed them across his skin.

His breath caught; goose bumps rose. She traced them with her tongue. Then he was spinning toward her instead of away, so close, her breasts slid across his chest and together, they gasped.

The cloth hit the floor with a *plop* as her hands lifted, palms skimming his belly, his ribs, then clutching his shoulders as he lowered his head and took her mouth.

Desperation laced the kiss. She might never again know a moment in this man's arms. Returning to Lassiter Morant would mean the end of them. It certainly might mean the end of her.

And that would be all right. As long as Ethan remained safe.

She tangled her fingers in the curling length of his hair, ran her thumb along the curve of his neck, then placed her mouth there. She tasted sweat and dust, life and death—the promise of the past, the ashes of their future.

She fumbled at his belt, her fingers trembling too much to unbuckle it. He set his hands atop hers, and she closed her eyes. Would he deny her now? She didn't think she could bear it.

He moved away, and she reached out, clasping nothing. Her eyes snapped open. He stood at the door. She bit her lip. She would not beg him to stay. She hadn't begged since Michael died. Begging didn't help. Then she heard a click—the lock—and she had to blink through foolish tears when he strode past her, trailing a finger down her arm as he went to the front door and did the same.

He pressed his chest to her back, wrapped his arms around her, and drew her against him. Tracing the curve of her shoulder with his mouth, he set his fingers on her belt. His didn't tremble. Her trousers fell, catching on the tops of her boots. She lifted a foot to kick them off, and his hand slid from her hip to her thigh.

"Wait." His mouth replaced his hand. He nibbled, then ran his tongue over the swell of her buttock. Her legs wobbled. "Sit."

One-word orders seemed all she was capable of understanding, perhaps all he was capable of uttering.

The exam table was the closest flat area, so she hitched herself onto it, again trying to kick free her boots. But he was there, on his knees, the moon casting his hair with threads of silver, showing her what he would look like when he was old.

Achingly beautiful.

Or perhaps that ache in her chest was merely the knowledge that she would probably never see him like that, and oh, how she wanted to.

Her boots hit the ground; his jeans slid away with a rustle, her socks on a whisper. He set his palms atop her knees, and she stilled as he opened his hands, her legs, and leaned forward, his tongue running from knee to thigh.

She held her breath as he kissed her center; then she couldn't remain upright anymore. Her shoulders met the table—ice cold when everything else seemed on fire.

He murmured soothing nonsense across her belly, scraped her hip with his teeth, then set his tongue where he'd already kissed. Her entire body tightened.

"Shh," he whispered. "Everything will be all right."

A sob threatened. She bit it back, but he knew, he heard, and he gathered her close, lifted her up. She wrapped her legs around his waist.

He carried her to the mattress. They fell as one. Her seeking mouth found his. His straining body settled into hers as he rose above her, his face so stark in the brilliant moonlight, she had to close her eyes, force herself to keep breathing.

He traced the silvery marks on her breasts—the ones that had not gone away when their son did—with the tip of his finger, then the tip of his tongue. Once the action would have made her writhe in agony; now she writhed with anything but.

Each time she touched him with passion, he touched her with tenderness. The contrast took her higher, brought him closer. By the time she rose above him, they were slick with sweat, panting, gasping. She trembled on the edge of oblivion, refusing any longer to be tamed. She met him stroke for stroke. All she smelled, all she tasted and saw, all she knew was him as together they fell.

And fell. And fell. And fell.

His cheek pressed to her breast. His face was wet. So was hers. When he rolled onto his back, she kept her eyes closed. If he stared into them now, he would know. Not that she'd leave; she was too good for that. But that she loved him. Always had, always would, couldn't stop.

And he couldn't know. If she died, Ethan needed to go on. Otherwise, what had been the point of anything?

So she remained close until he slept; she even tried to kiss him awake, shook him, too, whispered, "Ethan?" and curled her fingers around him.

If he'd woken, she would have loved him again. There was no man alive who wouldn't sleep the sleep of the dead for hours after that. But he never moved; he barely breathed.

She put on the clothes she'd taken off. They were filthy; she deserved nothing less. Boots in hand, she closed the door softly behind her before she shoved her feet inside. As she started toward the livery, a distant whinny drew her attention.

Horse and rider stood in stark silhouette against the shimmering, white moon. She knew them well.

They waited for her.

Ethan woke feeling better than he had in . . .

Had he ever felt this good?

He lay there, eyes closed, as he tried to remember why. It didn't take long.

He and Annabeth had shared all their secrets. She'd seen him at his worst, nursed him through the nightmare, and still she had agreed to stay in Freedom with him.

Their attempts to hang for a murder they had not committed only strengthened his belief in their future. He'd die for her and she for him. That vow was more binding than any *I do*.

A shadow fell over his face. Annabeth. Had to be.

His lips curved in welcome; his member stirred with the same. He began to lift his arms to embrace her and—

"Whatcha doin' thar?"

Ethan groped for a sheet to cover his nakedness. There wasn't one. He drew up his knees and hugged them so tightly, they crackled as he met Sadie Cantrell's very interested eye. "What are you doing here?"

"Asked ye first. How come ye be sleepin' downstairs? Naked?"

"I . . ." He thought it fairly obvious what he'd been doing, considering his and his wife's clothes were all over the floor. However, when he glanced about, Ethan saw not a single one of his wife's garments. Or his wife.

"Where's Annabeth?" Sadie shrugged. "How'd you get in?"

"Walked."

"The doors were locked."

"Not the back one."

Ethan closed his eyes as the significance of his wife's missing clothes, along with his missing wife and the no-longer-locked door, became clear.

Annabeth was gone.

CHAPTER 28

Lassiter Morant motioned for Annabeth to mount in front of him. When she hesitated, he cocked his gun and pointed it at Freedom with a smirk. "Bang-bang, they're all dead."

Annabeth had seen him do worse, so she climbed on, and they galloped west. He kept a swift pace until they were well away from town. Even then, he didn't slow the horse enough for conversation. Annabeth didn't mind. When he did, she'd have to explain why she'd gone to Freedom and hadn't come back.

How much did he know? What would he do? Maybe she should just kill him and be done with it. Unfortunately, she didn't have her Colt, or anything else with which to do the job but her bare hands.

She might be a tall woman, a strong woman, but Lassiter was taller, stronger, and a helluva lot meaner. Folks had been trying to kill him for a long time; no one had succeeded.

Deep in thought, she didn't at first notice that they'd passed the place where Lass always paused to blindfold her. Unease prickled across her skin. She doubted Lass had suddenly decided she was one of them. His behavior suggested just the opposite. But there wasn't much she could do other than keep her wits about her. No gun. No horse. No help. She was in even more trouble than usual.

Her eyes watered as the wind whipped past. The sun hovered on the horizon, and everything appeared craggy and gray. As the flat Kansas plain tilted downward, they wound through gullies that most would believe ended nowhere. Except these led to a deep, wide gorge with only a single entrance concealed by thorny, overgrown brush.

The horse picked its way along the narrow, winding path that led to Morant's Wonderland. They emerged into the protected hideaway. The just-born sun hovered at the edge of the world, casting shadows the shade of Ethan's eyes whenever he kissed her. She wanted to see his eyes again, but she didn't think she ever would.

It was early yet, and the others still slept around the campfire—or at least pretended to.

"What were you up to in Freedom?" Lassiter's voice rumbled against Annabeth's back as he reined in.

She listed away from his broad, damp chest, and he turned his head, slapping her in the cheek with his chestnut hair. He'd gathered the length at the nape to keep it from trailing in the breeze. Lass didn't like to wear a hat; sometimes she thought the hours of sun beating on his uncovered head had addled him.

Many believed that an outlaw became an outlaw because he was too stupid to do anything else. But an outlaw who was an outlaw for as long as Lass had been was a perfect combination of ruthless and cunning. He was still breathing because so many others weren't. Annabeth had to remember that.

"Anna!" he snapped, calling her by the name she had given him, a name no one else had ever called her. "Did you sell me out?"

A chill came over Annabeth. If the eyes reflected the soul, then Lassiter's was dead. She'd listened to him promise mercy and then shoot a man in the back. The last lawman who'd gotten anywhere near him had died at the end of a rope, and it hadn't been a quick snap of the neck, but a purposeful, long, drawn-out choking that had taken days.

"I can explain," she began.

"Doubtful." He shoved her off the horse; she landed hard, but she scrambled up when he followed. "You didn't come back . . ." He stepped in close; she had to grit her teeth to keep from stepping away. "And I got worried."

Annabeth's skin prickled. Lass didn't worry about anyone but himself.

"Started thinkin' what kind of town could it be where people went in and never came back out?" He tugged on her shortened hair. "Like they fell down the rabbit hole into Wonderland."

Right now, Annabeth wished that she had.

His fascination with that book was almost childlike—a trait that should have made Lass endearing but instead made him more frightening. Because his favorite character was the Queen of Hearts, and there'd been several times she'd heard him murmur in his sleep, "Off with her head." Personally, Annabeth thought he was more of a Mad Hatter—minus the hat.

"Freedom isn't like Wonderland," Annabeth said. "Nothing worth seeing there."

Lass's full lips lifted, causing another chill to trickle over her despite the steadily climbing heat of the awakening sun. The only times Annabeth had seen Lassiter Morant smile had been right before, or sometimes after, he killed someone.

"Not even your husband?"

Despite having learned well the futility of hope, Ethan listened all day for his wife's footsteps, her voice, someone—anyone—calling her name.

Sadie left, but Ethan wasn't alone for long. The marshal returned with questions. There *had* been a murder.

"Why would Mrs. Lewis be in your bedroom?"

Ethan, who couldn't keep his gaze from hopping between one citizen and another as they filed past the front window—none of them were his wife—spread his hands. "We had a relationship."

"Which ended when your wife returned."

Not a question, but Ethan answered anyway. "Yes."

"Then why would she be here?"

"To talk to me. Seduce me. Kill me. Or maybe my wife."

"She didn't have a weapon."

"Unless you count the one in her chest."

The marshal frowned. "Was it hers?"

"I never saw it. But I never saw the rifle either."

"You think she took her own life?"

If Ethan hadn't heard Annabeth cough after saying she'd never seen that knife before, he would have considered it. That would be just like Cora to dramatically end her own life in his bedroom.

Except he had heard that cough.

"No," Ethan said. "I don't."

The marshal sighed. "Me either. Could I speak to your wife?"

"She's resting."

Eversleigh eyed the mattress leaning against the wall. He didn't ask the obvious question: Upon what was she resting? Instead he frowned, pulled on his hat brim, and left.

For that, Ethan was almost pathetically grateful. But then he was pathetic. He'd believed last night had meant something. A promise. A vow. A new beginning, not another goddamn end.

Ethan opened the medicine cabinet and reached for a blessed blue bottle, but there were none. He would make more.

He found several empties, washed them inside and out, set them in a row. After retrieving the glazed crock he used only for making laudanum, he set it on the stove. Steeling himself, he climbed the steps. In his bedroom, he averted his eyes from the bloodstain that had seeped into the wood. That mark would never go away.

"Out damned spot," he muttered, then yanked open his nightstand drawer.

Inside rested a basket of dried poppies along with the needle he used to pierce the heads before he set them in the heated crock. He turned with the basket in one hand, the needle clutched between two fingers of the other, and the downstairs door opened.

"Doc?"

The marshal had returned. Ethan placed the items on the dresser and strode to the head of the stairs. The lawman stood at the bottom, Annabeth's gun in his hand. "Figgered yer wife might want this back."

Ethan stared at the Colt and frowned.

"Doc?" Eversleigh lifted the weapon along with his brow.

"Thank you. Just put it . . ." Ethan waved his hand at the desk.

The marshal set it down and departed, but Ethan continued to frown. Annabeth would not have left without a weapon. She wasn't that foolish. Had she taken his?

He opened the armoire, stood blinking at the sight of his weapons right where he'd left them. A prickle raced the length of his spine. He forgot all about the poppies as he hurried down the stairs and out of the house to the stable.

"Sure 'nuff." The stable boy ran his hand over the nose of a lovely roan. "This is yer wife's horse righchere."

"She didn't take another?"

The kid's face scrunched. "Why would she do that?"

For many reasons, none of which Ethan planned to explain. He tried a different tactic. "Are any horses missing?"

"'Course not! What kind of job would I be doin' if folks come for their mount and it ain't here?"

"When was the last time anyone took a horse and went anywhere?"

"That'd be you, Doc. But yer back and so's . . ." He pointed to Ethan's gelding, which hung its head over the stall and snuffled for attention. Ethan absently scratched between the animal's eyes as he considered.

Annabeth was gone, but she'd left behind her gun and her horse. Certainly she could have walked away, but without food, water, or a weapon, that was suicide.

Had she been taken? By whom? For what reason?

At a loss, Ethan returned home. He was no tracker—that was Mikey's talent. Unfortunately, he had no idea where his brother had gone after he'd left here last month. Other than with Fedya—a man who disappeared quicker than free whiskey on a Saturday night.

Ethan remained inside as the day waned. A few folks needed doctoring—cut hand, broken finger, loose bowels—nothing serious.

Night descended, and Ethan let the mattress fall to the floor. Dust puffed at the impact. He barely noticed. Instead he lay down and stared at the ceiling.

What if he contacted the army? Maybe they had an idea where their best sniper had gone. One never knew when he might be needed.

Ethan snorted. Fedya had spent the past five years wandering. He'd changed his name. His appearance. His occupation. Even if someone had known at one time where he was, he doubted they would any longer. Fedya would have made certain of it.

Panic pulsed at the base of Ethan's throat. The more he thought about it, the less he believed that his wife had left on her own. Which left two possibilities.

Moses Farquhar or Lassiter Morant.

Ethan didn't much care for either one.

Lass backhanded Annabeth. She landed on her ass in the dust. She figured the bruise on her rump would be almost as colorful as the one that would bloom on her face.

He climbed onto his horse. The ten men around the fire no longer pretended to sleep. They sat up and watched the show. If Lass's eyes were dead, most of theirs were dying.

"How is it that you never mentioned your husband, the doctor?"

Annabeth didn't like the way Lass glared at her from on high. She particularly didn't like the way his hands clenched on the reins, causing his mount to prance far too close. She got to her feet again. Being trampled to death in the dust was too damn humiliating.

"Why would I? I left him before; I just left him again." Lass tilted his head, and Annabeth pressed the advantage. "I didn't go there to scout the bank. I filed for divorce. I wanted to end it forever." She stopped talking before she said something that would give her the urge to cough. So far everything out of her mouth had been the truth.

Lass breathed in as if he could smell her fear. She could have sworn he fed on it. Like with the damnable *Eat Me* cake in his book, his chest would expand and he would grow so tall, his head would brush the sky. She wished she could pour the potion from the *Drink Me* bottle down his throat, watch him shrink, then step on him like a bug.

"Ain't there more you should tell me?"

Annabeth breathed in herself, striving for calm. "I can't think what."

"Oh, maybe that your husband was a spy. Just like you are now."

Annabeth froze; the other men shifted and murmured. Annabeth managed to keep herself from glancing around for an escape route. There wasn't one. And she knew better than to take her eyes off a wild animal ready to strike.

"You aren't going to deny it?" he asked.

"Would it help?"

He lifted his face to the speck of bright blue sky visible at the top of the rabbit hole. The rock face above them narrowed so sharply, it was impossible to enter unseen and equally difficult to get a good shot from the top at any inhabitants on the bottom.

"When you didn't come back, I had some of the boys ride to the nearby towns. In Freedom, everyone was talkin' about the doctor and his back-from-the-dead, redheaded wife. Made me angry." Lass's fingers clenched on the reins again. Again, Annabeth took a step back. The horse followed. "You're mine."

She didn't answer. She wasn't his, never would be or could be. Because she was forever Ethan's.

"I went to the doc's place, found you . . ." His voice lowered, and the next words were the growl of the animal within. "In his bed."

If Lass had discovered her in Ethan's bed, she'd be dead. Annabeth considered what might have happened. A dark house, a darker room, a woman asleep. Lass had mistaken Cora for Annabeth and stabbed her. Although, if that were the case, the blood would have been on the bed and not the floor. That it was on the floor changed everything. Cora Lewis—five foot nothing when standing—could never be confused with Annabeth.

"Why did you kill her?" Annabeth asked.

"What did you expect me to do? Let her scream and bring down the law?"

"You could have tied her up, gagged her . . ." Oh, what Annabeth wouldn't have given to see the woman gagged. "You'd have been gone before anyone found her."

He shrugged and waved away the seamstress's life as if he'd done nothing but swat a fly. "She told me everything she knew. About the doc, about you." His lip curled. "Bein' married."

"I won't be for long. I filed for divorce so I could . . ." Annabeth cleared her throat. "Come back to you. Free and clear."

"I know what you were. What you are. Spy. Liar. Detective."

Obviously Ethan had told Cora about his past. A relationship based on lies was no relationship at all. At least he'd learned that much. Still, she wished he'd kept her secrets out of it.

"Miz Lewis was a sneaky bitch," Lass continued. "Can't say I blame her, considering. She crept around, listened at keyholes. Told me everything she heard."

So Ethan hadn't shared her secrets, hadn't talked about her or betrayed her to Cora Lewis. Why that made Annabeth so happy, she couldn't say.

"You're a traitor, Anna."

She'd been called that before, but it had never held quite the same ring. In Lassiter's words, she heard a death knell.

He lowered his voice so only she could hear his whisper. "If I let a traitor live, you know what'll happen."

"Chaos," she muttered.

"I wouldn't be able to sleep at night."

He was right. If he let her live now that it was known who she was, what she'd done, it would be only a matter of time until one of his own men killed him in his sleep and took over. Outlaws were like that.

She was glad she'd seen Ethan again, helped him, held him. She hoped her promising to stay and then sneaking out in the night, combined with the divorce papers her lawyer would deliver, would make him angry enough to move on.

Annabeth stood in the bright sun and waited for the bullet that would kill her. She'd forgotten whom she was dealing with.

"Tie her," Lassiter Morant ordered.

Annabeth released an annoyed huff as his thugs grabbed her. "Can't you just shoot me?"

Lass smiled. "What do you think?"

CHAPTER 29

A man-shaped shadow emerged from the rear of the house and crept toward the stairs. As Ethan hadn't heard the door open, a floorboard creak, the scuff of a boot, or a single breath, he didn't think the intruder was a patient. He cocked the gun in his hand, and the shadow froze.

"Turn around," Ethan ordered. "Keep your hands where I can see them."

The figure complied. Silver moon shadows flickered over his face, but Ethan didn't recognize the fellow. Of course he wouldn't know Lassiter or Moses from Adam.

"Farquhar?" Ethan asked, then uncocked the weapon without waiting for an answer. He doubted Lassiter Morant would have turned without going for his gun. "I planned to wire the Pinkerton Detective Agency in the morning and have them contact you."

"They wouldn't even admit that they know me."

"Do they know you?"

Had the man invented his affiliation? Hoodwinked Annabeth? Gotten her involved in something dangerous for . . . what reason?

"Would your superior have admitted that he'd ever heard of you?" Ethan thought about John Law and laughed. "That's what I thought. Now, where's Annabeth?"

"If I knew that, I wouldn't need you."

"Why do you need me?"

Ethan hesitated. "Why are you here?"

It was too much of a coincidence that Ethan had been prepared to search out a man who suddenly appeared.

"There was a murder. The two of you went missing."
The dark figure shrugged. "I've been stopping by every
few days to see if . . ."

"They'd hung us?"

"Glad they didn't."

"Me too," Ethan muttered.

Ethan hadn't wanted Annabeth to be with Farquhar.
The way she said the man's name, the way he'd said
"Annie Beth Lou," their long history, and all she had
done for him, made Ethan think they were much more
than they let on, but the alternative to her disappearing
with Farquhar was much worse.

"Where can I find Lassiter Morant?"

It was Farquhar's turn to laugh. "I'll assume that
Annabeth told you her mission or you wouldn't even
know his name."

Ethan didn't comment.

"So you understand that if I had any idea where he
was, I'd be there arresting him and not here talking
to you."

Ethan stared out the front window at the silent,
deserted streets. "If she isn't with me and she isn't
with you—"

"Doesn't mean she's with him."

"She left without her Colt. Hell, she left without a
horse."

Farquhar shifted. "You'd better tell me what happened. From the beginning."

"Which beginning?" There'd been almost as many of
those as there'd been endings.

"She came back," Farquhar murmured. "And she
swore she never would. She stayed, even though staying
was too damn dangerous. Why?"

Ethan sighed and began to speak. He told Farquhar a lot, but he didn't tell him everything. Some
things were Ethan's and Annabeth's alone. However, when he got to the part about the knife, the man
cursed.

"Carved handle?" Ethan nodded. "Flowers? Roses,
daisies, larkspurs, and such?"

Ethan had no idea what a larkspur looked like, but he had seen the others. "How did you know that?"

"Morant owns one book, *Alice's Adventures in Wonderland.*"

As Ethan had never heard of it, he shrugged.

"Written by an Englishman. Some fellow who calls himself Lewis Caroll. A girl falls down a rabbit hole into another land. Cakes that grow her large, drinks that make her small. Talking rabbits and cats. Flowers, too, apparently."

"Sounds like a lot of nonsense."

"It's a story for children. But Morant loves it. Calls his hideout Wonderland. According to Annabeth, he carved the flowers from the novel into his knife handle."

"She knew the knife was his." Hence her cough.

"Which explains why she's gone."

Ethan rubbed his scar. Beneath it, his head had begun to throb. "Explain it to me."

"The knife was a threat. Come back or else."

Ethan dropped his hand. "Or else what?"

"Nothing good," Moses said.

"We have to find her."

"If she's with Lassiter Morant, she's in Wonderland."

"His hideout," Ethan said.

"No one can find it."

"I wouldn't be so sure of that."

They tied Annabeth to the nearest tree. Hell, the only tree. This was still Kansas, after all. Just because Lass called the hideout Wonderland didn't mean it had suddenly sprouted greenery and talking flowers.

Once they had her secured, the men gathered around Lass and began to whisper. The leering glances thrown Annabeth's way gave her no doubt about what her fate would be. Until now, no one had looked at her with anything other than respect. She was Lass's woman, and no one touched her but him.

Those days were done.

Her gaze flicked from outlaw to outlaw, cataloging

their weapons. All she needed was for one of them to get close and get careless; then she'd put an end to their fun.

"Me first," Lass announced. "When I've had enough, y'all can draw straws."

"Aw, Lass, there won't be nothin' left to draw straws fer once you've had enough."

Lass's eyes met Annabeth's, and he smiled. Annabeth hoped he was the one who got careless. Unfortunately, he'd never been anything but careful so far.

"I wouldn't do that to you, boys. I'll make sure you each get a chance. But first . . ." He reached for his belt. "I'm gonna show you how it's done."

As he released his buckle, the sound of a horse being ridden hard down the narrow trail had every man drawing his pistol. Annabeth's gaze fixed on the entrance, hoping the rider was rescue; then again—considering the guns—hoping it wasn't. She should have known better. If anyone but Lass and his men knew the location of Wonderland, she wouldn't be here at all.

Delbert Haney reined in his lathered horse. "Railroad payroll comin' on tomorrow's stage. We gotta ride."

Lass scowled at Annabeth, as if she'd purposely ruined his plans. Everyone else's eyes shifted to Lass. What would he do? Killing Annabeth the way that he wanted took time they didn't have and might lose them the chance to rob the stage.

Business? Or pleasure?

Annabeth, who'd spent months gauging Lassiter's moods, reading his face, peering into his eyes and seeing nothing but death, saw it there again. For just an instant, he considered shooting her now, not saving her for later.

Do it, she thought. *Please.*

The smile that had faded with the arrival of Delbert blossomed. He uncocked his gun. "You'd better still be breathing when I come back." Several full canteens landed in her lap.

Annabeth didn't answer. He couldn't make her drink water when he wasn't here, and in this heat, she wouldn't last two days without it. In this heat, she might not last one.

"You refuse to drink," Lassiter continued, "or somehow hang yourself with that rope . . ."

Annabeth frowned at the bindings on her hands and feet, as well as the one that securely lashed her middle to the tree. What did he think she was, a magician?

Lass snapped his fingers, and she met his gaze. "You die before I kill you, and he dies. I'll walk right into that no-account town and gut him like a downed buffalo."

The man's lips curved, and Annabeth understood he was going to do that anyway. No one touched Lassiter Morant's woman. At least while she was still his woman. Apparently, once she'd been labeled traitor and spy, other labels no longer applied. Confusing, but then Lassiter was crazy.

"Lass!" The men milled about near the entrance, mounted, ready, impatient. She'd hate to be her if they missed the stage. Hell, she'd hate to be her if they didn't.

Morant wheeled his horse far too close to Annabeth's bound feet. Grass, dirt, and rocks sprayed over her boots and a hoof ticked against her toe. She yanked her legs to her chest as he raced to join them. The thunder of retreating horses filled the small, secluded area. Dust rose up beyond the scrub that shaded the trail and then moved east.

She was going to have to live, to endure whatever came next. Either find a way to escape, or—

"No," Annabeth murmured. If she escaped, Lass would only follow. How long before she found a newly carved knife buried in Ethan's chest?

She couldn't let that happen. The only way to keep Ethan safe was to kill Lassiter Morant.

"How are you gonna find Wonderland when half a dozen Pinkerton detectives couldn't?" Farquhar asked.

"I didn't say I'd find it." Ethan struck a match, lit the lamp. "My—" He turned and the word *brother* stuck in his throat as the lamplight illuminated his companion. "What the hell is that?" Ethan pointed to Farquhar's neck.

"What does it look like?" Farquhar pulled at the collar. Which belonged on a priest.

"You're not a priest," Ethan said, though he wished the man were. Then Ethan wouldn't continue to imagine just how close Farquhar and Annabeth had once been, might still be.

Foolish jealousy, but he couldn't help himself. Annabeth had betrayed Ethan to Moses Farquhar at Chimborazo; she worked for him now. If he was truly a priest, Ethan might be able to squash the ever-present desire to throttle him.

"You're right; I'm not a priest," Farquhar agreed. "But let's hope no one but you figures that out."

Ethan narrowed his gaze. "What are you up to?"

"Nothing I'm going to tell you about."

Ethan couldn't imagine anyone appearing less priestly than this golden-haired, green-eyed, far-too-smooth and clever man. If it weren't for the hook in his nose, Farquhar would be as pretty as Fedya. Although now that Ethan thought of it, Fedya'd had a crook in his nose the last time he'd seen him that hadn't been there before.

"I need to locate my brother," Ethan said.

"He was the best scout you blue belly's had. He could find anything." Farquhar blinked as he caught up. "Anyone." The Pinkerton priest started for the door.

"Wait," Ethan said. "How are you going to find him?"

Farquhar cast Ethan a withering glance. "What kind of spy do you think I am?"

"I . . . What?"

"Your brother is now known as Mikhail, and considering his size, he's kind of hard to miss. Fedya, on the other hand, slips off now and again. Or at least he did until recently, when he decided to keep one name and stay in one place."

"Where are they?" Ethan asked.

"Colorado."

Ethan wasn't certain how Moses Farquhar wrote a telegram that convinced Fedya and Mikey—he still couldn't think of his little brother as Mikhail—to board the next train from Colorado to Kansas. But they arrived within two days.

Two days where Ethan barely slept or ate. But at least he didn't drink from a blue bottle—and not because they were empty. He spent half his time filling them. The other half he spent staring at them, when he wasn't staring north, waiting for the cloud of dust that would signal incoming riders.

It appeared early Wednesday morning. Ethan stepped onto his porch, glancing toward the hotel as Farquhar emerged and started his way. At least he'd left his collar behind.

Fedya and Mikey dismounted; Ethan led them inside. He could feel folks watching through their windows. If the stage into Ellsworth hadn't been robbed of the railroad payroll, requiring the marshal's presence in the posse, the lawman would not only have been watching them, but joining them.

Ethan wouldn't have minded, but he thought Fedya might. He had no idea what the man had been up to since the war, but considering the dead sheriff that had ended their last meeting, it probably wasn't completely—or even remotely—legal.

Despite what had to have been a long, dirty trip, Fedya's black suit coat, which would look more at home in a gambler's hell, appeared pristine. His ruffled white shirt was slightly limp and his black boots just a bit dusty, but those imperfections served only to make his immaculate black gloves shine. In contrast, Mikey looked like a farmhand—homespun shirt, tattered trousers, cracked boots, stained hat.

The four of them stood in the front hall. Mikey inched into the corner nearest the door, removed the hat, and wrung it in his large hands as he peered outside. His gray eyes and dark hair were very like Ethan's own, but there the similarities ended.

Or perhaps not. Right now the two of them rubbed raised ridges on the same sides of their foreheads. Mikey's was much larger and deeper, but more of his was covered by hair than Ethan's.

"What happened to you?"

Ethan lowered his hand. The former sniper was still handsome enough to cause women to stare. Ebony hair, sapphire eyes . . . Ethan could go on and on, but he might just nauseate himself.

"None of your concern."

Fedya's gaze narrowed; then he shrugged, removed his gloves and flicked dust from his cuff. "I'm merely curious."

"You know what they say about curiosity," Ethan murmured, and was treated to another narrow-eyed glare.

"I am not a cat."

At their last visit, Ethan *had* threatened to kill Fedya the next time they met. And that was before Fedya had tattled to Annabeth. Nevertheless—

"I won't," Ethan said.

Fedya peered at his fingernails and murmured, *"Sicher nicht."*

Farquhar cast a glance at Ethan, who shrugged. "I have no idea what he said." He wasn't even sure what language the man had said it in.

"I said, 'certainly not,'" Fedya translated.

"Certainly not what?" the detective asked.

Blue eyes met green. "He most certainly will not kill me."

From the corner, Mikey growled.

Without removing his gaze from Farquhar's, Fedya said, "Do not worry, Mikhail. Everything is all right."

Ethan had to tighten his lips to keep from correcting his brother's name. Mikey was now Mikhail, and he probably always would be. Unless Ethan wanted to attempt to cure him as he had been cured, and he wasn't sure about that.

"If everything were all right, you wouldn't be here," Ethan said.

"Pravda." Ethan cast the man an exasperated glance, and Fedya smirked.

The only language besides English that Ethan understood anything of was Gaelic, and it annoyed him when

Fedya said things he did not comprehend, which was no doubt why the man did it.

"Maybe we could stick to English," Farquhar suggested.

"I will do my best, but sometimes the words just "— Fedya waved a long-fingered, clever hand—"slip out."

Ethan grunted, causing Fedya's smirk to widen, until he asked, "How's your wife?" Then Fedya's expression froze.

"Did I not tell you to forget about her, about me, the instant we left?"

"You knew that wasn't going to happen."

"How did you find me?" Fedya asked.

Ethan jerked a thumb at Farquhar. The Pinkerton spread his hands. "Did you think I wouldn't keep an eye on you?" He glanced at Mikey, who was scowling mightily and rubbing at his scar as if he could erase it by touch alone, then lowered his voice. "On him?"

Ethan frowned. "You know each other?"

"We've met," Moze admitted.

"Where? Why?"

"I didn't just stroll into Castle Thunder without an escort," Fedya answered.

Ethan's eyes widened. "Him?"

"Oui," Fedya said.

"You were a very busy boy," Ethan murmured to Farquhar.

"My job." Farquhar looked away, discovered Mikey's steely gaze upon him, and looked back.

"How close an eye did you keep?" Fedya wondered.

"Don't worry. I couldn't care less who you've fleeced."

"Then why the eye upon me?"

"Never know when I might need a sniper or a scout. Like now."

"But, Alexi—" Mikey began, and Fedya silenced him with a glance.

"You're still using that name?" Ethan asked.

"It has become my own."

"And your wife? How's her—?"

"Her *pregnancy* is going well thus far," Fedya interrupted.

Pregnancy? Was that the truth or another lie? As Fedya never coughed or twitched or did anything else that might give him away, it was impossible to tell. If the man didn't want anyone to know the truth, about him or his "wife," no one would know. Because if anyone learned a truth he didn't want known, he would just—

"Mikhail," Fedya murmured.

Mikey no longer stood in the corner. For such a large man, he moved both quickly and quietly. He snatched the detective by his shirtfront and lifted him several feet off the ground.

"Put him down," Ethan said.

Mikey ignored him. He hadn't taken orders from Ethan since he'd forgotten who Ethan was.

"What do you know of me?" Fedya demanded.

Farquhar attempted to speak, but Mikey was holding him too tightly. The detective turned an ugly shade of puce.

"Can't speak if he's dead," Ethan pointed out.

"Precisely," Fedya answered.

"How many men have you had my—" Ethan bit his lip before the word *brother* slipped out. That always upset everyone. "Have you had *him* kill?"

"Too many to count."

Farquhar's eyes bulged. Ethan wasn't certain if that were a result of his lack of air or Fedya's answer.

"A dead Pinkerton detective isn't going to go unnoticed."

"You'd be surprised," Fedya said.

"No doubt," Ethan answered, and Fedya laughed. For an instant, it almost felt like the old days.

In prison.

They'd been friends—until everything had gone badly and they'd wound up hating each other. Or Ethan had wound up hating Fedya. He wasn't certain how Fedya felt about him.

Fedya waved his hand, and Mikey opened his.

Farquhar crumpled to the ground, where he rubbed his throat and gasped for air like a fish upon a riverbank. Fedya didn't even look at the man as he spoke. "You asked us here to help our friend."

Ethan blinked, frowned, glanced at Farquhar, then at Fedya. "You came for me?"

"Who else?"

"Annabeth?"

"She's here?" Fedya looked around, a picture of perfect innocence. Except Ethan knew he wasn't perfect, or innocent, and never had been. "Since when?"

"Since you sent her. We'll discuss that once I have her back."

"What did you expect me to do, *mon ami*? Nothing?"

Farquhar peered back and forth between the two of them. "What are you talking about?"

"Shh," Fedya murmured, and Farquhar did. "You said we must get Annabeth back," Fedya continued. "Where has she gone?"

"It's a long story," Ethan said.

Most of which Fedya didn't know. Considering Fedya, he'd probably discovered some on his own. Though Ethan doubted he knew that Annabeth had betrayed them or he wouldn't be saying her name with such fondness. Should he tell the man the truth or shouldn't he?

Ethan wrestled with the question. Apparently, his indecision showed on his face, for Farquhar found his voice at last. "Shut up, Walsh."

"I don't like him." Fedya tilted his head as he gazed at the detective who still sat on the floor. "Do we need him?"

"No," Ethan began, but then Fedya flicked a finger and Mikey started forward. "Yes! We do. We need him."

Fedya cast a disgusted glance at Ethan before calling Mikey off. "Water the horses, Mikhail."

Mikey lumbered out.

"You need to stop making him kill people," Ethan said.

"I don't make him do anything."

"Suggesting?"

"It's a difficult world. Only the strong survive."

Fedya was no doubt right, but Ethan still didn't like the idea of his little brother as an assassin.

"Would you rather he was dead?" Fedya murmured.

"No," Ethan admitted. Mikey might not remember him; he might think Fedya was his brother. The sight of him might make Ethan want to weep. But Mikey was alive, and it was because of Fedya that he'd stayed that way.

Considering it was Fedya who had killed him in the first place, that only seemed fair. And it only seemed fair to be honest about everything, even to a man who didn't know what honesty was.

"Annabeth betrayed us."

Farquhar cursed. As he still didn't seem capable of standing, it was easy to ignore him.

Fedya lifted a dark brow and waited. Ethan had taught him that, or maybe it had been Mikey, during the time they'd spent in prison. According to the gospel of John Law, there was power in silence. Folks often felt compelled to fill it, and a patient man could learn much without ever asking anything.

Even though Ethan knew what Fedya was doing, he filled the silence. Not because he felt compelled to, but because he wanted to.

"The trap—Lee and Davis. That was her doing. She was a spy."

"Interesting."

Ethan considered the information many things. Interesting was the least of them.

"You already knew, didn't you?"

Fedya shrugged. "It was a long time ago. There has been enough blame and anger. What good does it do? Can we change the past?"

"No," Ethan agreed. He only wished that he could. "When did you become so . . . ?" Ethan searched for a word.

"Smart?" Fedya suggested. "Mature? Virtuous?" Ethan gave a derisive huff, and Fedya smiled. "Stones and glass houses, Doctor. As I recall, you were a spy, as well."

"Annabeth still is," Ethan muttered.

"She and Cat would get along well."

"Cat?"

"O'Banyon."

"The bounty hunter?" That would explain the gunshot wound.

"Former. She is now my wife."

Trust Fedya to marry a legendary bounty hunter.

"Does her being a bounty hunter have something to do with the dead sheriff?" Ethan asked.

"He wasn't a sheriff but an outlaw by the name of Rufus Owens. He killed the man you'd hired to be your sheriff and took his place."

"Why?"

"He was tired of being chased by bounty hunters. He thought he was safe until one turned up here."

"Cat tried to arrest him?"

Fedya's gaze darkened. "More or less."

"But he fell out the window."

Fedya's lips quirked. "More or less."

As Ethan had suspected, he would never know the whole truth of the dead sheriff.

"Your wife is Cat O'Banyon?" Farquhar asked.

Fedya hauled the detective to his feet. "My wife is Catey Romanov. If I hear any whisper of Cat O'Banyon—"

"No one will hear it from me."

"I don't ever want to hear from you or see you again," Fedya continued. "I am a businessman. I have my own gambling hall and saloon. I came here only to help my old friend, not to perform any tricks for you. I am not a show pony."

"Anymore," Ethan murmured, and received an icy glance from Fedya.

At one time, the man now known as Alexi Romanov had traveled the country as Fedya, the amazing sharpshooting boy. Which was how he'd become the Union's best sniper.

"Daylight's wasting," Fedya said. "Tell me everything."

CHAPTER 30

Mikhail couldn't wait to leave the town behind. Too many people staring, too many buildings too close together. And that man. That doctor. Who peered at Mikhail with light eyes full of so much dark. Whenever Mikhail saw him, he wanted both to run to him and away from him.

Which made no sense attall. Or maybe it did.

Alexi thought Mikhail didn't remember Castle Thunder, and Mikhail let him. Because he knew that the place upset his brother. Hell, it upset Mikhail.

His memories of the prison were fuzzy. He was never really certain what was real and what was a dream. He remembered only waking there—hurt and alone, missing Alexi, needing to find him with a desperation he couldn't ignore. He never could recall how it was he'd come to be in Castle Thunder in the first place, nor how or why he'd been hurt, not even how he'd escaped. He remembered only tracking Alexi and finding him.

The doctor had healed Mikhail, but whenever he looked at the man, all he remembered was pain. So he stopped glancing the doctor's way.

Over the past few years, there had been hard times, sad times, bloody times. With Alexi, there always were. But they were together, and they had Miss Cathy—Alexi called her Catey now, but Mikhail could never remember that—and a baby on the way.

Alexi said Mikhail would be the baby's uncle and that was an important job. Mikhail would protect the child, even though Miss Cathy was nearly as dangerous as Alexi. Still, three was always better than one or even two. They were a family, and there weren't nothin' stronger than that. Which was why he didn't mind searchin' for the doctor's wife.

Even though the doctor himself gave Mikhail the worst kind of headache.

Farquhar hadn't spent the last two days staring at blue bottles as Ethan had. Instead he'd been preparing to leave as soon as their scout arrived. Water, food, weapons, bedrolls awaited them at the stable.

They rode out of Freedom within an hour of Fedya's and Mikey's riding in. Ethan could almost like the man for that.

Almost, but not quite. He couldn't forget Farquhar's having recruited Annabeth as a spy. Twice. What kind of man did that?

One who had no scruples, no kindness, no charity. One who couldn't be trusted. Ethan made sure Farquhar rode in front of him so he could watch the detective every second. It wasn't until they'd been riding for several hours that he caught Fedya doing the same thing.

A sense of camaraderie that he hadn't experienced since the war came over him. Ethan didn't miss the blood and the death and the artillery, but he had missed that.

Mikey followed the route of one horse carrying two riders. According to him, every other trace that led out of Freedom belonged to one horse and one rider.

Ethan had never understood how his brother saw such things. To Ethan, a trail was a trail. But for Mikey, each one told a story that only he could read. Oddly, the ability had not been lost with the loss of himself but rather enhanced.

The four men rode across the prairie, stopping every so often so Mikey could climb from his horse and scowl at the marks on the ground.

"How does he do that?" Farquhar asked, gaze on the swaying knee-high grasses that appeared exactly the same all the way to the horizon.

"No one knows," Fedya answered. "Him least of all."

"From the moment he could walk," Ethan said, "he followed me. I'd try to hide." He shrugged. "Little brothers, who needs them? But he found me every time. Once"—Ethan paused as Mikey again stopped, dismounted, scowled—"a child disappeared. Her parents feared the Shawnee had taken her. The law refused to look."

The Shawnee Indians had relocated from South Carolina to Pennsylvania to Ohio and then on to Kansas and eventually Indian Territory. When Ethan and Mikey had been children in Pennsylvania, there had still been a few bands that refused to move.

"Where was she?" Farquhar asked as Mikey got back on his horse and continued on; the three of them did the same.

"With the Shawnee," Ethan said. "But the Indians were so impressed that Mikey found them, they gave her back." Fedya and the detective appeared dubious, and Ethan lifted one hand. "I swear."

They rode through the excruciating heat of midday. Farquhar stayed close to Mikey, which gave Fedya and Ethan the opportunity to talk. Ethan had not thought he would ever speak to the man again, but suddenly he wanted to.

"How is he?" Ethan asked.

"The same."

"He's remembered nothing from his life . . . before?"

"He remembers everything, Ethan. An entire life that he and I lived."

"A life that never happened."

Fedya shrugged. "For him it did."

The two of them remained silent for several moments; then Fedya continued. "Wouldn't you rather forget the war? Castle Thunder? Everything that happened then and there?"

Ethan had thought so. But if he forgot that, he would forget Annabeth. Once he'd believed that would be for the best, but he believed that no longer. Perhaps because he'd tried every way that he knew to forget her, yet still she remained. In his mind, his dreams, his heart.

"No," Ethan answered. "I would not."

Fedya's glance said he understood. His sending Annabeth to Ethan proved it. While Ethan had first wanted to strangle him for interfering, the urge had passed.

"Thank you," he said.

Fedya's brow lifted. Ethan waited for him to say something sarcastic—in any language—but he didn't.

"You need not worry about Mikhail. Catey loves him as I do. She's never known him any other way than the way he is now."

"I just wish . . ." Ethan began, and Fedya finished. "Me too."

"There might be a way to cure him."

"Cure?" Fedya said, as if the word were as foreign as some of his own.

Quickly Ethan shared what had happened to him—the injury, his memory loss, its return.

"You think if we re-create the situation that caused Mikey to lose his memory, he might regain it?"

"I don't know." Fedya opened his mouth, shut it again, sighed. "Ask," Ethan urged.

Fedya slid his gaze to Ethan's face, then set it back between his horse's ears. "You will not kill me?"

"I told you that I wouldn't. Besides, that threat was entirely too optimistic on my part."

"Not really," Fedya muttered.

"To think I could kill the Union's greatest sniper, who happens to have a very large, vicious bodyguard? Definitely overreaching."

"You'd be surprised."

Something in Fedya's voice made Ethan frown. "What are you talking about?"

The man hesitated, then shook his head. "We are discussing you and the reason you threatened the 'Union's once-greatest sniper.'"

"Courage, courtesy of a bottle."

"*Oui*," Fedya murmured. "You don't seem in thrall to the bottle any longer."

"She cured me."

"Saved you."

"Yes."

Again Fedya turned his gaze forward, though he seemed to see all the way back home. "They do that."

As the sun tumbled toward the western horizon, Farquhar drew even with them. "I've been this way before. There's nothing but washouts and scrub."

"Which might be why you've never found your outlaw," Fedya said. "Looks deceive."

If anyone knew the truth of that, it was Fedya.

Less than an hour later, Mikey dismounted, but he didn't kneel and contemplate dirt. Instead, he stared into a snarl of scrub and thorns. The three men joined him.

"Lose them?" Farquhar asked.

Mikey cast him a glare. Farquhar swallowed and lifted a hand to his bruised throat. His brother's gaze passed over Ethan as if he weren't there, honing in on Fedya. "Horse went in here. Then a bunch came out and went . . ." He pointed to the east.

"That can't be right," Farquhar murmured. "No horse can get through there. A bunch certainly couldn't."

Fedya pointed to the ground where dozens of hoofprints headed in the direction Mikey had indicated. They seemed to appear right at the edge of the scrub.

"But how—"

Mikey pulled back what seemed to be a solid nest of thorns. The thicket swung away like a door, revealing a narrow path coiling downward.

"Rabbit hole," Farquhar muttered.

"Sure 'nough." Mikey moved forward.

Ethan put a hand on his brother's arm. "No."

Mikey jerked away; Fedya stepped between them, setting his own hand on the same arm. Mikey quieted instantly.

Fedya turned to Ethan. "What do you think?"

"Outlaw gang." Ethan held up one finger. "Many horses going that way." He pointed where Mikey had. "Stage robbed yesterday near Ellsworth."

"Which happens to be that way," Farquhar murmured.

"They haven't come back?" Ethan asked.

"No," Mikey answered, and the ache in Ethan's chest eased a bit at the first word his brother had said to him since he'd become someone else's brother. It was a start.

"Didn't we come to get the man's wife, Alexi?"

"We did," Fedya answered.

"Then why don't we get 'er?"

Ethan blinked. "She's . . . ?"

Mikey lifted his chin, indicating the entrance to the rabbit hole. "In there."

Fedya shouted something behind him that Ethan couldn't hear. He was already halfway down the spiraling path.

"Shit," Annabeth muttered.

Someone was coming.

She'd been chewing at the ropes that bound her wrists. Her mouth was sore and her jaw ached. The rope looked exactly the same as it had when she'd started.

She'd have to return to her original plan. Hope that one of the men was so eager to rape her that he barely removed his pants, let alone his weapons, and that this particular fool was either the first to draw the short straw for her favors or that she survived until a big enough fool did.

Not the best plan, but the only one she had.

Annabeth squinted at the opening through which whoever was arriving should appear. She didn't see enough dust to indicate the entire gang. The arrival sounded like a single person. Had all but one of Lassiter's gang been killed in their robbery attempt?

She couldn't be that lucky. Except . . .

A skitter and thud was followed by the rattle of rocks rolling down the trail. Then a man stepped out.

Annabeth closed her eyes. Opened them again. She had been in the sun for days. Her water was nearly gone. She hadn't eaten. That still didn't explain what Ethan was doing here.

Unless he wasn't.

"Beth," he whispered, and ran to her.

His hands felt real when they cradled her face, his lips the same when they brushed hers. But she knew better. Not only was Wonderland impossible to find, but why would Ethan come after her this time when he hadn't the last?

"You're not real," she said.

"Now you sound like me." He kissed her forehead, then tugged at the knots on her wrists. "What the hell did you do to these?"

She opened her mouth, and he lifted a hand to her lips. A sweet gesture—she nearly puckered up—then he plucked a rope fiber from between her teeth. "You'd have chewed through them eventually." He frowned at her black eye. "Someone's gonna pay for that."

"Now you sound like me," she said.

He tugged a knife from his pocket, slicing through the rope at her wrists, her ankles, and her waist. Then he hauled her to her feet. As she hadn't stood on them for two days, she swayed. Ethan lifted her into his arms. Annabeth started to think that maybe, just maybe, this was real.

When she saw Lassiter Morant blocking the exit, she knew that it was.

CHAPTER 31

A man stood at the foot of the rabbit hole alone, no horse, which was how he'd approached without them hearing. He scowled as if he'd like to kill them both. Considering the gun in his hand, he probably would.

"Let me go," Annabeth murmured.

Ethan released her legs. Her feet hit the earth with a dull thud. He kept his arm around her waist, afraid she'd sink into the dirt. Maybe she should. According to Fedya, those nearer the ground made the smallest targets.

"Get down," he whispered.

She wavered, but she didn't fall. "No."

"What the fuck?" the man muttered, coming toward them.

Ethan stepped around his wife, wishing he hadn't foolishly left his own pistols with his horse. Although what good they would have done him now, he had no idea. The man had the drop on them.

Not that Ethan was exceptionally fast on the draw. He could shoot. Sometimes he might even hit something. But his best weapon had always been his brain.

"Lassiter Morant?" Ethan extended his hand. Maybe the fellow would holster his gun long enough to shake. Stranger things had happened.

Instead, Morant wrinkled his nose at Ethan's palm as if he'd smelled something foul and kept the gun pointed at Ethan's chest. "How did you find this place? It's . . . it's . . . impossible."

"Not really." Ethan lowered his hand to his side.

"Oh," Annabeth whispered, as understanding dawned.

Only Mikey could find the impossible. Which meant Mikey was here and, therefore, so was Fedya. Ethan expected a bullet to pierce Morant's brain momentarily. Both Ethan and Annabeth stepped to the side, out of the line of fire.

The gun shifted, following them, along with the outlaw's confused expression. Ethan was equally confused. What in hell was Fedya waiting for? Except . . . if the trio Ethan had arrived with had remained at the entrance to the rabbit hole, the outlaw would not be here. Where were they?

"How did that stage robbery work out for you?" Annabeth asked. "You seem short a few men. All of them, in fact."

"I rode ahead. Wanted to get back to"—Morant smirked—"you."

"Let him go," Annabeth blurted. "I'll do anything you want. You can . . . do anything you want."

"Oh, I plan to." The smirk widened. "He can watch."

Risking a glance upward, Ethan saw nothing, no one. He wasn't surprised. Neither Mikey nor Fedya had survived this long by allowing themselves to be seen by the enemy.

"You said if I was breathing when you returned, you wouldn't hurt him."

"And you believed me? Oh, Anna, you fool."

Ethan disliked the man's calling her a fool almost as much as he disliked Morant's shortened version of her name. At least the bastard wasn't calling her Beth.

Annabeth shrugged. "Worth a try."

"You think I'd leave you?" Ethan murmured. "You are a fool."

Her lips tightened. "I left you. I went to him, chose him. You're the fool."

Ethan just rolled his eyes and returned his gaze to the man with the gun.

"She did come willingly," Lassiter said. "She's part of my gang. She's stolen, cheated, lied, and a whole lot more."

"Me too," Ethan said. "You both must think I'm an imbecile. My wife just said you threatened my life. Of course she went with you."

"I didn't threaten you until we got here."

"Bullshit," Ethan returned. "That knife was a threat louder than words."

"How did you—?" Annabeth began, then muttered, "Ass."

Ethan hoped she was referring to Farquhar and not to him.

"You wanted her back," Ethan continued. "I understand that. Who wouldn't?"

"I didn't want her back; I wanted her dead."

Ethan shifted again. What in hell was taking Fedya so long to shoot this guy?

"If you'd wanted her dead, why didn't you kill her before now?"

"She doesn't get to die fast and easy. She betrayed me."

"She was my wife first."

"She'll be my whore last."

"Watch what you say," Ethan murmured.

"Or what?" Morant asked. "You think I let her in my gang because she could ride a horse? I let her in because she rode me."

Morant stepped so close, the barrel of the gun brushed Ethan's shirt. Huge mistake. Ethan had been taught to disarm fools like this by a master.

He grabbed the barrel with one hand, pushed it away, and twisted. The gun went off; the bullet plowed harmlessly into the dirt. Ethan used his other hand to break Lassiter Morant's nose.

The outlaw fell backward, blood spurting. Ethan handed the weapon to his wife and followed. He wanted to hit him again and again, but Lassiter's nose wasn't the only thing Ethan had broken. Ethan cradled his screaming hand.

"Are you crazy?" Annabeth asked, pointing Morant's gun at Morant's head. "He could have shot you."

Oddly, things had moved too fast for Ethan to even consider that. He'd wanted to stop the outlaw's words with his fist, so he had. Luckily, Morant had been stupid enough to get close, and Ethan had spent time in prison with Fedya, a man who knew just what to do in this situation.

"He insulted my wife."

"That wasn't an insult. You can believe what he told you."

"Oh, I believe him. I just don't care."

"If you believe him, why did you hit him?"

"Someone had to. I was hoping for a bullet from Fedya, but that didn't happen."

Gunfire erupted in the distance.

"My men are gonna kill you both." The threat in the outlaw's words was negated by the nasally whine of his voice through a blood-clogged nose.

Annabeth cocked the gun. "I'm gonna kill you if you give me the slightest reason."

"Bitch," he muttered.

Annabeth appeared bored. "I've been called worse than that by better than you."

Ethan considered his left hand, which he'd already curled into a fist as the right was pretty much worthless. Morant wouldn't be able to talk at all with a broken jaw.

"You have better uses for that hand," she said.

Ethan looped his left arm around her shoulder. She was right.

The gunfire slowed, picked up again, ended. Distant shouts were followed by a whole lot of silence. Just when Ethan was about to take the path upward, the sound of hoofbeats came downward; Fedya and Farquhar appeared.

"Mikey?" Ethan asked as they dismounted.

Please let him be okay, he thought, then realized that his definition of "okay" had changed. All Ethan wanted was for Mikey to be as he'd been the last time he'd seen him. He didn't care if his brother called himself Mikhail and didn't know Ethan from General Grant.

"Guarding the door." Fedya gave a graceful, Gallic shrug. "Such as it is."

"Where are my men?" Morant asked.

"In hell, I imagine."

"All of them?"

Fedya spread his hands. "I'm not sure how many you have."

"Eleven."

"Then, yes. All of them." He narrowed his eyes on Lassiter's face. "Nice work." He lowered his gaze to Ethan's hand. "I must teach you how to break noses without injuring yourself."

"And I'll teach you how to hit people in the head before I have to." Fedya's gaze slid away, and Ethan frowned. "Where the hell were you?"

"Searching for an elevated position," Farquhar said. "You know, so we could save her like we wanted to and not get trapped in here. Like you."

"The only reason I was trapped was because you wandered off and let the bastard in."

"He has a point," Fedya murmured.

"Shut up," Ethan and Farquhar said at the same time.

"You'd have been searching a long time." Annabeth waved her free hand—the other still held Lassiter's own weapon steady on him—at the narrow opening above them. "There's a reason this place is called a rabbit hole. It's hard to get a decent shot from up there. Though I suppose if anyone could have, that someone would have been you."

"Perhaps," Fedya agreed.

"We're alive; they're dead," Annabeth continued. "We win."

"I'm not dead," Morant snarled.

"You will be," Ethan said.

"No one ever saw me do anything. I made sure of it."

"You killed Cora Lewis."

"Prove it."

Farquhar drew from his pocket the carved knife he'd "confiscated" from the sheriff's office. "Look familiar?"

"No."

"One of my top detectives saw you carve it. I'm sure

she'll swear to that, as well as anything else she knows about you."

Lassiter's gaze flicked to Annabeth's. "I will kill you."

"You can try."

Lassiter exploded off the ground. The sun sparked off a second knife. Ethan leaped in front of Annabeth. He didn't realize he'd blocked both her shot and Farquhar's until the detective cursed and Annabeth shoved Ethan in the back.

The knife sped toward Ethan's chest. He lifted his only good hand, hoping he could stop its decent, as well as turn Morant around so that someone, anyone, had a shot. But Ethan had never been much good at anything with his left hand.

The boom of a gun echoed around the cavernous space. The outlaw fell backward. He no longer had to worry about a broken nose. If he were still alive, he might have worried about his missing face.

Mikey stood near the entrance, rifle still at his shoulder. He lowered it and hurried to join them.

Farquhar's gaze narrowed on Fedya. "Thought you were the sniper."

Fedya peered at his nails. "Times change."

CHAPTER 32

"M a'am." Mikey ducked his head.

Annabeth could tell by the expression in his gray eyes that he didn't remember her. But why should he? Her days as Nurse Annabeth had occurred before his injury.

"Hello. I'm Annabeth."

"Mikhail," he said. "Yer the doc's wife?"

"Yes. Thank you for finding me."

"It's what I do best."

She almost said "I know," but that would only confuse him. Instead, she patted him on the arm and smiled. But that only seemed to confuse him, too, because he wandered off, rubbing at his head.

"I blamed you for his death," Ethan murmured. Annabeth wasn't certain whom he was talking to—perhaps all of them.

Fedya muttered something derogatory in a language that sounded quite pretty. When they glanced at him, he shrugged. "He is not dead."

"I know." Ethan returned his gaze to Mikhail, who'd started cleaning his boots with his knife. "He's . . . fine."

Annabeth peered at her husband. "I think you might finally believe that."

"I do." Ethan faced the former sniper. "I'm sorry."

Fedya tilted his head, and his ebony hair slid over his ridiculously blue eyes. "I think you might mean that."

"I was wrong about a lot. Especially you."

"It was war. Terrible things happened to us all." Fedya glanced at Annabeth and smiled the smile that had seduced a thousand women but had never had any effect on her. "The only way to move on is to devote your life to something good. I must return to my life. I miss her." Fedya snapped his fingers, and Mikhail came toward them.

"Wait," Moze said. "I don't know why I never thought of this before." He stared at Mikhail as if he'd just dug into an anthill and discovered gold. "He can find anything."

"He is not a show pony either," Fedya said.

Moze ignored him as he moved his gaze to Annabeth. "He can find anyone."

"Luke," she whispered. She'd wished she could ask for Mikey's—for Mikhail's—help so many times, and now that he was here, she hadn't even thought of it.

"Who is Luke?" Fedya asked.

"My brother. He's the reason I..." Annabeth paused, not wanting to go into all that she had done.

"Annabeth's brother was one of Mosby's Rangers. He went missing at Mount Zion Church," Ethan said. "The intelligence came out of Chimborazo."

"Ah," Fedya murmured.

"Then she exchanged you for him," Ethan continued. Fedya gave a half bow. "Except the man they brought wasn't him."

Fedya glanced at Farquhar, who hunched his shoulders. Fedya's gaze narrowed. "Do you know where Luke is?"

Farquhar shook his head, then looked down. Both Fedya and Mikhail took a step toward the detective, who took a quick step back.

"Stop," Annabeth ordered.

"He's lying," Fedya said. "Believe me, I know lying."

"I'm not! Annie Beth Lou, I—"

Fedya flicked a finger, and Mikhail lifted Moze by his collar; his feet dangled and kicked. "I would hazard to guess that all the men he sent after Morant were unsuccessful. No one ever got as close as you did to what he was after. *Oui?*"

"Oui," Annabeth agreed.

"And if he would have told you he'd found your brother, or at least had some word of him, you would have left your post and gone searching?" Fedya cast her a glance, and she nodded. "So he kept what he knew to himself and let you continue to . . ." He waved a hand at the dead Lassiter Morant.

Annabeth turned her gaze to Moze, a man she'd known all her life, a man she'd trusted. "Is this true?"

Moze tried to speak, but couldn't.

"Mikhail," Fedya murmured, and the big man released his prisoner.

Moze spent a few minutes catching his breath. But finally he gasped. "I knew you'd succeed. You were so damn close."

"You lied?"

"I'm a spy. That's what I do. What you do."

True enough. She just hadn't thought he'd lie to her.

"She almost died," Ethan said. "I thought you cared about her."

"I do."

"You have a damn interesting way of showing it."

"I took her in when you cast her out."

"I tried to find her," Ethan muttered.

Annabeth's heart lurched. "You . . . what?"

"I looked everywhere. I even got in touch with *my* old superior. He couldn't find you, either."

"And why was that?" Fedya kept his sharp blue gaze on the detective.

"Because Yankees can't find their ass with both hands," Moze snapped.

"Perhaps." Fedya's smile gave Annabeth a chill. "Or perhaps you made certain every attempt at locating Annabeth was thwarted."

"I—" was all Moze managed before Annabeth punched him in the chin. He fell to the ground.

"I quit," she said.

"I could not have done that any better myself," Fedya said. "Perhaps now we could focus on the question at hand?"

"What question?" Moze got to his feet, rubbing at his jaw.

"Where is Annabeth's dear brother?"

"I . . . uh . . ."

Fedya sighed. "Must she hit you again?"

Moze glanced at Annabeth, then looked quickly away. The way he was behaving, she wanted to hit him again.

"There's word among the Indians of a man with hair of fire," Moze blurted.

"Now we know why Joe was so damn fascinated with your hair," Ethan observed.

"I thought he was fighting Indians." Annabeth said.

"He was. But not long after he arrived, some white women and children were taken. He was with the group that rode out to get them back."

"Did they?"

"Yes. Only Luke wasn't with them when they returned. Army thought he was dead, maybe escaped. They didn't care enough to find out which."

His disappearance so soon after being "galvanized" might explain why there'd been no record of Luke Phelan in Kansas.

"How long have you known this?"

"Not long."

As Moze was the one who'd taught her how *not* to answer a question, Annabeth lifted a brow.

"I found another man who was with that party," he explained. "Said Luke exchanged himself for the captives."

"And then?"

"There wasn't any word of him, not a whisper until several of the tribes started talking about the white ghost with hair of fire who lives in the hills and talks to the spirits."

"What does that mean?" Annabeth asked. Moze spread his hands. "I'll take Mikhail, and we'll—"

"Too late," Fedya murmured, and when she glanced at him, he pointed upward. At the rim of Wonderland, a puff of dust drifted west. "Mikhail has already left."

———

They buried the outlaws at the bottom of their hidden Wonderland, then pulled shut the thorn gate and rode away.

Fedya headed for Colorado, where his wife and soon-to-be child awaited.

Moze tugged a priest's collar from his pack and positioned it around his neck.

"What are you up to?" Annabeth asked.

"If I live through it, I'll tell you." He sighed. "I'm sorry, Annie Beth Lou. You seemed better when you were working, and you were damn good at it. I wanted Morant so badly. But I should have told you the truth."

Ethan stood a few yards away with their horses. His cool, gray gaze, which he kept trained on Moze, made the Pinkerton uncomfortable, but he deserved it. Still—

"If you had, I might never have gone back to Freedom. And, Moze . . ." Annabeth waited until he met her eyes. "I needed to go back."

He seemed about to say something else, then merely nodded and left, taking most of the outlaws' horses along for company.

Annabeth and Ethan headed toward Freedom.

She experienced a tingle of déjà vu as they rode into town in the depths of the night. The moon cast the silent street in every shade of silver.

They dealt with their own horses, as the stable boy snored softly, then strolled toward home. Ethan took her hand. Annabeth let him.

Inside the house, everything seemed exactly the same, except for the mattress against the wall and the papers on the desk.

Ethan crossed the room, lifted them with his unbroken hand; the other was wrapped in dirty strips of cloth, which didn't do much but remind him not to use it. As if the pain didn't already. He tilted the sheets toward the moonlight. "Divorce papers."

Annabeth stilled. She'd forgotten about them.

"I wanted you to be happy," she said. "To have what

you always dreamed of. What I couldn't give you. A wife, a child, a family."

He stepped so close, his body skimmed hers. "Why can't you give me that?"

She turned away. She couldn't look at him while she admitted the truth. "It's not that I can't. It's that . . ." She took a breath. "What Lassiter said was true. I slept with him to gain his trust. I pretended to be—no, I was—his mistress for months, and he wasn't the first. I'm not the woman you knew. I won't ever be her again."

She waited; she wasn't sure for what. Then the silence was split by the screech of papers being torn—once, twice, again. Annabeth spun as the pieces tumbled to the ground. How he'd torn them with one good hand, she wasn't quite sure. He must have used his teeth.

"I told you before that I don't care." He crossed the room, cupped her neck. "I'll keep telling you if you like, or we could just forget the past five years ever happened."

Annabeth didn't even have to think about that. "Let's forget."

He kissed her softly, sweetly, the way he had the first time at Chimborazo. Back then all they'd had were secrets. Later all they'd had were lies. But now . . .

Now they had a world of possibilities.

The door opened. For the first time in a long time, Annabeth did not reach for her gun. She didn't have one. She didn't need it.

"Doc?" One of the townsfolk stuck his head in, relief flowing over his face at the sight of them. "Thank God yer both back. We need your help. Hurry!"

Ethan extended his good hand; Annabeth put hers into it.

"My bag," he murmured, and she snatched it as, together, they followed the man into the night.

Toward the life they had always wanted.

Read on for a look at the first novel in Lori Austin's
Once Upon a Time in the West series,

BEAUTY AND THE BOUNTY HUNTER

Available from Signet Eclipse.

By the time they reached the hotel, Alexi was behaving so strangely, Cat's skin started to itch. Was someone watching them? Following them? Was that target she felt on her back real?

"How long should we stay?" she asked.

"Until full dark at least."

Cat understood why, but she didn't like it. She wanted out of this town.

Yesterday.

They strolled through the lobby, heads together, murmuring like the lovebirds they weren't. Alexi nodded to the clerk, who'd been here when the Signora arrived but obviously hadn't been when Jed did since the man stared at them without recognition.

"Jed and Meg Nelson." Alexi held out a hand. "Room 12."

The clerk handed over the key after a quick glance at the register. Knowing Alexi, his scribbled name was so illegible it could be anything, even Jed and Meg. Another trick of their trade. One never knew when an identity might need to be changed middodge.

Once Cat was inside, her gaze circled the room, which was exactly the same as hers down the hall—right down to the deck of cards sitting in the center of the table.

She crossed to the window, through which a tepid breeze blew. Tossing off her bonnet, she stuck her head out, knocking the "baby" against the casing. She wasn't used to having all this extra front.

She reached around to remove her costume, and Alexi snapped, "Leave it."

Cat started and glanced over her shoulder. He was closer than she'd thought. Very close. "Why?"

"All we need is for someone to knock on the door and you've . . ." He waved vaguely in the area of her midsection.

"Lost the baby?"

He winced, and she heard what she'd said. The words gave her a strange, hollow feeling. But what was his excuse?

Cat tilted her head. She couldn't decipher his expression. His face seemed so . . . different.

The bruises, she thought. She'd never once seen Alexi with a bruise on his face. It changed him, made him vulnerable. She wasn't sure she liked that any more than he appeared to.

Come to think of it—she tilted her head in the opposite direction—she'd rarely seen Alexi with a bruise anywhere. And she'd seen everywhere.

The memory of that seeing, the touching, the tasting suddenly hit her so hard, she swayed.

He cursed. French? Spanish? Italian? She wasn't certain, but whatever language, the words, the tone, and the cadence were both beautiful and brutal. Kind of like Alexi himself.

She brushed her fingertips across his face. "Why did you let him hurt you?"

"Sometimes," he said, "the hurt just happens."

She narrowed her eyes. She didn't think he was talking about Langston anymore.

He peered at her as if trying to see into her mind, her heart, her soul. "Don't you agree?"

Cat froze, hand still in the air. She'd never shared a single word about her hurts. As she didn't plan to start now, she sidled away.

Alexi crossed to the table, where he picked up the deck of cards and began to shuffle. She became entranced, seduced by the grace, the rhythm. How could she have forgotten? In Alexi's hands, cards did whatever he wanted them to. Kind of like women.

"When you say 'knock,'" Cat murmured, bringing them back to their earlier conversation, happy to pretend the other had never happened, "you mean 'bust in here and drag us back to jail'?"

"No." He didn't look up; he just kept shuffling the cards. "As long as you keep that kid in place, and Meg on your face, we'll be fine."

Why was he irritated with her? She'd just saved his life.

Cat paced in front of the window. The urge to peer from it again was nearly overwhelming. What was out there that was bothering her? If there was a rifle, and considering the prickling of her skin, there might be, she should stay away from the window.

She sat. First on the bed. Then on the chair. Then on the bed again. Alexi ignored her, seemingly captivated with the cards.

Cat went to the door, put her hand on the knob. Alexi tsked, and she turned away. Her gaze went again to the window, and from this angle, with the horizon framed like a picture, she saw what was wrong. She couldn't believe she hadn't noticed it before, but she'd been Meg, and Meg wouldn't recognize that vista. Only Cathleen would.

She had not been back to the farm since she had left it nearly two years ago. It took Cat only an instant to decide that she was going back now. Or at least as soon as she could get away from Alexi.

"Deal," she said. Alexi glanced up, expression curious, hands still shuffling, shuffling, shuffling. "If we have to stay in here, we can at least make it interesting."

His lips curved. "Faro?"

Cat took a chair at the table. "You know better."

Cat loathed Faro, known by many as "Bucking the Tiger." Every saloon between St. Louis and San Francisco offered the game, and most of them cheated. Stacked decks, with many paired cards that allowed the dealer, or banker, to collect half the bets, as well as shaved decks and razored aces were common.

Alexi wouldn't stoop to such tactics; he'd consider mundane cheats beneath him. Besides, he'd already taught her how to spot them, so why bother? Certainly he cheated, but with Faro, Cat had never been able to discover just how.

He'd swindle her at poker too if she wasn't paying attention, but at least with that game, she had a better-than-average chance of catching him.

Alexi laid out five cards for each of them. "Stakes?"

"We can't play just to pass the time?"

He didn't even bother to dignify that foolishness with an answer.

For an instant Cat considered forgoing the wayward nature of the cards and, instead, getting him drunk. But she'd attempted that before. Alexi had remained annoyingly sober, and she had been rewarded with a three-day headache, which Alexi had found beyond amusing.

She had more tolerance now—Cat O'Banyon had drunk many a bounty beneath the table—but she still doubted she could drink this man into a stupor. Sometimes she wondered if he sipped on watered wine daily just to ascertain no one ever could.

Which meant her only other choice was this.

Cat lifted her cards. She gave away nothing; neither did Alexi. After pulling her purse from her pocket, she tossed a few coins onto the table. With a lift of his brow, he did the same.

They played in silence as the day waned. The room grew hot. In the way of cards, first Alexi was ahead, then Cat. She watched him as closely as he watched her. Neither one of them cheated.

Much.

Cat arched, rubbing absently at the ache in the small of her back with her free hand.

"Stop that." Alexi flicked a glance from his cards to her face then back again.

"What?"

"You're not expecting." He set two cards onto the

table, then took two more with stiff yet fussy movements. "Stop acting like it."

There was something in his face she'd never seen before. Was he scared? Had coming a hair from a hanging frightened him at last? Or was she merely seeing in Alexi a reflection of herself?

Cat bit her lip to keep from looking at the window. Instead she continued with the game.

When the sun began to slant toward dusk, and the pile of coins on both sides of the table lay about even, Cat lifted her eyes. "Wanna make this interesting?"

"*Khriso mou*," Alexi murmured. "When you say things like that . . ." He moved a card from the right side of his hand to the left. "I get excited."

"How about we raise the stakes to . . ." She drew out the moment, and even though he knew exactly what she was doing, as he was the one who had taught her to do it, eventually his anticipation caused him to lean forward. Only then did Cat give him what he sought. "Anything."

"Anything?" he repeated.

"*Oui*." He cast her an exasperated glance as she purposely mangled one of his favorite words. "I win this hand, you give me anything I ask. You win—"

"I get anything I ask."

"You've played this before."

"Not with you."

She doubted he'd played it with anyone. What moron would promise anything?

Only someone with little left to lose or . . .

Cat considered her cards without so much as a flicker of an eyelash. Someone with a hand like hers.

"All right," he agreed. "Who am I to turn down anything?"

Not the man she knew and—

Cat brought herself up short. Not the man she knew and what?

Well, not the man she knew.

Alexi turned his cards faceup. Cat kept her face blank as she placed hers facedown.

"You win."

ALSO AVAILABLE FROM
NEW YORK TIMES AND *USA TODAY*
BESTSELLING AUTHOR

LORI AUSTIN

Beauty and the Bounty Hunter
Once Upon a Time in the West

Cathleen Chase is no killer—but as Cat O'Banyon, she is
a ruthless bounty hunter. Catching one lowlife after
another, she keeps searching for the only man she really
cares to find: the man who killed her husband.

But when that man places a bounty on her head, Cat is
forced to team up once again with con artist Alexi
Romanov. He's difficult to trust, even more difficult to
resist—and just like before, the two of them together are
nothing but trouble.

"Austin knows how to keep the pages turning."
—Kaki Warner

Available wherever books are sold or at
penguin.com

facebook.com/LoveAlwaysBooks

LOVE
ROMANCE
NOVELS?

For news on all your favorite romance authors, sneak peeks into the newest releases, book giveaways, and much more—

"Like" Love Always on Facebook!

 LoveAlwaysBooks